REDLAND LIBRARIES

YEAR ONE

By Nora Roberts

HOMEPORT

THE REEF

RIVER'S END

CAROLINA MOON

THE VILLA

MIDNIGHT BAYOU

THREE FATES

BIRTHRIGHT

NORTHERN LIGHTS

BLUE SMOKE

MONTANA SKY

ANGELS FALL

HIGH NOON

DIVINE EVIL

TRIBUTE

SANCTUARY

BLACK HILLS

THE SEARCH

CHASING FIRE

THE WITNESS

WHISKEY BEACH

THE COLLECTOR

THE LIAR

THE OBSESSION

COME SUNDOWN

By Nora Roberts
Trilogies and Quartets

THE BORN IN TRILOGY
BORN IN FIRE
BORN IN ICE
BORN IN SHAME

THE BRIDE QUARTET
VISION IN WHITE
BED OF ROSES
SAVOUR THE MOMENT
HAPPY EVER AFTER

THE KEY TRILOGY
KEY OF LIGHT
KEY OF KNOWLEDGE
KEY OF VALOUR

THE IRISH TRILOGY
JEWELS OF THE SUN
TEARS OF THE MOON
HEART OF THE SEA

THREE SISTERS ISLAND TRILOGY
DANCE UPON THE AIR
HEAVEN AND EARTH
FACE THE FIRE

THE INN AT BOONSBORO TRILOGY
THE NEXT ALWAYS
THE LAST BOYFRIEND
THE PERFECT HOPE

THE SIGN OF SEVEN TRILOGY
BLOOD BROTHERS
THE HOLLOW
THE PAGAN STONE

CHESAPEAKE BAY QUARTET
SEA SWEPT
RISING TIDES
INNER HARBOUR
CHESAPEAKE BLUE

IN THE GARDEN TRILOGY
BLUE DAHLIA
BLACK ROSE
RED LILY

THE CIRCLE TRILOGY
MORRIGAN'S CROSS
DANCE OF THE GODS
VALLEY OF SILENCE

THE DREAM TRILOGY
DARING TO DREAM
HOLDING THE DREAM
FINDING THE DREAM

THE COUSINS O'DWYER TRILOGY
DARK WITCH
SHADOW SPELL
BLOOD MAGICK

THE GUARDIANS TRILOGY
STARS OF FORTUNE
BAY OF SIGHS
ISLAND OF GLASS

eBooks by Nora Roberts

CORDINA'S ROYAL FAMILY
AFFAIRE ROYALE
COMMAND PERFORMANCE
THE PLAYBOY PRINCE
CORDINA'S CROWN JEWEL

THE DONOVAN LEGACY
CAPTIVATED
ENTRANCED
CHARMED
ENCHANTED

THE O'HURLEYS
THE LAST HONEST WOMAN
DANCE TO THE PIPER
SKIN DEEP
WITHOUT A TRACE

NIGHT TALES
NIGHT SHIFT
NIGHT SHADOW
NIGHTSHADE
NIGHT SMOKE
NIGHT SHIELD

THE MACGREGORS
THE WINNING HAND
THE PERFECT NEIGHBOR
ALL THE POSSIBILITIES
ONE MAN'S ART
TEMPTING FATE
PLAYING THE ODDS
THE MACGREGOR BRIDES
THE MACGREGOR GROOMS
REBELLION/IN FROM THE COLD
FOR NOW, FOREVER

THE CALHOUNS
SUZANNA'S SURRENDER
MEGAN'S MATE
COURTING CATHERINE
A MAN FOR AMANDA
FOR THE LOVE OF LILAH

IRISH LEGACY
IRISH ROSE
IRISH REBEL
IRISH THOROUGHBRED

BEST LAID PLANS
LOVING JACK
LAWLESS

SUMMER LOVE
BOUNDARY LINES
DUAL IMAGE
FIRST IMPRESSIONS
THE LAW IS A LADY
LOCAL HERO
THIS MAGIC MOMENT
THE NAME OF THE GAME
PARTNERS
TEMPTATION
THE WELCOMING
OPPOSITES ATTRACT
TIME WAS
TIMES CHANGE
GABRIEL'S ANGEL
HOLIDAY WISHES
THE HEART'S VICTORY
THE RIGHT PATH

RULES OF THE GAME
SEARCH FOR LOVE
BLITHE IMAGES
FROM THIS DAY
SONG OF THE WEST
ISLAND OF FLOWERS
HER MOTHER'S KEEPER
UNTAMED
SULLIVAN'S WOMAN
LESS OF A STRANGER
REFLECTIONS
DANCE OF DREAMS
STORM WARNING
ONCE MORE WITH FEELING
ENDINGS AND BEGINNINGS
A MATTER OF CHOICE

*Nora Roberts also writes the In Death series
using the pseudonym J. D. Robb*

NAKED IN DEATH
GLORY IN DEATH
IMMORTAL IN DEATH
RAPTURE IN DEATH
CEREMONY IN DEATH
VENGEANCE IN DEATH
HOLIDAY IN DEATH
CONSPIRACY IN DEATH
LOYALTY IN DEATH
WITNESS IN DEATH
JUDGEMENT IN DEATH
BETRAYAL IN DEATH
SEDUCTION IN DEATH
REUNION IN DEATH
PURITY IN DEATH
PORTRAIT IN DEATH
IMITATION IN DEATH
DIVIDED IN DEATH
VISIONS IN DEATH
SURVIVOR IN DEATH
ORIGIN IN DEATH
MEMORY IN DEATH
BORN IN DEATH

INNOCENT IN DEATH
CREATION IN DEATH
STRANGERS IN DEATH
SALVATION IN DEATH
PROMISES IN DEATH
KINDRED IN DEATH
FANTASY IN DEATH
INDULGENCE IN DEATH
TREACHERY IN DEATH
NEW YORK TO DALLAS
CELEBRITY IN DEATH
DELUSION IN DEATH
CALCULATED IN DEATH
THANKLESS IN DEATH
CONCEALED IN DEATH
FESTIVE IN DEATH
OBSESSION IN DEATH
DEVOTED IN DEATH
BROTHERHOOD IN DEATH
APPRENTICE IN DEATH
ECHOES IN DEATH
SECRETS IN DEATH

NORA ROBERTS
YEAR ONE

piatkus

PIATKUS

First published in Great Britain in 2017 by Piatkus

1 3 5 7 9 10 8 6 4 2

Copyright © 2017 by Nora Roberts

The moral right of the author has been asserted.

A CIP catalogue record for this book
is available from the British Library.

ISBN: 978-0-349-41493-5 (hardback)
ISBN: 978-0-349-41494-2 (trade paperback)

Printed and bound in Australia by McPherson's Printing Group

Papers used by Piatkus are from well-managed forests
and other responsible sources.

Piatkus
An imprint of
Little, Brown Book Group
50 Victoria Embankment
Carmelite House
London EC4Y 0DZ

An Hachette UK Company
www.hachette.co.uk

www.littlebrown.co.uk

THE DOOM

It is the still, small voice that the soul heeds,
not the deafening blasts of doom.

—William Dean Howells

CHAPTER ONE

— Dumfries, Scotland —

When Ross MacLeod pulled the trigger and brought down the pheasant, he had no way of knowing he'd killed himself. And billions of others.

On a cold, damp day, the last day of what would be his last year, he hunted with his brother and cousin, walking the crackling, frosted field under skies of washed-out, winter blue. He felt healthy and fit, a man of sixty-four who hit the gym three times a week, and had a passion for golf (reflected in a handicap of nine).

With his twin brother, Rob, he'd built—and continued to run—a successful marketing firm based in New York and London. His wife of thirty-nine years, along with Rob's and their cousin Hugh's wives, stayed back, tucked into the charming old farmhouse.

With fires snapping in stone hearths, the kettle always on the boil, the women chose to cook and bake and fuss over the coming New Year's Eve party.

They happily passed on tromping the fields in their wellies.

The MacLeod farm, passed from father to son for more than two hundred years, spread for more than eighty hectares. Hugh loved it nearly as much as he did his wife, children, and grandchildren. From the field they crossed, distant hills rose in the east. And not that far a cry to the west rolled the Irish Sea.

The brothers and their families often traveled together, but this annual trip to the farm remained a highlight for all. As boys they'd often spent a month in the summer on the farm, running across the fields with Hugh and his brother, Duncan—dead now from the soldier's life he'd chosen. Ross and Rob, the city boys, had always thrown themselves into the farm chores assigned by their Uncle Jamie and Aunt Bess.

They'd learned to fish, to hunt, to feed chickens, and to gather eggs. They'd roamed, forests and fields, on foot and on horseback.

Often, on dark nights, they'd crept out of the house to hike to the very field they walked now, to hold secret meetings and try to raise the spirits within the little stone circle the locals called *sgiath de solas*, shield of light.

They'd never succeeded, nor had they ever chased down the haints or faeries young boys knew traveled the forests. Though on one midnight adventure, when even the air held its breath, Ross swore he'd felt a dark presence, heard its rustling wings, even smelled its foul breath.

Felt—he would always claim—that breath blow into him.

In adolescent panic, he'd stumbled in his rush to flee the circle, and scraped the heel of his hand on a stone within.

A single drop of his blood struck the ground.

As grown men, they still laughed and teased over that long-ago night, and treasured the memories.

And as grown men, they had brought their wives, then their children, back to the farm on an annual pilgrimage beginning on Boxing Day and ending on the second of January.

Their sons and their sons' wives had left only that morning for London, where they would all see in the New Year with friends—and spend another few days on business. Only Ross's daughter, Katie, who was seven months along with twins of her own, had stayed back in New York.

She planned a welcome-home dinner for her parents that was never to be.

But on that bracing last day of the year, Ross MacLeod felt as fit and joyful as the boy he'd been. He wondered at the quick shiver down his spine, at the crows circling and calling over the stone circle. But even as he shook it away, the cock pheasant, a flurry of color against the pale sky, rose in flight.

He lifted the twelve-gauge his uncle had given him for his sixteenth birthday, followed the bird's flight.

It might be that the heel of the hand he'd scraped more than fifty years before stung for an instant, throbbed an instant more.

But still . . .

He pulled the trigger.

When the shot blasted the air, the crows screamed, but didn't scatter. Instead, one broke away as if to snatch the kill. One of the men laughed as the darting black bird collided with the falling pheasant.

The dead bird struck the center of the stone circle. Its blood smeared over the frosted ground.

Rob clamped a hand on Ross's shoulder, and the three men grinned as one of Hugh's cheerful Labs raced off to retrieve the bird. "Did you see that crazy crow?"

Shaking his head, Ross laughed again. "He won't be having pheasant for dinner."

"But we will," Hugh said. "That's three for each, enough for a feast."

The men gathered their birds, and Rob pulled a selfie stick out of his pocket.

"Always prepared."

So they posed—three men with cheeks ruddy from the cold, all with eyes a sparkling MacLeod blue—before making the pleasant hike back to the farmhouse.

Behind them, the bird's blood, as if heated by flame, soaked through the frozen ground. And pulsed as the shield thinned, cracked.

They trooped, successful hunters, past fields of winter barley stirring in the light wind, and sheep grazing on a hillock. One of the cows Hugh kept for fattening and finishing lowed lazily.

As they walked, Ross, a contented man, thought himself blessed to end one year and start another on the farm with those he loved.

Smoke puffed from the chimneys in the sturdy stone house. As they approached, the dogs—their workday done—raced ahead to wrestle and play. The men, knowing the ropes, veered off toward a small shed.

Hugh's Millie, a farmer's wife and a farmer's daughter, drew a hard line at cleaning game. So on a bench Hugh had built for that purpose, they set up to do the job themselves.

They talked idly—of the hunt, of the meal to come—as Ross took a pair of the sharp sheers to cut the wings off the pheasant. He cleaned it as his uncle had taught him, cutting close to the body. There were parts that would be used for soup, and those went into a thick plastic bag for the kitchen. Other parts into another bag for disposal.

Rob lifted a severed head, made squawking sounds. Despite himself, Ross laughed, glancing over. He nicked his thumb on a broken bone.

He muttered, "Shit," and used his index finger to staunch the trickle of blood.

"You know to watch for that," Hugh said with a *tsk*.

"Yeah, yeah. Blame it on goofball here." As he peeled back the skin, the bird's blood mixed with his.

Once the job was done, they washed the cleaned birds in icy water pumped from the well, then carried them into the house through the kitchen.

The women were gathered in the big farm kitchen with air rich from the scents of baking and warmth from the fire simmering in the hearth.

It all struck Ross as so homey—a perfect tableau—it tugged at his heart. He laid his birds on the wide kitchen counter and grabbed his wife in a circling hug that made her laugh.

"The return of the hunters." Angie gave him a quick, smacking kiss.

Hugh's Millie, her curly red mop bundled on top of her head, gave the pile of birds an approving nod. "Enough to roast for our feast and more to serve at the party. How about we do some pheasant and walnut pasties there. You're fond of them, I recall, Robbie."

He grinned, patting the belly that pudged over his belt. "Maybe I need to go out and bag a few more so there'll be some for everyone else."

Rob's wife, Jayne, drilled a finger into his belly. "Since you're going to make a pig of yourself, we're going to put you to work."

"That we are," Millie agreed. "Hugh, you and the lads haul out the long table into the big parlor for the party, and use my mother's long lace cloth. I want the good candlestands on it as well. And get the extra chairs from the closet and set them out."

"Wherever we set them, you'll want them moved again."

"Then you'd best get started." Millie eyed the birds, rubbing her hands together. "All right, ladies, let's boot the men along and get started ourselves."

They had their feast, a happy family group, roasted wild pheasant seasoned with tarragon, stuffed with oranges, apples, shallots, and sage, cooked on a bed of carrots and potatoes, tomatoes. Peas and good brown bread from the oven, farm butter.

Good friends, old friends as well as family, they enjoyed the last meal of the year with two bottles of the Cristal that Ross and Angie had brought from New York just for this occasion.

A light, thin snow blew outside the windows as they cleared and washed up, all still basking in the glow, and in anticipation of the party to come.

Candles lit, fires snapping, more food—two days in the making—set out on tables. Wine and whiskey and champagne. Traditional cordials along with scones and haggis and cheeses for the Hogmanay celebration.

Some neighbors and friends came early, before midnight struck, to eat and drink and gossip, to tap toes to the music of pipes and fiddles. So the house filled with sound and song and fellowship as the old clock on the wall struck its midnight notes.

The old year died on the last chime, and the New Year was greeted with cheers, kisses, and voices raised in "Auld Lang Syne." All this Ross hugged sentimentally to his heart with Angie tucked against his side, and his brother's arm linked with his.

As the song ended, as glasses were raised, the front door swung open wide.

"The first-footer!" someone exclaimed.

Ross watched the door, expecting one of the Frazier boys or maybe Delroy MacGruder to step in. All dark-haired youths of good nature, as tradition required. The first to enter the house in the New Year must be so to ensure good luck.

But all that swept in was wind and the thin snow and the deep country dark.

As he stood closest, Ross walked to the door himself, looked out, stepped out. The chill running through him he attributed to the bluster of wind, and the odd, holding silence under the wind.

Air holding its breath.

Was that a rustle of wings, a long shadow—dark over dark?

With a quick shudder, Ross MacLeod stepped back in, a man who would never enjoy another feast or welcome another New Year, and so became the first-footer.

"Must not have latched it," he said, closing the door.

Chilled still, Ross stepped over to the fire, held his hands to the flame. An old woman sat beside the fire, her shawl wrapped tight, her cane leaning against the chair. He knew her as the young Frazier boys' great-granny.

"Can I get you a whiskey, Mrs. Frazier?"

She reached out with a thin, age-spotted hand, gripping his hand with surprising strength when he offered it. Her dark eyes bored into his.

"'Twas written so long ago most have forgot."

"What was?"

"The shield would be broken, the fabric torn, by the blood of the Tuatha de Danann. So now the end and the grief, the strife and the fear—the beginning and the light. I ne'er thought to live for it."

He laid a hand over hers, gentle, indulgent. Some, he knew, said she was one of the fey. Others said she was a bit doddering in the mind. But the chill stabbed again, an ice pick in the base of his spine.

"It starts with you, child of the ancients."

Her eyes darkened, her voice deepened, sending a fresh frisson of dread down his spine.

"So now between the birth and the death of time, power rises— both the dark and the light—from the long slumber. Now begins the blood-soaked battle between them. And with the lightning and a mother's birth pangs comes The One who wields the sword. The graves are many, with yours the first. The war is long, with no end- ing writ."

Pity moved over her face as her voice thinned again, as her eyes cleared. "But there's no blame in it, and blessings will come as magicks long shadowed breathe again. There can be joy after the tears."

With a sigh she gave his hand a small squeeze. "I'd have a whiskey, and thanks for it."

"Of course."

Ross told himself it was foolish to be shaken by her nonsensical words, by those probing eyes. But he had to settle himself before he poured the whiskey for her—and another for himself.

The room hushed with anticipation at the booming knock on the door. Hugh opened it to one of the Frazier boys—Ross couldn't say which—who was greeted with applause and pleasure as he stepped in with a grin and a loaf of bread.

Though the time to bring luck had come and gone.

Still, by the time the last guests left at near to four a.m., Ross had forgotten his unease. Maybe he drank a little too much, but the night was for celebration, and he only had to stagger up to bed.

Angie slipped in beside him—nothing stopped her from cleansing off her makeup and slathering on her night cream—and sighed.

"Happy New Year, baby," she murmured.

He wrapped an arm around her in the dark. "Happy New Year, baby."

And Ross fell into sleep, into dreams about a bloody pheasant dropping to the ground inside the little stone circle, of crows with black eyes circling thick enough to block out the sun. A wolf howl of wind, of bitter cold and fierce heat. Of weeping and wailing, the bong and chime marking time rushing by.

And a sudden, terrible silence.

He woke well past midday with a banging head and queasy stomach. As he'd earned the hangover, he forced himself to get up, fumble his way into the bathroom, hunt up some aspirin in his wife's little medicine bag.

He downed four, drank two glasses of water to try to ease his scratchy throat. He tried a hot shower and, feeling a little better, dressed and went downstairs.

He went into the kitchen where the others gathered around the table for a brunch of eggs and scones and bacon and cheese. And where the smell, much less the sight, of food had his stomach doing an ungainly pitch.

"He rises," Angie said with a smile, then tipped her head, studying his face as she brushed back her chin-swing of blond hair. "You look rough, honey."

"You do look a bit hingy," Millie agreed, and pushed back from the table. "Sit yourself, and I'll get you a nice cup."

"Glass of ginger for what ails him," Hugh prescribed. "It's the thing for the morning after."

"We all knocked back more than a few." Rob gulped his tea. "I'm feeling a little hollow myself. The food helped."

"I'll pass on that for now." He took the glass of ginger ale from Millie, murmured his thanks, and sipped it carefully. "I think I'll get some air, clear my head. And remind myself why I'm too old to drink until damn near dawn."

"Speak for yourself." And though he looked a little pale himself, Rob bit into a scone.

"I'm always going to be four minutes ahead of you."

"Three minutes and forty-three seconds."

Ross shoved his feet into wellies, pulled on a thick jacket. Thinking of his sore throat, he wrapped a scarf around his neck, put on a cap. And taking the tea Millie offered him in a thick mug, he walked out into the cold, crisp air.

He sipped the strong, scalding tea and began to walk as Bilbo, the black Lab, fell into companionable pace with him. He walked a long way, decided he felt steadier. Hangovers might be a bitch, he thought, but they didn't last. And he wouldn't spend his last hours in Scotland brooding about drinking too much whiskey and wine.

A hangover couldn't spoil a bracing walk in the country with a good dog.

He found himself crossing the same field where he'd downed the last pheasant of the hunt. And approaching the small stone circle where it had fallen.

Was that its blood on the winter-pale grass under the skin of snow? Was it black?

He didn't want to go closer, didn't want to see. As he turned away, he heard a rustling.

The dog growled low in his throat as Ross turned to stare into the copse of old, gnarled trees edging the field. Something there, he thought with a fresh chill. He could hear it moving. Could hear a rustling.

Just a deer, he told himself. A deer or a fox. Maybe a hiker.

But the dog bared his teeth, and the hair on Bilbo's back stood up.

"Hello?" Ross called out, but heard only the sly rustle of movement.

"The wind," he said firmly. "Just the wind."

But knew, as the boy he'd been had known, it wasn't.

He walked back several paces, his eyes scanning the trees. "Come on, Bilbo. Come on, let's go home."

Turning, he began to stride quickly away, feeling his chest go tight. Glancing back, he saw the dog still stood stiff-legged, his fur ruffled.

"Bilbo! Come!" Ross clapped his hands together. "Now!"

The dog turned his head, and for a moment his eyes were almost feral, wild and fierce. Then he broke into a trot toward Ross, tongue happily lolling.

Ross kept up a quick stride until he reached the edge of the field. He put a hand—it shook a little—on the dog's head. "Okay, we're both idiots. We'll never speak of it."

His headache had eased a bit by the time he got back, and his stomach seemed to have settled enough to allow him some toast with another cup of tea.

Sure the worst was over, he sat down with the other men to watch a match on TV, dozed off into fragments of dark dreams.

The nap helped, and the simple bowl of soup he had for dinner tasted like glory. He packed his bags as Angie packed hers.

"I'm going to call it an early night," he told her. "I'm pretty ragged out."

"You look . . . hingy." Angie laid a hand on his cheek. "You might be a little warm."

"I think I've got a cold coming on."

With a brisk nod, she walked off to the bathroom, rummaged around. She came back with two bright green tablets and a glass of water.

"Take these and go to bed. They're p.m. cold tablets, so they'll help you sleep, too."

"You think of everything." He downed them. "Tell everybody I'll see them in the morning."

"Just get some sleep."

She tucked him in, making him smile. Kissed his forehead.

"Maybe a little warm."

"I'll sleep it off."

"See that you do."

In the morning he thought he had. He couldn't claim a hundred percent—that dull, nagging headache was back and he had loose bowels—but he ate a good breakfast of porridge and strong black coffee.

One last walk, then loading up the car got his blood moving. He hugged Millie, embraced Hugh.

"Come to New York this spring."

"Might be we will. Our Jamie can see to things around here for a few days."

"Tell him good-bye for us."

"That we will. He'll likely be home before long, but . . ."

"Plane to catch." Rob gave his hugs.

"Oh, I'll miss you," Millie said as she pulled both women close. "Fly safe, be well."

"Come see us," Angie called out as she got into the car. "Love you!" She blew a kiss as they drove away from the MacLeod farm for the last time.

They returned the rental car, infecting the clerk and the business-man who rented it next. They infected the porter who took their bags when tips exchanged hands. By the time they reached and passed through security, the infection had passed to an easy two dozen people.

More still in the first-class lounge where they drank Bloody Marys and relived moments from the holiday.

"Time, Jayne." Rob rose, exchanged one-arm hugs and backslaps with his brother, a squeeze and kiss on the cheek with Angie. "See you next week."

"Keep me up on the Colridge account," Ross told him.

"Will do. Short flight to London. If there's anything you need to know, you'll have it when you land in New York. Get some rest on the plane. You're still pretty pale."

"You look a little off yourself."

"I'll perk up," Rob told him and, gripping his briefcase with one hand, gave his twin a quick salute with the other. "On the flip side, bro."

Rob and Jayne MacLeod carried the virus to London. On the way, they passed it to passengers bound for Paris, Rome, Frankfurt, Dublin, and beyond. In Heathrow, what would come to be known as the Doom spread to passengers bound for Tokyo and Hong Kong, for Los Angeles, D.C., and Moscow.

The driver who shuttled them to their hotel, a father of four, took it home and doomed his entire family over dinner.

The desk clerk at the Dorchester cheerfully checked them in. She *felt* cheerful. After all, she was leaving in the morning for a full week's holiday in Bimini.

She took the Doom with her.

That evening, over drinks and dinner with their son and daughter-in-law, their nephew and his wife, they spread death to more of the family, added it with a generous tip to the waiter.

That night, ascribing his sore throat, fatigue, and queasy stomach to a bug he'd caught from his brother—and he wasn't wrong—Rob took some NyQuil to help him sleep it off.

On the flight across the Atlantic, Ross tried to settle into a book but couldn't concentrate. He switched to music, hoping to lull himself to sleep. Beside him, Angie kicked back with a movie, a romantic comedy as light and frothy as the champagne in her glass.

Halfway across the ocean he woke with a violent coughing fit that had Angie shooting up to pat his back.

"I'll get you some water," she began, but he shook his head, holding up a hand.

He fumbled to get his seat belt off, rose to hurry to the bathroom. His hands braced on the basin, he coughed up thick yellow phlegm that seemed to burn straight out of his laboring lungs. Even as he tried to catch his breath, the coughing struck again.

He had a ridiculous flash of Ferris Bueller speculating about coughing up a lung as he hocked up more phlegm, vomited weakly.

Then a sharp, stabbing cramp barely gave him enough time to drag down his pants. Now he felt as if he shat out his intestines while sweat popped hot on his face. Dizzy with it, he pressed one hand to the wall, closed his eyes as his body brutally emptied out.

When the cramping eased, the dizziness passed, he could have wept with relief. Exhausted, he cleaned himself up, rinsed his mouth with the mouthwash provided, splashed cool water on his face. And felt better.

He studied his face in the mirror, admitted he remained a little hollow-eyed, but thought he looked a bit better as well. He decided he'd expelled whatever ugly bug had crawled inside him.

When he stepped out, the senior flight attendant cast him a concerned look. "Are you all right, Mr. MacLeod?"

"I think so." Mildly embarrassed, he covered with a wink and a joke. "Too much haggis."

She laughed obligingly, unaware she'd be just as violently ill in less than seventy-two hours.

He walked back to Angie, eased by her to the window seat.

"Are you okay, baby?"

"Yeah, yeah. I think so now."

After a critical study, she rubbed a hand over his. "Your color's better. How about some tea?"

"Maybe. Yeah."

He sipped tea, found his appetite stirred enough to try a little of the chicken and rice that was on the menu. An hour before landing, he had another bout of coughing, vomiting, and diarrhea, but judged it milder than before.

He leaned on Angie to get him through customs, passport secu-

rity, and to handle pushing the baggage cart out to where the driver
from their car service waited.

"Good to see you! Let me take that, Mr. Mac."

"Thanks, Amid."

"How was your trip?"

"It was wonderful," Angie said as they wove through the crowds
at Kennedy. "But Ross isn't feeling very well. He picked up a bug
along the way."

"I'm sorry to hear that. We'll get you home, quick as we can."

For Ross the trip home passed in the blur of fatigue: through the
airport to the car, loading the luggage, the airport traffic, the drive
to Brooklyn and the pretty house where they'd raised two children.

Once again he let Angie handle the details, appreciating her arm
around his waist as she took some of his weight while guiding him
upstairs.

"Straight to bed with you."

"I'm not going to argue, but I want a shower first. I feel . . . I need
a shower."

She helped him undress, which struck him with a wave of ten-
derness. He leaned his head against her breast. "What would I do
without you?"

"Just try to find out."

The shower felt like heaven, made him believe absolutely he'd gotten through the worst. When he came out and saw she'd turned
down the bed and set a bottle of water, a glass of ginger ale, and his
phone all on the bedside table, his eyes actually stung with tears of
gratitude.

She hit the remote to lower the shades on the windows. "Drink
some of that water, or the ginger ale, so you don't get dehydrated.
And if you're not better in the morning, it's to the doctor with you,
mister."

"Already better," he claimed, but obeyed, downing some ginger ale before sliding blissfully into bed.

She tucked and fussed, laid a hand on his brow. "You're definitely running a fever. I'm going to get the thermometer."

"Later," he said. "Give me a couple hours down first."

"I'll be right downstairs."

He closed his eyes, sighed. "Just need a little sleep in my own bed."

She went downstairs, got some chicken, along with a carcass she'd bagged, out of the freezer, and began the task of running it under cool water to speed up the defrosting. She'd make a big pot of chicken soup, her cure for everything. She could use some herself, as she was dog-tired and had already sneaked a couple of meds behind Ross's back for her own sore throat.

No need to worry him when he was feeling so low. Besides, she'd always had a tougher constitution than Ross, and would probably kick it before it took serious hold.

While she worked she put her phone on speaker and called her daughter, Katie. They chatted happily while Angie ran the cold water and made herself some tea.

"Is Dad around? I want to say hi."

"He's sleeping. He came down with something on New Year's."

"Oh no!"

"Don't worry. I'm making chicken soup. He'll be fine by Saturday when we come to dinner. We can't wait to see you and Tony. Oh, Katie, I got the most adorable little outfits for the babies! Okay, a few adorable little outfits. Wait until you see. But I've got to go." Talking was playing hell with her sore throat. "We'll see you in a couple days. Now don't come by here, Katie, and I mean it. Your dad's probably contagious."

"Tell him I hope he feels better, and to call me when he wakes up."

"I will. Love you, sweetie."

"Love you back."

Angie switched on the kitchen TV for company, decided a glass of wine might do her more good than the tea. Into the pot with the chicken, the carcass, then a quick run upstairs to look in on her husband. Reassured, since he was snoring lightly, she went back down to peel potatoes and carrots, chop celery.

She concentrated on the task, let the bright chatter of the TV wash over her, and stubbornly ignored the headache beginning to brew behind her eyes.

If Ross felt better—and that fever he had went down—she'd let him move from the bedroom to the family room. And by God, she'd get into her own pajamas because she felt fairly crappy herself, and they'd snuggle up, eat chicken soup, and watch TV.

She went through the process of making the soup on automatic, disposing of the carcass now that it had done its work, cutting the chicken meat into generous chunks, adding the vegetables, herbs, spices, and her own chicken stock.

She turned it on low, went back upstairs, looked in on Ross again. Not wanting to disturb him, but wanting to stay close, she went into what had been her daughter's room and now served as a room for visiting grandchildren. Then dashed to the guest bath to vomit up the pasta she'd had on the plane.

"Damn it, Ross, *what* did you catch?"

She got the thermometer, turned it on, put the tip in her ear. And when it beeped stared at the readout in dismay: 101.3.

"That settles it, chicken soup on trays in bed for both of us."

But for the moment, she took a couple of Advil, went down to pour herself a glass of ginger ale over ice. After sneaking quietly into their bedroom, she pulled out a sweatshirt and a pair of flannel pants—adding thick socks because she felt chills coming on. Back in the second bedroom she changed, lay down on the bed, pulled around her the pretty throw that had been folded at the foot of the bed, and almost immediately fell asleep.

And into dreams about black lightning and black birds, a river that ran with bubbling red water.

She woke with a jolt, her throat on fire, her head pounding. Had she heard a cry, a shout? Even as she fumbled to untangle herself from the throw, she heard a *thud*.

"Ross!" The room spun when she leaped up. Hissing out an oath, she raced to the bedroom, let out her own cry.

He was on the floor by the bed, convulsing. A pool of vomit, another of watery excrement, and she could see the blood in both.

"Oh God, God." She ran to him, tried to turn him on his side— weren't you supposed to do that? She didn't know, not for sure. She grabbed his phone off the nightstand, hit nine-one-one.

"I need an ambulance. I need help. God." She rattled off the address. "My husband, my husband. He's having a seizure. He's burning up, just burning up. He's vomited. There's blood in it."

"Help's on the way, ma'am."

"Hurry. Please hurry."

CHAPTER TWO

Jonah Vorhies, a thirty-three-year-old paramedic, smelled the soup cooking and turned off the burner before he and his partner, Patti Ann, rolled MacLeod out of the house and loaded him into the ambulance.

His partner jumped in the front, hit the sirens as he stayed in the back, working to stabilize the patient while the wife looked on.

And held on, Jonah thought. No hysterics. He could almost hear her willing her husband to wake up.

But Jonah knew death when he saw it. Sometimes he could feel it. He tried not to—it could get in the way of the work—tried to block out that *knowing*. Like, sometimes he knew that some guy who brushed by him on the street had cancer. Or some kid running by would fall off his bike that very afternoon and end up with a greenstick fracture of his right wrist.

Sometimes he even knew the kid's name, his age, where he lived.

It could be that specific, so he'd made it a kind of game for a while. But it spooked him, so he stopped.

With MacLeod, the knowing came on fast and strong, wouldn't let him block it out. Worse, this came with something new. A *seeing*. The seizure had stopped by the time he and Patti Ann had arrived but, as he worked and called out details for Patti Ann to radio in, Jonah could *see* the patient in bed, rolling over, vomiting on the floor. Calling for help before he fell out of bed and began to convulse.

He could *see* the wife rushing in, hear her voice as she cried out. He could hear it, see it all as if watching it on a big screen.

And he didn't fucking like it.

When they rolled up to the ambulance bay, he did his best to turn off that screen, to do whatever he could to help save the life he knew was already gone.

He rattled off vitals, the details of symptoms, of emergency treatment given so far, as Dr. Rachel Hopman (he had a pretty serious crush on the doc) and her team double-timed the patient toward a treatment room.

Once there, he took the wife's arm before she could push through those double doors. And released it as if burned because he'd seen she was dead, too.

She said, "Ross," and put a hand on the door to push it open.

"Ma'am. Mrs. MacLeod, you need to stay out here. Dr. Hopman's the best. She's going to do everything she can do for your husband."

And for you, pretty soon now, for you. But it won't be enough.

"Ross. I need to—"

"How about you sit down? You want some coffee?"

"I—no." She pressed a hand to her forehead. "No, thanks. No. What's wrong with him? What happened?"

"Dr. Hopman's going to find out. Is there someone we can call for you?"

"Our son's in London. He won't be home for a couple of days. My daughter . . . But she's pregnant, with twins. She shouldn't be upset. This will upset her. My friend Marjorie."

"Do you want me to call Marjorie?"

"I . . ." She looked down at the purse she clutched, the one she'd grabbed automatically, just as she'd grabbed her coat, yanked on shoes. "I have my phone."

She took it out, then just stared at it.

Jonah stepped away, snagged a nurse. "Somebody needs to look after her." He gestured toward Mrs. MacLeod. "Her husband's in there, and it's bad. I think she's sick, too."

"There's a lot of sick going on around here, Jonah."

"She's running a fever. I can't tell you how high." He could: 101.3 and rising. "The patient's running one. I have to get back on the roll."

"Okay, okay, I'll check on her. How bad?" she asked, lifting her chin toward the treatment room.

Against his will, Jonah saw inside, watched the woman he hadn't worked up the guts to ask for a serious date look at the clock, and called it.

"Bad" was all he said, escaping before Rachel came out to tell the wife that her husband was dead.

Across the East River, in a loft in Chelsea, Lana Bingham cried out, soaring on the long, rolling orgasm. As cry slid to moan and moan to sigh, her fingers unclenched from the bedsheets, lifting so she could wrap her arms around Max as he came.

She sighed again, a woman replete and loose and content with her lover's weight on her, his heart still drumming its mad beat against hers. She ran her fingers, lazily now, through his dark hair.

He probably needed a trim, but she liked when it had some length, when she could twine the ends around her finger.

Six months since they'd moved in together, she thought, and it only got better.

In the quiet aftermath, she closed her eyes, sighed yet again.

Then cried out as something, something wild and wonderful, burst through her, in her, over her. Stronger than the orgasm, deeper, and with a ferocious mix of pleasure and shock she'd never be able to describe. Like light exploding, a lightning strike to her center, a flaming arrow to her heart that flashed through all of her. She all but felt her blood glow.

On her, still inside her, Max's body jerked. She heard his breath catch even as, for an instant, he hardened again.

Then it all quieted, smoothed, soothed to no more than a glimmer behind her eyes until even that faded.

Max pushed up on his elbows, looked down at her in the light of a dozen flickering candles. "What was that?"

A little dazed yet, she blew out a long breath. "I don't know. The world's biggest postcoital aftershock?"

He laughed, lowered his head to brush his lips to hers. "I think we're going to have to buy another bottle of that new wine we opened."

"Let's go for a case. Wow." Under him she stretched, lifting her arms up and back. "I feel amazing."

"And look the same. My pretty, pretty witch."

Now she laughed. She knew—as he did—she was a dabbler at best. And was perfectly happy to stay one, to try her hand at little charms and candle rituals, to observe the holidays.

Since meeting Max Fallon at a winter solstice festival, and falling for him—hard—before Ostara, she'd made some attempt to work more seriously on the Craft.

But she didn't have the spark and, to be honest, knew few who

did. Most—try pretty much all—she knew or met at festivals, rituals, meetings, ranked as dabblers, just as she did. And some were
just a little crazy by her gauge. Others were way too obsessed.

Some might even hit dangerous, if they actually had power.

Then, oh yes, then, there was Max.

He had that spark. Hadn't he lit the bedroom candles with his
breath—something that always aroused her? And if he really focused, he could levitate small things.

Once he'd floated a full cup of coffee across the kitchen and set
it down right on the counter in front of her.

Amazing.

And he loved her. That was the kind of magick that mattered to
Lana above all else.

He kissed her again, rolled off. And picked up an unlit candle.

Lana rolled her eyes, gave an exaggerated groan.

"You always do better when you're relaxed." He did a slow scan
of her body. "You look relaxed."

She lay comfortably naked, her arms behind her head, her long
butterscotch hair spread over the pillow. Her bottom-heavy lips full,
curved.

"If I were any more relaxed, I'd be unconscious."

"So give it a try." He took her hand, kissed her fingers. "Focus.
The light's in you."

She wanted it to be, because he did. And because she hated dis-
appointing him, she sat up, shook back her hair.

"Okay."

Preparing herself, she closed her eyes, leveled her breathing. She
tried, as he'd *tried* to teach her, to draw up the light he believed she
held.

Oddly, she thought she felt something stir inside her and, surprised by it, opened her eyes, released a breath.

The wick shot light.

She gaped at it while he grinned.

"Look at you!" he said, with pride.

"I— But I didn't even . . ." She had managed to bring a few candles to flame, after a couple minutes of fierce concentration. "I wasn't even ready to start, and . . . You did it."

Amused, and secretly a little relieved, she poked a finger into his chest. "Trying to boost my confidence?"

"I didn't." He laid his free hand on her bare knee. "I wouldn't do that, and I'll never lie to you. That was all you, Lana."

"But I . . . You really didn't? And you didn't, I don't know, give me some sort of boost?"

"All you. Try it again." He blew out the candle, and this time put it in her hands.

Nervous now, she closed her eyes—more to calm herself than anything. But when she thought of the candle, of lighting it, she felt that *rising* inside her. When she opened her eyes and simply thought of the flame, the flame appeared.

"Oh, oh God." Her eyes, a bright summer blue, reflected the candlelight. "I really did it."

"What did you feel?"

"It was . . . like something lifting inside me. Lifting up, spreading out, I don't know exactly. But, Max, it felt natural. Not a big flash and *boom*. Just like, well, breathing. And still, you know, a little spooky. Let's keep it between just us, okay?"

She looked at him through the light.

She saw the pride and the interest on that handsome, poetic face, with the edgy cheekbones under the scruff, as he'd worked through the day without shaving.

She saw both in his eyes, pure gray in candlelight.

"Don't write about it or anything. At least not until we're sure it's not a fluke, a just-this-one-time thing."

"A door opened inside you, Lana. I saw it in your eyes, just as I saw the potential for it in your eyes the first time we met. Even before I loved you, I saw it. But if you want it to stay between us, it does."

"Good." She rose, stepped over to place her candle with his. A symbol, she thought, of their unity. She turned, candlelight swaying behind her. "I love you, Max. That's my light."

He stood, lithe as a cat, gathered her close. "I can't imagine what my life would be without you in it. Want more wine?"

She tipped her head back. "Is that a euphemism?"

He smiled, kissed her. "I'm thinking wine, and we order in because I'm starving. Then we'll see about euphemisms."

"I'm in for all of that. I can cook."

"You certainly can, but you did that all day. You've got the night off. We talked about going out—"

"I'd rather stay in. With you." Much rather, she realized.

"Great. What are you in the mood for?"

"Surprise me," she said, turning to pick up the black pants and T-shirt she'd worn under her chef's coat—sous chef to be exact—he'd stripped off her when she'd come home from the restaurant.

"Two double shifts this week, so I'll be happy to stay home, eat something—anything—somebody else cooked."

"Done." He pulled on the jeans and dark sweater he'd worn to work—writing in his office in the loft. "I'll open the wine, and surprise you with the rest."

"I'll be right out," she promised, going to the closet.

When she'd moved in with Max, she'd tried to limit her space to half the closet, but . . . She loved clothes, adored fashion—and since she spent so much of her time in a white tunic and black pants, indulged herself outside of work.

Casual, she thought, could still be pretty, even a little romantic for an evening at home. She chose a navy dress with swirls of red that would float a bit just below her knees. And she could come up with her own surprise—some sexy underwear—for when they got to the euphemism part of the night.

She dressed, then studied her face in the mirror. Candlelight flattered, but . . . She laid her hands on her face and did a light glamour—something she'd had the talent for since puberty.

She often wondered if whatever spark she had depended more on vanity than real power.

That was fine with Lana. It didn't shame her a bit to be or feel more pretty than powerful. Especially since whatever she had of each attracted a man like Max.

She started out, remembered the candles.

"Don't leave them unattended," she murmured, and turned back to put them out.

She stopped, considered. If she could light them, could she *unlight* them?

"It's just the reverse, right?" Saying it, thinking it, she pointed at one, intended to walk over and try.

The flame died.

"Oh well . . . Wow." She started to call Max, then realized he'd probably get wound up in it all, and they'd end up practicing and studying instead of having their quiet dinner at home.

Instead, she simply moved from candle to candle in her mind until the room fell dark. She couldn't explain what she felt, or how that door Max spoke of had so suddenly opened.

Something to think about later, she decided.

She wanted that wine.

While Lana and Max enjoyed their wine—and an appetizer of melted Brie on toasted baguette slices Lana couldn't stop herself from making—Katie MacLeod Parsoni rushed into a hospital in Brooklyn.

The tears hadn't come yet because she didn't believe, refused to believe, her father was dead, and her mother suddenly was so ill as to be in ICU.

With one hand pressed to her belly, her husband's arm around her now nonexistent waist, she followed directions to the elevator that led to Intensive Care.

"This isn't happening. It's a mistake. I told you, I talked to her a few hours ago. Dad wasn't feeling well—a cold or something—and she was making soup."

She'd said the same thing over and over again on the drive to the hospital. Tony just kept his arm around her. "It's going to be all right," he said, as he could think of nothing else.

"It's a mistake," she repeated. But when they reached the nurse's station, she couldn't get a word out. Nothing came. She looked up helplessly at Tony.

"We were told Angie—Angela MacLeod was admitted. This is her daughter, Kathleen—my wife, Katie."

"I need to see my mother. I need to see her." Something in the nurse's eyes had panic bubbling in Katie's throat. "I need to see my mother! I want to talk to Dr. Hopman. She said—" And that Katie couldn't say.

"Dr. Gerson's treating your mother," the nurse began.

"I don't want to see Dr. Gerson. I want to see my mother! I want to talk to Dr. Hopman."

"Come on now, Katie, come on. You've got to try to calm down. You've got to think of the babies."

"I'm going to contact Dr. Hopman." The nurse came around the desk. "Why don't you wait over here, sit down while you wait. How far along are you?"

"Twenty-nine weeks, four days," Tony said.

Now tears came, slow drops running. "You count the days, too," Katie managed.

"Of course I do, honey. Sure I do. We're having twins," he told the nurse.

"What fun for you." The nurse smiled, but her face went grave when she turned to walk back to the desk.

Rachel answered the page as soon as she could—and sized up the situation quickly when she saw the man and woman. She was about to have a grieving pregnant woman on her hands.

Still, she thought it better all around she'd gotten there ahead of Gerson. He was an excellent internist, but could be brusk to the point of rudeness.

The nurse on the desk gave Rachel the nod. Bracing herself, she walked over to the couple.

"I'm Dr. Hopman. I'm so sorry about your father."

"It's a mistake."

"You're Katie?"

"I'm Katie MacLeod Parsoni."

"Katie," Rachel said and sat. "We did all we could. Your mother did all she could. She called for help, and got him to us as quickly as possible. But he was too ill."

Katie's eyes, the same dark green as her mother's, clung to Rachel's. Pleaded. "He had a cold. Some little bug. My mother was making him chicken soup."

"Your mother was able to give us a little information. They were in Scotland? But you didn't travel with them?"

"I'm on modified bed rest."

"Twins," Tony said. "Twenty-nine weeks, four days."

"Can you tell me where in Scotland?"

"In Dumfries. What does it matter? Where's my mother? I need to see my mother."

"She's in isolation."

"What does that mean!"

Rachel shifted, her gaze as calm and steady as her voice. "It's a precaution, Katie. If she and your father contracted an infection, or one passed it to the other, we have to guard against contagion. I can let you see her for a few minutes, but you need to be prepared. She's very ill. You'll need to wear a mask and gloves and a protective gown."

"I don't care what I have to wear, I need to see my mother."

"You won't be able to touch her," Rachel added. "And you can only see her for a few minutes."

"I'm going with my wife."

"All right. First, I need you to tell me everything you can about their time in Scotland. Your mother said they only got back today, and had been there since the day after Christmas. Do you know if your father was ill before they left?"

"No, no, he was fine. We had Christmas. We always go to the farm the day after. We all go, but I couldn't because I can't travel right now."

"Did you speak to them while they were gone?"

"Of course. Almost every day. I'm telling you they were fine. You can ask Uncle Rob—my father's twin brother. They were all there, and they were fine. You can ask him. He's in London."

"Can you give me his contact number?"

"I'll do that." Tony gripped Katie's hand. "I've got all that, and I'll give you whatever you need. But Katie needs to see her mom."

Once the family members were gowned and gloved, Rachel did what she could to prepare them.

"Your mother's being treated for dehydration. She's running a high fever, and we're working on bringing that down." She paused outside the room with its glass wall, a fine-boned woman with what would have been an explosion of black curls had they not been clamped ruthlessly back. Fatigue dogged her deep chocolate eyes, but her tone remained brisk.

"The plastic curtaining is to protect against infections."

All Katie could do was stare through the glass, through the film of the plastic inside the room, to the woman in the narrow hospital bed.

Like a husk of my mother, she thought.

"I just talked to her. I just talked to her."

She gripped Tony's hand, stepped inside.

Monitors beeped. Green squiggles and spikes ran across the screens. Some sort of fan hummed like a swarm of wasps. Over it all she heard her mother's rasping breaths.

"Mom," she said, but Angie didn't stir. "Is she sedated?"

"No."

Katie cleared her throat, spoke louder, clearer. "Mom, it's Katie. Mom."

Angie stirred, moaned. "Tired, so tired. Make the soup. Sick day, we'll have a sick day. Mommy, I want my lambie jammies. Can't go to school today."

"Mom, it's Katie."

"Katie, Katie." On the pillow, Angie's head turned right, left, right, left. "Mommy says Katie, bar the door. Bar the door, Katie." Angie's eyes fluttered open, and her fever-bright gaze rolled around the room. "Don't let it come in. Do you hear it, rustling in the bushes? Katie, bar the door!"

"Don't worry, Mom. Don't worry."

"Do you see the crows? All the crows circling."

That bright, blind gaze landed on Katie—and something Katie recognized as her mother came into it. "Katie. There's my baby girl."

"I'm here, Mom. Right here."

"Dad and I aren't feeling our best. We're going to have chicken soup on trays in bed and watch TV."

"That's good." Tears rushed into Katie's throat, but she pushed the words through them. "You'll feel better soon. I love you."

"You have to hold my hand when we cross the street. It's very important to look both ways."

"I know."

"Did you hear that!" Breath quickening, Angie dropped her voice to a whisper. "Something rustling in the bushes. Something's watching."

"Nothing's there, Mom."

"There is! I love you, Katie. I love you, Ian. My babies."

"I love you, Mom," Tony said, understanding she thought he was Katie's brother. "I love you," he repeated, because he did.

"We'll have a picnic in the park later, but . . . No, no, storm's coming. It's coming with it. Red lightning, burns and bleeds. Run!" She shoved herself up. "Run!"

Angie dissolved into a violent coughing fit that sprayed sputum and phlegm on the curtain.

"Take her out!" Rachel ordered, pressing the button for the nurse.

"No! Mom!"

Over her protests, Tony dragged Katie from the room.

"I'm sorry. I'm so sorry, but you have to let them try to help her. Come on." His hands shook as he helped her take off the gown. "We're supposed to take all this off here, remember?"

He pulled off her gloves, his own, disposed of them as the nurse rushed into the room to assist.

"You have to sit down, Katie."

"What's wrong with her, Tony? She was talking crazy."

"It must be the fever." He steered her—he felt her shaking against him—back to the chairs. "They'll get the fever down."

"My father's dead. He's dead, and I can't think about him. I have to think about her. But—"

"That's right." He kept his arm around her, drew her head to his shoulder, stroked her curly brown hair. "We have to think about her. Ian's going to be here as soon as he can. He may even be on his way. He's going to need us, too, especially if Abby and the kids can't come with him, if he couldn't find enough seats on a flight back."

Just talk, Tony thought, just talk and keep Katie's mind off whatever just happened inside that horrible plastic curtain. "Remember, he texted back he'd managed to book a hopper to Dublin, and got a direct from there. Remember? And he's working on getting Abby and the kids on a flight out of London as soon as he can."

"She thought you were Ian. She loves you, Tony."

"I know that. It's okay. I know that."

"I'm sorry."

"Aw, come on, Katie."

"No, I'm sorry. I'm having contractions."

"Wait, what? How many?"

"I don't know. I don't know, but I'm having them. And I feel . . ."

When she swayed in the chair, he gathered her up. He stood—holding his wife and their babies, feeling the world fall apart under him—and called for help.

They admitted her and, after a tense hour, the contractions stopped. The ordeal following the nightmare, and the conclusion of hospital bed rest and observation, left them both exhausted.

"We'll make a list of what you want, from home, and I'll run and get it. I'll stay right here tonight."

"I can't think straight." Though her eyes felt gritty, Katie couldn't close them.

He took her hand, covered it with kisses. "I'll wing it. And you have to do what the doctor said. You have to rest."

"I know, but . . . Tony, can you just go check? Can you go see how Mom's doing? I don't think I can rest until I know."

"Okay, but no getting up and boogying around the room while I'm gone."

She worked up a wan smile. "Solemn oath."

He rose, leaned over, kissed her belly. "And you guys stay put. Kids." He rolled his eyes at Katie. "Always in a hurry."

When he stepped out, he just leaned against the door, struggled against the gnawing need to break down. Katie was the tough one, he thought, the strong one. But now he had to be. So he would.

He made his way through the special care section—the place was a maze—found the doors to the waiting area, check-in, elevators. Tony suspected Katie would have to stay long enough for him to learn his way around.

As he stepped to the elevators, a slightly built, pretty black woman in a white lab coat and black Nikes stepped off.

His mind cleared. "Dr. Hopman."

"Mr. Parsoni, how's Katie?"

"It's Tony, and she's trying to rest. Everything's good. No contractions for the last hour, and the babies are both fine. They want to keep her at least overnight, probably for a few days. She's asking about her mom, so I was coming up to check."

"Why don't we sit down over here?"

He'd worked in his family's sports equipment store since childhood—managed the main branch now. He knew how to read people.

"No."

"I'm so sorry, Tony." She took his arm, guided him to the chairs. "I told Dr. Gerson I'd come down, but I can have him paged, have him come talk to you."

"No, I don't know him, I don't need that." He dropped down, lowered his head into his hands. "What's happening? I don't understand what's happening. Why did they die?"

"We're running tests, looking for the nature of the infection. We believe they contracted it in Scotland, as your father-in-law had symptoms before he left. Katie said they stayed on a farm, in Dumfries?"

"Yeah, the family farm—a cousin's farm. It's a great place."

"A cousin?"

"Yeah, Hugh, Hugh MacLeod. And Millie. God, I need to tell them. Tell Rob, tell Ian. What do I tell Katie?"

"Can I get you some coffee?"

"No, thanks. What I could use is a good, stiff drink, but . . ." He had to be strong, he remembered, and wiped at his tears with the heels of his hands. "I'll settle for a Coke."

When he started to get up, Rachel put a hand on his arm. "I'll get it. Regular?"

"Yeah."

She walked over to the vending machines, dug out change. A farm, she thought. Pigs, chickens. A possible strain of swine or bird flu?

Not her area, but she'd get the information, pass it on.

She brought Tony the Coke. "If you'd give me the contact information on Hugh MacLeod and for Ross MacLeod's brother, it may help us."

She took it all, keyed them into her phone. The cousin, the twin brother, the son, even the nephews, as Tony offered them.

"Take my number." She took his phone, added it to his contacts list. "Call me if there's something I can do. Are you planning on staying with Katie tonight?"

"Yeah."

"I'll set that up for you. I'm sorry, Tony. Very sorry."

He let out a long breath. "Ross and Angie, they were . . . I loved them like my own ma and pop. It helps to know they were with somebody good, somebody, you know, caring, at the end. It'll help Katie knowing that, too."

He walked back to Katie's room, walked slowly, even deliberately taking a wrong turn once to give himself more time.

When he went in, saw her lying there, staring up at the ceiling, her hands protectively cradling the babies inside her, he knew what he had to do.

For the first time since he'd met her, he lied to her.

"Mom?"

"She's sleeping. You need to do the same." Leaning over the bed, he kissed her. "I'm going to run home, pack us some things. Since the food probably sucks in here, I'll pick us up some lasagna from Carmines. Kids gotta eat." He patted her belly. "And need some meat."

"Okay, you're right. You're my rock, Tone."

"You've always been mine. Be back before you know it. No wild parties while I'm gone."

Her eyes glimmered, her smile wobbled. But his Katie had always been game. "I already ordered the strippers."

"Tell them to keep it on till I get back."

He walked out, trudged to his car. It started to snow in anemic wisps he barely felt. He slid into the minivan they'd bought only two weeks before, in anticipation of the twins.

Lowering his head to the wheel, he wept out his broken heart.

CHAPTER THREE

By the end of the first week of January, the reported death count topped a million. The World Health Organization declared a pandemic spreading with unprecedented speed. The Centers for Disease Control and Prevention identified it as a new strain of avian influenza, one that spread with human-to-human contact.

But no one could explain why the birds tested showed no signs of infection. None of the chickens, turkeys, geese, pheasants, or quail—confiscated or captured within a hundred-kilometer radius of the MacLeod farm—revealed any infection.

But the people—the MacLeod family in Scotland, their neighbors, the villagers—died in droves.

That detail the WHO, the CDC, and the NIH kept under tight wraps.

In the scramble for vaccines, distribution ran through complex and maddening loops. Delays incited rioting, looting, violence.

It didn't matter, as the vaccines proved as ineffective as the fraudulent cures selling briskly on the Internet.

Across the globe, heads of state urged calm and called for order, promised assistance, spoke of policies.

Schools closed, countless businesses locked their doors as people were urged to limit contact with others. The sale of surgical masks, gloves, over-the-counter and prescription flu remedies, bleach, and disinfectants soared.

It wouldn't help. Tony Parsoni could've told them, but he died in the same hospital bed as his mother-in-law less than seventy-two hours after her.

Plastic barriers, latex gloves, surgical masks? The Doom scoffed at all and gleefully spread its poisons.

In the second week of the New Year, the death toll topped ten million and showed no sign of abating. Though his illness went unreported, and his death was kept secret for nearly two days, the President of the United States succumbed.

Those heads of state fell like dominoes. Despite extreme precautions, they proved just as susceptible as the homeless, the panicked, the churchgoer, the atheist, the priest, and the sinner.

In its wave through D.C. in the third week of the Doom, more than sixty percent of Congress lay dead or dying, along with more than a billion others worldwide.

With the government in chaos, new fears of terrorist attacks lit fires. But terrorists were as busy dying as the rest.

Urban areas became war zones, with thinning police forces fighting against survivors who looked at the end of humanity as an opportunity for blood and brutality. Or profit.

Rumors abounded about odd dancing lights, about people with strange abilities healing burns without salve, lighting fires in barrels for warmth without fuel. Or lighting them for the thrill of watching the flames rise. Some claimed to have seen a woman walk through a wall, others swore they'd seen a man lift a car with one hand. And another who had danced a jig a full foot off the ground.

Commercial air travel shut down in week two in the vain hope of stopping or slowing the spread. Most who fled before the travel bans, leaving their homes, their cities, even their countries, died elsewhere.

Others opted to ride it out, stockpiling supplies in homes and apartments—even office buildings—locking doors and windows, often posting armed guards.

And had the comfort of dying in their own beds.

Those who locked themselves in and lived clung to the increasingly sporadic news coverage, hoping for a miracle.

By week three, news was as precious as diamonds, and much more rare.

Arlys Reid didn't believe in miracles, but she believed in the public's right to know. She'd worked her way from a predawn newsreader in Ohio, doing mostly farm reports and a few remotes at local fairs and festivals, to a fluff reporter at a local affiliate in New York.

She gained popularity, if not many opportunities for hard news.

At thirty-two, she'd still had her eye on national news. She hadn't expected to get it by default. The star of *The Evening Spotlight*, a steady, sober voice through two decades of world crises, went missing before the end of the first week of the pandemic. One by one, in the pecking order of replacements, came death, flight, or, in the case of her immediate predecessor, a sobbing breakdown on air.

Every morning when Arlys woke—in her nearly empty low-rise only a few blocks from the studio—she took stock.

No fever, no nausea, no cramping, no cough, no delusions. No—though she didn't actually believe the rumors—strange abilities.

She ate from her meager supplies. Usually dry cereal, as milk had become nearly impossible to find unless you could stomach the powdered stuff. And she couldn't.

She dressed for a run, as she'd discovered running could be necessary, even in broad daylight, even for a handful of blocks. She strapped her briefcase cross-body. Inside, she kept a .32 she'd found on the street. She locked her door and hit the streets.

Along the way, if she felt reasonably safe, she took pictures with her phone. Always something to document. Another body, another burned-out car, another broken shop window. Otherwise, she kept up a steady jog.

She kept in good shape—always had—and could kick into a sprint if needed. Most mornings the streets remained eerily quiet, empty but for abandoned cars, wrecks. Those who roamed the nights looking for blood had crawled back into their holes with the sunlight like vampires.

She used the side door, as Tim in security had given her a full set of keys and swipes before he'd disappeared. She always used the stairs, as they'd had a couple of power outages. The climb up five flights helped make up for missing her five-times-weekly hour at the gym.

She'd stopped letting the echoing silence of the building bother her. The lunchroom and the commissary still had coffee. Before she started a pot, she ground extra beans for the plastic bag in her briefcase. Only a day's supply at a time—after all, she wasn't the only one still coming to work who needed that good jolt.

Sometimes Little Fred—the enthusiastic intern who, like Arlys, continued to report to the TV station every day—restocked. Arlys never questioned where the bouncy little redhead acquired the coffee beans, the boxes of Snickers, or the Little Debbie snack cakes.

She just enjoyed the largess.

Today, she filled her thermos with coffee and decided on a Swiss Roll.

Taking both, she wound her way to the newsroom. She could've taken an office—plenty of them available now—but preferred the open feel of the newsroom.

She hit the lights, watched them blink on over empty desks, blank screens, silent computers.

She tried not to worry about the day she hit the switches and nothing happened.

As always, she settled down at the desk she'd chosen, crossed her fingers, and booted up the computer. The Wi-Fi in her apartment building had hit the dirt two weeks earlier, but the station still pulled it.

It ran painfully slow, often hiccupped off and on, but it ran. She clicked to connect, poured her coffee, settled back to drink and wait—fingers still crossed.

"And so we live another day," she said aloud when the screen came up.

She clicked on her e-mail, drank, and waited until it fluttered on-screen. As she did several times a day, she searched for an e-mail from her parents, her brother, the friends she had back in Ohio. She'd had no luck phoning or texting in more than a week. The last time she'd been able to reach her parents, her mother had told her they were fine. But her voice had sounded raw and weak.

Then nothing. Calls didn't go through, texts and e-mails went unanswered.

She sent another group e-mail.

Please contact me. I check my e-mail several times a day. You can phone my cell, it's still working. I need to know how you are. Any information from you and your location. I'm really getting worried.

Melly, if you get this, please, please, go check on my parents. I
hope you and yours are well. Arlys.

She hit send and, because there was nothing else she could do,
locked it in a corner of her mind and got to work.

She brought up *The New York Times*, *The Washington Post*. Reports had thinned, but she could still dig out some meat.

The former Secretary of State—now president, through the line
of succession—spoke by videoconference with the Secretary of
Health and Human Services, the current head of the CDC (the former had died on day nine of the pandemic), and the newly ap-
pointed head of the WHO. Elizabeth Morrelli succeeded Carlson
Track, who succumbed to illness. Questions regarding the details
of Dr. Track's death had not been answered.

Arlys noted that Morrelli issued a statement claiming that through
global efforts, a new vaccine to combat H5N1-X should be ready
for distribution within a week.

"Funny, that's what Track said ten days ago. Bullshit in a her-
metically sealed bunker is still bullshit."

She read about a group of people hoarding food, water, and supplies in an elementary school in Queens firing on others who tried
to break in.

Five dead, including a woman carrying a ten-month-old baby.

On the other end of the spectrum, a church in the Maryland sub-
urbs was handing out blankets, MREs, candles, batteries, and other
basics.

Reports of murders, suicides, rapes, maimings. And a scattering
of reports on heroism and simple kindnesses.

Of course, there were the lunacy reports of people claiming to
have seen creatures with luminous wings flying around. Or of a man
impaling another man with flaming darts shot out of his fingertips.

She read reports of the military transporting volunteers believed to be immune to secured facilities for testing. Where are they? she wondered. And quarantines of entire communities, mass burials, blockades, a firebomb hurled onto the White House lawn.

The fanatical preacher Reverend Jeremiah White, who claimed the pandemic to be God's wrath on a godless world and proclaimed the virtuous would survive only by vanquishing the wicked.

"They walk among us," was his latest cry, "but they are not as us. They are as from hell, and must be driven back to the fire!"

Arlys made notes, checked other sites. More going dark every day, she thought as she surfed.

Checking her watch, she brought up Skype to connect with a source she trusted more than any other.

He gave her his rubbery grin when he came on-screen. His hair sprang everywhere at once, a Billy Idol white slick around his pleasantly goofy face.

"Hey, Chuck."

"Hey, Awesome Arlys! Still five-by-five?"

"Yeah, and you?"

"Healthy, wealthy, and wise. Did you lose any more?"

"I don't know yet. I haven't seen anyone else this morning. Bob Barrett's still not showing up. Lorraine Marsh lost it yesterday."

"Yeah, saw that."

"I'll pick up her afternoon report because I don't see her coming back. We've still got some crew. Carol's in the booth, and Jim Clayton's been coming in every day for the last ten or so. It's pretty surreal when the head of broadcasting shows up to pick up as gaffer or whatever needs filling in. And Little Fred's still stocking the commissary, writing some copy, playing gofer, doing some on-air."

"She's totally cute. Why don't you set me up with her?"

"Happy to. Give me your address and I'll bring her right to you."

He gave her that grin again. "Wish I could, but the walls have ears. The fucking air has them. Your friendly neighborhood hacker needs his Batcave."

"Batman wasn't friendly, he was a brilliant psycho. And Spider-Man didn't have a cave."

He gave her a cackling chuckle. "Only another reason I'm your biggest fan. You can school me on superheroes. Favorite report you read this morning?"

"The one about the naked woman riding a unicorn in SoHo."

"Man, I'd love to see a naked woman, with or without unicorn. It's been awhile."

"I'm not stripping down for you, Chuck. Not even for the buzz you're going to give me."

"We're pals, Arlys. Pals don't require naked."

"So, what's the buzz?"

The grin faded away. "You caught today's tally?"

"Yeah." Both the *Times* and the *Post* ran a daily updated total of reported deaths. "We've topped a billion by five hundred million, three hundred twenty-two thousand, four hundred and sixteen."

"That's the official count for the media. The real count's more than two."

Her heart jumped. "More than two billion? Where'd you get that number?"

"I've gotta keep that under the vest. But it's real, Arlys, and it's going up a lot faster than the people in charge of this clusterfuck are saying."

"But . . . Jesus God, Chuck, that's nearly a third of the world population. A third of the world population wiped out in weeks?" Sick, she scribbled the number down. "And that doesn't count the murders, the suicides, the people killed in crashes, fires, stampedes, the ones who've died of exposure."

"It's going to get worse, Arlys. In the saga of revolving POTUS? Carnegie's out."

"Define 'out.'"

"Dead." He rubbed his eyes, a pale and cagey blue in a lightly freckled face. "They swore in the new one about two this morning. Secretary of Agriculture—the ones ahead of her already hit by the Doom. Fucking farm lady is now running what's left of the free world. If you report that, the jackboots are going to come kicking down your door."

"Yeah. I'll kill the comp like you told me if I decide to go on air with it. Agriculture." She had to flip back through notes to the list she'd made. "She was eighth in line."

As she spoke Arlys crossed out those who came between, and saw she'd already crossed out several following.

"If she doesn't make it, we're down to the Secretary of Education, and after him, there's nobody left."

"Honeypot, the government's finished. Not just here, all over hell and back again. It's a hell of a way to get rid of asshole dictators, but it's a way. North Korea, Russia—"

"Wait. Kim Jong-un? He's dead? When?"

"Two weeks ago. They're claiming he's alive, but that's bogus. You can take it to the bank. If there's still one open. But that's not the biggest buzz. It mutated, Arlys. Carnegie—POTUS for a day? Well, three days. He had sores, sores broke out all over his body—and inside delicate orifices—before he showed the expected symptoms of the Doom. He was sealed tight, under watch twenty-four-seven, tested three times a day, and it still got him."

"If it's mutated . . ."

"Back to the drawing board with two billion plus and counting. But here's the big boom: They don't know what the fuck it is. The bird flu line? It's bullshit."

"What do you mean?" Arlys demanded. "They identified the strain. Patient Zero—"

"It's bullshit, Arlys. The dead guy in Brooklyn, maybe. But the

Doom ain't no bird flu. Birds aren't infected. They've been testing chickens and pheasants, and all kinds of our feathered friends, and nothing. And four-legged animals? They're just fine and just dandy. It's just humans. Just people."

Her throat wanted to close, but she forced out the words. "Biological warfare? Terrorism."

"No buzz on that, just nada, and you bet your fine ass they've been looking. Whatever the hell it is, nobody's ever seen it before. What's left of the powers-that-be? They're lying, falling back on the let's-not-cause-panic bullshit. Well, fuck that. Panic's here."

"If they can't identify the virus, they can't create a vaccine."

"Bingo." Chuck shot up a finger, made a check mark in the air. "They've got another route, and it doesn't inspire confidence. I'm hearing chatter about military roundups, pulling people who are— so far—asymptomatic out of their homes, and taking them to places like Raven Rock, Fort Detrick. They've set up checkpoints, and they're doing neighborhood sweeps, closing off urban areas. If you plan to get out of New York, sugarcake, do it soon."

"Who'd report the news?" But her stomach clenched. "And how would I talk to you every day?"

"I figure I've got time before they come knocking, and I've got an escape hatch. If you use this, Arlys, no shitting around, get gone. Get supplies you can carry and get out of the city. Don't fuck around."

He paused, shot her that grin again. "On that note. Hit it, Frank!"

Arlys closed her eyes, let out a weak laugh when she heard Sinatra crooning "New York, New York."

"Yeah, I'm spreading the news."

"He sure made it. Skinny guy from Hoboken. Hey, I'm a skinny guy, too. It's got a ring, right? Hoboken."

His grin stayed wide, but she saw his eyes—his intense and serious eyes. "Yeah, I did a fluff piece there a million years ago."

"Podoken Hoboken. It ain't no Park Avenue, but its number-one boy sure went places. Anyway, gotta book. I was hackedy-hacking till three in the a.m. Three in the morning's past even this boy's bedtime. Keep it real."

"You, too, Chuck."

She ended the call, pulled up a street map of Hoboken.

"Park Avenue," she mumbled. "And found it. Number One Park Avenue, maybe? Or . . . Park crosses First Street. Park and First, three a.m. if I get out of Manhattan."

She got up, paced, trying to absorb all Chuck had told her. She trusted him—nearly everything he'd told her up to that morning had been verified. And what hadn't been officially verified had swirled into the anonymous-sources category.

Two billion dead. Mutated. Yet another dead president. She needed to do some research on Sally MacBride—Ag Secretary turned POTUS, according to Chuck. She'd be ready if and when the change of power was announced.

If she went on the air with that, the uniforms—or the men in black—would certainly swarm the station. Take her in for questioning, maybe shut it all down. In the world that had been she'd have risked questioning, risked being hauled into court to protect a source. But this wasn't the world that had been.

She'd stick with officially verified reports for her morning edition, that and her own observations. Then she'd write up copy from Chuck's intel. Monitor the Internet—Little Fred could help her with that. If she could name another source, even from the deep Web, she'd protect herself and Chuck. And the station.

She knew there were people who depended on the broadcasts—for help, for hope, for truth when she could find it for them.

She sat back down, poured more coffee, wrote copy, refined it, rewrote, printed it. She'd have Fred set it in the prompter.

She took the copy with her to wardrobe, picked a jacket before

going in to do her own makeup and hair. The world might be ending, but she *would* look professional when she reported same.

In studio, she found the bouncy, redheaded Little Fred chatting
with the sad-eyed cameraman.

"Hi, Arlys! You were working away and I didn't want to break
your rhythm. I got some apples and oranges, put them in the break
room."

"Where do you find this stuff?"

"Oh, you just have to know where to look."

"I'm glad you do. Can you set my copy up?"

"Sure thing." She lowered her voice. "Steve's feeling low. He saw
some asshole shoot a dog last night. By the time he got down to the
street, the guy was gone, and the dog dead. Why do people have to
be so mean?"

"I don't know. But there are people like Steve who'd go down on
the street to try to help a dog, so that's the other side of it."

"That's true, isn't it? Maybe I can find him a dog. There are so
many strays now."

Before Arlys could comment, Little Fred dashed off to load the
prompter.

Arlys walked behind the anchor desk, fit on her earpiece.

"Am I coming through?"

"We've got you, Arlys."

"Good morning, Carol. I've got ten minutes of hard, another ten
of soft. Little Fred's loading it up."

They talked production, added in copy Carol and Jim had
written, worked out the opening story, the close—the unicorn
got the close—and calculated they could offer a full thirty-minute
report.

"When we get through this, Arlys," Jim said in her ear, "and the
world's sane again—relatively—you're keeping that anchor desk on
The Evening Spotlight."

The big guns, she thought. And thought, too, of what she'd learned from Chuck. It would never happen.

"I'll hold you to it."

"Solemn oath."

Fred set the written copy on the desk, and a mug of water. "Thanks." Arlys checked her face, smoothed her long bob of deep brown hair, ran through some tongue twisters when she got the thirty-seconds mark.

At ten, she rolled her shoulders, at five turned to the camera, waited for Steve to give her the go.

"Good morning. This is Arlys Reid in New York with your *Morning Report*. Today, the World Health Organization estimates the death toll from H5N1-X at more than one billion, five hundred million. Yesterday, President Carnegie held meetings with officials from the WHO and the CDC, including the heads of both organizations and scientists who are working around the clock to create a vaccine to combat the virus."

I'm lying, she thought as she continued. Lying because I'm afraid to tell the truth.

Lying because I'm afraid.

CHAPTER FOUR

While Arlys gave her report, Lana listened to the ugly news layered on ugly news as she looked out the window.

She loved the loft's floor-to-ceiling windows, loved being able to look out at what had become her neighborhood. How many mornings had she or Max run across to the little bakery for fresh bagels? Now, instead of a display window filled with tempting pastries and cakes, boards covered the glass and obscene graffiti covered the boards.

She tracked her gaze down to the corner deli where she'd so often joked with the cheerful woman behind the counter. Doris, Lana remembered. Her name was Doris, and she'd always worn a white cap over tight, tight gray curls and bright, bright red lipstick.

Only the day before, Lana had looked out this same window to see the once-busy, family-run deli reduced to charred brick, still-smoking wood, and smashed glass.

Surely for no reason other than vicious glee.

So many shops and restaurants she and Max had patronized, had enjoyed, were closed now or had been destroyed by looters or vandals.

Other lofts and apartments were empty or locked up tight. Did the locked ones hold the living or the dead?

No one walked the sidewalks this morning. Not even those who sometimes ventured out to scavenge for food or supplies before they locked themselves in again. Not a single car drove past.

They came at night, with the dark. The self-dubbed Raiders. Was there any other word for them? Lana wondered. They came out, roaming in packs like rabid wolves, roaring along the streets on motorcycles. Firing guns, heaving rocks or firebombs through windows. Smashing, burning, looting, laughing.

The night before, awakened by the shouts, the gunshots, Lana had risked a look. She'd seen a pack of Raiders all but on the doorstep of their building. She'd watched two argue, fight, draw knives while others circled to cheer on the blood. They left the vanquished bleeding on the street—but not before kicking him, stomping on him.

Max had called the police. His own growing powers helped him boost the signal, as phones—landlines or cells—rarely connected now.

They'd come, clad in riot gear, a full hour after the call. They had bagged the body and taken it away—but hadn't bothered to come in and interview her or Max.

She could see the blood on the street from the window.

How could the world have gone so dark, so cruel? And at the same time when such light had come into her? She felt it bloom, felt it glow, felt that rush of power whenever she opened herself to it.

She knew it was the same for Max, that blooming, that discovery.

She'd seen for herself there were others. The woman she'd watched leap off the roof of the building across the street. Not in despair, but to soar joyfully on luminous, spreading wings.

Or the boy of no more than ten she'd watched skipping down the street, turning the streetlights off and on with his waving arms.

She'd seen the dance of tiny lights, watched some flutter close enough to her window that she could make out their figures—male, female.

Wonders, she thought. From this very window she'd witnessed wonders. And viciousness. Human cruelty that rampaged with guns and knives and wild eyes. The dark side of magicks that tossed lethal balls of fire or struck others down with black, screaming swords.

So even as her light grew, the world died, in front of her eyes.

With a shuddering heart, Lana thought of the numbers reported by the woman on TV. More than a billion and a half dead. A billion and a half lives wiped away, not by terrorism, not by bombs and tanks or mad ideology. But by a virus, germs, some microscopic bug scientists labeled dispassionately with letters.

And people more succinctly, to her mind, called the Doom.

Arlys Reid was now Lana's primary touchstone with the world outside the loft. She clung to the daily broadcasts because the reporter seemed so calm, so impossibly calm as she spoke of horror.

And hope, Lana reminded herself. The continuing work on a cure. But even when it came—would it come?—nothing would ever be the same again.

The Doom spread its poison so fast, while magicks, both the dark and the light, rose up to fill the void death created.

What would be left at the end of things?

"Lana, come away from the window. It's not safe."

"I shielded it. No one can see in."

"Did you bulletproof it?" Max strode to her, pulled her back.

She turned into him, squeezed her eyes shut. "Oh, Max. How can this be real? There's smoke to the west. It's all but blocking out the sky. New York's dying, Max."

"I know it." Enfolding her, he stared over her head, at the smoke, at what looked to be birds, black against the gray, circling. "I finally got ahold of Eric."

Lana drew back quickly. Max had been trying to reach his younger brother for days. "Thank God! He's all right?"

"Yes. He hasn't been able to reach our parents, either. With them traveling in France when this hit . . . There's no way to know. I haven't been able to push the signal that far. Yet."

"I know they're all right. I just know they are. Where is Eric?"

"Still at Penn State, but he says it's bad, and he's going to try to get out tonight. He's going to head west, get away from the city. He's got a group of people to travel with and they're stockpiling supplies. He was able to give me the location before the signal dropped. I just couldn't hold it any longer."

"But you reached him, and he's all right." She held on to that, and to Max's hands. "You want to go, find him."

"We have to get out of New York, Lana. You said it yourself, the city's dying."

She glanced back at the window. "All my life," she told him. "I've lived here all my life. Worked here, met you here. It's not our home anymore. And you need to find Eric. We need to go, find him."

Relieved she understood, he rested his cheek on the top of her head. He'd found his place here, in this city, considered it his power center—for the writing he loved, the magicks discovered inside him. Here, he'd truly begun, studying, practicing the Craft, building a satisfying career. Here, he'd found Lana; and here, they'd started to build a life together.

But now the city burned and bled. He'd seen enough to know it would take them into hell with it if they stayed. Whatever else he might risk, he wouldn't risk Lana.

"I need to find Eric, but you—keeping you safe—that's the most important thing to me."

She turned her head to brush her lips over his throat. "We'll keep each other safe. Maybe one day we'll come back, help rebuild."

He said nothing to that. He'd been outside the loft, he'd scavenged the streets for supplies. His hopes of coming back had already died.

"One of Eric's group's family has a vacation home in the Alleghenies, so they're heading there. It's fairly isolated." Max continued to watch out the window where birds—were there more of them now?—circled in the rising smoke. "It should be safe there, away from urban areas. I've mapped out the route."

"It's a long way from here to there. Reports—the reliable Arlys Reid—say the tunnels are blocked. And the military has barricades up now, trying to keep people contained."

"We'll get through." Drawing her back, he gripped her shoulders, ran his hands down her arms as if to transfer his determination to her. "We'll get out. Pack up what you need, only what you need. I'm going to go out, get some supplies. Then we're going to steal a car—plenty of them abandoned. I can start it."

He looked down at his hands. "I can do that. We'll head north, get into the Bronx."

"The Bronx?"

"The main problems are the tunnels and bridges. We'll need to get over the Harlem River, but the last I heard, people aren't being stopped from going into the Bronx."

"How do we get there?"

"The Park Avenue Bridge looks like the quickest." He'd been studying maps for days. "It's a train route, but a truck or SUV could handle it. It's only a little more than three hundred feet, so we're off nearly as soon as we're on. And we keep going north until we can cut west into Pennsylvania. We have to get out of New York. Worse is coming, Lana."

"I know. I can feel it." Gripping Max's hand, she turned toward the TV. "She's saying that the government, the scientists, the officials are all claiming they're close to a vaccine, but I don't feel that. I don't feel that, Max, as much as I want to."

Resolved, Lana stepped back. "I'll pack, for both of us. We won't need much."

"Warm clothes," he told her. "And wear something you can move in, run in, if necessary. We'll pack up food—but keep that light for now, too. Flashlights, extra batteries, water, a couple of blankets. We can get more supplies once we're on the road."

She looked at the wall of shelves—floor to ceiling like the windows—and the dozens and dozens of books—some with his name on them.

Understanding, he shrugged. "I've read them anyway. I'm going out, getting us a couple of backpacks. Meanwhile, pack one bag, Lana, for both of us."

"Don't take any chances."

He cupped her face, kissed her. "I'll be back in an hour."

"I'll be ready." But as her nerves skittered, she held on another moment. "Let's just go now, Max, together. We can get whatever we need once we're out of the city."

"Lana." Now he kissed her forehead. "A lot of people who took off unprepared ended up dead. We're going to keep our heads, do this step-by-step. Warm clothes," he repeated, and went to put on his own coat, pulled on a ski cap. "An hour. Bolt the door behind me."

When he went out, she turned the locks he'd installed since the madness began.

He'd come back, she told herself. He'd come back because he was smart and quick, because he had power inside him. Because he'd never leave her alone.

She went into the bedroom, stared at the clothes in her closet. No fun or pretty dresses, no stylish shoes or sexy boots. She felt a little pang, imagined Max felt the same pang about leaving the books.

Necessity meant leaving things they loved—but never each other.

She packed sweaters, sweatshirts, thick leggings, wool trousers, jeans, flannel shirts, socks, underwear. One blanket, one big, warm throw, two towels, a small bag for basic toiletries.

In the bathroom she sighed over her collection of skin-care products, hair products, makeup, bath oils. Convinced herself that one, just one, jar of her favorite moisturizer equaled necessity.

She walked out into the living room as Arlys Reid ended her broadcast with a report of a naked woman riding a unicorn on Madison.

"I hope it's true," Lana murmured, shutting off the TV for the last time.

For sentiment, she selected her favorite photo of her and Max. He stood behind her, his arms around her. Her hands crossed over his. He wore black jeans and a blue shirt rolled to his elbows, and she a floaty summer dress—with the lush green of Central Park around them.

She packed it, frame and all, between the towels. And slipped in a copy of his first published novel, *The Wizard King*.

For hope, she went into his office, took his flash drive where he backed up his work in progress. One day, when sanity came back to the world, he'd want it.

She set out the two flashlights kept in the skinny kitchen closet, the spare batteries. She gathered bread she'd made only the day before, a bag of pasta, another of rice, bags of herbs she'd dried, coffee, tea. She used a small soft-sided cooler for the few perishables, some frozen chicken breasts.

They wouldn't starve—for a while at least.

She unrolled her knives, the gorgeous Japanese blades she'd saved up for—months of scrimping, but so worth it.

She probably shouldn't take them all, but she admitted leaving any behind would break her heart more than abandoning her wardrobe. Besides, they were tools.

She rolled them up again, set them aside. Her tools, she thought, so she'd carry them in her backpack. Her tools, her weight.

However foolish it was, she went in, neatly made the bed, arranged the throw pillows.

She dressed—warm clothes, thick socks, sturdy boots.

When she heard Max's knock—seven times, three-three-one— she all but flew to the door, yanking at the locks. Then flung herself into his arms.

"I wouldn't let myself worry while you were gone." She pulled him inside. "So it all crested and ebbed the second I heard your knock."

Tears swam into her eyes, shimmered—and she burst into laughter when he held out a burgundy backpack with candy-pink trim.

He grinned back at her. "You like pink. They had one in stock."

"Max." Blinking away the tears, she took it. "Wow. Already heavy."

"I loaded them both up—yours and my manly camo."

Though he didn't tell her his held a 9mm and extra clips he'd found in a looted storeroom.

"I got each of us a multi-tool and a kit for filtering water, some bungee cords." He took off his hat, shoved his fingers through his hair. "We're New Yorkers, Lana. Urbanites. We're going to be strangers in a strange land out there."

"We'll be together."

"I won't let anyone hurt you."

"Good. I won't let anyone hurt you, either."

"Let's pack up the rest. We might have to hike awhile before we find something drivable. I want to be out of New York before dark."

As they added to the backpacks, he eyed her knife roll.

"All of them?"

"I didn't take a single pair of Manolos. That stings, Max. It stings."

He considered it, then chose a bottle of wine from the rack, slipped it into his pack. "Seems fair."

"It does. You have a knife on your belt. That's a knife sheath, isn't it?"

"It's a tool. And a precaution," he added when she said nothing. After a moment, he unzipped the front pocket of the pack, took out the gun and holster.

Shocked, sincerely, to see a gun in his hand, she stepped back. "Oh, Max. Not a gun. We've both always felt the same way about guns."

"A strange land, Lana. A dangerous one." He clipped it on his belt. "You haven't been out in nearly two weeks." He took her hand, squeezed it. "Trust me, it's necessary."

"I do trust you. I want to get out, Max, get somewhere guns aren't necessary, and knives aren't a precaution. Let's go. Let's just go."

She started to put on the cashmere coat—blue as her eyes—he'd given her for Christmas, but at his head shake, switched to her parka. At least he didn't quibble about the cashmere scarf she wrapped around her neck.

He helped her shoulder her backpack. "Can you handle it?"

She made a fist, bent her arm at the elbow. "I'm an urbanite who uses the gym. Or used to."

With it, she picked up her purse, put it on cross-body.

"Lana, you don't need—"

"I'm leaving my food processor, my Dutch oven, my worn exactly once Louboutin over-the-knee boots, but I'm not leaving without my purse." Rolling her shoulders to adjust the pack, she gave him a steady, challenging stare. "Doom or no Doom, there are lines, Max. There are lines."

"Were those the boots you walked into my office wearing—with one of my shirts?"

"Right. That makes worn twice."

"I'll miss them as much as you."

It was good, she thought, good they'd made each other smile before they left their home.

He hefted the bag she'd packed. Opened the door.

"We keep moving," he told her. "Just keep moving north until we find a truck or an SUV."

As her smile dropped away, she only nodded.

They moved toward the stairway at the end of the common hall. The door of the last unit opened a crack.

"Don't go out there."

"Keep moving," Max ordered when Lana stopped.

The door opened a little wider. Through the opening, Lana saw the woman she knew casually as Michelle. Worked in advertising, some family money, divorced, active social life.

Now Michelle's hair, the mad tangles of it, flew around her face as if in a wild wind.

Behind her dishes, glassware, pillows, and photos flew in circles.

"Don't go out there," she repeated. "There's death out there." Then she grinned, horribly, as she whirled her fingers in the air. "I can't stop! I just can't stop! We're all mad here. All. Mad. Here."

She slammed the door.

"Can't we help her?" Lana asked him.

Max just took her arm, pulling her to the stairwell. "Keep moving."

"She's one of us, Max."

"And some like us couldn't handle what turned on inside them. They've gone mad, like she has. Immune to the virus, doomed anyway. That's the reality, Lana. Keep moving."

They walked down three floors to the narrow lobby.

Mail slots gaped open, their doors broken off or hanging out like tongues. Graffiti smeared the walls. She smelled urine, harsh and stale.

"I didn't know they'd made it into the building."

"Up to the second floor," Max told her. "Most of the tenants took off before that. I'm not sure if anyone's still in the building below the third floor."

They stepped out into the winter sunlight and snapping wind. Lana smelled smoke and ash, food gone rotten, and what she knew was death.

She kept moving, said nothing as they walked quickly through what had been her little world of streets and shops and cafes.

In its place lay destruction, desolation, and deserted streets scattered with wrecked and abandoned cars. A terrible quiet made their footsteps echo.

She yearned for the engines, the horns, the voices, the clashing, crashing music of the city. She mourned it as she walked north.

"Max, God, Max, there are bodies in that car."

"Some were too sick to get out or to the hospital, but tried anyway. I see more every time I come out. We can't stop, Lana. There's nothing we can do."

"It's wrong to leave them like this, but everything about this is wrong. Even if they started dispensing a vaccine tomorrow . . ." She heard it in his silence, as truly as if he had spoken. "You don't think there'll be a vaccine."

"I think there are more dead than reported, and will be more to come. I don't think they're close to finding a cure."

"We can't think like that. Max, we can't—"

As she spoke, a girl—she couldn't have been more than fifteen—jumped out of a smashed display window, a bulging knapsack on her back.

Lana started to speak, reassuring words on her tongue. The girl smiled as she yanked a toothy knife out of her belt.

"How about you dump the backpacks, the bags, and keep walking? Then I won't cut you."

Shock as much as fear had Lana cringing back. Max shifted in front of her.

"Do us all a favor," he suggested. "Turn around, walk away."

The girl, pale hair spiking out beneath a wool cap, sliced the knife in the air. It whistled in the silence. "Your bitch won't look so pretty when I put a few holes in her. Dump your shit unless you want to bleed."

When the girl lunged, jabbing with the knife, Lana reacted instinctively. She threw up a hand, fear screaming inside her head.

With pain widening her eyes, the girl jerked back, cried out. Those few seconds gave Max time to pull out the gun on his hip.

"Back off. Walk away."

"You're one of them." Eyes, full of hate now, narrowed on Lana. "You're an Uncanny. You did this. You did all this. You're fucking filth." She spat at their feet and ran.

"Max, my God—"

"Move! She might have friends."

She broke into a jog with him, noting he kept the gun out. "What did she mean by—"

"Later. There, that silver SUV. See it?"

She saw it, saw its bumper crumpled by a sedan. Just as she saw the bodies sprawled on the street beside them.

Max shoved the gun back in its holster, gripped her hand. Now she had to sprint to keep up with his longer legs.

"Max. The blood . . ." It soaked into the street.

"Ignore it."

As he wrenched the door open, the roar of an engine broke the silence. "Get in!"

Lana had to step through blood and over death to throw herself awkwardly into the car. She couldn't block the short scream at the thunder of gunfire and sat trembling as Max launched himself behind the wheel, heaving the bag into the back. She watched the bag slap then bounce onto an empty car seat.

A line of colorful plastic rings jingled as he held a hand out to the starter. A motorcycle streaked around the corner, racing toward them. The girl rode pillion behind a man whose red-streaked black hair flew in the wind.

"Get the Uncannys!" she screamed. "Kill them!"

A group of four, possibly five, people swarmed after them, firing at the SUV. Sweat shimmered on Max's face as he clenched his jaw. "Come on, come on," he urged.

Thinking of the life they might have had, the world that might have been, Lana closed her eyes. At least they'd die together, she thought, gripping his arm.

The engine sprang to life. Max shoved it into Drive, stomped on the gas.

"Hold on," he warned and, wrenching the wheel, steered away from the mob, tires screaming.

Lana jolted when the side mirror exploded from a bullet, and the SUV bumped hard over the curb, banged back. It kissed the side of another wrecked car before Max floored it.

They streaked down the street with the motorcycle in pursuit.

Max didn't slow when they came to more wrecks, more abandoned cars, but threaded through them at a dangerous speed. Sparks flew when he veered close enough for metal to skim against metal.

She risked a look behind. "I think they're gaining. My Jesus, Max, the girl—that same girl—she has a gun. She's—"

Bullets singed the air. She heard glass breaking.

"Taillight," he said grimly, cut the corner at Fiftieth Street and had the SUV rocking, pushed east. "I might have to slow to get across town, Lana, to get through abandoned cars. He's got more maneuverability. Do what you did back on the street."

In full panic, she pressed her hands to the sides of her head. "I don't *know* what I did. I was terrified."

He spun the wheel, spun it back, bumped over an already flattened messenger bike. "Scared now? Knock them back, Lana. Knock them back or I don't know if we'll make it."

A bullet hit the rear window, shattering glass. Lana threw out her hand. Threw her fear with it.

The front wheel of the bike shot straight up; the rear lifted. As it began to flip, the girl flew off. Lana heard her screaming before she slammed onto the hood of a car. The man held on, fighting for control. But the motorcycle tumbled, flipped, and then both it and its driver skidded and rolled over the street.

"God, I killed them! Did I kill them?"

"You saved us."

He slowed a little, weaving across town. He had to take a jog north at Broadway as a clog of wrecked cars blocked the east-side route. Behind them, Times Square, once a crowded, chaotic world of its own, stood silent as a grave.

He slowed at every intersection, checking to see if the way held clear. Turned east.

How many times, Lana wondered, how many times had she taken a cab or the subway to Midtown to shop or have lunch or go to the theater?

A sale at Barneys, a hunt through the shoe paradise of Saks's eighth floor. A stroll in Central Park with Max.

Over now, only memories now.

Of the few signs of life she did see, people moved furtively, not with that brisk, I've-got-places-to-go New York pace. No tourists with their heads tipped back marveling at skyscrapers.

Smashed windows, overturned trash cans, broken streetlights, a dog, so thin its ribs showed, hunting for food. Would he go feral, she wondered, hunt for human flesh?

"I don't know the population of New York."

"It was closing in on nine million," Max told her.

"We've come nearly fifty blocks, and I haven't seen fifty people. Not even one person a block." She took a breath, tried to steady herself. "I didn't believe you when you said they weren't reporting all the dead. I do now. Why did that girl want us dead, Max? Why did they come after us that way, try to kill us?"

"Let me get us out of the city first."

He turned onto Park. The wide avenue gave them no clearer path, only provided more room for more cars. She imagined the panic that had caused the pileups, the rage that had overturned buses, cars, the fear that had boarded up windows, even six and seven stories above the streets and sidewalks.

A corner food cart on its side was picked to the bone. A limo burned out to a husk still smoked. Abandoned cranes rose and swayed like giant skeletons. Max threaded through it all, hands tight on the wheel, eyes tracking.

"A little clearer now," he said. "Most would've headed for the tunnels, the bridges, even after they put up barricades."

"It's still beautiful." Lana's throat tightened on the words. "The old brownstones, the mansions."

Even with doors ripped off hinges, windows shattered, the beauty held stubbornly on.

Eyes scanning, Max drove quickly down the wide, once gracious avenue. "It'll come back," he said. "Humans are too stubborn not to rebuild, not to resettle a city like New York."

"Are we human?"

"Of course we are." To comfort both of them, he covered her hand with his. "Don't let the fear and suspicion of the brutal and ignorant make you doubt yourself. We'll get out of Manhattan, and then we'll head north, north and west, until we find a clear way over the river. The farther away from urban areas, the better the chances."

When she only nodded, he squeezed her hand. "If we can't find a way over, we'll find somewhere safe to settle in until spring. Trust me, Lana."

"I do."

"Less than twenty blocks now before the bridge." He flicked a glance at the rearview, frowned. "There's a car moving back there, coming up fast."

In response, Max increased their speed.

Swiveling, Lana looked back. "I think it's the police. The lights— and now sirens. It's the police, Max, you should pull over."

Instead, he gunned it. "Old rules don't apply anymore. Some cops are rounding up people like us."

"No. I haven't heard any reports of that. Max! You're driving too fast."

"I'm not taking any chances. I've talked to others like us, and we're being rounded up when they can find us. That girl's not the only one blaming us. We're nearly there."

"But even once we—" She broke off, squeezing her eyes shut when he whipped around a flipped-over truck.

"Slow them down," he snapped.

"I don't—"

"Do what you did before, but less. Slow them down."

With her heart banging in her throat, she held up a hand, tried to imagine pushing the car back, just pushing it backward.

She saw it fishtail, then miraculously slow. How is this happening? she thought. A few weeks ago she could barely light a candle, and now . . . now she was the one burning with light.

"Keep it up. Just hold it. We only need a couple minutes."

"I'm afraid if I . . . It could be like the motorcycle. I don't want to hurt anyone."

"Just hold steady, there's the bridge. And fuck me! They've lifted the span. I didn't think of it. I should've thought of it."

Losing her focus, she turned and saw the span of the lift bridge raised high. And the gap between it and the road.

"We have to turn off!"

"No. We have to lower it." He gripped her hand again. "Together. We can do it together. Focus, Lana, you know how. Focus on bringing it down, or we're done."

He thought too much of her abilities, of her spine. But his hand held tight to hers, and she felt his power vibrate. Whatever she had, she pushed toward him.

She trembled from the effort, felt everything inside her shift and . . . expand. And with a jolt, like blowing on a candle, the span began to lower.

"It's working. But—"

"Stay focused. We're going to make it."

But they were going too fast, and the span was lowering so slowly. Behind them, sirens screamed.

Together, she thought. Live or die. Closing her eyes, she pushed harder.

She heard a *thud*, felt the car jump and shake.

"Lift it!" Max shouted.

Through the buzzing in her ears, the buzzing through her body, she pushed again. Opened her eyes. For a moment, she thought they were flying.

She whipped around, saw the span lifting, foot by foot behind them. The pursuing car screeched to a stop at the far edge.

"Max. Where is this coming from? How can we do these things? This power, this kind of power, it's terrifying and . . ."

"Exhilarating? A shift of balance, an opening. I don't know, but can't you feel it?"

"Yes. Yes." An opening, she thought, and so much more.

"We got out," Max reassured her. He brought her hand to his lips, but didn't slow down as they zoomed over the tracks. "We'll find a way over. Get some water out of the pack, take some deep breaths. You're shaky."

"People . . . people are trying to kill us."

"We won't let them." When he turned his head to look at her, his eyes burned dark gray and fierce. "We've got a long way to go, Lana, but we're going to make it."

She let her head fall back against the headrest, closed her eyes to try to steady her pulse, to clear the fear haze from her mind.

"It's so strange," she murmured. "All the time I've lived in New York, this is the first time I've been to the Bronx."

His laugh surprised her as it rolled out, so rich, so easy. "Well, it's a hell of a first trip."

CHAPTER FIVE

Jonah Vorhies wandered the chaos of the ER. People still streamed or stumbled in, as if the building itself offered miracles. They came in hacking and puking, bleeding and dying. Most from the Doom, some from the Doom's by-product of violence.

GSWs, knife wounds, broken bones, head injuries.

Some sat quietly, hopelessly, like the man with the boy of about seven in his lap. Or the woman with glassy, feverish eyes praying with a rosary. Death spread so thick in them, so black, he knew they wouldn't last the day.

Others raged, screaming, demanding, spittle flying out of snarling mouths. He thought it a shame their last act in life would be one of such ugliness.

Fights broke out regularly, but rarely lasted long. The virus so destroyed the body that even a world champ would drop after giving or receiving a couple of punches.

The medical staff, what was left of them, did what they could.

There were beds available, he knew. Oh, there were plenty of beds, open ORs, treatment rooms. But not enough doctors, nurses, interns, orderlies to treat and stitch and staunch.

No beds in the morgue—he knew that, too. No vacancies there, and bodies piled up like grim Lincoln Logs.

Most of the medical staff? Dead or fled. Patti, his partner of four years. Patti, the mother of two who'd loved head-banging rock, horror movies (the grislier the better), and Mexican food—don't spare the Tabasco—had fled, kids in tow, to Florida during week two. She'd fled because her father—avid golfer living the good life in Tampa—had died, and her mother—retired teacher, literacy volunteer, ardent knitter—was dying.

He'd seen the Doom in Patti, along with her fear, her grief, when she'd said good-bye. He'd known he'd never see her again.

Her, or the cute nurse who'd liked scrubs with kittens or puppies on them. The gum-snapping orderly, the eager intern who hoped to be a surgeon, and dozens, dozens more.

They dropped like flies, some at home, some struggling to work. He'd brought in a few himself—by himself now. Like the hospital staff, paramedics, EMTs, firefighters, cops had all seen their ranks decimated.

Dead or fled.

Rachel lived—pretty, dedicated Dr. Hopman. He'd see her fighting against the tide of the Doom. Overworked, exhausted, but never panicked. He'd come to look for her, to look into her.

She gave him hope.

Then he'd stay away, locked in his apartment, locked in the dark because hope hurt.

But he'd come back, looking for that tiny spark, that bit of light in a cruel world. And all he saw was death, pressing at him, clawing at him, mocking him for his ability to see it and do nothing.

So he wandered the ER, wandered out of it, accepting the decision he'd made in the dark. This would be his last time to search for hope.

He looked to treatment rooms, saw death. Looked at supply rooms, saw the ravages there.

Maybe he'd take a tour, one last tour.

Outside of the ER, the hospital echoed like a tomb. Maybe that was appropriate, he thought. Maybe that was a sign. And God knew the quiet soothed.

Everything would be quiet soon.

He walked into the staff break room—he had some good memories in there he wanted to take with him. He saw Rachel sitting at one of the tables, drawing her own blood.

"What're you doing?"

She looked up. Worry, fatigue, still no panic. Still no Doom.

"Close the door, Jonah." She capped the sample, labeled it, set it with others in a rack. "I'm drawing blood. I'm immune. More than four weeks, and I'm asymptomatic. I've been exposed multiple times, and show no signs of the virus. Neither do you," she observed. "Sit down. I want a sample."

"Why?"

Calmly, she opened a fresh syringe. "Because everyone I've treated—every single patient—has died. Because I believe you brought Patient Zero into my ER: Ross MacLeod."

When his legs went watery, Jonah sat.

"I . . ."

"I sent a report to the CDC weeks ago when I looked at the timeline, but I never heard back. They're dying, too. I can't get through, but I'll try to send another report tomorrow. I want time before they get to us. Take off your jacket and roll up your sleeve."

" 'Get to us'?"

"They're in New York now—New York City, Chicago, D.C., L.A., Atlanta, of course." She snapped on the rubber tourniquet. "Make a fist," she said before she swabbed the inside of his elbow. "Doing sweeps. Looking for immunes like you and me, taking them in for testing. Whether or not they want to be taken."

"How do you know?"

She smiled a little, sliding the needle in with barely a prick. "Doctors talk to doctors. I have a friend doing her residency in Chicago. Had. I think she's dead now."

When her voice broke, she sat a moment, breathing in and breathing out until she steadied.

"They came in—hazmat suits, tested staff. She didn't pass, but they took away the ones who did. That was three days ago. Her brother worked at Sibley in D.C. They've taken that over. A combination task force sort of thing. CDC, NIH, WHO. They moved the sick to other area hospitals. Culled some out for observation, testing. The immune are in quarantine. Military quarantine. Her brother managed to get out and contact her, warn her. She did the same for me."

"I've been listening to the news when I can get it." When he could stand it. "I haven't heard any of this."

"If anyone in the media knows, they'll keep a lid on it. Or find themselves in some holding area. That's my guess." She capped and labeled his blood sample, put a cotton ball and a Band-Aid on the tiny needle mark.

She sat back, looked into his eyes. "Healy's immune, too."

"I don't know Healy."

"Right, why would you? Lab rat—a good one. He's been running his own tests. We ran plenty on the infected—starting with MacLeod. But we're—he's—running them on the immune now. While he can."

Rachel looked around the break room like a woman who'd just surfaced from a deep pool.

"We're a small hospital in Brooklyn, but they'll get to us. If anyone finds my initial report, they'll get to us faster, and I'll be in quarantine, a test study.

"You, too," she added, then pressed her fingers to her exhausted eyes. "You should stay away from here."

"I just came to say good-bye."

"Good thinking. We're not doing any good. You bringing in the infected, me trying to treat them. A hundred percent mortality rate once infected. A hundred percent."

She covered her face with her hands, shook her head when he touched her arm. "Minute," she murmured, blowing out a long breath before she lowered her hands again. Her eyes, deep, dark brown, shimmered, but tears didn't fall.

"I wanted to be a doctor all my life. Never wanted to be a princess or a ballerina, a rock star, a famous actress. A doctor. Emergency medicine. You're there when people are sick and scared, hurt. You're there. And now? It doesn't make any difference."

"No." He felt the darkness close around him. "It doesn't."

"Maybe our blood will. Maybe Healy finds a miracle. Long odds, but maybe. But I'm going to do what I can while I can. You should go." She laid a hand on his. "Find a safe place. Don't come back here."

He looked down at her hand. He knew it to be strong, capable. "I had sort of a crush on you."

"I know." She smiled at him when he looked back up at her. "Kind of a shame neither one of us acted on it. I—for various reasons— avoided entanglements. What's your excuse?"

"Couldn't get my guts up for it."

"Our mistake. Too late now." She drew her hand back, rose and picked up the rack of samples. "I'm going to take these up to Healy, stand as his lab assistant since he's all that's left in his department. Good luck, Jonah."

He watched her go. No hope, he thought. He'd seen no hope in her. Strength, yes, but that spark of hope had died. He understood.

He rolled down his sleeve, put on his jacket. He didn't want to go back through the ER, through all that death, but knew it would help him follow through on the decision he'd made.

He ignored the screaming, the retching, the terrible racking coughs, and stepped out into the air. He'd thought to finish this inside. If he had the balls, he'd have gone to the morgue to end it. Make it easy on everyone. But he just couldn't face that.

Right here, he considered, at the doors of the ER? But hell, they had enough to do. In his ambulance? That seemed like good closure.

Behind the wheel, or in the back? Behind the wheel, or in the back? Why was it so hard to decide?

The act itself? No problem. He'd handled enough suicides and attempted suicides to know the best way. His grandfather's old .32. Barrel in the mouth, pull the trigger. Done.

He just couldn't live seeing death all around him. Hopeless, inevitable death. He couldn't keep looking at the faces of neighbors, coworkers, friends, family, and seeing death in them.

He couldn't keep locking himself in the dark to stop seeing it. Couldn't keep hearing the screams, the gunfire, the pleas for help, the mad laughter.

Eventually his depression and despair would turn to madness. And he feared, actively feared, that the madness would turn him into one of the vicious who hunted others and caused more death.

Better to end it, just end it and go into the quiet.

He reached into his coat pocket, felt the reassuring shape of the gun. He started toward the ambulance, glad he'd had the chance to see Rachel, to help her, to say good-bye. He wondered what Healy would find in his blood. Something tainted with this horrible ability?

Cursed blood.

He turned at the blast of a horn, but kept walking even as the minivan squealed up, bumped onto the curb. More death for the death house, he thought, hunching his shoulders at the call for help.

No help for it.

"Please, please. Help me."

No more death, he vowed. He wasn't going to look at any more death.

"The babies are coming! I need help."

He couldn't stop himself from looking back again, and watched the woman drag herself out of the bright red van, cradling her pregnant belly.

"I need a doctor. I'm in labor. They're coming."

He didn't see death, but life. Three lives. Three bright sparks.

Comforting himself that he could kill himself later, he went to her.

"How many weeks?"

"Thirty-four weeks, five days. Twins. I'm having twins."

"That's good baking time for a two-pack." He got an arm around her.

"Are you a doctor?"

"No. Paramedic. I'm not taking you through the ER. It's full of the infected."

"I think I'm immune. Everyone else . . . But the babies. They're alive. They're not sick."

Hearing the fear in her voice, he tuned his own to easy reassurance. "Okay, it's going to be okay. We're going to go in that door up there. I'll get you to Maternity. We'll get you a doctor."

"I— Contraction!" She grabbed on to him, digging her fingers in like claws, breathing in hisses.

"Slow it down."

"You slow it down," she snapped, hissing her way through it. "Sorry."

"No problem. How far apart?"

"I couldn't time them once I started driving. About three minutes when I left. It took me, I don't know. Ten minutes to get here. I didn't know what else to do."

He got her inside, steered her toward the elevators. "What's your name?"

"Katie."

"I'm Jonah. You ready for twins, Katie?"

She looked up at him, huge green eyes, then dropped her head on his chest and wept.

"It's okay, it's okay. It's all going to be all right."

Bringing babies into this dark, deadly world? He hadn't thought of it. Told himself not to think beyond getting her to Maternity.

"Did your water break?"

She shook her head.

The elevator doors opened onto an empty reception area. That same echoing silence made him realize he might find no help for her there.

He led her back—empty rooms, unmanned desk. Didn't anyone have babies anymore?

He steered her into one of the birthing suites. "Prime digs," he said, working to keep cheer in his voice. "Let's get your coat off, get you in bed. Who's your OB?"

"He's dead. It doesn't matter, he's dead."

"Let's get your shoes off." He pressed the nurse's call button before he crouched down, pulled off her shoes.

They wouldn't bother with a gown. He didn't know where to find one, didn't want to waste time looking. She was wearing a dress anyway.

"Here you go." He helped her into bed, stopping when she dug her fingers into his arm again. Pushed the call button again.

"Are they all dead?" she asked when the contraction passed. "The doctors, the nurses?"

"No. I was just talking to a doctor downstairs, a friend of mine, before I walked out and you drove up. I'm going to see if I can find one of the OB nurses."

"Oh God, don't leave me."

"I won't. I swear, I won't. I'm going to see if I can find a nurse, and I'm going to get a couple of warming trays for the babies. Good baking time," he said again, "but they're preemies."

"I tried to get to thirty-six weeks. I tried, but—"

"Hey." Taking her hand, he waited until her teary eyes met his. "You're right on the edge of thirty-five. Damn good job. Give me two minutes, all right? Don't push, Katie. Breathe through it if you have another before I get back. Don't push."

"Hurry. Please."

"Promise."

He stepped out, then ran.

He didn't know this wing, had only been in it a handful of times, and only as far as the desk. He tried to take heart when he saw three infants behind the glass in their nursery cribs. Somebody had to be on the floor. Somebody had to be caring for the babies.

He hit a pair of double doors, stepped into an OR. A doctor— he hoped—gowned, gloved, holding a scalpel. A nurse, and a pregnant woman on the table, eyes closed.

"I've got a woman in labor with twins. I—"

"And I'm trying to save the life of this woman and fetus. Get out!"

"I need— She needs a doctor."

"I said get out! I'm it. I'm what's left, and I'm fucking busy here. Nurse!"

"Go!" She ordered as the doctor made the incision.

"Page Dr. Hopman. Just do that. Page her."

Jonah rushed out, grabbed two warming trays, pushed them back to the room where Katie panted through a contraction.

"Keep breathing, keep breathing. I'm going to set these up so they'll be ready."

"Doctor," she managed.

He turned on the trays, shed his coat, rolled up his sleeves. "It's going to be you, me, and the twins. We're going to be fine."

"Oh God. Oh God. Have you ever delivered a baby?"

"Yeah, a few times."

"Would you say that even if you hadn't?"

"No. I've even delivered a preemie. It's my first multiple, but hey, if you can do one, you can do two. I'm going to wash my hands, get gloved. Then we'll see where we're at, okay?"

"I'm out of choices." She stared up at the ceiling, as she'd done when her mother had been dying. "If it goes wrong for me, promise me you'll take care of them. You'll take care of my babies."

"It's not going to go wrong, and I'm going to take care of them. And you. Solemn oath." He crossed his heart, stepped into the bath to scrub his hands.

"What are you naming them?" he called out.

"The girl's Antonia. My husband . . . he wanted a girl especially. Before we knew we were having twins, he hoped for a girl. The boy's Duncan for my father's father."

"Nice. Good, strong names." He pulled on gloves, took one deep, long breath. "One of each, huh? Best of the best."

"He died here. My Tony. My parents, too, and my brother. Four people I loved died in this hospital, but I didn't know where else to go."

"I'm sorry. But your babies aren't going to die, and neither are you. Ah, I gotta get your underwear off, and take a look at things."

"Modesty isn't anywhere on my list."

He rolled the panties away. "I need you to scoot up a little."

"'Scoot,' my ass."

"Yeah, it's your ass I need you to scoot."

He smiled when she laughed. "Funny guy."

"You should hear my full stand-up routine. I gotta get personal, and I know it's uncomfortable. Breathe through."

He inserted fingers to measure her while she blew at the ceiling.

"You're fully dilated, Katie. I'll apologize to Antonia when she gets here. I poked her head."

"Duncan. He's first. His head?"

"Yeah." And thank God it was his head, not *his* ass.

"One's coming."

"Ride it out. You're really close. You—there she blows. Water broke."

"It hurts. Oh, Christ Jesus, Mother of Mary, it hurts!"

"I know."

"What do you know? You're a man." She turned her head, closed her eyes, let out a long, cleansing breath. "We were going to have Adele playing during delivery. And Tony and I were going to have both our moms in with us. His mom's dead now, and his father. My brother, Tony's brother and sister. The babies only have me."

"Duncan's crowning, Katie. I can see his head. He's got hair! It's dark. Do you want the mirror?"

She let out a sob, covered her eyes, and held up a hand for him to wait. "I loved him, so much. Tony. My parents, my brother, his family. My family. They're all gone. The babies. The babies are all I have left of my family. I'm all they'll have." She wiped her eyes. "I want the mirror, please. I want to see them born."

He adjusted it until she nodded. Coached her through the next contractions, then through the pushing.

She didn't speak of loss again, but bore down like a warrior in battle.

Duncan, with his dark hair and waving fists, came into the world yelling. His mother laughed, held out her arms.

"He's got good color, and damn good lungs." Jonah wiped off the down, laid the baby in Katie's arms. "I'm clamping off the cord."

"He's beautiful. He's perfect. Is he perfect? Please."

"We're going to weigh him and get him in the warming tray. He sure looks perfect."

"He . . . He's going for the breast!"

"Well, he's a guy."

"The books say, especially with preemies . . . He's latched right on! He's hungry. And— Oh God, she's coming. She's coming."

"Antonia doesn't want to get left behind. Let me put him in the tray."

"No, no. I've got him. He's hungry. I need to push!"

"Okay, a good one now. You can do better."

"I'm trying!"

"Okay, hold it. Relax, relax, breathe. I'm going to need one more. One good, strong one. She's ready. Look at the mirror, Katie. Push her out."

She sucked in her breath, let it out in a low, keening wail. Jonah cupped the head, turned the shoulders, and Antonia slipped into his hands.

"There she is."

"She's not crying, she's not crying. What's wrong?"

"Give her a second." Jonah cleared out the baby's nose, mouth, rubbed the tiny chest. "Come on, Antonia. We know you're no crybaby, but your mom wants to hear from you. She's just taking her time. She's fine. The light's in her, not the dark. I see life, not death."

"What—"

"And there." Jonah grinned as the baby let out a high wail, an insulted, annoyed little sound. "She's pinking right up. Just wanted to take stock first, that's all. She's a beauty, Mom."

Katie cuddled her. "Look at her sweet little head."

"Yeah, her brother hogged all the hair. Give her some time, she'll outdo him there. Cutting the cords. If he's finished his snack, I want to clean him up, weigh him, check a couple of things. You've got another round with the placenta."

"It's got to be easier than delivering twins."

Jonah took Duncan, carefully cleaned him, checked his heart rate and reflexes, weighed him. "He comes in at six pounds, two ounces. That's a solid weight, even for a full-term single. Good job, Katie."

"She's watching me. I know that's probably not true, but it's like she's looking at me. Like she knows me."

"Sure she does." Staring at the baby in his hands, Jonah felt . . . triumph, and a quiet, steady love.

"I want to put Duncan in the warmer for a bit. I need your girl, too. I'm going to hunt you up something cold to drink," he told Katie as he cleaned Antonia. "Some food if I can find it. And your girl weighs in at five pounds, ten ounces. Good for her."

"Contraction."

"Okay, let's get it all out. Nice and clean. Got a pail here. Just shove it out, champ."

When it was done, Katie lay back, said nothing while Jonah wiped the sweat from her face. Then she gripped his hand.

"You said you could see life, not death. Light, not dark. And when you did, when you said that . . . you were different. I could see something different."

"I was a little caught up in the moment." He started to step back, but she tightened her grip, looked at him.

"I've seen things in the last weeks. Things that don't make sense, things out of books and fantasy movies. Are you one of them? One of what they're calling the Uncanny?"

"Look, you're tired, and I've got to—"

"You brought my son and my daughter into the world. You

gave me a family again. You gave me . . ." Tears streamed out as her voice quavered. "You gave me a reason to go on living. I'll be grateful to you every day for the rest of my life. Grateful every time I look at my children. I have children. If part of the reason I have them is you having something, being something, I'm grateful for that, too."

When his eyes teared, he found himself clinging to her hand like a lifeline. "I don't know what I am. I don't know. I can see death coming in someone, or injury. I can see how it'll happen, and I can't make it stop."

"You saw life in my babies, and in me. You saw life. I know what you are. You're my personal miracle."

He had to sit on the side of the bed, to gather himself. "I was going to kill myself."

"No. No, Jonah."

"If you'd driven up five minutes later, I'd be dead. I didn't think I could take seeing any more death. Then you drove up, and I saw all that life. I guess you're my personal miracle, too."

Katie eased herself up. "Can you hold on to me a minute?"

"Sure. Sure, I can."

She laid her head on his shoulder.

He heard footsteps coming fast and brisk—heard Rachel call his name.

"In here. Doctor," he told Katie. "Better late than never."

"Who needs a doctor?"

Rachel came to the door, looked in at him, over at the warming units. "Well, look here. Did you do this?"

"She helped a little," Jonah said.

"It looks like excellent teamwork. I'm Dr. Hopman," she began, then Katie turned her head. "Katie? It's Katie Parsoni, isn't it?"

"Yes. Dr. Hopman." Tears spilled faster now. Katie held out a hand even as she clung to Jonah. "You're alive."

"Yes, and so are you and your babies. I'm just going to take a look at them, and you."

"Duncan—six pounds, two ounces," Jonah told her. "Antonia—five, ten. I forgot to get their lengths."

"You did the important work. How are you feeling, Mom?" she asked as she went over to examine Duncan.

"Tired, hungry, grateful, sad, happy. I feel everything. Dr. Hopman was with me when my mother died. She took care of my mother. My father, too."

"Jonah brought them to the hospital," Rachel said, glancing back at him. "Ross and Angela MacLeod."

"MacLeod." Chicken soup on the stove. The first. Patient Zero. "It's like a circle," he murmured.

"We're looking at two healthy babies." Rachel crouched down, examining the placentas, the umbilical cords. "Good. Good."

"How soon can they travel?" Jonah demanded.

"I need to have a look at Katie, and I'm going to try to find somebody in Peeds to examine the babies."

"She's fine, and so are they. I can see it, just like I could see her mother wasn't fine while you were working on her dad. Like I could see you were immune. I had sort of a sense before . . . before all this. But it's more now. I don't expect you to believe me, but—"

"I do," Rachel corrected. She rubbed her eyes. "I've seen things. Things I didn't believe at first, but you see enough and you're an idiot if you don't believe. I'd also be a lousy doctor if I didn't examine a woman who just gave birth to twins."

"Once you do, I need to know when they can travel. And when you can be ready to go."

"Where am I going?"

"I don't know yet, but I know you're immune. So are Katie and those babies. You said they're doing sweeps, taking immunes into quarantined areas, testing them."

"What?" Katie gripped his shoulder. " 'They'? Like the government? They're detaining people who aren't sick?"

Rachel let out a sigh. "Jonah."

No more bullshit, he thought. No more despair. "She has a right to know. She has babies to think of. You're a doctor. There are people who don't have the virus who need doctors. Who need goddamn smart, adaptable doctors. They're going to try rounding up people like me, too, and I'm damned if I'm going to end up somebody's experiment.

"It's a circle," he repeated. "Her parents to me, me to you, you to Katie, Katie to me. And now the babies. It means something. When can they travel, when can you leave?"

Tired to the bone, Rachel looked at the babies, at the woman weeping silently, at the man who so suddenly looked hard as steel.

"Maybe tomorrow depending on what kind of travel you mean. They have roads blocked."

"I can get a boat."

"A boat?"

"Patti—she was my partner," he told Katie. "She had a boat. It's not much of one, but it'll do. We get to the boat, we get in the boat, we use it to get across the river. And we start heading . . . whatever direction looks best. Stick to rural areas where we can. I'm not sure until we get out. Nobody's putting those kids in some testing ground."

"Nobody's touching my babies." Like a tap wrenched off, tears stopped. "Nobody. We can go now."

Rachel held up a hand. "Tomorrow. I'm going to examine you, and we're going to keep an eye on your babies for twenty-four hours. If there are no complications, we can leave tomorrow. We need supplies. We need diapers and clothes, blankets. We may need formula for the twins."

"Duncan already breastfed."

"Seriously?" Rachel let out a laugh. "More good news. We still need supplies. I can get some of what we need here. I'll go, and clear them to go—if they check out medically—because a woman and her day-old infants could use a doctor. Though Jonah could probably handle most anything. I'll go because you're right. This?" She gestured to include the five of them. "This means something. And because maybe, out there, I can start feeling like a doctor again."

She moved to the bed. "Go hunt up something for the new mother to eat. Maybe a cold drink, definitely some water. And find her something clean to change into. Find us some caps and preemie diapers for the babies. We'll see how resourceful you are, Jonah."

"Consider it done." He rose. "I'll be back," he told Katie.

"I know you will."

"All right, Katie, let's have a look."

"Dr. Hopman?"

"Rachel. It's Rachel, since we appear to have formed an alliance."

"Rachel, when you're done, can I hold my babies?"

"Absolutely." And the spark that had died inside her over the past horrible days rekindled.

ESCAPE

How shall man escape from that which is written;
How shall he flee from his destiny?

—Ferdowsi

CHAPTER SIX

While Katie nursed her daughter for the first time, Arlys Reid decided to take her show on the road. For days now she'd depended on Chuck's reports, on what she could dig out of the shaky Internet, with the few observations from her quick hikes to and from the studio mixed in.

She'd wanted to be a reporter, she told herself as she checked the batteries in her tape recorder. It was time she went out on the street and reported.

She didn't check with her producer, her director. Whatever happened, the decision would be hers—and part of that decision, she knew, weighed from holding back the worst of what Chuck had told her that morning.

Help wasn't coming.

As she got up to put on her coat, Fred looked over from her desk. "Where are you going?"

"Out. To work. I need you to cover for me, Fred. Just say I'm taking a nap or something. I want to get a man-on-the-street segment. If I can find one who doesn't want to rob, rape, or kill me."

"Not going to cover." Fred stood up. "I'm going with you."

"Absolutely not."

Little Fred—all five feet, one inch of her—just smiled. "Absolutely am. I've spent plenty of time out there. Somebody's got to get the Ho Hos and chips, right? And two's better than one," she added, swinging on a bright blue jacket covered with pink stars. "There's a market—well, kind of a hole-in-the-wall place—across Sixth on Fifty-first. It's boarded up, but some of us know you can pull back a couple of the boards and squeeze in."

She pulled a pink cap with a tail ending in a bouncing pom-pom onto her curly mop of red hair. "There's still food, so we can pick up a few supplies. Nobody takes more than they need. We made an agreement."

" 'We'?"

"It's like . . . the neighborhood. Who's left. You don't take more than you need so everybody gets a share."

"Fred." Arlys shouldered on her briefcase and studied the little redhead with the perky, freckled face. "That's a story. You're a story."

Eyes of soft, quiet green clouded. "You can't broadcast it, Arlys. Some people, if they find out there's food they'll take it all. Hoard it."

"No address—not even the area." To seal it, Arlys crossed a finger over her heart. "Just the story. One about people working together, helping each other. A bright spot. Who doesn't need a bright spot right now? You could give me some details—not names or locations—just how you came to the agreement, how it works."

"I'll tell you while we're out for the MOS."

"All right, but we stick together." Arlys thought of the gun in her bag.

"You got that. And don't worry. I've got a way of seeing if somebody's friendly or an asshole. Well, some assholes aren't looking to kill you or anything. They're just assholes because they always were."

"Can't argue with that."

They started out.

"You know, Jim's not going to like you taking chances."

Arlys shrugged. "He'll like if I get a story out of it. There are real people out there, just trying to get through another day. How do they do it? What happened to them? People need to hear about other people getting through. It helps them get through."

"Like not taking more than you need from the market."

"Like that." As they walked down to the lobby, Arlys outlined a general plan. "We head west to Sixth, keeping an eye out for anyone on the street. A group of people, we steer clear. Groups can turn into mobs."

"Mostly at night," Fred commented. "But in the daytime, too."

"I haven't been out at night in three weeks except to get the hell home after the evening broadcast. I used to love walking at night."

"You just have to know where to walk, have to go out in the safe zones."

" 'Safe zones'?"

"Where more good people go than bad. Some of the bad, they're not really bad. They're just scared and desperate. But some are scary bad, and you need to stay away, know how to hide."

It could be, Arlys thought, her MOS was right in front of her. "How do you know about safe zones?"

"You talk to people, and they've talked to people," Fred told her when they reached the lobby. "I didn't say anything because if we broadcast it maybe the bad ones will find the safe zones. I thought, if we have to shut down, when we do, I'll tell everybody else so they can try to get to one."

"You amaze me, Fred."

"Sometimes they can help if somebody wants to get out of the city. But a lot of people still here don't want to give up the city, even if they have to fight."

Arlys unlocked the door.

"Aren't you going to wear a mask?"

"You know they don't do any good, don't you?" Arlys looked over at Fred. "You know as well as I do if you're going to get it, you get it."

"They make some people feel safe. I thought that's how you felt."

"Not anymore."

They stepped out and Arlys locked the door. "We're not going to get separated, but just in case, do you have your key?"

"Don't worry," Fred assured her.

Arlys nodded and they began to walk through air that carried the stench of burning and blood and piss.

"How many people do you estimate, Fred, you've seen or spoken with in these safe zones? I won't go on air with it. Off the record."

"I don't know exactly. I know they're trying to keep a count, but it changes. People come, people go. People are still getting sick. Still dying. We—they—try to take the bodies into green areas, parks, at dawn. It's still cold enough so, you know."

"I know." But when the temperatures warmed again, the decay would be horrific. And those who had died indoors . . .

She'd caught the smell in her own building. The smell of decay.

"You can't really have funerals or memorials, exactly. There are so many," Fred added. "Somebody says some words, and . . . You have to burn them. There are rats, you know, and dogs and cats and . . . They can't help it, so you have to burn them. It's clean, and it's kind, I think."

"You've been to these . . . memorials?"

Fred nodded. "It's so sad, Arlys. But it's the right thing to do. You have to try to do the right thing, but there are so many. A lot more than they say."

"I know."

From under her pom-pom cap, Fred slanted a look up at Arlys. "You know?"

"I have a source, but . . . It's like not broadcasting the safe zones. If I go on air with everything he tells me, they'll stop me. And they might get to him."

"You wouldn't tell. You wouldn't reveal a source."

"I wouldn't tell, but there might be a way to trace him from me. I can't take the chance. I have a protocol—he gave me—if I ever go on air with what he asked me to hold back? I have to destroy the computer I'm working on, my notes, everything. And go."

"Go where?"

"I can't tell you."

"Because he told you in confidence."

"That's right. But if—"

"*Shh!* Hear that?" Even as she spoke, Fred grabbed Arlys's arm, yanking her back from the corner of Sixth. "In here."

As Fred dragged her through the broken display window of what had once been a shoe store, Arlys heard the engine.

"It sounds like a motorcycle. Raiders?"

"They like motorcycles. You can get around the wrecks." Fred put her finger to her lips, drew Arlys away from the broken glass, into the shadows.

Arlys started to speak, but Fred shook her head fiercely.

She heard the sound of more glass breaking, wild laughter. Then the roaring engine thundered by, began to fade again.

Fred put her hand up, a wait signal, for several seconds more. "Some of them can hear like bats. And sometimes they travel in groups. You can't take chances."

After letting out a breath, Arlys looked around. The empty shelves ran up the walls on both sides. If there had been display tables, someone had hauled them off.

A few shoes scattered around the floor, a couple of handbags, some socks.

"I'm surprised they left anything."

"The bad ones take what they want, bust the rest up. They'll pee on things, even poop on them. They don't want the stuff, but they don't want anybody else to have it. Mostly right now, they do stuff like this."

She led Arlys out again, walked to the corner, looked long north and long south before jogging across the street.

"They get drunk or high," she continued, "set fires, shoot off guns. They ride around looking for somebody who doesn't hide quick enough, or run fast enough. They hurt them. Or kill them."

"But they're starting to hunt."

"Hunt people?"

"Starting to go through buildings where people live. Or lived. It's the dead that keep them out of some places. But it won't keep them out much longer. They do the same thing, bust things up, take what they want, and look for people to hurt. Raiders."

She stopped by an empty car.

"This wasn't here yesterday. See, they tried to get through, but the street's mostly blocked. They didn't take their things. See, they tried to take too much, and couldn't take it with them if they had to run. The market's just down here."

"Is this a safe zone?"

"It's safe enough if you're not stupid." She smiled when she said it.

She stopped at a boarded storefront. Arlys frowned at the symbols painted over the boards. "What does all this mean?"

"Oh . . . You could say it's for good luck. Somebody's inside now. It's okay," she said quickly. "It's not one of the Raiders or the bad ones."

"How do you know?"

But Fred had already eased two boards apart. "Blessings," she said. "It's like a password," she told Arlys, and stepped inside.

The boards closed behind Arlys, pitching them into full dark. Not even a crack of light showed. Then one flashed on.

"Who's with you, Fred?"

"Hi, T.J. This is Arlys. We work together. It's okay. She's one of the good ones."

"Are you bringing her into one of the zones?"

"Not now anyway. She's looking for an interview, and I figured since we were out, I'd get a couple cans of soup for back at the station. How's Noah?"

When his answer was silence, Fred took a step forward. "T.J., you know I wouldn't bring anyone who means harm."

"You can cause it without meaning to."

"Would you mind getting that light out of my eyes?" Arlys spoke coolly. "Then I can answer for myself."

It lowered slowly.

"I don't know how much longer we'll be able to broadcast. There are only a handful of us still working, still able and willing to. Communication matters, information matters, even when it's thin. I don't know how many people can still access a broadcast, but for everyone who can, they can relay that information to someone else. My guess, and we can hope it's pessimistic, is we've got a few days, maybe a week before we go dark. I want to do my job until that happens. Then I'm going to find some other way to do my job."

"What's this interview bull?"

"I want to go on with a story, a personal one. I want people to hear—not from me, but from someone who's getting through this. I want to go on with that story. Because it matters. It's about all that matters now."

"You want to tell a story?"

"I want you to tell yours," Arlys corrected. "I want you to speak to and for all the others out there, hanging on. What you think, what you feel, what you've done. Maybe one person hears it, and it helps them hang on."

"Talk to her, T.J. It's the right thing to do."

"No names," Arlys added. "I'll call you something else. No location. I won't say where we spoke. I have a recorder with me. Anything you say is off the record, I turn it off."

"You're going to go on with this tonight?"

"I'm going to ask to go on with it when I get back, ask for it to run every hour until the evening report. Tomorrow, if I can, I'm going to try to talk to someone else, get their story, and do the same thing. This isn't going to be the end because we're not going to let it be the end. The Raiders aren't going to pick us clean. We're going to get through. I want you to tell me how you did, how you are."

"You want to hear my story? I'll tell you my story."

"Can I get my recorder? And my flashlight?"

"Go ahead."

She reached in her briefcase, found the flashlight by feel, took her recorder out of her pocket before turning the light on, aiming it in the direction of T.J.'s voice.

A big guy, she thought, a broad-shouldered black man with fierce black eyes. The stubble thickening on his head told her he'd likely shaved it routinely until recently.

"You'll call me Ben."

"All right, Ben. I'm turning on the recorder. This is Arlys Reid. I'm speaking to Ben. I've asked him to tell me, tell all of us, his story. The pandemic has changed everything for everyone. How do you cope?"

"You get up in the morning, and do what you have to do. You get up, thinking for just a split second, everything's the way it was. Then you know it's not. It's never going to be, but you get up and keep going. Three weeks and two days ago, I lost my husband. The best man I ever knew. A police officer, decorated. When things started to go bad, he went out every day, trying to help people. To serve and protect. It cost him his life."

"He was killed in the line of duty?"

"Yeah, he was. But not by a bullet or a knife. That would've been easier for him. He got infected, he got sick. By that time, the hospitals were so overloaded . . . He wouldn't go. No point in it, he told me. He wanted to die at home, in our home. His worry was he'd infected me, but I didn't get sick."

He paused a minute, seemed to gather himself.

"I did everything I could for him, for two terrible days. Two days, that's all it took when we realized we couldn't keep pretending it was just exhaustion from working doubles, but the Doom. I'm not going to talk about those two days. I'll just say he died like he wanted. At home. And I took him . . . where I took him to rest."

"I'm so sorry, Ben."

"Everybody thinks their loss is the worst that can happen to them. And this, this fucking scourge, it's taken from everybody. We all had the worst that can happen."

"But you got through it. You're still getting through it."

"I wanted to die, too. I wanted to get sick and die, but I didn't. I thought I could take his gun, take his service weapon, and that'd be a way to die. I thought about that while people were rioting in the streets, when people started acting like animals. And I thought of what he'd say to me, I thought how disappointed in me he'd be for not cherishing life, and doing something to help. And still, I wavered."

He fell silent for nearly thirty seconds, but Arlys said nothing, gave him the time, the space.

"Where I live," he continued, "the building, people were dying or running or going out to join the animals in the streets. I thought: There's nothing left but the dark now. But I could hear my husband's voice in my head saying: Don't you do it. Don't you give up."

"And you didn't."

"Nearly did. I went out one day, started to. Maybe I'd get some food, maybe I'd just keep walking. I didn't know. And there was a boy sitting on the stairs. He lived in the building. I didn't know his name—I'm not going to say his name."

"We'll call him John."

"All right. John was sitting there crying. Both his parents and his brother, all dead. He couldn't stay in his apartment. You can imagine why."

"Yes."

"He thought I meant to harm him at first. He didn't run. He was going to stand and fight, that scared, grieving little boy. He'd fight, and what was I doing but wallowing? So I sat down on the steps, and we talked awhile. I took his mama first, and we were going to take her to where I'd laid my husband. When we went out with her, somebody came up. I'm not going to say a name," he added, but Arlys saw his gaze cut to Fred. "She asked if she could help us. She knew others who could help. So we got that help and we laid John's family to rest.

"And he came to live with me. So we get up in the morning, and we have some breakfast. We do some reading, and some math and such. It's important a boy still learns. I'm teaching him to fight, in case he needs to. We play games because play's as important as learning. We get up and do what we have to do, and that's how we get through it. When he's ready—it's only been a couple weeks—I'm going to get him out of the city. Get him out and find someplace clean. And we'll get up in the morning there, and do what needs to be done. We'll build a life, because death can't be all there is."

He looked at Arlys now, right into her. "This won't be the end of it," he said, repeating her words. "We won't let it be the end of it."

"Thank you, Ben. I hope your story reaches people who need to hear it. I needed to hear it. This is Arlys Reid, grateful for everyone who's doing what needs to be done."

She switched off the recorder. "Don't wait until he's ready. Get John out as soon as you can."

"His name is Noah." T.J.'s eyes flicked between the two women before fixing on her. "You know something you're not telling."

"I know it's going to get worse here. I know if I had a child depending on me, I'd get him out. Fred said there are people who can help you with that. Pack and ask them to help you. You should go with them," she said to Fred.

"I'll stick with you. You know who to contact, T.J. Honest, if Arlys says you should go, you should go. For Noah."

"I'll go talk to him. He knows it's coming. I'm going to miss you, Fred."

He moved over, wrapped arms around her, towering over her.

"Miss you back, and Noah. But, you know, if it's meant, we'll find each other again."

"I want it to be meant." He held out a hand to Arlys. "I thought it would make me angry to tell my story. It didn't. Watch out for yourself."

"I intend to. Good luck, T.J."

He picked up the bag he'd brought in to gather supplies, took one last look, and slipped out through the boards.

"It's going to be a good segment. A powerful one. I think he was here because he needed to tell his story, and he needed you to tell him to get Noah and go."

"Lucky all around."

"Not lucky. Meant. I have something to tell you—off the record."

"Okay, let's grab that soup, and you can tell me on the way back to the station. I want to put this together."

"I really better show you, and here, where it's safe. Don't freak, okay?"

"Why would I . . ."

Arlys trailed off, her jaw dropping, when Fred wiggled her fingers and sparkling lights danced around her.

"How did you—"

"I wanted you to be able to see better." Now she held her hands out to the sides.

Before Arlys's dazzled eyes, iridescent wings flowed out of Fred's back, shimmering right through the jacket she wore. And she rose a foot from the floor, circling in the air with the wings waving.

"What is this? What *is* this?"

"I got a little freaked at first—it just sort of happened one day. Then it was like, this is so beyond all coolness. It turns out I'm a faerie!"

"A what—a faerie? That's crazy. Would you stop doing that!"

Fluid as water, Fred lowered to the ground, but the wings remained. "It's so much fun, but okay. You can't report on this, Arlys—I mean not about me. They call us the Uncanny—I can't figure out if I like that or not, but it's growing on me. I can tell by the way you do the stories, you're like: Oh, yeah, right. But hey." Fred lifted up again. "Oh, yeah, right!"

"It's not possible."

"It shouldn't be possible that more than a billion people are dead in a month. But it *is* possible. And this? Me? Others like me? It's not only possible, it's as real as anything else. Maybe it's some sort of balance. I don't know. I can't figure it out, either, so I accept."

"Others. Like you?"

"Faeries, elves, witches, sirens, sorcerers—and that's just people I've met since."

As if the idea delighted her, Fred fluttered up another foot in the air.

"We have to be careful. Magickal people have the good and the bad, too. So we've got the bad who'd do us harm—and the regular people, who don't get it, who would, too."

She lowered again, touched a hand to Arlys's arm. "I showed you and I'm telling you because something inside me said I should. I've always trusted the something inside me, even when I didn't know it was there."

"Maybe I fell asleep at my desk, and this is all a dream."

On a laugh, Fred gave her a light punch on the arm. "You know you didn't, and it's not."

"I . . . we really need to talk about this."

"Yeah, sure. We have to get back, get that segment up. Maybe after the evening broadcast, when we shut down for the day. We can have some wine and talk about it. I've got some wine squirreled away."

"I think it's going to take a lot of wine."

"Okay, but let's get that soup. You should punch up your makeup, redo your hair before you go on the air."

"Right."

"You freaked?"

"I'm pretty freaked."

Fred smiled. "But you'll do what you need to do. You won't betray me, just like you won't betray your source, or T.J. and Noah. You've got integrity."

Back at the station, Jim called it something else. He called it recklessness and gave Arlys and Fred a heated lecture. A lecture that would have annoyed Arlys down to the core if she hadn't seen the worry on his face, heard it under the anger.

But he couldn't fault the interview. He listened to it twice, then sat back. "It's exceptional. You let him narrate it, let him speak from the heart. A lot of reporters would have inserted a lot of questions, tried to steer him. You didn't."

"It was his story, not mine."

He turned in his chair, stared out the window in the office he rarely used. He'd called them in there—on the carpet—because he'd been pissed and scared.

"It's never supposed to be about you. Before everything went to hell, a lot of journalists had forgotten that. I got caught up in it myself, might have overlooked that quality in you."

He swiveled around again. "Let's get this on the air. You need an intro."

"Already in my head. I'd like it to run every hour until the evening report."

"That's what we'll do. And don't do anything like this again without checking with me first. And don't take this pip-squeak out there. Sorry, Little Fred, but you're not exactly Wonder Woman."

"More like Tinker Bell," Arlys mumbled, making Fred laugh.

"Exactly. Now, let's go do our jobs."

Arlys dictated the intro to Fred while punching up her makeup, smoothing her hair. At the anchor station she waited for the green, for the cue.

"This is Arlys Reid, bringing you what I hope will be a recurring segment. Every day, in the midst of tragedy and despair, people go on. Every one of those who go on lives with loss, lives with uncertainty. Every one has a story to tell, of a life that was, a life that is. This is Ben's story."

They cut the camera, ran the audio.

She listened to the words again, found they struck her just as deeply. She thought of the big man and the young boy, and hoped they found their way to somewhere clean.

"We'll replay Ben's story in one hour," she concluded, "to remind us all of hope and humanity. This is Arlys Reid, signing off for the hour."

Fred applauded. With a sigh of satisfaction, Arlys rose, signaled Fred as she headed to the newsroom. "I'm going to talk Jim into letting us go out with a handheld camera tomorrow."

"Awesome!"

"We won't put anyone's face on who doesn't want it on, but we can get some B roll. If anyone else you know wants to talk to me, let them know I'm going to make it happen. And that wine, Fred? Let's take it to my place when we sign off for the night. You can stay over. I think we're going to need to talk, a lot."

"Like a sleepover! Love it."

How anybody could be that cheerful considering the state of the human race, Arlys couldn't understand. Then again, she thought: faerie. Were faeries always cheerful? How could a woman she'd known nearly a year be something that wasn't supposed to exist?

Thinking about it made her head spin.

She needed to do the job, see what she could dig up for the evening report.

She didn't find much, but knew when she reported on a sighting of a woman causing flowers to pop up and bloom through the snow in Wisconsin, she wouldn't do it with a smirk in her voice.

She opted to change her jacket for the evening report, switch out earrings, sweep her hair into an updo. No point boring people with the same visual.

She'd had her quota of coffee for the day—take only what you need, she reminded herself—and opted for water.

She settled back at the anchor desk, checked her copy, rolled her shoulders. She'd be ready for that wine.

She put on her sober, professional face, took her cue. Into the first segment, she heard a minor ruckus off camera. And Jim's voice into her ear.

"Bob Barrett just walked in the studio. I think he's drunk. I'm coming down, see if I can distract him."

She kept going, saw movement out of the corner of her eye.

Now Carol's voice came through her earpiece. "Jim's not going to get here in time. I can cut away."

"Arlys Reid!" Bob's rich baritone slurred his words as he walked— more like staggered—toward her.

"It's all right, Carol. It's Bob's desk."

"Damn right." He stepped onto the platform, dropped down beside her.

He smelled of . . . gin, she decided, and stale sweat. His craggy face gleamed with more sweat, showed sickly pale under the studio lights.

Bloodshot eyes bored resentfully into hers.

"Twelve years I sat at this desk."

"And rock steady. Do you want to finish this evening's report?"

"Aw, fuck the evening report. The world's gone to hell and everybody knows it. Ben's story?" He snorted out a disgusted laugh. "Don't pluck my heartstrings, rookie. I'll give them a story."

Arlys froze when he pulled out a gun and waved it toward Jim as Jim started sprinting to the desk. "You want to stay back there, Jim boy. You all want to stay back. And, Carol, sweetheart, if you cut the feed, I'll know it. Cut it, and I put a bullet in this pretty girl's head."

Arlys tried to swallow on a throat that had gone dead dry. "It's your desk, Bob," she repeated.

CHAPTER SEVEN

When she'd been a fledgling reporter with dreams of conducting hard-hitting, insightful interviews with heads of state, Arlys had imagined herself in life-and-death situations, and how her courageous and intrepid on-the-spot reporting would impact the nation.

Now, as she faced a drunk, potentially crazy colleague with a gun, her mind went blank. Panic sweat rolled greasily down her spine.

"Didn't take long for you to sit your fine, young ass down in *my* chair, did it? Backstabbing bitch."

She heard her own voice: tinny, indistinct, as if on a bad connection. "Everyone here knows, everyone in the viewing audience knows I've only filled in until you could get back."

"Don't bullshit a bullshitter, little girl."

The "*little* girl" woke her up, pissed her off enough to snap her back. Later, when she analyzed it, she'd admit the foolishness, the sheer knee-jerk aspect of her reaction, but it got her up and running again.

"You're better than that, Bob. You're too good, too experienced to fall back on sexist insults and baseless accusations."

She added the visual equivalent of a *tsk-tsk* with the angle of her head, the subtle frown.

"You criticized Ben's story, and my reporting, and said you had your own story. I'm certain everyone watching would like to hear it as much as I would."

"You wanna hear my story?"

"Very much." Keep him talking, keep him talking. Maybe he'd pass out.

Or she'd just drown in a pool of her own panic sweat before he shot her.

"Twenty-six years I've been in this business. Twelve years I sat at this desk. Do you know why *The Evening Spotlight*'s the top-rated news hour?"

"Yes, I do. Because people know they can trust you. Because you're a steady hand, a calm voice."

"I didn't just read the news, I found it, I fought it out, I reported it. I earned this desk." He smacked the desk with his fist, hard enough to make the papers on it jump. "I earned it every single day. Night after night, I let the world know the truth. I'm going to give the world—what's left of it—the truth tonight."

Gun hand waving, he swung back to face the camera.

"It's over! Are you fucking listening out there? Over! The human race is finished, and in its place come the weird and the strange, demons from hell. If you don't die choking on your own bile, they'll hunt you down. I've seen them, oozing out of shadows, slithering through the dark. Maybe you're one."

When he swung the gun toward Arlys again, numbness set in. He wasn't going to pass out. She couldn't run.

"You're speaking of what's been termed the *Uncanny.*"

"Fuck that! They're evil. What do you think caused this plague? Them! Not some goddamn bird, not some mutating virus. They set it on us, and they're watching us die like sick dogs. They've taken over the government, destroyed governments around the world, and they feed pitiful, third-rate reporters like you bullshit about a cure that's never coming. They'll enslave the immune."

On a jerk, he pivoted back to the camera. "Run! Run if you can. Hide. Fight to spend your last days on Earth in freedom. Kill as many as you can."

"Bob." Arlys reached out a hand, but at the flash in his eyes, let it drop to the desk. "You're a veteran journalist. You know you have to provide evidence, to give facts to substantiate—"

"Corpses rotting in the streets! That's your evidence. Demons scratching at the windows," he whispered. "Grinning as they float. Red eyes staring. I turned off the lights, but I could still see the eyes. They'll poison the water. They'll starve us out. And you sit here and spout their lies. You sit here and pretend a miraculous cure's coming, that there's some sort of pathetic hope because a man took in one stray kid and plays games with him? People need to listen to *me*! Destroy them while you can. Run while you can.

"You could all be demons. Every one of you. Maybe we need a demonstration. You! Redhead. What the hell's your name again?"

"I'm Fred. I'm not a demon."

He chortled. Arlys could think of no other word for the wet, sick sound of his laugh.

"Says she's not a demon. Of course she says that. I don't think they bleed. Not red like humans. We can test that right now."

"Don't hurt her, Bob." Now Arlys did put a hand on his arm. "That's not who you are."

"The public has a right to know! It's our job to tell them, show them the truth."

"Yes. Yes, it is, but not by hurting an innocent intern who comes in every day, even through all this, to help us do just that. She could've gotten out of the city weeks ago, but she stayed and came into work. Jim, he's the head of our division. He lost his wife in this, Bob, but he's here, working in the control booth. Every day. Steve is working the camera, every day. Carol is in the booth, every day. All of us trying to keep the station up and running so we can inform and communicate."

Now Bob's eyes filled with tears. "There's no point anymore. No point. False hope's just a lie in soft focus. You lie in soft focus. I have two dead ex-wives now, and my son . . . my son's dead. It's all over, and they're coming for the rest of us, so there's no point. I'd be doing you a favor."

He turned the gun back to Arlys, cocking his head. "Think about what the demons might do to a young, pretty woman like you. Do you want to risk that?"

"I don't believe in demons."

"You will." He turned to the camera. "You all will, when it's too late. It's already too late. This is Bob Barrett, signing off."

He put the gun under his chin, pulled the trigger.

Blood splattered, a shock of warm and wet, on Arlys's face even as Bob fell back in the coanchor chair.

She heard—that same bad connection—Fred's scream, the shouts. For three banging seconds, her vision grayed.

She lifted a trembling hand. "Don't cut the feed."

She felt Jim's hands grip her. "Come with me, Arlys. Come on with me."

"No, no, please." She tipped her face to his, saw tears sliding down his cheeks. "I need to . . . On me, Steve," she told the cameraman. "Please. Bob Barrett built an illustrious, admirable career as a journalist with his ethics, his integrity, his no-bullshit style, his dedication to serving the ethos of the Fourth Estate, to serving the truth. His son, Marshall, was . . . seventeen."

"Eighteen," Jim corrected.

"Eighteen. I didn't know Marshall had died, and can only speculate how Bob suffered with his great, personal loss in the last several days. Today, he succumbed to his grief, and we who try to serve the truth, who try to mirror his ethics and integrity, suffer a great, personal loss. He shouldn't be remembered for his last moments of despair. And even in them, even in them, he showed me I still have a long way to go to reach his level. In tribute to him, I'm going to serve up the truth."

She knuckled a tear away, saw the red smear of blood, let out a breathy moan.

"I have to." She looked directly at the camera, hoped—prayed—Chuck was watching. "I have information from a source I consider absolutely reliable. I've had this information since early this morning, and I withheld it. I withheld it from my boss, from my coworkers, and from all of you. I apologize, and offer no excuse. Contrary to the information and numbers given to the media by the World Health Organization in conjunction with the Centers for Disease Control and Prevention and the National Institutes of Health, the death count as of this morning from H5N1-X is more than two billion. This is one-third of the world population, and does not include deaths from murder, suicide, or accidents connected to the virus."

Under the desk, she forced her hands to release their fists, continued to stare into the camera.

"Again, contrary to what is being reported, the progress on the vaccine has stalled as the virus has, again, mutated. There is no vaccine at this time. Moreover, the virus itself has not yet been identified. Previous reports categorizing H5N1-X as a new strain of avian flu are false."

She paused, fought to find her center. "All evidence indicates that only humans are affected. Recently sworn-in President Ronald Carnegie contracted H5N1-X, and succumbed to it yesterday. Former Secretary of Agriculture Sally MacBride has been sworn in as president. President MacBride is forty-four, a Yale graduate—summa cum laude—and prior to accepting the cabinet position had served two terms in the United States Senate from the state of Kansas. President MacBride's husband of sixteen years, Peter Laster, died in week two of the pandemic. Her two children—Julian, age fourteen, and Sarah, age twelve—are reported to be alive and in a safe location. I can't, at this time, verify the veracity of that information."

She reached for the water bottle she'd set out of camera range, look a long drink. She saw Carol weeping silently, Jim's arm around her. Fred stood beside them, a hand stroking Carol's back as she nodded at Arlys.

"I have further information that military forces—I can't verify under what authority—have begun sweeps to find those of us who appear to be immune, and to quarantine the immune in unspecified locations for testing. This will not be voluntary. It will be, essentially, martial law.

"I don't believe in demons. That isn't a lie. But I have seen what was once the unbelievable. I've seen the beauty and the wonder of it. I believe what we've termed the Uncanny—there is light and dark in them, as there is light and dark in all of us—will also be swept up and detained and tested. And, I fear, that what H5N1-X leaves us, all of us, will not destroy us, but the fear and violence it breeds in those of us who give in to it—the forced restrictions on freedom—could."

She paused, took a breath, looked over at Jim, gave him a signal to be ready to cut the feed. With a nod, he murmured to Carol. She shook her head.

"I'll do it," Carol murmured, walking off to go back to the booth.

"I held this information knowing if and when I broadcasted it, it would very likely be the last broadcast from this station. That I would endanger my coworkers. And further, I let myself lower the bar on my expectations of the human race. I told myself it wouldn't matter if you knew, if I told the truth. I apologize for that. And I commend everyone with me in this studio for risking everything to get the truth. To all of you, don't give in to fear, to grief, to despair. Survive.

"I'll find a way to reach you again, with truth. For now, this is Arlys Reid, signing off."

She sat back, hitched in a breath. "I'm sorry, Jim."

"No, forget that." He moved to her when she looked over at Bob, slumped in his chair, blood soaked through his shirt.

"Oh God. Oh God."

"Come away now. I'll take care of him. I'll take care of him."

"I had to do it." Shaking, quaking, she let him steer her away. "Bob killed himself. He was wrong, he was wrong, but he was right about the lies. I was part of the lies. I couldn't keep lying after . . . Now they'll shut us down. You did so much to keep us up, and—"

"It was going to happen sooner or later. You got the truth out before we go dark. You need to go, Arlys. If you go home, they'll likely come for you there."

"I . . . I have a place nobody knows about."

"All right. What do you need?"

"I need to destroy the computer I've been using. My source told me how."

"All right. Do that. Fred, get Arlys some supplies."

"I'm going with her," Fred told him.

"Enough for two then," Jim said without missing a beat. "Fred, you can get both of you some clothes out of wardrobe." As he spoke, Jim unbuttoned the blood-spattered jacket Arlys wore. "I'll take care of the rest. We probably don't have a lot of time."

Arlys went straight to the computer, her hands shaking. She couldn't destroy her notes, just couldn't, so she stuffed them into her briefcase before following the steps Chuck had outlined.

Basically, he'd explained, she'd give the computer a virus, and everything on it would be wiped away. Then she was to remove the hard drive, and . . . smash the shit out of it, in Chuck's words, with a hammer.

Even with that, some genius cyber freak might dig out something, but—according to Chuck—by then it wouldn't matter.

She had to change her shirt—more of Bob's blood—clean off the blood and the TV makeup. Fred rushed in, snagged some eyeliners, lipsticks, mascaras.

"Nobody's going to use it around here so we might as well take it."

"Really? I think pretty faces are going to be the least of it."

"Pretty's never least." Fred stuffed makeup in her pockets. "Jim says we should hurry, we should go."

She grabbed her coat on the fly, found Steve waiting. He offered two backpacks. "These got left behind when people stopped coming back."

"Thanks." Arlys shrugged hers on, looking over at Jim and Carol. "Come with us. You should all come with us."

"I've got things to do here. If they come before I'm done, I know ways out."

"I'm with Jim," Carol told her. "We're going to close down right."

"I need to go home. I'm going to give them a hand, then I'm going home. Good luck." Steve offered a hand.

Arlys ignored it, wrapped her arms around him, then the others.

"We're going to—"

"Don't tell us," Jim interrupted. "We can't tell anyone what we don't know. Be careful."

"We will. I'll find a way," she promised.

"If anyone can."

They went out, down the stairwell.

"You were really brave. With Bob. He just, you know, lost it, and you were really brave."

"I wasn't. It was mostly shock. And then it was shame because he said I was lying, and I was, even if he didn't know about what, I was lying."

"I think you need to cut yourself a break there."

"A journalist—"

"Kind of an apocalypse going on right now," Fred reminded her, "so everybody gets cut a break."

When they reached the lobby, the dark of night had fallen. Arlys headed for the door, paused.

"I didn't question why nobody's busted in here. I've just been glad no one did. Did you do something? Like with the market?"

"I had help. It's a lot bigger than the market. You probably didn't look up high enough to see the symbols. It won't last forever, but it's holding so far."

"You're full of surprises, Fred. Will it keep out the cops, the military, whoever tries to get in?"

"I didn't think of that!" Doing a hip wiggle, Fred punched Arlys's arm lightly. "I think so. I'm not absolutely a hundred percent, but yeah, they'd mean harm, right? Maybe some of them, it's just duty, but even then . . . I think ninety percent. No, eighty-five."

"I'll take it. Let's go."

"Where, exactly?"

"Hoboken."

"Yeah? I went to an art fair there once. How are we getting there?"

"We're taking the PATH."

"None of the subways are running."

"The tracks are still there. We're hiking it. We head to the Thirty-third Street station, go down, follow the tracks. It'll take us awhile." They slipped out, headed west again, trying to keep out of the glow from any of the streetlights still operating. "But we've got time. My source isn't going to meet us until three a.m."

"We're meeting up with your source? Excellent! I never met with a source."

"Don't get too excited. I'm counting on having understood his code about where and when—and that he watched the broadcast so he knows I'm coming. If any of that didn't pan out? We'll have to keep going. I need to get to Ohio."

"I've never been to Ohio." Fred shot Arlys a sunny smile. "I bet it's nice."

Lana wept in her dreams. She sat under a dead tree with skeletal branches jutting toward a starless sky. Everything dark and dead, her own body and mind aching, exhausted.

Nowhere to go, she thought, in a world so full of hate and death, so swollen with grief.

She was too tired to go on pretending, to walk another step. She'd lost everything, and the hate would hunt her to the grave. What point was there in fighting it?

"You don't have time for this."

Lana looked up.

A young woman stood over her, hands fisted on her hips. Raven black hair cut short and sharp formed a dark halo around her head. Though she wore black, she was light. Luminous. In the moonless dark, she shimmered with light.

She stood slim and straight, a rifle slung over her shoulder, a quiver on her back, a knife sheath on her belt.

With them, she carried a palpable strength and an almost care-less beauty.

"I'm tired," Lana told her.

"Then stop wasting your energy on tears. Get up, get moving."

"For what? To what?"

"For your life, for the world. To your destiny."

"There *is* no world."

The woman crouched so they were eye to eye. "Am I here? Are you? One person can make a world, and we're two. There are more. You have power in you."

"I don't want it!"

"It doesn't matter what you want, but what is. You hold the key, Lana Bingham. Get up, go north. Follow the signs. Trust them. Trust what you have and are, Lana Bingham." The woman smiled on Lana's name, and Lana felt a flash of knowing, of recognition, that rippled away. "You have all you need. Use it."

"I . . . Do I know you? Do I?"

"You will. Now get up. You need to get up!"

"Lana, you have to get up." Max shook her shoulder. "We need to get going."

"I . . . all right."

She sat up in the lumpy bed in the musty-smelling room. They'd found a run-down motel far enough off the main road that Max felt it was safe enough to stop, to sleep for a few hours.

God knew they'd needed it.

"There's bad motel-room coffee." He gestured to the pot on the TV stand. "It's better than none—barely." He took her face in his hands. "It's still shy of dawn. I'm going to go out, see if there's any-thing in the vending machines. Ten minutes. All right?"

"Ten minutes."

She took the coffee into the bathroom, splashed water on her face. It smelled metallic; but like the coffee, it was better than none.

She looked in the mirror, saw hollow eyes, pale skin. She did a subtle glamour—not for vanity this time, but for Max. If she looked too tired, too weak, he wouldn't push.

After yesterday, she understood they needed to push.

They'd finally gotten across the river on the 202, just after the all but deserted city of Peekskill. Deserted, she'd discovered, as they hadn't been the only ones trying to get across.

Wrecked cars, abandoned cars, some with bodies at the wheels.

They'd had to leave the SUV less than halfway across and carry their belongings around an overturned semi blocking the way. She'd realized while some had fled west—or tried—others had been rushing east.

Barricades erected on the east side lay smashed. Someone, she thought, had gotten through. But to what?

It took them eight hours to travel from Chelsea and make that final crossing of the Hudson River.

They took another car—bald tires, but a half tank of gas—and began to head west, then north, sticking to back roads, avoiding populated areas—or what had been populated.

When she insisted he needed to stop, rest, eat, they turned toward what looked like an abandoned house in an area with a winding two-lane road. Boarded windows, unshoveled snow. But as they bumped along its pitted drive, a woman, wild-eyed and armed with a shotgun, stepped out on the sagging porch.

They drove on.

They hadn't stopped until full dark, at a two-pump gas station alongside the dingy motel called Hidden Rest.

Lana made chicken and rice on a hot plate in the motel's office. The dust and grime on the check-in counter told her they were the first guests, more or less, for weeks.

But they ate, and they slept.

Now they'd keep going. They'd find Eric, and Max would figure out what to do next.

She heard the seven-knock signal, gathered up the bag they'd brought in when Max opened the door.

"I'm ready."

"Got some chips and sodas, a few candy bars. And we've got another car," he told her. "It's in better shape than the last one, though dead out of gas. But I got one of the pumps going, so we can fill it up once we get it to the pump."

"Okay. You need to eat something besides chips and candy." She pulled an orange out of her bag.

"Split it with you," Max said.

"Deal."

"Let's get the car moved, loaded, and gassed up first. You look rested."

She smiled, glad she'd done the glamour. "Who wouldn't look rested after a night in this palace?"

She walked out with him, shivering in the cold despite her jacket. "It smells like snow."

"Yeah, we could get some, so gassed up or not, if we see a four-wheel, we switch again."

"How much farther, do you think?"

"About three hundred and fifty miles. If we can use major roads, we'll make decent time. If we can't . . ."

He let that lay, picked up a red can marked *gas*, then led her about thirty feet down the road where a car sat crookedly on the skinny shoulder.

"They almost made it," she murmured.

"Wouldn't have made any difference if the pumps had been turned off. I managed to move it magickally about ten, twelve feet, but that's about all I could do. We could probably do better together, but this is just as fast."

She said nothing, as she knew he pushed himself too far, too hard. Power, they'd both learned, didn't come free.

He gave the tank the gallon of gas, stowed the can in the trunk. "I can drive awhile."

He slanted her a look. "We tried that yesterday."

Until yesterday, she'd never driven a car. She lived in New York. "I need the practice."

He laughed, kissed her. "No argument. Practice by driving back to the gas station."

They got in, and Max nodded to the ignition button. "You do it—you need practice there, too."

She'd left the starting of engines, gas pumps, and boosting of electricity to him. But he had a point—she needed to practice.

She held a hand over the ignition, focused. Pushed. The engine sprang to life.

Riding on the flash of power, she grinned at him. "Practice, my ass."

He laughed again, and oh, how the sound of it steadied her. "Drive."

She gripped the wheel like a falling woman grips a rope, squealed and inched, lurched, and swerved her way to the gas station.

"Don't hit the pumps," Max warned. "Ease up, a little to the left now. Stop!"

She hit the brakes hard so the car jerked, but she'd done it.

"Put it in Park. Engine off."

They both got out. Max put the nozzle in the tank, flipped it on. At the hum, he put an arm around Lana. "We're in business."

"I never knew I'd be thrilled to smell gas fumes, but—" She broke off, pressing a hand to his chest. "Did you hear—"

Even as she spoke, he spun around, shoving her behind him. He pulled out the gun from his hip.

A young dog, barely more than a puppy, gamboled across the lot, tongue cheerfully lolling, eyes bright.

"Oh, Max!" She started to crouch down to greet the dog, but Max called out.

"I know you're back there. Come out, and I want to see your hands up."

Lana stood stock-still even as the dog scrambled his front paws up her legs, wagging and yipping.

"Don't shoot. Jeez! Come on, man, don't freaking shoot me."

At the sound of the voice—male with a twang of an accent—the dog raced back, raced around the man who stepped out from behind the scrubby brush at the edge of the lot.

"Hands are up, dude. Way up. Just a couple fellow travelers here. No harm. Don't hurt the pup, okay? Seriously, man, don't plug the pooch."

"Why are you hiding back there?"

"I heard the car, okay? Wanted to check it out. Last time I wanted to check it out when I heard a car, asshole tried to run us over. I barely grabbed up Joe and got us clear."

"Is that what happened to your face?"

His narrow face showed some yellowing bruising under his left eye, some still purple around the scruffy beard dangling off his jaw.

"Nah. A couple weeks ago I hooked up with this group. Seemed okay. We're camping out, got some brews. Second night, they beat the crap out of me and stole my stash. I had some prime stuff, man, and I *shared*. But they wanted it all. Left me there, took my pack, my water, the works. After they took off, that's when Joe here came up. So we hooked up. No way he's going to kick the shit out of me. Look, just don't hurt him."

"No one's going to hurt him." Lana crouched down, and Joe flew to her, covering her face with kisses. "No one's going to hurt Joe. You're so sweet!"

"He's a good dog, that Joe. Can't be more'n three months, I figure. Some Lab in him. Can't say what else. Could ya not point the gun at me? I really don't like guns. They kill people, whatever the NRA says. Used to say."

"Take off your pack," Max ordered. "Empty it out. And your coat, turn out your pockets."

"Oh, man, I just restocked."

"We're not going to take anything. But I'm going to make damn sure you don't have a gun of your own."

"Oh. No problem! I got a knife." Hands still up, he pointed at the sheath on his belt. "You need one when you're hiking and camping rough. I had a tent, those bastards took it. I gotta put my hands down to take off the pack, okay?"

At Max's nod, he shrugged off the pack, unzipped it, pulled out a space blanket, a pair of socks, a hoodie, a harmonica, a small bag of dog food, a couple of cans, some snack food, water, two paperback books.

"I'm hoping to find me another bedroll, maybe a truck—four-wheel drive. I haven't found anything I could get started. Snow's coming in. I'm Eddie," he said as he kept pulling things out. "Eddie Clawson. That's what I got," he added. "Can I put my coat back on? It's freaking cold out here."

He was thin as a rail—a long, bony man, no more, Lana thought, than twenty-two or -three. His hair, dirty blond, trailed down in tangled, half-assed dreds from an orange ski cap.

Every instinct in her told her he was as harmless as his dog.

"Put your coat back on, Eddie. I'm Lana. This is Max." She started to walk toward him.

"Lana."

"We have to trust someone, sometime." She stooped over to help him pick up his supplies. "Where are you going, Eddie?"

"No clue. Had a compass. They took that, too. I guess I'm just looking for people, you know? Who aren't dead or trying to kill me, who won't beat the shit out of me for a bag of weed. How about you?"

He looked up when Max stepped over to study him up close.

"Dude, you've got fifty pounds on me easy—and it looks like muscle. And you got a gun. I ain't going to try anything. I just want to get somewhere nice. Where people aren't crazy. Where are you heading?"

"Into Pennsylvania," Max told him.

"Maybe you've got room for two more. I could help you get there."

"How?"

"Well, to start." Eddie hauled up his pack, jaw-pointed at the car. "That's a nice ride and all, but it ain't four-wheel drive and snow's coming. Main roads are mostly blocked, and the side roads, a lot of 'em haven't been plowed since the last snow. I bet there're some chains inside the gas station."

"Chains?" Lana said, baffled. Eddie grinned.

"City, aren't you? Snow chains. You might need 'em on the way. And a couple shovels wouldn't hurt. Sand if we can find it. Or a couple buckets of this gravel maybe. I'm handy," he told them. "And I'm gonna be straight. I don't want to travel alone. It's getting weirder than shit. The more people traveling together the better, I figure."

Max looked at Lana, got a smile. "Let's see if we can find some chains."

"Yeah?" Eddie lit up. "Cool."

CHAPTER EIGHT

Eddie found chains, some tools—whoever had abandoned the gas station had left behind a well-stocked toolbox.

Then he dug out a three-gallon gas can, filled it.

"Don't generally like carrying gas in the trunk," he said as he stowed it there. "But, you know, circumstances. Say, okay if me and Joe go relieve ourselves before we hit the road?"

"Go ahead," Max told him.

"He's all right, Max. I just don't sense any harm in him."

"I've got the same sense. We're both still getting used to having more than we did. And for now, at least, we're going to have to deal with strangers. But he fell in with a group of strangers, and I think he's telling the truth about them turning on him, beating him, leaving him for what he had on him. We're going to need to hone what we have, hone that sense we've started to develop. Because he won't be the only one we come across."

"You're worried about Eric, because you don't know who he's with."

"He'll be with us soon. Get in the car, it's cold. And I want to start it before he gets back. No point showing him, showing anyone, right now, what we have."

They got in. Max watched in the rearview, held his hand over the ignition to start it when he saw Eddie and the dog trotting back.

"Jump in, Joe." Eddie slid in after the dog. "Gonna say thanks again. It's going to feel good making some miles sitting down instead of on my feet."

As Max pulled out of the lot, Lana swiveled around to look at Eddie. "How far have you come?"

"Don't know exactly. I was up in the Catskills. Friend of mine got an off-season caretaker job at this half-assed resort up there. Like something out of the movie—you know the *Dirty Dancing* movie with the cabins and all that?"

" 'Nobody puts Baby in a corner.' "

"Yeah, that's the one. This place wasn't as nice as in the movie. Kinda run-down, you know? But I went up to help him out—we were doing some repairs, too.

"We didn't watch much TV, and the Internet was pretty much jackshit, but then we heard about people getting sick when we went into the town nearby one night to toss back some beer."

Joe stretched out over his lap, and Eddie stroked and petted with his long, bony fingers.

"I guess that was about three weeks ago—lost track. I called home—had to go into town for that, too—the next day because I couldn't get through that night. Cell reception was buggy back at the resort, and the owners shut down the landline phones in the winter. Cheap bastards. Anyway, I couldn't reach my ma, and got more worried. Then I got ahold of my sister. She said how Ma was real sick in the hospital, and Jesus, I could hear Sarri was sick, too."

He kept stroking the dog, but turned to stare out the side window. "I went back, to pack up, tell Bud—my friend—and I could see he wasn't feeling good. This bad cough. But we packed up, started out before nightfall—left his truck there because he wasn't feeling up to driving by then. He got sicker, sick enough I detoured off to find a hospital."

He shifted back to look at Lana. "It was crazy, man, just nuts. This little Podunk town, and everybody's trying to get out any way they can. I could see, like, boarded-up houses and shops—and some busted into—but they had a hospital, and I got Bud to it."

He took a slow breath. "I couldn't just leave him that way, but my ma and Sarri . . . I couldn't reach either of them when I tried from that place. Called half a dozen people before I got one to answer. My second cousin Mason. He said—God, he sounded bad, too. He said my ma and his both were gone, and Sarri was in the hospital and it didn't look good. He couldn't get out, he said not to come home, it was bad there. Nothing I could do. No point trying to call my old man. He took off not long after Sarri was born, and I wouldn't know where to . . . Anyway. Bud didn't make it. Sarri or Mason, either."

"I'm sorry, Eddie."

After swiping at his damp eyes, he went back to stroking Joe. "I just started driving, wasn't thinking straight. Then I got to this place in the road, all blocked with cars so I couldn't get through. Turned the truck around, headed another way. I just kept hitting roads that were blocked up, then the truck broke down on me. Better than two weeks, I guess, I've been on foot. Learned to stay clear of your bigger towns—bad shit happening, man, serious shit. Back roads are better. I think about heading home—that'd be a little spot called Fiddler's Creek, outside of Louisville. But I don't think I could stand it knowing my ma and my sis are dead. Don't think I could stand going home knowing they're not there. You lose anybody?"

"I lost my parents a few years ago," Lana told him. "I'm an only child. Max can't reach his parents—they're in Europe. We're going to meet up with his brother."

"I pray he's well. I'm not much good at praying, though my ma tried to make me a God-fearing churchgoer. But I've been practicing just lately, so I'll pray he stays well."

Max flicked a glance in the rearview. "Thanks."

"I figure we got to try looking out for each other now." Eddie rubbed his bruised jaw. "Some don't see it that way. Sure glad you do. You're city—it shows. What city?"

"New York," Max told him.

"No shit? I heard it was, like, real bad there. When'd you get out?"

"Yesterday morning, and it *is* bad."

"It's bad everywhere," Lana added. "More than a billion people dead from this virus. They keep saying the vaccine's coming, but—"

"You ain't heard."

She turned again to look at Eddie, saw his eyes had gone big, wide as an owl's. "Heard what?"

"Right out of New York, too. I found me and Joe a little farmhouse yesterday. My ribs were aching like a bitch, and I thought maybe they'd let me sleep in the barn or something. Nobody there. They'd cleared out, so I stayed in the house. Had a generator, so I got that going, had my first hot shower in a week, and goddamn that was sweet. Had a TV, and I figured to watch some of the DVDs they had—left all that behind. But I turned it on and it surprised the shit out of me I got this news on there. The girl giving the report—ah . . . funny name."

"Arlys? Arlys Reid?" Lana asked.

"Yeah, yeah. I thought I'd watch awhile, see what was what maybe. Plus, she's pretty hot. And while she's talking, this guy comes up, sits down. Skunk drunk. I've seen him before. Bob Somebody."

"Bob Barrett? He's the anchor—the main guy," Max said.

"Yeah, well, the main guy was skunk drunk, and pulls out a freaking gun."

"Oh my God!" Lana turned around as far as she could. "What happened?"

"Well, like this." Shifting, Eddie got comfortable for the story. "He's waving the freaking gun around, spouting off a bunch of crap, threatens to shoot the hot chick. Gloom about the Doom, you know what I'm saying? It's like watching a damn movie now, scary shit, but you can't *not* watch, right? She lets him bullshit on—chick's got balls—and it looks like maybe she's going to talk him down, maybe. Then he puts the gun . . ." Eddie stuck his index finger under his scraggly beard. "And *bam*. Right on the air. Guy shoots half his face off right on TV."

Snow began to drift down, slithering over the windshield. Max turned on the wipers.

"That ain't the worst," Eddie continued. "The hot chick—Arlys? She says to, you know, keep it rolling, to put the camera on her. I guess so people who can watch won't be looking at the dead guy. She's got blood on her face where it splattered like, but she starts talking. She's talking about how she hasn't been telling the whole truth, but now she will. How she has this—what do you call it—this source? And how it's not like a billion dead, it's more than two."

"'More than two'?" As it jumped, Lana pressed a fist to her heart. "But that can't be true."

"If you'da been watching her, you'd believe it. More than two, she said, and how there's no vaccine coming because it—the Doom—it keeps, like, mutating. And how the guy who was president after the other guy died? He's dead, too, and some woman—like, the agriculture woman—is president now. How they're starting to round up people like, well, I gotta figure like us."

Max's eyes narrowed in the mirror. "What do you mean 'like us'?"

"Who aren't sick. Who aren't getting sick. They're rounding us up, taking us places to test us and shit. Whether or not we're okay with it. Martial law and all that happy shit, man. Hell, I saw that for myself a couple times the last week or two. Freaking tanks heading east, big convoys of military trucks and shit. It's why I started going west. Anyway, she said all that, and how it would probably be the last broadcast, 'cause they'd get shut down for her saying all this, letting it all out. And when she finished, the station went blank.

"I don't know if the people still working shut it down or if the military or whatever did. But it was still off the air when I tried later. I thought about staying there, hiding out there, but I got antsy. Me and Joe got antsy and headed out early this morning. Started walking and walked into you guys."

"Two billion people." Lana's voice came out in a shaky whisper. "How could anything kill so many so fast?"

"It's global," Max said flatly. "We're global. People travel—or did—all over the world every day. It passes from person to person, and the next person spreads it wherever he goes. A handful of infected—maybe not knowing they're sick—get on a plane to China or Rio or Kansas fucking City, and the rest of the passengers are exposed, the flight crew, the people at security, in the airport gift shops, bars. And they all spread it. It wouldn't take long."

"You're saying . . . We're saying," Lana corrected, "that it's going to keep spreading, keep killing until . . . Until there's no one left but people like us. Immune."

"That's the word I couldn't pull out," Eddie said. "*Immune.* I have to figure I am because I was with Bud the whole time. Before he got sick and after. And where I took him, the hospital? A lot of sick people there. But I didn't get sick. Yet."

"From what I've read, and heard," Max told him, "you start showing symptoms between twelve and twenty-four hours after exposure."

"I guess I should feel good about that. I guess I do," Eddie continued. "Even though it all sucks out loud."

"What happens next?" Lana turned to Max. "You're good at figuring out what happens next."

"Not fiction but real this time."

"You're good at what happens next," she repeated. "I haven't been prepared for the worst. I imagined we'd spend a few weeks in the mountains until things got back to normal, or as normal as they could be. But now . . . There isn't going to be anything resembling normal, and I need to know what to expect."

"If it keeps on spreading, there could be two billion more," Max said flatly. "It's impossible to say how many will be left. Half the world population? A quarter? Ten percent? But it's possible to speculate that, as we've already seen beginning, the infrastructure will collapse. Communications, power, roads. Medical facilities overrun with virus patients will struggle to treat them, and other patients. People with injuries, with cancer or other conditions. More of the looting and the killings we saw ourselves in New York. The government collapses or reforms into something we don't know."

He took a hand off the wheel to squeeze hers. "Getting out of the city was the right call. Cities will fall first. More people spreading the virus, more people looting or reverting to violence. More infrastructure to collapse. More people to panic, the military coming in to try to keep order. And that chain of command frays as those in authority fall to the virus."

"It's the old 'head for the hills.'"

Max nodded at Eddie. "You're not wrong. You find a place, a safe one—or as safe as you can—and you supply it, maintain it, defend it."

"Defend it against who?"

Max gave Lana's hand another squeeze. "Against anyone who tries to take it. You hope like-minded people come together, build communities and their own infrastructure, laws and order. You scavenge, you farm, you hunt. You live."

If she'd hoped Max would offer a less dire scenario, she had to admit the one he painted sounded all too real. "And if you're like the two of us, and haven't the first clue how to hunt or farm?"

"You find other ways to contribute, and you learn. We've gotten this far. We'll survive the rest."

"My ma kept a garden—grew some nice vegetables every year. I can get things to grow, I'd guess, and show you how it's done. I hunted some as a kid, but that was awhile back. I'm one of those rare country boys who don't much like guns. But I know how to use one."

"It's still possible they could have a breakthrough on the vaccine," Lana insisted.

"It is," Max agreed. "But if there are already two billion dead, there'll be more before they can dispense and inoculate, even if they broke through tomorrow. The center can't hold, Lana. It's already breaking down. Hell, the Secretary of Agriculture is now president. I don't even know who that is."

"Sorry to interrupt," Eddie began, "but we ought to stop and put those chains on before it gets any thicker on the road."

Max eased to the shoulder as the snow continued to fall. "You'll have to show me how."

"And me," Lana added. "If I'm going to have to learn what I don't know, I might as well start now."

"No problem, nothing to it."

He showed them how to unkink the chains—simple enough even if the cold, the snow, the wind added a nasty element to the chore. Then how to fit the chains over the top of the tire. Though her fingers felt numb even with gloves, Lana insisted on doing one herself.

She had to learn.

She stayed out to watch and observe when Max got behind the wheel to ease the car forward enough to expose the rest of the tire. And, after watching Eddie, listening to his step-by-step, she connected the chains, using the closer link to tighten them.

"Is that right?"

Eddie checked her chain. "Aced it, first time out. She beat you to it, Max."

Max glanced over and smiled as he finished the connection. "She had a head start."

With a cackle, Eddie walked around the car to fix the last chain. "That'll do her." He looked to the pup, who squatted on the shoulder.

"You finished there, Joe?" When he opened the door, the pup jumped right in. "I can drive if you want a break."

Max shook his head. "I'm good."

"You let me know when you want to rotate. Until you do I'm gonna catch a nap in the back with Joe. Didn't sleep so good last night after the news show."

He started to yank the space blanket out of his pack, but Lana took out a cotton one of her own. "Use this. It's soft."

For a moment, Eddie just stared down at the blanket. Then he got in, waited for Lana to sit, close her door.

"I was scared for a couple minutes you were going to just shoot me, take my stuff. Maybe hurt the pup, too. Then I could see, pretty quick, that wasn't going to happen. I could see you weren't that kind."

"You're not that kind, either," Lana told him.

"No, ma'am, I'm not. But I guess you could say we took a chance on each other. I'm real glad we did. It's a nice blanket."

He lay down on the backseat, long, skinny legs tucked up and the puppy curled against him. "I appreciate it," he said and shut his eyes.

Lana didn't sleep. Instead she reminded herself she'd learned to put on snow chains. She'd cooked a decent meal from meager supplies—on a hot plate in an ugly motel office. She could start a fire, for light or for heat, with her breath. She could start an engine with her will.

And with that will, with the power that grew in her, she was learning to move things—small things now, but that would change. With Max, she'd raised the span of a bridge—and she'd pushed enough power to slow down other cars, even to slap back against those who wished them harm.

She had learned that, and she would learn whatever else she needed to learn.

If Max's speculation became reality, she'd use her will, her wits, her magicks, and her mind to do whatever had to be done to keep them safe.

And, she thought as the man and the little dog in the backseat snored softly and almost in unison, they'd already started to build a community.

"I love you, Max."

"I love you. Sleep awhile. We've still got a long way to go."

"I'll sleep when you sleep. You may need me."

"When we find our place, and we will, will you marry me?"

Reaching out, she touched his cheek. "Yes."

She watched the sun come up, chasing away the dark, and let it fill her with hope.

It took longer to reach the Thirty-third Street station than Arlys had calculated. They'd had to stop, find concealment several times on the trip. More than once she knew they'd made it because Fred heard the engines, the footsteps, the gunfire before she did.

Faerie ears, she supposed.

In the gateway of Times Square, once thriving, crowded, boldly lit, the enormous screens and digital billboards loomed like blank, black doorways to the unknown. A sudden flash, an explosive jag of horizontal lightning, struck just south of Herald Square and shot the madness into sharp relief.

Bodies, wild-eyed dogs feasting, the rubble of shops, the jumble of cars, buses, and vans spread across Herald Square—as if an angry hand had heaved them together over the street and sidewalks.

Someone, something laughed.

Someone, something screamed.

Arlys grabbed Fred's hand and, in the eerie afterglow of the flash, ran. At the entrance leading down into the dark, she stopped, catching her breath and fighting to clear the panic.

Keep your head, she ordered herself. Stay alive.

Her companion might have wings and better hearing than a schnauzer, but Fred still struck Arlys as too cheerful to be cautious.

"Listen, we don't know who or what might be down here. In the terminal, in the tunnels. We've got a long hike, and one without an easy escape route if we need one. I've got a gun, but I've never actually shot anything."

"I really don't think you should."

The scream came again, and the terror in it rolled down Arlys's spine.

"If we have to defend ourselves, we're going to. We're going to walk as fast as we can, as safely as we can, and you can keep those insanely good ears of yours peeled."

"I can see really well in the dark, too."

"Another plus. We stick together, just like we did on the way here."

Arlys took out her flashlight, aimed it down the steps. She looked over—they stood at the corner of Macy's.

She thought, There will never be another holiday parade, never another sale.

There will never be another miracle on this or any other street.

"Let's go."

She had to steel her own nerves to walk down and down. Every step had her heart thudding faster, louder.

What was she doing here? What was any sane person doing here?

"Do you hear anything?" she whispered to Fred.

"I don't hear a thing. We're good."

They crossed in the dark, following the single beam of light, boosted themselves over the turnstiles.

"I always wanted to do that." Fred's voice, even lowered, echoed. "For the fun, not for the not paying."

Arlys put her finger to her lips, playing the light everywhere, fearing she'd see more dead bodies littering the terminal, the tracks.

Or worse, live ones poised to attack.

Using the flashlight, she followed the signs for the PATH to Hoboken.

She scanned the platform, the tracks, the platform across the tracks. Her heartbeat leveled a bit—until she had to face the fact they needed to go down farther and into the tunnels.

No turning back, she thought. Once they started down the— ha-ha—*path*, there'd be no turning back.

"This is it." She sat, let herself drop down. Even with her knees soft, the descent stole a little of her breath.

Fred sprouted her wings and floated down like a feather.

"I might be able to fly with you for short distances. I haven't tried it with a person yet," Fred admitted. "But I've taken a few dogs that way to this shelter we started. I wish I could've gone by first, gotten one to take with us."

Since one of Arlys's fears was running into a family pet gone feral, like the ones gnawing bodies on the street, she was fine without a dog.

"You know about the third rail?"

"Arlys, I might be a pretty new faerie, but I'm twenty-one, not two. You have to stop worrying so much."

"I feel responsible."

"For doing the right thing? You are. I was really proud of what you did. It's when I knew, for sure, I was going with you. There've been some rumblings."

"Rumblings?"

"We're—the people like me, the magickal people—we're not very organized yet. A lot of us are just figuring out what we are. And some, when they figure it out, go a little nuts, or they go full evil. So we've mostly been trying to make those safe zones and help people, help the dogs and cats and other pets that got left behind or let loose when their owners got sick. But we've had a few working scrying mirrors or crystals, and have been trying other spells, to find out what's really going on."

Arlys had no idea what a *scrying mirror* was. "Crystals? Like a fortune-teller at a carnival?"

"Some of them probably had latent power, but anyway, yeah, like that—and other ways. We figured out it was worse than what they were telling us, but it's hard to say how much worse, since there are a lot of conflicting reports, you know? Lots of chatter. But we figured worse and going to get even more worse. That's why we've been trying to help people get out when we can. And when you told everybody everything you knew tonight, I knew I'd help you."

She stopped, tapped Arlys's arm. Arlys switched off her light, and let Fred guide her through the dark until her back was pressed to cold tiles.

She didn't speak, didn't ask, but put her hand on the butt of the gun.

She heard the leading edge of male laughter, with enough mean in it to tell her they wouldn't be friendly.

"Did you see that asshole squirm!"

She caught the light now—two beams cutting through the dark, growing closer, brighter.

Now and again they sliced over the walls. If they swept over her or Fred, could she use the gun? Could she aim and shoot another human being?

"Pissed himself. Fucker pissed himself!"

"Don't see why we can't hunt another down here. Plenty of asshole fuckers in the tunnel."

"Come on, most of those are crazy. It's more fun to *make* them crazy, then kill the fuckers. Let's get a woman this time, and not one of the hags down here. We do her a couple times, then nail her on the tracks, do her again before we gut her."

"You're a sick bastard."

More laughter. She heard their boots ring on the ground. Saw their silhouettes behind the beams of light.

Could they see hers?

"Let's get two. I don't want your sloppy seconds."

A beam skimmed the wall an inch from her face; her hand tightened on the butt of the gun.

If they hadn't been so busy laughing about their plans to rape, torture, and kill, they would have seen her.

They walked on, close enough she could have reached out and touched them. Continued along the tracks, arguing about the best hunting ground.

Beside Arlys, Fred quivered. "I don't know enough to stop them," she whispered. "I don't have enough yet to know how. I hope someone does. They can't hear us now, or see the light."

Trusting her, Arlys turned on the flashlight.

She counted her paces. Fifty. A hundred. A hundred and fifty.

This time Fred gripped her arm, fingers digging hard. "Do you smell that?"

"I smell musk and urine and beer puke."

"Blood. A lot of blood, and . . . death. But no sound, no movement."

In another twenty paces, Arlys smelled it. She knew the scent as it had streaked over her face, even into her hair, from Bob Barrett.

Then her light picked up something on the tracks. Beside her Fred let out a muffled sob, but kept going.

A body, Arlys realized as they came closer. A body nailed to the ground through his hands and feet. His mouth hung slack in a battered face, showed broken teeth. And all the blood that had spilled out of him when they'd sliced him across the belly formed a gleaming, dark pool.

When Fred lowered to her knees, Arlys swallowed down her rising gorge, tugged at her.

"We have to go. He's gone, Fred. You can't do anything for him."

"I can. I can say a prayer his soul finds peace. I can do that for him."

Arlys straightened, stood by—now with the gun in her hand.

She didn't have to ask herself if she could aim it or fire it at another human being, not when she looked at what human beings had done to a boy who looked barely twenty.

Damn right she could.

CHAPTER NINE

Fred rose, letting out a breath that shuddered with tears.
"He was younger than me."

"I wish—" Arlys cut herself off. Wishing solved nothing. "We have to keep going."

"I know, and I know it doesn't matter to him now, but I wish we didn't have to leave him alone here, too. That's what you were going to say."

"But we have to. You take the flashlight." Arlys intended to keep the gun in her hand now. "There are probably more like those two. If you sense anything, we hide. If hiding doesn't work, we run. If running doesn't work, we fight."

She curled a hand around Fred's arm as they walked. "If fighting doesn't work for me, and you can get away—"

Even in the dark, Fred's shock gleamed. "I won't leave you!"

"If only one of us can get out, one of us gets out. I need you to go to Park and First in Hoboken. Be there at three a.m. My source's name is Chuck. Get to Chuck, tell him what happened."

"I can do some things. I'm still learning, but I can do some things."

"You do whatever you can to get to Chuck. If he doesn't show by five, find a safe place. Find more like you, Fred, and get out."

"Would you leave me behind?"

"Yes."

"You're not telling the truth. I can hear it in your voice. We're both going to get to Chuck. You have to think of the positive, of the light, or the dark takes over."

You have to prepare for the worst, Arlys thought, the incomprehensible worst or you could die in the dark.

They kept walking, following the beam of the light as the track switchbacked. The musky stench grew stronger, as did the lacing of piss, the sudden, gagging odor of vomit. And again, blood.

Arlys felt herself growing almost immune to it when the light caught a stain, a pool, a trail. And worse, when Fred played the light over the wall.

NEW YORK IS OURS!
THE RAIDERS

Written in blood, it served as warning and triumph, as did the dripping skull beneath it.

"Like the two we saw back there," Fred whispered. "They like to kill. Some of them follow the Black Uncanny. The magickals who hunt humans, and us. I don't know why."

"There is no why. It's just—" Arlys let out a stifled scream, stumbled back.

"It's just a rat," Fred told her as it scuttled away from the light.

"There are lots of them down here. Don't worry. You don't have to be afraid of rats."

"Just a personal phobia." One that turned her skin to ice, churned her stomach. The boy on the tracks. The rats would find him. "We can't stop."

But they did when, in a few more yards, they came to a subway car on the tracks. Graffiti covered the outside, like an obscene mural. The skull symbol, snarling exclamations to KILL! to RAPE THE CUNTS! A drawing of a man with a hugely exaggerated penis dragging a naked woman by the hair.

But worse, far worse, was the stench. Arlys saw the cause through an open door of the car, and the scatter of decomposing bodies.

And the rats.

She dragged Fred away. "It's too late to pray for their souls."

This time Fred let out a scream as a figure—Arlys could barely identify it as a man—leaped into the open doorway. Blood stained his face, the thick and filthy beard that stubbled over his chin. He wore smeared glasses over wild eyes, a long coat, painted with gore, that hung on his bony body.

He held a knife, stained like the coat. And grinned.

"This is my place. You can't have it. These are my dead. You can't have them. I'll burn you!"

Arlys raised the gun in a hand that shook, gripped Fred's arm with the other.

"We don't want your place. We're going away."

"There's no *away*! There's only the end of the world! First the petulance. Then the fire. See?"

He held up a dirty hand with nails that curled like claws. A golf ball of fire burned in it.

"I'm the end of the world!" His laugh, as wild as his eyes, burst out as he flung the ball.

Arlys felt the shocking heat fly past her face, heard the sizzle as it struck the wall behind them.

"There's no away!" he screamed when Arlys, her hand clamped on Fred's arm, ran. "There's only hell."

Another ball smacked and sizzled on the ground beside her. She kept running. And tripped over something on the tracks.

She went mad for a moment, lost her mind at the stench, at the horrible *give* of the rotten corpse under her. At the scrabbling rats that ran over her back, over her hands.

"Get them off! Get them off me!"

She rolled, plunged her hand down into what had once been another human being, then shoved herself back on the ground using the heels of her hands and feet.

"They're all over me!" She flailed, slapping at her own arms, torso, legs, struggling when Fred's arms came around her.

"You're okay. They're not on you. You're okay."

Her head spun, and rolling again, she vomited while Fred held back her hair, tried to soothe.

"Oh God, God, God, this can't be real. How can any of this be real?" Arlys managed to push up to her knees, started to wipe at her face. And, realizing what was coating her hands, gagged as she stripped off her gloves.

She crawled until she felt the wall, sat with her back propped against it. Her heart hammered in her chest, terrible pressure.

"You're breathing too fast. I think you're hyperventilating, okay? You have to slow down, Arlys. You really have to."

She gulped in air—too hard, too fast—felt her head loll, forced herself to expel it. Sucked in more, but slower.

"I can't lose it. Can't lose it. Not here. Not now."

"I should've had the light on the ground. It's my fault."

"No." Though her head still spun, the horrible pressure in her chest eased a little. "Nobody's fault. We have to go, but I dropped the gun. We have to find it. We need it. We have to—"

"I'm going to find it. Stay here. Keep breathing, and I'll find it."

Arlys nodded. She'd be useless until she stopped shaking, until her ears stopped ringing. So she closed her eyes, ordered herself to stop thinking, to just breathe in and out.

She heard Fred's sound of distress, started to push her rocky legs to standing.

"It's okay. I found it. Just stay there. I can see you. I can see pretty well in the dark, remember? I've got the flashlight, too, now. I'd dropped it, but it's okay."

She patted Arlys's cheek as she said the last.

"We can take a break."

"No." Arlys shook her head, clenched her teeth, and stood up. She had to brace against the wall a moment with her head and stomach spinning. "We have to keep going. We have to get out of here. I need the gun."

Carefully, Fred put it into Arlys's hand.

"I'm covered with . . ."

"Maybe I can fix it. I can try."

"We need to get farther away from the crazy man with the fireballs first. I can stand it if you can."

She put one foot in front of the other. She thought about just ditching her coat—maybe the coat had taken the worst—but she wanted distance first.

"Something's coming." Fred barely breathed it in Arlys's ear. "Something bad."

She switched off the light and, in the darkness, pulled Arlys along the wall, into one of the narrow depressions.

"What are you doing?"

"It's bad, what's coming. It's magickal and black. I'm using a

Sharpie, trying to write the symbols on the wall. Trying to remember the right ones. Don't talk. Try not to breathe. Don't move. Pray."

As they huddled, Arlys saw the light coming. But not a light, she thought. Lights weren't black.

Yet this was—black yet luminous. And along the top of the tunnel.

Movement now with it, a figure forming.

A man, black hair flowing, black coat spread like wings as he flew along the roof of the tunnel.

A woman lay limp in his arms—arms, legs, head dangling.

Scratches, gouges, even teeth marks scored her naked body.

As he came closer, Arlys saw his eyes burned red.

When he passed, she might have allowed herself a shudder, but he stopped, spun in midair. Hovering, he searched the dark with those red eyes.

The woman in his arms moaned. He smiled down at her.

"Some life in you yet. All the better."

He flew on until that black light vanished in the dark.

Arlys drew a breath to speak, but Fred put fingers on her lips. They stood in the black, in silence, for another full minute.

"I don't know how far he can hear or see."

"What . . . what was that?"

"I think a sorcerer. I don't know. Evil. The really evil. She was alive, Arlys. I couldn't help her. I'm not strong enough."

Who was? Arlys wondered. What could be? "Why didn't he see us, sense us? The symbols?"

"I think they helped. Let's hurry, let's go. I think they helped shield us, and you smell like . . ."

"Death."

"Yeah. It's like a shield, too."

"Then we keep it. Oh, thank God. The tracks are going down. We're going under the river."

It was steep and tricky, and slowed progress.

She'd said before they'd gone in they couldn't know who or what waited in the tunnels. And still, she hadn't fully believed.

Now, she feared.

All that mattered was getting to the end, getting back up into air that didn't carry the stench of death.

"We're close. We're close now." Oddly, knowing that, Arlys's fear doubled. "We're hitting the big U-turn the tracks make before the Hoboken exit. We double back, see? And we have to start checking the platforms, looking for—"

They came out of nowhere.

She heard Fred scream as someone—or something—dragged them apart. Another grabbed Arlys from behind, lifting her off her feet.

"Bitch stinks! But she's got a nice rack on her."

She held on to the gun with sheer will as a hand squeezed her breast.

"Let's get them up, strip them down!"

Arlys rammed back with an elbow, fought to kick. Then froze when she felt a knife pressed to her throat, felt blood trickle down from where it bit in.

"Rather fuck you once while you're still breathing, but I'm not particular. How do you want it, bitch?"

Arlys closed her eyes. "I can give you a better ride while I'm breathing."

He laughed, licked her ear. "Good choice."

She let herself go still.

Fred screamed, a high, bright, somehow musical sound. As it echoed along with the attackers' laughter, Arlys forced out a little laugh of her own, turned as if into the man's arms.

And pressing the gun to his crotch, fired, fired again.

He shrieked, fell back, and the knife tore down the sleeve of her coat.

"What the fuck? I'll kill her. Kill both of you."

Arlys swung the gun toward the voice, but feared she'd hit Fred if she shot.

"I'm hurt, I'm hurt. She shot my fucking balls off! Kill them!"

Arlys kicked out at the hand that grabbed at her ankle, stomped on it, and filled the tunnels with another shriek.

"Run, Arlys! Just run!"

She heard the awful sound of fist striking flesh and bone, Fred's gasping moan.

She couldn't shoot, but she could fight. Even as she gathered herself to leap forward, the tunnel filled with light, blinding and brilliant.

Arlys whipped a hand in front of her eyes to block it out. Eyes watering from the glare, she saw Fred trying to crawl, and the man looming over her swatting at the air with his hand, with his knife. Reaching for the gun in his belt.

She didn't think, simply fired. Again and again and again, even when he fell, even when the gun clicked on empty.

"Stop, Arlys, stop! You might hurt them. Stop, stop! It hurts me!"

Face white as bone under a gathering bruise, Fred crawled toward her. "Please help me."

That got through. Arlys lowered the gun, rushed toward her friend. "What can I do?"

"I'm okay. I'm okay. It's too bright. It's too bright."

As Fred spoke, the light softened. Sweetened, Arlys thought as she saw dozens of tiny flickers of light dancing over them.

"What . . . what are they?"

"Like me. But mini." Fred slumped against Arlys. "I called them. I didn't know I could, but I did. They came to help."

Behind them, the first man moaned and clawed toward his knife with his uninjured hand. Arlys made herself walk over, pick up the knife, wipe her own blood from the blade.

She wanted to kill him, and the want of it sickened her. Instead she stomped, without remorse, on his good hand.

Left him shrieking while she went to his dead companion, took his knife and gun, shoved everything into the side pockets of her backpack.

"Can you walk?" she asked Fred.

"Yeah."

"Can you run?"

"It's my face, not my legs."

"There may be more of this kind, or the even worse kind. We don't have far, but—I think we should jog it. We need the flashlight."

Fred picked it up, but stuck it in the side of her pack. "Not right now. They can stay with us."

"Even better. Let's go, fast as we can."

Arlys paced herself to Fred's shorter legs, but they kept up a good speed.

"You didn't leave me. You said you would."

Locking away the fear, Arlys kept her gaze straight ahead in the faerie light. "I guess you were right. I wasn't telling the truth."

"You saved me. You had to take a life to save me."

Arlys kept running and thought of bright, brilliant light over dark, dark deeds.

At the Hoboken station, Arlys hauled herself up to the platform while Fred floated up.

Arlys wanted to scrub her hands, her face, strip off her ruined jacket. The sting in her arm told her the knife had done more than tear the material.

But she wanted to get aboveground again more.

She heard echoing voices, but couldn't risk finding out if they were friend or foe. So she hurried Fred up the stairs to the street.

The dancing lights circled, then whisked away.

"They'll come back, or others will," Fred told her, "if we need them."

"Best backup ever." Then the tears scorched her throat. "I have to get somewhere, somewhere I can wash my hands—my face. My . . . I have to get somewhere I can fall apart for a few minutes."

"We'll find somewhere. Lean on me now." Fred circled an arm around Arlys's waist.

"You're hurt. We need to get you some ice or frozen peas or a raw steak. Does that actually work?"

"I don't know. Nobody ever punched me in the face before. It really hurts. It really hurts when it happens. It's not as bad now."

They limped along the street, and Arlys prayed they wouldn't have to fight again. She didn't know if she had any fight left.

They stopped in front of a shop, windows boarded, door bolted, called Cassidy's Closet.

"I bet there's a washroom for employees." Fred studied the door. "Maybe some clothes. Maybe a coat you can change into."

"It's shut up tight. If we had some tools, maybe . . ."

"Faeries—experienced ones—can get into locked places. I might be able to. I just have to find it, and hold it, and . . ."

Fred shut her eyes, cupped her hands as if about to catch rainwater in her palms. Her wings fluttered out. She began to glow.

"Find it, inside me," she murmured, "hold it. Bring it. Offer it. Be with me, children of light and air, of the forests and the flowers. Open locks so we may enter."

Nearly numb to it all, Arlys heard locks and bolts *click* and *clank* and fall.

Bruised, filthy, triumphant, Fred fluttered up on her wings to circle in the air.

"I did it! It's the first time I did it on my own!"

"You're a wonder, Fred. An absolute wonder." Cautiously, Arlys reached for the door. "But stay behind me, just in case."

Arlys led with the gun, and Fred threw in some light.

No doubt the secondhand clothing store had been picked over, but it didn't appear to have been looted or vandalized.

"There's no one here." Fred carefully closed the door, locking it again. "I'd know. I didn't sense the two—the last two—because we, well, smelled, and it made me a little sick. You know?"

"Yeah, I know. Let's see if there's somewhere to wash up."

As they wandered through, Fred looked around, stopping herself from touching anything because her hands were filthy. "Nobody broke in and trashed the place."

"Maybe people are more civilized in Hoboken. Or maybe more got out quicker, or are holed up. Chuck must be holed up."

"I almost forgot about him."

"Let's hope he didn't forget to watch tonight's broadcast. Here! We got a little washroom back here."

"Yay! I've got to pee so bad."

Fred yanked down her pants, dropped down on the toilet.

Arlys braced herself, walking to the little sink, looking in the fancy little mirror over it.

Worse, even worse than she'd imagined. Blood on her face, gore in her hair, the jacket covered with both. She gagged again, fought down the bile. Ripped off her backpack, then the jacket.

"I might be able to fix it."

"Even if you could, I . . ."

"I get it. I'm going to take it out, find you something warm to wear. I think I can clean myself up without the soap and water. If not, I'll be back to do that when you're done. And, um, your pants, too, Arlys."

"I know."

"I'll take the jacket out so . . . Arlys, your arm's bleeding. You're cut!"

She made herself look, pulled off her ruined shirt. "It's not really bad."

"I'm not a healer. I mean magickally. But we should find some antiseptic and a bandage."

"It's not bad," Arlys repeated, and though her chin wobbled, she managed a smile. "I'm going to say it."

"It's just a scratch?"

"Right. Just a flesh wound."

She turned on the sink, relieved when water actually pumped out and, pumping the lemon-scented liquid soap in her hand, started scrubbing.

She scrubbed her hands, her arms—though it stung the thin slice on her forearm. She stripped down to her underwear, scrubbed at her legs. Then wedged her head into the little sink to wet down her hair, scrub it, rinse, scrub, rinse until she could see it run clean.

Then she sat on the chilly floor, wet hair dripping, and wept and wept.

"Sorry it took so long, but I . . . Oh, Arlys!"

Clean again, smelling like a forest in spring, Fred dropped the clothes in her hands and knelt down to gather Arlys close.

"I killed a man. I killed him. Maybe I killed both of them. I—"

"You saved me. You saved us both."

"I don't know this world. I don't know how to live in it."

"I don't think anybody does, not really. It's why we need each other. You're strong and brave. I think this world needs people like you. And like me."

"I'm just tired. I'm so tired."

"Me, too. Maybe you can change, and we'll rest for a while. This feels like a kind of safe zone, and we've got plenty of time before three."

"Yeah."

"But first, I found a first-aid kit, so we can bandage your arm."

"You need some ice."

"I couldn't find any, or frozen peas. Maybe Chuck'll have some. I took some of the Motrin I found in a desk in this tiny office, so that'll help."

With her arm bandaged, Arlys pulled on thick black leggings. She folded the jeans Fred had brought as an alternate into the backpack. It wouldn't hurt to have a spare.

She went for a long-sleeved tee and a black hoodie over it.

Feeling nearly human, she studied the options for coat or jacket.

"This is really nice. It's cashmere." Arlys held up the black peacoat style.

"It'll look great on you."

"Yeah, I'm really worried about fashion."

"When you start reporting, you'll want to look good."

"I love your optimism." Arlys tried the coat, found it was a good fit. Then she folded it, sat on it, and drank one of the sodas Fred had packed, ate an apple.

"What are you doing?" she asked Fred.

"I'm leaving a note for Cassidy, in case she comes back. I'm telling her what we took—leaving the tags here—and how if the world comes back, we'll pay her. Signed Arlys and Fred, with a whole lot of gratitude."

"Yes, you're a wonder." After stretching out on the floor, Arlys used the folded coat as a pillow. "Thirty minutes, then we should go." Arlys set her no-fail internal alarm. "If Chuck doesn't show, we can come back here, figure out what to do next."

"Thirty minutes, check."

But Arlys didn't hear her, as she'd dropped out.

She woke in thirty, feeling worse than she had before she slept. But in forty, they were outside, following the map she'd drawn.

"Not completely civilized." Arlys gestured to a shop, a restaurant, a market—all obviously looted.

"I don't think many people are left. You can barely feel the air stir. I hope they got somewhere safe."

But Arlys imagined at least some of the homes and apartments— locked and boarded—held the dead.

They reached the rendezvous point twenty minutes early.

"I don't think we should wait in the open," Arlys began.

"Too late."

At the voice out of the dark, she whirled, dragged the gun out.

"Whoa, whoa, wait, Annie fricking Oakley. It's Chuck."

She knew the voice now, and he came out of the shadows, hands up, with that silly and wonderfully elastic grin on his face.

"Chuck." Arlys lowered the gun, digging deep to hold back fresh tears. "You're early."

"You, too. And you got company."

"This is Fred." Arlys put a protective arm around her. "I couldn't have gotten out without her."

"Yeah, I want to hear about all that. But let's get inside. It's been pretty quiet around here the last week, but you never know."

"There's a lot you never know."

"It's really nice to meet you." Fred offered a hand.

"You did the weather some these last few weeks. You give good weather. We're not going all that far."

He started to walk, fast on long legs. "I'd have brought you in closer, but I had the Old Blue Eyes moment, and went with it."

"It worked."

"I knew you'd latch on. Didn't figure it would all blow up to-night."

"I'm so sorry."

"Hey, no sweat there. You did what you had to do, and it was real. Jeez, way real. Anyway, I'm glad you're here. I like the quiet, but even for me, it's been too dead around here. Pun sort of intended."

"We've got to get out, Chuck. I mean away from here. They're too close. What's in the tunnels."

"You came through the PATH tunnel?" For a moment he had to stop, to gape at them. "Jesus, you've got steel, both of you. I don't think I could've handled it."

"I'm not sure I would've if I'd known, but I know we can't stay."

"Figured it. Been working on a get-out-of-Dodge plan for a while. Few more things to tie up. Probably by tomorrow afternoon. You look like you need some sleep. This is us."

He stopped at a corner building, four stories, brick. Old and distinguished.

"We've got the basement."

"I just knew you'd live in the basement. Anyone else still here?"

Chuck shook his head as he pulled out keys, opened a series of locks. Then stepped inside a hallway, keyed a code into a wall panel.

"Everybody is dead or fled. It's my uncle's place—one of his properties. He's got a big-ass house on Long Island. Or did. He died the end of week one."

"I'm sorry." Fred rubbed Chuck's arm.

"Hell of a guy. Lights," he called and they flashed on. "I like my toys."

"I'll say."

Arlys stared. The enormous and well-finished space resembled some sort of high-tech HQ. Computers, monitors, stations, some sort of communication system. Some counters and swivel chairs, the biggest wall screen she'd ever seen, and a leather recliner.

One corner held a kitchen—stainless-steel appliances, cluttered counters.

"Bedroom's through there—haven't been using it much. You guys can take that. Bathroom's attached, but I've got another one over there."

Fred wandered, head clocking back and forth, eyes more than a little dazzled. "You must be really rich."

"Well, my uncle was. Who's rich these days? I guess you are if you've got supplies and a roof over your head. So we're rolling in it. You want eats?"

"No, not me." Arlys pressed the heels of her hands to her eyes.

"Want a beer, and to talk about it?"

"Not now. I don't think I can now. If I could get some sleep first."

He gestured toward the bedroom.

Arlys walked toward it, turned around. "Thank you, Chuck."

"Hey, there's no buds like cyber buds. Go crash, and we'll talk on the flip side."

Fred watched her go. "She needs sleep and some quiet." Then she smiled at Chuck. "I wouldn't mind a beer."

"Sure thing."

"And I can tell you some of it. I can tell you so she doesn't have to. Unless she wants."

"Got my napping couch over there. Have a seat. I've got some chips and salsa to go with the beer."

Fred dumped her pack, her coat, sat down on the big leather couch, sighed. "She really likes you, and trusts you. I can see why. Um, do you maybe have some ice? There were men in the tunnel, and they tried to . . . One of them punched me."

Chuck gave her a long, quiet look as she cupped her bruised jaw. "A lot of people suck, that's why I like the quiet."

"A lot more don't."

"Maybe. I'll set you up, Red Fred. Ice, beer, chips, and salsa."

"Is it really spicy salsa?"

"Set your mouth on fire."

"That's my favorite kind."

CHAPTER TEN

With Max at the wheel, they crossed the Susquehanna. The tire chains bit through the snow—an inch, then two—as they pushed west.

He picked up the 414, kept to the rural areas, passing a scatter of homes and little farms as the hills rolled and forests thickened. A few times, with Eddie asleep in the back, he worked with Lana to ease an abandoned or wrecked car onto the shoulder of the winding two-lane road.

"Maybe we should find a place to stop. You've been driving more than three hours, and the roads are getting worse."

"We've barely hit a hundred miles today. I want more before we break."

In the back, Eddie stirred, rubbed his eyes, and sat up. "Ain't letting up, is it? Storm's coming in from the west, looks like, so we're heading into worse. Want me to take the wheel for a spell?"

"Not yet."

He made it another twenty miles before he had to stop for a three-car pileup.

"Well." Eddie scratched his beard. "Looks like we've got some work to do. Lana, you mind taking Joe to do some business while me and Max see about pushing this mess out of the way?"

A warning look from Max told her he wasn't ready to share what they could do with their new companion.

She took the dog, trudged through the snow to a stand of trees.

Max and Eddie walked toward the wrecked cars.

Behind the wheel of the hatchback, the body of a man slumped.

"That's a bullet hole in the windshield there, and in him, too, I guess." Though he'd gone a little pale, Eddie moved closer. "I don't know much, but I know this dude hasn't been dead long. I mean not like a couple of days."

"Somebody put some bullet holes in this Subaru, too. And there's some blood on the seat."

Pulling lightly at his scraggle of a beard, Eddie let out a sigh. "Gun rack in the truck there—and no guns in it. I ain't no CSI type, but I watched it some on TV. Looks to me like the truck dude shot at these two, killed the one here, wounded the other. Wrecked the shit out of the truck, so he couldn't drive it."

"I'd say you're right."

"So, you know . . ." Eddie looked around, searching for tracks, afraid he'd find them. "Maybe we should clear this mess out of the way, quick as we can, and get the hell out of here. In case."

The hatchback rolled easily once in neutral with Eddie guiding the wheel and Max pushing from the rear.

Lana walked back as they worked on the Subaru.

"Tire's flat. Looks like the wheel's bent, too." Eddie rolled his shoulders. "Gonna take more muscle."

"I'll help."

"Don't you strain nothing," Eddie warned. This time, he cut the wheel, left the door open, and put his back into it from the front.

It only took Lana one shove to know muscle alone wouldn't be enough. She added a different kind of push, and though she tried to keep it light, the car jerked forward.

"We got her!" Eddie called out. "Just a little more."

Max, his hair covered with snow, laughed under his breath. "Ease back, Amazon Queen."

They pushed again, had the car bumping over the shoulder, and stopping crookedly in the shallow ravine beside it.

Eddie shot Lana a grin. "Stronger than you look."

She only smiled, flexed.

"We can get around the truck," Max said.

"Yeah, room enough to squeak by. Give me a minute first."

Eddie slid down to the ravine, pulled the keys out of the Subaru, stomped through snow to the back to open it. "Could be some useful things got left behind. Should check the other car, too."

"I'll do that." Max thought of the body. Lana didn't need to see it. "You help Eddie."

She slithered down, opened the suitcase in the back while Eddie poked through a big cardboard box.

"Got food," he said. "Looks like somebody grabbed stuff out of the pantry."

"Just take the box. There are clothes in here—men's clothes. And . . ." She took out a framed photo of a man in his thirties, a woman of about the same age. He wore a tux with a white rose boutonniere, and she a billowy white dress.

"Their wedding photo," she murmured. "But only men's clothes. He must have lost her to the virus."

"We oughta take the suitcase, too."

"Yes." She put the photo back inside. She wouldn't leave it to fade in the back of a car.

Between them, they managed to haul the box of provisions to the road while shoving and pulling the suitcase. Max joined them with a duffel bag and a rifle.

"In the trunk. The gun and there's ammo in the duffel, some warm weather clothes, a roll of cash stuffed in a boot. For all the good that does anyone now."

"Gonna check the truck."

Eddie jogged to it while Lana and Max started to pack the new finds in the car. Eddie came back with a half bottle of Jack Daniel's and three cans of Bud.

"I suspect somebody was driving under the influence, and maybe that caused the wreck." He wedged them into the car, turned in a circle.

"Pretty country. Damn pretty country. Find a stream, build yourself a cabin. Life wouldn't be half bad." He grinned over at the dog, who leaped through the snow, rolled in it. "He sure likes it."

Max opened the driver's door, leaned in to start the car while Eddie called the dog. "You drive," he told Eddie. "I'll navigate."

"Sure thing. You oughta take yourself a nap, Lana. You look tired out."

The glamour is wearing off, she thought. And the truth was, she felt tired out. The new provisions took up some of the backseat, but she managed to curl up, and tuned out almost immediately.

As he drove—competently, to Max's relief—Eddie struck up conversation.

"You guys been together awhile?"

"We met about a year ago, moved in together a couple months later."

"When it's right, it's right. Haven't found the right yet. Not really looking, but I appreciate female company, if you know what I mean. Is she out?"

Max looked back. "Yeah. You're right, she's tired. We've pushed it pretty hard."

"Likely have to keep pushing. What we saw back there? That's how it is now for some. Kill you soon as look at you. I don't get why when what makes sense is we need each other, but that's how it is. You had to see plenty of that back in the city."

"Too much of it. People are scared and pissed off, desperate."

"And some are just no damn good," Eddie added.

"And some are just no damn good."

They passed through a little township, its main street deserted but for parked cars. Its shops shut down or gaping open.

"You let me know when you want to find a pump, top off the tank."

"We've got enough for now. We're going to get off this when it dips south, head north toward Route Six. If it's clear, we can take that west. If not, there are back roads."

Eddie flicked Max an impressed look. "Got it mapped out in your head?"

"I do. And it's written down if anything happens to me. And if anything does, I have to trust you with her. I have to trust you to look out for her."

Under the bruise and the beard, Eddie's jaw tightened. "Nothing's going to happen. We're looking out for each other now. But you can trust me to take care of her if she needs it. I got no family left, dude. You could've left me back there. I guess you could say you're my people now."

"Take Fifteen north when you get to it. Let's try to get at least another fifty or sixty miles before we stop, find a pump. We're going to want one of the small towns, nothing too big."

"I got that."

Max kicked back, shut his eyes. As he drifted off, he heard Eddie singing some country song. Bluegrass? He wasn't familiar enough to know. But the clear, easy voice sang about angels, and soothed Max to sleep.

He woke with a start, felt their speed drop. Shoving up, he expected to see another wreck blocking the road. Instead he saw a snow-covered road, some houses, and a mini-mart with gas pumps.

"Six was a no go," Eddie said. "Had to double back, take the back roads. We're down to a quarter tank, so we better gas it up."

He pulled into the lot.

All three got out. "It looks like it's slowed down, the snow. I'll see what I can put together so we can eat something," Lana said.

"I sure could use that." Eddie glanced around as Max walked to a pump. "Quiet around here. Maybe everybody lit out."

"Maybe. Pumps are still on." Max put the nozzle in the tank.

"I'm going inside first, use an actual bathroom."

"Probably locked up," Eddie told Lana.

"We'll see." Because that she could deal with.

"Joe and I are fine with the great outdoors."

"Be quick," Max ordered. "And careful."

He studied the street—theirs weren't the only tracks in the snow—the near buildings. Nothing stirred but a trio of deer nibbling at seeds spilled from a wrecked bird feeder across the road.

He considered trolling for another SUV. The snowfall had slowed, but a four-wheel drive would serve better, especially where they were headed.

Maybe after he gassed up, they'd hunt one down, reload. At least they'd leave a full tank for another traveler. He relaxed a little when Lana came out again, carrying a bag.

"I still feel wrong about just taking things, but I did it anyway. Not much left in there, but I found some potato rolls stuffed into the freezer section. When they thaw out, I can make some sandwiches."

"That'll give us time to get somewhere more secluded." Max replaced the hose, closed the tank. "Too open here."

"It feels wrong, doesn't it? More like a photograph than life."

She bent down, scrubbed at the pup's head when he raced back. "In you go, Joe."

He leaped in the back as Eddie walked back. He glanced behind him.

"I thought I heard a—"

The shot that rang out shattered the stillness, a hammer against glass.

She saw Eddie jerk, saw his face go white, and the blood bloom on his flapping army green coat. Before she could rush forward, Max shoved her into the passenger seat.

"Get in, get in!"

He grabbed Eddie as Eddie stumbled forward, all but throwing him in the back.

The next shot shattered the right taillight.

"Get down. Lana, get the hell down." Max ducked around the front of the car.

Two men ran into the lot from the back, still firing.

Enraged, Lana threw out power, heaving it at them even as Max pulled the gun from his hip and fired back. Both men flew backward, guns firing in the air.

Max yanked the driver's-side door open, hit the starter and the gas even before he slammed the door shut. He spun, fishtailed, feared for a moment he'd flip the damn car, but the chains bit in.

In the rearview, he saw the men struggle to their feet, take aim, but their bullets thudded into the snow behind them.

Others came out of some of the houses, armed, watching with cold eyes as he drove away.

"Are you hurt? Lana?"

"No, no, are you?"

"No. Eddie, how bad?"

"I'm shot!" He pressed a hand between his collarbone and right shoulder. "I'm fucking shot. And Jesus, Jesus *Christ*, it fucking hurts."

"Lana, strap in, goddamn it," Max snapped as she started to crawl between the seats.

"I have to see how bad it is. If I can help."

"I can't stop yet. I can't stop until we're sure they're not coming after us."

She wedged into the back, hauled up the dog currently whining and licking Eddie's face. She plopped Joe on the front seat. When he immediately tried to wiggle back, Max snapped again.

"Sit!"

Joe didn't sit so much as curl up and cry.

"I need to see, need to see." Lana unbuttoned the jacket.

"You're going to see I'm shot! What the hell, man? We weren't hurting anybody."

"Quiet now, just quiet." With hands that surprised her by staying steady, she ripped open his shirt, then yanked off her scarf, used it to put pressure on the wound. "I'm going to stop the bleeding, that's the first thing. You're going to be all right. As soon as we're far enough away, Max's going to find a place we can stop, and we'll get you inside, take care of this. I think I can help."

"Like you helped back there, knocking those assholes on their asses like with your mind or something? You're one of those, those others? Both of you?"

Lana looked at him, into his shocked eyes. "We're not going to hurt you."

"Hell, you just saved my life. Unless I'm dying anyway."

"You're not dying. I . . . Max, I feel like I can help."

Eddie moaned, gritted his teeth. "If you'd get that bottle of Jack—I mean the whiskey—that'd be a start."

"Good idea. You need to press down on this while I do. Even though it hurts." She put his hand on the bloody scarf, pressed. "Like that."

She turned, unwedged the bottle from the floor, unzipped the duffel, dug through until she found a T-shirt. Lifting herself up a little, she pulled out the multi-tool Max had given her, cut through the shirt until she could rip it and make a couple of thick pads.

She opened the Jack Daniel's bottle, nudged Eddie's hand and the scarf away.

"Brace yourself." And she poured the whiskey on the ugly little wound.

He let out a sound that tore at her, but she doused it, then pressed a fresh pad against the wound while Eddie, eyes glassy, fought for breath.

"I'm sorry, I'm sorry."

"I was looking to drink it."

She put the bottle in his trembling hand so he could.

"I screamed like a girl."

"You screamed like a man having whiskey poured on a bullet wound." She got a hand under him, felt the hole in the coat, the wet. "Press that pad, keep the pressure on." She pressed the second one to his back. "It went through. The bullet went through. I think that's good."

"It ain't so good when you're the one it went through. Coming out makes a bigger hole. Pretty sure."

"We'll take care of it. Max."

"I'm looking. They're not following, so I'm looking."

She took a breath, looked into Eddie's eyes again. "I think I can help, help slow the bleeding. I've never done anything like this before."

"Me, either." He gripped her hand. "Probably going to hurt."

"I don't know."

"Let's find out." He closed his eyes.

She didn't know what stirred in her, but it reached up and out, it quivered to help. She kept one hand gripping his, the other pressed on the exit wound. Let it flow out.

It hurt. She heard the pain, felt it, saw it black and pulsing. She opened herself to whatever rose and stirred and flowed—white and cool against the black and hot.

"Stop." Eddie gripped her arm now, squeezed, shook. "Stop!"

She shivered back. Whatever flowed and stirred in her stilled.

"Stop," he said again. "You look as bad as I feel. It's better. Whatever you did there, it's better. I don't feel so shaky, and it hurts—Christ knows—but it's not as bad."

"Let me try to—"

"Lana." Max spoke quietly, but firmly. "You can't push too hard, too fast. You need to re-gather." He slowed the car. "There's a house—not much of one. It looks deserted. We'll try it."

He turned in slowly, sat, waited.

"I'm going to go check it out. Lana, you come and get behind the wheel. If there's trouble, you go. I'll find you." He turned to look at her. "I'll find you."

She nodded, but when he got out, walked down to the house, she stayed where she was.

"No way we're leaving him," Eddie said.

"No, we're not leaving him."

"So, ah, hey. You guys like gods or something?"

"No." Gently, she brushed his hair back from his face. "Witches."

"Witches? Huh."

Max jogged back. "Nobody here. Doesn't look like anybody's been here for a couple of weeks. It's a dump, but it'll do."

He drove around the back, through the snow until he felt certain the car wouldn't be seen from the road.

He helped Eddie out and, when his legs buckled, picked him up and carried him inside. Lana's first thought was the kitchen was a small nightmare of filth, garbage, bugs, and mouse droppings.

They'd deal with it.

The living room wasn't any better, nor was the bedroom Max turned into.

"Wait, don't lay him down on that. We have to keep the wound clean." She stripped off the ratty blanket, the stained sheets. "Just wait."

She dashed back out, dug out the sheets she'd packed, the towels. Inside, she yanked the sheets over the mattress, spread one of the towels over the bottom sheet.

"We have to get his coat and his shirt off."

"Help him stand," Max told her.

Between the three of them, they got him stripped down.

"Okay." She pressed a folded washcloth to the exit wound as Max laid Eddie down. "The bleeding's nearly stopped, so that's good. Maybe there's some antiseptic or alcohol. We make sure the wounds are clean. I think they need to be closed, but I don't have enough, Max. I don't have enough to do that. I can't find that in me."

"We'll sew him up. I'll find something."

"Oh, man" was all Eddie could manage.

"You'll get through it." Lana spoke briskly as she walked across a narrow hall into a disgusting bathroom. She ignored the smell, the stains—more to deal with later—and pried open the rusted medicine cabinet.

"Alcohol, hydrogen peroxide, a roll of bandages. No tape. No soap in here. The way this place looks, there may not be any anywhere in here."

"Scissors, needles, thread," Max called out. "Somebody sewed. A lot of scraps of material if we need them. I'll find soap."

"I brought some if you can't. In the suitcase."

They hunted for what they needed. Max scrubbed off a tray to set it all on. Lana washed her hands until they felt raw.

On the bed, Eddie lay quiet, the dog pressed to his side. His face shined, pale and clammy, but stayed cool to the touch. No infection, Lana thought. At least not yet.

She knew she hurt him, cleaning the wound and using the alcohol liberally until she felt, just felt, it held clean. Then she looked at the needle and thread, steeled herself.

"I've got this part." Max touched her shoulder. "I've got this. We could all use some food when this is done."

"I can't cook in that kitchen until it's clean and sanitized."

"I'll do this, you start on that."

"All right. Hang in, Eddie."

He managed a wan smile for her, which faded when she left. "Any way we could skip this part?"

"I don't think so."

"Figured. Don't suppose you've got a joint on you."

"Sorry. But I'm going to put you into a trance. You may feel some, but if it works, it should be like you're floating above it."

"You can do that?"

"I think so. It'll go faster if you trust me."

"Dude, can't deny I'd rather have the joint, but if I don't trust you by now, my ma raised a complete asshole. Don't insult my ma."

"Okay. Look at me. Just look at me."

Within an hour, Max walked back to the kitchen. She'd hauled out garbage, he noted, washed up the counters, the stove top, the floor. The refrigerator door, propped open, revealed a clean if battered interior.

And she stood, hair bundled up, wearing thick, yellow rubber gloves that nearly reached her elbows as she dumped dirty water into the sink.

Love, the strong grip of it, steadied him.

"How is he?"

"Sleeping. He's going to be fine—a lot of that's thanks to you."

Gloves and all, she all but melted into his arms. "I thought he was dead. When I saw the bullet hit him, I thought he was dead. We barely know him, but . . . he's part of us now. He's ours now."

"He's ours. You could use some rest. I'll finish cleaning in here."

"You can finish cleaning," she agreed with alacrity and stripped off the gloves. "There was a dead mouse, still in the trap, under the sink."

"I'll take care of it."

"I had to. The smell . . ." She shuddered. "I tossed it outside, trap and all. So you can finish cleaning. I've sanitized an area and the stove—I used bleach—so I can start cooking. I've got the makings, with what we found in that car, for some soup, pretty hearty soup."

"I thought I loved you before we left New York."

"Thought?"

"I thought I loved you as much as a man could love, but I was wrong. Every hour, Lana, there's more."

"I feel it." She pressed to him again. "From you and for you. I think it's part of what keeps building inside me. It's love, Max."

She laid her hands on his face, let herself fall into the kiss, into the love.

"I'm scared," she told him. "So scared, and yet there's this part of me, inside me, opening and stretching, and it's not . . . it's not afraid."

"We'll find our place."

"Anywhere we're together. Well." She drew back, smiled at him. "Maybe not here. Will you do something for me?"

"There's nothing you could ask I wouldn't do for you."

"I should've thought of something harder, but could you go get our last bottle of wine? I could use a glass."

Later, with her soup simmering, and the kitchen as well as the bathroom cleaned to her specifications, Max dragged the garbage she'd heaved out the back door toward a small shed.

No point in having her walk outside, possibly see a rat or mouse or some other creature gnawing at the trash. If they needed to stay for another day, to give Eddie more recovery time, she'd likely insist on cleaning the rest of the damn dump.

He couldn't blame her.

The door of the shed squealed on bad hinges.

Max found the owner of the house.

He'd been dead at least a couple of weeks, and the vermin had found him.

No need to tell her, no need for her to see. Though he felt a pang, he heaved in the garbage, shut the door. Laying his hand on the door, he offered a blessing and a thanks for the shelter.

"Max!"

He latched the shed, turned, and smiled, as he'd heard pleasure and not alarm in her voice.

"Eddie's awake. And he's hungry! No fever, no infection."

"I'll be right there."

He offered up more thanks. They'd leave in the morning, and drive the rest of the way to where Eric waited.

They'd find their place, he thought again.

They'd make one.

SURVIVAL

Friends who set forth at our side,
Falter, are lost in the storm.
We, we only, are left!

—Matthew Arnold

CHAPTER ELEVEN

Jonah Vorhies worked nearly around the clock, using the predawn hours to slip onto the Marine Basin Marina and onto his dead partner's boat.

It made him a little sick to break into what had been Patti's, to see pieces of her scattered around the old cruiser she'd loved. But it gave him hope, and it gave him purpose.

He stowed extra blankets, medical supplies, food.

He planned for a short, direct trip across the Narrows and up the Hudson, but prepared for complications. On board he would have newborns and a woman who'd just given birth to twins. A doctor, too.

Rachel.

She, too, had given him hope when he'd believed all hope was lost. She hadn't hesitated to do all she could to ensure the health and safety of Katie and her babies.

He wondered if those new lives in the middle of so much death had also given Rachel hope and purpose.

Had made her willing, as he was, to take risks.

They'd be taking newborns, barely two days old, across a river in the dead of winter. Out of New York and the increasing violence, away from potential detainment.

But to what? None of them could be sure.

Still, when he walked through the hospital for what he knew would be the last time, he understood they had no choice.

He could see death, his curse, in so many he passed. And there were fewer staff, fewer patients than even the day before.

More of them in the morgue.

But when he stepped into Katie's room, and she looked at him with absolute trust, he knew he'd get them to safety.

Whatever the cost.

"Rachel?"

"She went to try to scavenge more supplies."

Dressed in clothes he'd brought her, with the bag he'd packed at her feet, she stood. "Jonah, there's only one baby left in the nursery. Her mother—she was getting an emergency C-section when you delivered the twins—she died. And the nurse . . . she's sick. But the baby's healthy. Rachel examined her. It's been two days. She'd probably show symptoms by now if she had the virus."

"You want to take her."

"She doesn't have anyone."

"Okay."

Katie closed her eyes, opened them as a tear spilled. "Rachel said you'd say that. She's getting some supplements, but I can nurse her. I have plenty of milk."

"Does she have a name?"

"Her mother's name was Hannah. I think she should be Hannah."

"Pretty." He smiled, ignoring the fear of now having three infants to save. "How are these two?"

He moved to the rolling crib where the swaddled twins slept.

"I just fed them about a half hour ago. Rachel said they're really healthy—as healthy as full-termers."

"Let's get them bundled up. You, too."

Jonah worked Duncan's arms into the gift-shop sweater while Katie dressed Antonia. The baby's skin, so pink and white against his fingers, seemed impossibly soft. He'd rarely worked on infants as a paramedic, but he had the training and re-swaddled Duncan in one of the blankets he'd gotten from Katie's apartment.

When he heard Rachel's footsteps—he knew her stride—the knots in his stomach released. She came in, a med bag over one arm, an infant in the other.

"Room for one more?"

"Sure. Get your coats. I've got the big guy."

He picked up Katie's bag and took the med bag as Rachel got her own bag out of the closet.

"There's some trouble out on the streets, but it's not as bad as it's been. It won't take long to get to the marina. We're going straight out, straight into the ambulance. Both of you and the babies in the back."

"We went on emergency power twice today," Rachel told him. "I don't know how much longer that's going to hold. And since that news report, there's barely any staff. I never asked you where we're going. I think I never actually believed we'd have to get out by boat."

"Only way. Even if we could get over a bridge to Manhattan—and they're blocked—we'd have to get over another to New Jersey. Patti kept her boat year-round in the Marine Basin Marina. Lived on it since her divorce, about eight years ago. Said it was cheaper than an apartment. And she loved it."

"I went to school with a girl who lived on a houseboat." Katie swayed with Antonia. "I went to a party on it once."

"Straight out," Jonah reminded them when they got to the main floor. "Straight out, straight in. A couple of those baby slings back there, best I could find. Didn't know we'd have Hannah the Hitch-hiker."

No one stopped them. Once outside, the night was eerily quiet. Katie told herself the sounds she heard in the distance were back-fires, not gunfire. Backfires.

"Get two of them in slings and hold on to the third." Jonah opened the rear doors. "I'm going to drive fast, and I may have to maneuver."

"We'll be fine. Need help, Katie?" Rachel asked.

"No, I've got it."

Once Katie had the sling on, the baby in it, Jonah passed her Duncan.

"Won't take long," he said again, then closed the doors.

He got behind the wheel, touched a hand to the gun he'd strapped to his hip.

Whatever it took.

One of the babies woke and let out some fussy cries as he pulled out, but the movement soothed it, Jonah supposed. He drove fast, avoiding the expressway. He'd done a couple of test runs, and there was no getting through on major roads.

He slowed for turns when he could, but he knew the sounds he heard for what they were. He wouldn't risk having a bullet hit the ambulance or one of his passengers.

He heard the sirens, saw the flashing lights barreling toward him, and his heart thudded. But it passed at ridiculous speed, nearly side-swiping the ambulance.

Not cops, he'd seen that. Just as he'd seen, in his mind, the wreck, the blood, the broken bones seconds before the driver lost control and flipped going around a turn.

He didn't stop. He had purpose. Only one purpose.

He swerved when a man ran into the street, tried to grab the side door. And saw death, terrible death, before an enormous wolf leaped out, clamped gleaming teeth on the man's throat. The single high-pitched scream snapped off like a light.

"Jonah."

"We can't stop." He flicked a glance back at Rachel. "We're nearly there."

The ambulance squealed into the marina, bumped along beside the dock. "I moved the boat earlier tonight. A lot of them are gone, some of them are wrecked. Same deal here. Get out, straight to the boat, straight down to the cabin. It's warmer."

Safer, he hoped.

He hit the brakes, shoved out to rush back to open the doors. He snagged bags, grabbed Duncan.

"Fast!"

He led the way through the near dark.

"There. White cabin cruiser, red lettering: *Patti's Pride.*"

He tossed bags onto the boat, then picked up Katie, got her over the side. "Take Duncan, go straight down."

"I'll deal with the lines," Rachel said before he could grab her. "My father had a boat—it'll be faster."

He nodded, pulled the baby out of the sling—he'd forgotten which was which—and got on board.

"Cast off, cast off."

Rachel unhooked the bow, jogged back to the stern. She heard footsteps running toward her, a quick cackle of laughter. She whirled, prepared to fight. But there was Jonah, an infant in one arm, a gun in his other hand.

"Back off."

The man, his hair blowing in the wind under a pirate hat, grinned. "Avast! Just want a taste."

"Touch her, and you'll find out what a .32 slug tastes like in your throat. Rachel."

Quickly, she unhooked the line, boosted herself on board. She took the baby, spoke calmly. "I'll pull us out."

She hurried to the wheel while Jonah stood, watching the man make feints toward the boat, do a jig.

"You don't need two wenches! Share the spoils, laddie! Share the spoils."

As the boat pulled away, he feinted again, lost his balance, and tumbled off the dock. He surfaced, cackling and trying to paddle after them.

Jonah saw death in the man, but not by drowning. He turned away, went to Rachel.

"Take the baby down."

"Do you know how to steer a boat, and in water this rough?"

"I've been out on it plenty. Patti let me drive it a couple times."

Rachel kept her legs braced against the pitch of the boat. "Give Katie the baby. I've got the wheel, you navigate. Keep the gun handy."

He couldn't argue, not with the way she handled the boat. "We're going across the Narrows, around the west tip, and up the Hudson."

"All right." As the boat pitched, she held steady. "To where?"

"Not sure yet. Let's say as far as we need to. I fueled it up, so as far as we need to."

He went down to the cabin where Katie sat on Patti's narrow daybed, cradling two infants. He laid the third beside her.

"You've got three babies to tend to. I'm going up with Rachel, but if you need help, call out."

"We'll be fine."

Under his feet, the boat rocked. "Remember the ambulance ride? This may be like that."

"We'll be fine," she repeated.

He went back up, stood beside Rachel.

"Are they patrolling the rivers?" she asked him.

"I don't know for sure. I don't know why they would at this point, but the world's fucked-up crazy." Icy fingers of wind slapped at his face, roughened the black water. "There might be more like that idiot back there, but in boats. We're going to want to avoid everyone, and we're going to need to push for speed if we can't avoid."

Because he didn't like the feel of it in his hand, he put the gun back on his hip.

"I know the marina at Hoboken. My father," she reminded him. "He kept a boat there for a few years."

"Okay, Hoboken."

"We can't outrun a patrol boat in this. If . . . I might be able to pull off somewhere, get Katie and the babies off."

He laid a hand over hers. "It's Hoboken. Eyes on the prize."

In Hoboken, Chuck packed up all the equipment he thought he could carry. He hated leaving anything behind, but had always known this day would come.

Not along with an apocalypse, but eventually.

He'd planned what would fit, but had to adjust that now, as they had Fred along.

She was totally cute.

Not the reason he'd agreed to take her along, but it didn't hurt.

He'd given what he thought of as *his ladies* time to rest. Arlys had conked out for a full twelve hours, and totally cute Red

Fred had gone lights-out—after a couple of beers—for about the same.

Hardly a wonder, if their experience in the tunnels had been even half as fricking *harrowing* as Fred described.

And he believed every word. Why wouldn't he when he'd been eavesdropping on chatter from freaked-out civilians and freaked-out military.

Plus, he'd seen some serious shit going down on the monitor from hacking into street cams.

Serious crazy-time shit.

So, since he hadn't heard anything to make him think the military—and they were pretty much running the show right now—had ID'd him or his location, he got some sleep himself.

Seemed like the time to bank it.

He'd given them all another day to chill, to pack up, and for him to keep his ear to the cyber air.

But the time had come to say good-bye to his Batcave and some pretty awesome toys.

Arlys came out of the bedroom dressed, her hair pulled back in a tail. She was really hot, Chuck thought, but she sort of felt like his sister at this point.

He couldn't even fantasize about banging her without feeling, well, the ick.

"Fred's nearly ready, too. I could help you with all this, Chuck."

"Rather not have anybody else messing with my stuff. Just about done anyhow. We're all going to load it in our transpo. I've got to go get that. You guys could pack up some food, what's left of the beer."

"We'll take care of it."

"Great. I'll go get our ride."

"Chuck, we don't know how bad it is out there. I should go with you."

"Not to worry. I've got my way." With a tap of his finger to his temple, he saluted. "Back in ten."

"At least take one of the guns."

"Nah." He just winked and walked out.

After pressing her fingers to her eyes, Arlys dropped her hands. He'd made it this far, she thought. She'd just have to hope he kept on making it.

At least he stocked decent coffee, so she'd have one more hit before they left the odd and expansive basement. The safety of it. Safe, she thought, like a bomb shelter while the world blew itself to pieces outside the walls.

"Want one?" she asked Fred when she came out, red hair fresh and bouncy, makeup perfect.

"Chuck still has Cokes. Where is he?"

"He went to get the car. We need to pack up some food."

"Okay." Fred pulled out a box of Ring Dings.

"I was thinking more of basics."

"What's the point if you don't eat the fun while you can?" She grabbed a Coke, swigging as she packed a box. "Is he taking all that?"

"Appears to be."

"I hope he has a big car so we're not all smooshed."

"I hope he has a car that can get us out of here."

"Don't worry so much. We got here, right? We'll get there, too."

"I'm feeling edgy, therefore bitchy." Arlys grabbed some cans, wondered if anyone over the age of twelve actually ate alphabet soup besides Chuck—then reminded herself to be grateful for it.

"You're worried about Jim and everybody. I'm going to believe they got out, because we don't know they didn't. There's still good in the world, Arlys. I can feel the good just like I can feel the bad."

Arlys set down the coffee, pushed over a pile of Hostess pies. "Apple or cherry?"

"Why not both?" Fred opened her backpack, slid them in. "There's room."

"You're good for me, Fred."

In just under the allotted ten minutes, Chuck disengaged the locks, came in. "Let's load 'em up and head 'em out."

Arlys pulled on her coat, a cap, hefted the food box. And when she walked out, stopped. Blinked.

"Is that a . . ."

"Humvee—not militarized," Chuck added as he loaded a box of equipment. "I'm a hacker not a fighter. Cool, right? Like Arctic Circle cool."

"It's awesome!" Fred stuffed in bags and backpacks as Chuck went back for more.

"Who . . . who actually owns a Humvee?"

"I do." Chuck loaded more. "Always figured the world would screw itself, and why not have a monster ride to use to head for the hills? One more load."

Arlys went back, got the case of bottled water. Chuck grabbed the last load of equipment, took a sentimental look around.

Then he shut the door, locked it, and turned his back on home.

They weren't smooshed—it was a monster ride—but the equipment and supplies took up a lot of space. Arlys nudged Fred into the front with Chuck, settled in the back, and as he rolled and rumbled away, took out the pad and pencil he'd dug up for her.

She'd written out every detail she could remember from the last broadcast, from the trip through the tunnels. She'd written until her fingers numbed. Now she wrote about beginning this journey.

Maybe no one would ever read it, ever hear it. Maybe no one would care, or be left to care. But she needed to make a record.

"Going to head up Nine," he told them, "and see if we can get on Eighty. It's probably blocked, but this bitch has muscle. We may be able to clear the road."

Arlys pulled out the folder of maps she'd asked him to print off. "I worked out some alternates."

"Always prepared. Don't worry, cupcake. We're getting you to Ohio. That's the deal."

They made it as far as Ridgefield before they hit a serious road-block. An SUV with a dented rear fender was slowly backing away from a five-car pileup blocking the road.

Arlys laid a hand on the gun under her coat.

"They're good. I can tell," Fred said quickly. "They're not bad." Fred swiveled around. "They probably just want to get out like we do."

As she'd trusted Fred in the tunnel, Arlys trusted her now. She rolled down her window, put both hands out and up.

"We're trying to get through," she called out. "We're not looking for any trouble. I'm Arlys, and I'm with Fred and Chuck. Chuck thinks he can push the wreck out of the way."

"Can do," he confirmed.

For several seconds, the SUV didn't move, then it began to back up again, veering to the side until the driver's window faced Arlys and Fred.

"We're not looking for trouble, either. I can help move the wreck."

"I've got it."

"Chuck's got it," Arlys relayed. "If he can push them out of the way, you can follow us through."

A woman in the passenger seat leaned forward. "Arlys Reid?"

"Yes."

She nodded to the driver, who let out a long breath. "Okay. We'll wait here."

Chuck rolled his shoulders. "Watch me plow this road!"

He took it slow. Arlys had worried he'd ram the mess of five cars like a horny buck, but he eased into it, kept it steady, worked the wheel.

With the ringing squeal of metal, he pushed two cars back enough to angle and nudge one off to the shoulder.

Fred applauded.

"Video games," he claimed, backing up to get an angle on another. "Plus, I ran a snowplow for one of my uncle's businesses a few years."

He only had to push the other cars over a few feet.

"We can get through, they can get through. We're wider." He drove past the wrecked cars, eased over, stopped.

This time the SUV pulled up to Chuck's side.

"We appreciate it."

"No sweat, we both wanted through."

"Rachel," she said. "Jonah, and Katie in the back. We have three infants with us."

"Babies!" Fred shoved open her door, leaped out.

"Fred!"

"I want to see the babies." She waved a hand at Arlys, bounced over to peer in the back window. "Oh! They're beautiful! Are they all yours? Oh, babies are so full of light. What are their names?"

Slowly, Katie rolled down the window a few inches. "Duncan, Antonia, Hannah."

"You're blessed. Chuck, they have three babies. They need help. We should help. We're going to Ohio," she continued, before anyone else could speak. "If you want, you can follow us until we're not going the way you are. Chuck can maybe keep pushing things out of the way."

"Jonah?"

Jonah glanced at Katie, then back at Rachel, then nodded. "We'd be grateful. We're not heading anywhere in particular. We'll follow you."

"How far you want to go before you break?" Chuck asked.

"We've got almost a full tank. We just started in Hoboken."

"Hey!" Chuck poked a finger into his own chest. "I'm from Hoboken. We must've been right behind you. How about we try for the Pennsylvania border? You need to stop sooner, blink your lights, or when the sun's up, honk."

"Safety in numbers," Rachel added.

"Yeah, can't hurt."

As Chuck rolled forward, Arlys wrote down the names in her notepad.

Not just safety in numbers, she thought. Strength in them.

With pileups and jams of abandoned cars beyond even the Humvee's muscle to clear, the journey across New Jersey involved winding, back-tracking, detouring.

When they finally crossed into Pennsylvania, Chuck pumped a fist in the air, let out a *"Woot!"*

"Crossed ourselves another state line, ladies. I'm going to hunt up a pit stop. This big girl's getting thirsty."

They turned onto what proved to be the main street of what Arlys thought of as a hamlet—too small to be a town. Quiet as a tomb now, one buried in snow. A Christmas card, she thought, a traditional ideal. Her vision of it only sharpened when she watched a small herd of deer wander by what was billed as Arnette's Salon for Hair and Nails as if they roamed the forest.

People had known their neighbors here, she thought. Had gossiped with them and about them. Surely Arnette had often patronized Billy's Dine In or Out. Pie at the counter? she wondered. Surely there'd been a counter and a sassy waitress behind it pushing pie.

Where was Arnette now? And Billy? That sassy waitress?

They passed through, left it to the deer.

A half mile out, Chuck turned into a gas station/convenience store.

"Probably bathrooms inside." He gave the windows, the glass doors a long look. "Looks intact—small population around here. It's going to be locked up, but—"

"We'll get in." Arlys pushed open her door, stepped out into pristine snow. She walked to the SUV; Fred dashed to it.

"Can I take one? I mean hold one?"

"She's getting fussy." Katie lifted a baby into Fred's waiting arms. "I have to feed her."

"I don't mind. Oh, she's so sweet. What's her name?"

"She's Hannah."

"Sweet Hannah. I'll take her inside for you. Hannah's hungry," she crooned as the baby whimpered. "Maybe it's not locked. It's all right, Hannah," she soothed as she walked. "Your mama's going to feed you."

"It's nice to meet you." Arlys held out a hand to Rachel.

"It's really nice to meet somebody with a . . . Is that a Humvee?"

"Chuck's."

"It's open!" Fred looked back with a sparkling smile.

Faeries could get into locked places, Arlys remembered.

As Rachel bent to take a baby from Katie, Jonah called out.

"Don't go in! Wait." He jogged toward Fred. "Let me just check it out first."

"He's right." Arlys strode over to join them. "Wait, Fred. Just in case."

Jonah gave Arlys a long look when she took out the gun from under her coat. Then nodded. "I'll take left, you take right."

They moved in, down thinly stocked shelves, by a counter with its open and empty cash register. By tacit agreement she pushed open the door of the women's room, he the men's.

Once satisfied, Jonah shifted his gun to his left hand, held out his right. "Jonah."

She did the same. "Arlys. Okay, Fred!"

"Chuck says the pumps are on." Fred kissed the baby who now lay contentedly in her arms. "He's gassing up the Humvee."

"I guess this is as good a place as any to get acquainted." Jonah put his gun away as Rachel and Katie came in. "I'll fill up our tank."

"We need a chair for Katie." Fred beamed. "So she can sit and feed Hannah."

"There's one in the back." Arlys holstered her gun. "I'll get it."

"I could hold—which one is that?"

"This is Duncan."

"I can hold Duncan while you feed Hannah." Fred managed the exchange smoothly, then covered Duncan's face with little kisses.

"You're so good with them."

"I'm going to have half a dozen one day. Duncan's wide awake. Hello, Duncan! He says he needs to be changed."

"I'm not surprised."

"I can do it."

"That'd be great," Rachel said before Katie could speak. She handed Fred a diaper bag. "All the basics are in there."

"There's a changing table in the bathroom." Arlys rolled out a desk chair. "I didn't try the water, but if the pumps are running, there's got to be power."

"I hope so because our new mother needs a hot meal. Don't say you're fine, Katie. You've got three mouths to feed, and have to stay healthy and strong. There's probably a microwave in here."

Arlys pointed.

"Great. Maybe you could heat something up for her? I want to check out the over-the-counter meds they might have left. I'm a doctor."

"Now I'm even happier to meet you. I saw a couple of cans of beef stew."

"Perfect. I'll see about more baby supplies while I'm at it. Can't go overboard there with three."

Arlys scavenged the shelves—no point depleting their own supplies. She heated stew, canned ravioli, a can of chicken noodle soup in doubled paper bowls in the microwave. As she worked, she saw the men get in the vehicles, pull away from the pumps.

Getting them out of sight of the road, she thought.

Just in case.

She set the various choices on the checkout counter, took some stew to Katie.

"Thanks. She's slowing down, so nearly done."

"Fred?"

"She took Antonia to change." Eyes exhausted, Katie smiled. "She's wonderful."

"You have no idea. I have to say you look amazing for a woman who had triplets no more than days ago."

Katie looked down at Hannah. "Twins. Hannah was orphaned. Her mother died giving birth. She was alone in the hospital because everyone was sick or dead. So we took her with us. She's mine now."

Katie looked up, those exhausted eyes fierce. "Just as much mine."

"We'll help you protect the babies." Fred carried Antonia back. "All your babies."

"The babies and I wouldn't be here without Jonah and Rachel. Part of me believed they were the last decent people left on Earth. I think we were meant to meet you. Everything so horrible, and yet we met you. We met people who'd protect babies and help strangers. We'll help you."

"Yes, we will." Rachel came back with a bulging bag. "Over-the-counter meds, basic vitamins, and first aid. Look through it, take whatever you need. Well, minus the baby-care items."

Pushing a hand through her curly mop of hair, Rachel glanced toward the counter. "That up for grabs?"

"You bet."

"I'm starving."

"Arlys got cut on her arm." Fred jiggled the baby. "Could you look at it?"

Rachel smiled. "The doctor is in."

Arlys sat on a counter while Rachel cleaned and re-bandaged the cut.

"This could have used a few stitches. You're going to have a scar."

"Least of my worries."

"It's healing well."

"What kind of a doctor?"

"Emergency Medicine."

"Handier and handier." Testing her arm, Arlys looked over at Katie—nursing another baby and eating stew one-handed, while Fred sat on the floor snuggling the other babies.

"Did you deliver the twins?"

"No. Jonah did. He found Katie in labor, got her into the hospital. We were in crisis. The only OB left was trying to save Hannah and her mother, so Jonah delivered the twins. He's a paramedic."

"This *is* our lucky day."

"Ours, too." Rachel picked up a bowl of soup—the men had returned and grabbed up the raviolis. "We wouldn't have gotten this far today if you hadn't cleared the way. We need to stick together."

"Couldn't agree more. We're going to need to find real shelter tonight." Like Rachel, she again glanced toward Katie and the baby in her arms. "Somewhere warm."

"The town we just went through looked promising, but you want to push on. Why Ohio?"

"My parents, my brother. I'm hoping."

Nodding, Rachel ate more soup. "We push on."

CHAPTER TWELVE

Lana woke shuddering, on the edge of a scream. She clutched a fist to her chest, to the heart that felt it would leap out of her, leave her hollow.

Grief, drenching grief overwhelmed even fear.

A dream, some terrible dream she couldn't quite remember. She remembered the feelings in it—that grief, that fear. And . . . crows circling. Crows circling, shrieking. Blood on her hands, her face.

She looked down at her hands. Though they trembled, no blood stained them.

Stress, she told herself. Stress dreams, compounded by waking alone.

She huddled in the bed, assuring herself all was well. Better than well. The bed, warm and soft, stood in a room where a fire still simmered. A room where wide windows offered the spread of a snow-saturated forest, as quiet and peaceful as a church, on a rise of land.

They'd found Eric, and no stress dream could smear the joy of remembering how Max leaped from the car, grabbed his brother, embraced him.

They'd found Eric, alive and well. Found shelter beyond anything she'd believed still existed in the expansive mountain home tucked into the Alleghenies.

Hot food, good wine, a group of survivors banded together.

For the first time in weeks, she'd felt safe. For the first time in weeks, she and Max had loved each other with joy rather than desperation.

No, she wouldn't let a dream dredged from her weak and nervous subconscious spoil that. Though fatigue still dragged at her, she got out of bed. She indulged in a shower—oh, glorious body jets, soft-scented soap, and shampoo—and refreshed herself on their housemates.

Eric, of course, was eight years Max's junior. Handsome, eager, his eyes more blue than Max's gray, his smile quicker, flashier. And a little giddy now to have discovered the power inside him.

Had it come through the blood? she wondered, since Eric had never shown any interest in or talent for the Craft before.

The virus, she thought. It somehow grew from the virus—or filled the void left by it.

Along with Eric, there was Shaun, awkward and nerdy, thick glasses over brown eyes, floppy hair.

The college group included Kim, a stunning girl with gorgeous caramel-gold skin. Cool and cautious in Lana's estimation, but who could blame her? A genius, according to Eric.

Poe, football star who had had scouts sniffing around him. Tough faced, tough bodied. He'd been the one to push a plate of spaghetti to her when she and Max had found the house in the snowy dark.

And Allegra, with her ice-queen looks: pale skin, pale hair, frosty blue eyes. But her manner contradicted her looks, Lana thought. Warm and open, welcoming and kind.

And yet . . .

No *and yets*, Lana ordered herself as she switched off the shower. Allegra and Eric shared a bedroom, and their relationship had that fresh and shiny look of the new, so she would be warm and welcoming, too.

She dressed, studied herself in the mirror, and decided that while she might not feel fully rested, she looked it. She went out to find the others.

They owed the big, beautiful house to Shaun—or his parents. For a vacation home, they hadn't stinted on luxury: gorgeous wood floors, spacious rooms, fields of windows to let the forest and mountains in, generous decks. A small, in-house gym equaled a lovely dream after the rigors of the road. But her favorite aspect was the huge and exceptional kitchen.

She found Max and Eric in the great room, huddled together over coffee.

She walked to Eric, wrapped her arms around him, and hugged hard. She'd only met him twice before: once at a family wedding, and then when he'd spent a long weekend with them in New York the previous summer. But they'd clicked.

She moved from him to bend down and kiss Max.

"Want coffee?" Max asked.

"Actually, I want tea for some reason. Is it all right, Eric, if I hunt for some?"

"I know we've got it because Kim goes for it. You don't have to ask. We're all in this together."

"We're going to have to start thinking about inventorying the food," Max began, and Eric rolled his eyes.

"Man, you just got here. Relax a little."

"There are eight of us now," Max began, and because she knew Eric could get defensive when Max played big brother, Lana broke in.

"Speaking of, where's everyone else?"

"Poe's in the gym—he hits it every morning. Allegra's still conked. Probably the others, too. Mostly we don't get up this early. Except for Poe. Your pal Eddie took the dog out."

"How about if I do some more hunting around and see what I can make for breakfast. For eight."

"That'd be great." Eric beamed at her. "We've been mostly doing everyone for themselves, unless Poe cooks something. He's not bad, but he's nothing close to you. We picked up some supplies on the way here when we could. And there's a big freezer in that mudroom place. Shaun said his parents would've just had it stocked before . . . before everything went to hell."

His face lost its easy cheer as Eric lowered his voice. "They'd always come up after the holidays, after all that, and they'd spend about a month here. Have some friends up, and stuff."

He glanced toward the doorway. "The way it looks, they didn't make it."

"It must be hard on him," Lana murmured.

She found the freezer and the pantry well stocked. The refrigerator offered slimmer pickings. Max, she knew, had a strong point about inventory.

The eggs and milk wouldn't last long—and the milk would turn in any case. Since she had frozen blueberries in stock, she started gathering what she needed for pancake batter.

"What's the generator run on?" Max asked.

Eric, feet up on the table, shrugged. "I think Shaun said propane."

"He must know where his parents got it. If we can get a propane truck up here, keep the generator filled, we'll keep heat and light. We shouldn't be using more power than necessary."

"Christ, you sound like Kim."

"That makes Kim a sensible girl," Max countered.

"Look, with what I've got now . . ." Eric wiggled his fingers. "I can keep this place up and running."

"That may be, but basics are basics. Keeping the heat on, replacing firewood as we use it, going out for fresh supplies, keeping enough fresh drinking water in stock."

"We're going to have to learn how to hunt." Poe walked in, his dark skin shining from his workout.

"Not you, too?" Eric shook his head, got up for more coffee.

"We've got eight people and a dog to feed," Poe went on. "And it might be more people find us, need a place."

"This isn't the only place around here. Let them get their own."

"Eric." Surprised, disappointed, Lana nudged his arm.

"Seriously. Shaun's got about six acres here, he said, but there are other cabins. High-class ones like this, and more—what was it— *basic* ones."

"Has anybody scouted out those cabins?" Max asked. "To see if anyone's using them, or if there are more supplies we can use here?"

Poe turned to Max. "Kim and I talked about doing that today."

"It's a good idea. I'll go with you," Max offered. "And you're right about learning to hunt."

"Hunting what?" Shaun came in, pushing his glasses up on sleepy eyes. "You mean like shooting animals? Uh-uh, no way. I'm not shooting animals."

"Then you can go vegetarian." Poe shrugged. "But the rest of us are going to need fresh meat, and have to learn how to hunt it, dress it, cook it. Either way, we're going to have to learn how to grow shit, too, when spring comes around. I'm going to get a shower."

"Poe and Kim are always looking on the downside," Eric muttered.

"It sounded to me they're looking on the realistic side. Eric," Max said patiently, "we can't live off what's in that freezer long-term. The fact is, we might not be able to stay here long-term."

Eric's next shrug held a sulky edge. "I'm going to see if Allegra's up."

"Give him some time, Max," Lana whispered when Eric walked out. "They haven't been here long, either, so it's natural just to want to hold on to the relief. The rest? It's a lot to take in, a lot of adjusting."

"Taking in and adjusting is what's going to keep us alive."

"I don't want to shoot things." Shaun flopped down. "Maybe I could fish. My dad and I went fishing every summer."

He shoved his glasses up to cover eyes that glimmered with tears. Then Joe raced in from the mudroom with Eddie behind him. Shaun brightened, slapping his thigh to invite the dog over.

After breakfast, Eric and Allegra volunteered for cleanup, and Max joined Kim and Poe on their scouting expedition. Lana held Eddie back to check his wounds, change his bandage.

"I think it's healing pretty well, but I don't think we should take the stitches out yet."

"They're starting to pull some. That's probably good, I guess. Closing things up."

"Keep taking that antibiotic we got from that drugstore, and I'll take another look tomorrow."

"Yes, ma'am, Dr. Lana." He pulled his shirt back on, looked around the stone-tiled bathroom. "This is some place. I've never been inside a house like this. Fan-cee. Eight of us in here, along with Joe, and we don't feel crowded. But . . ."

"Supplies don't just regenerate. Max will find more."

"A lot of deer in the woods. Rabbits, too. Some streams close by where fishing's probably good."

"I get a little queasy at the idea of shooting a deer or a rabbit, which is hypocritical since I've cooked both."

"Don't much like it myself, but you gotta do what you gotta. This is a good place to be for now, but it's a fact we'd be better off finding a place where we could grow some crops, keep a couple of milk cows and some chickens. And more people. More hands to work, more hands for defense."

"I know Max feels the same."

"And, Lana?" He stepped to the door, glanced out, eased it shut. "There's more going on out there than deer and rabbits."

"What do you mean?"

"We walked a ways, right? Me and Joe. Felt good to be out in the air. And back in the woods I came across this like, circle of stones. Not like a campfire, exactly, but that's what I thought at first. But the ground in it, that was black and burnt but, no ash, no charred-up wood. And Joe, he got the shakes and wouldn't go near it. I got 'em, too, I admit it."

Rubbing idly at his wound, he kept his voice low.

"You know how the hair on the back of your neck stands up, and you get that cold right up your spine?"

"Yes." She experienced it as he spoke.

"Like that. Spit dried up in my mouth. We backed off because, man, it just wasn't right. It just wasn't, you know, natural. I'll cop all the way to wimpy, but I won't be walking back that way."

"You think it was magick, dark magick."

"I don't know about that stuff, but I know it wasn't right. I didn't want to say anything in front of everybody. Just don't know them yet, right?"

"Tell Max—just Max. He and I will go out there."

"I wish you wouldn't. Man, I wish you wouldn't, but I think you've, like, gotta. And if you've gotta . . ." He sighed. "I gotta."

"When he gets back then. For now, can you use a washing machine?"

"If I have to."

She patted his cheek. "I was thinking you could wash the clothes we've been wearing on the road while we have soap, water, and a machine. It's a nice machine in a nice little laundry room. You should hang them up to dry once they're washed, save the generator."

He let out a puff of air. "Yeah, okay. I guess I can do my bit."

While he did, Lana assigned herself to take inventory. She wrote down categories, amounts, pounds, number of cans. Then sat down to calculate how many meals, portions, days, weeks, what they had would last.

She glanced up, smiled, when Allegra came in.

"You and Eric sure know how to shine up a kitchen."

Graceful, she all but floated over in jeans and a bright red sweater. "It's the least we could do after that amazing breakfast. I might have to join Poe in the gym if you keep cooking like that."

Allegra wandered to a window. "They're not back yet?"

"No." Lana glanced toward the window. "Not yet."

"I'm sure they're fine. It really hasn't been all that long. I have to say I'm glad I'm not out there trudging through the snow. What are you doing?"

"Inventory—starting with food supplies. I'm going to hit other basics like toilet paper, soap, lightbulbs, whatever else I can think of."

"Oh, we have plenty, don't you think?" Strolling back, Allegra tapped one of the cans. "It's not like we're going to stay here forever. It's fine right now—middle of the winter—but it's so isolated. We'll go stir-crazy. I'm going to open a bottle of wine—something we have plenty of, too. Hey, it's five o'clock somewhere. Have you seen the wine cellar?"

"No."

"Talk about inventory. I'll go get us a bottle, and we can get to know each other. After all, I'm with Eric, you're with Max. We're like sisters."

"You're right. They'll be hungry when they get back. I've got some chicken thawing out. I thought I'd make tortilla soup for dinner."

"Sounds fantastic!" Allegra tossed back her hair and left to go down to the cellar.

Soups and stews, Lana thought as she rose. A good way to stretch supplies.

She got what she needed, started putting things together in a large stockpot from memory.

"Wow. It already smells good." Allegra, brandishing the wine, strolled over to get a corkscrew. "Eric said you're an actual chef. Professional."

"That's right. What were you studying?"

"Liberal arts. I still hadn't decided where to go with it. I guess it doesn't matter much now."

"I hope that's not true."

"Everything's changed." With a tug, Allegra drew the cork. "It's smart to make the best of it. I mean, really, what else can we do? Don't you wonder why we didn't get sick? What that means for us? For others like us?"

"Yes. Yes, I think about all of that." Lana rinsed beans in the sink. "But I don't know the answers."

"Eric told you he's changed. I know he told you he can . . . do things. He told me, even before you got here, that Max could do things. And you, a little. It must be more than a little now. It's more than a little for Eric."

"We're not going to hurt anyone."

"Oh, I know!" She touched a hand to Lana's arm, set down the glass of wine. "I won't tell the others if you don't want me to. Eric only told me because we're together. Is Eddie like you?"

"No."

"You see?" Scooting onto a counter stool, Allegra sipped her wine. "You have to wonder, right? Why some are, some aren't. What it means. It's like . . . I don't know. The virus, killing so many people, *still* spreading, I guess. Is it, like, a kind of cleansing?"

" 'Cleansing'?" The word, the idea, just horrified Lana.

"I don't know. Eric and I talk about it sometimes when we're alone. And with the others, too, because you have to think about it, wonder about it. I'm upsetting you. I can see it. I'm sorry."

"Not your fault. I've thought about it, but it's all happened so fast. It's been one day at a time. One hour for some of it."

Lana stirred the pot, wished she had fresh herbs. Wondered if she ever would again.

Resigned, she got out the chicken—remembered her knives were still wrapped and tucked away. Chose one from the block. Testing the edge, she found it to be good enough.

She sat at the counter—more sociable—with knife, chicken, and board. "I think, yes, the virus opened something. It's beyond co-incidence for it all to have happened at the same time. But why? I don't know if we'll ever be sure of that."

"We heard things on campus, and even after we left. How people, some people, were hunting the ones like you. And some like you were hunting people, and the ones like you, too."

"I don't understand why, why when so much is gone, we'd turn against each other."

"It's human nature." With a flip of her hair, Allegra shrugged. "It's terrible, but it is. You forgot your wine." Allegra got up to get it her-self, sat back down. "We'll talk about something else. I don't know what put me in this mood. Being stuck here, I guess. It's a nice house, sure, but stuck is stuck."

And safe is safe, Lana thought.

She picked up her wine, started to drink. The smell of it turned her stomach. She set it down again quickly. "It smells off."

"It does?" Brows together, Allegra sniffed her glass, then Lana's. "Really?"

"Yeah. Anyway, I need to sauté these chicken strips."

When she pushed off the stool, the room spun.

"Lana!" Allegra leaped up, started to reach out. Max ran in from the mudroom.

"What is it? What's wrong?"

"Nothing. Nothing. I got up too fast."

"She got dizzy. I thought she was going to faint. Are you all right?"

"Yes, yes, honestly. It was just a second." Lana let out a breath, took stock. "Absolutely fine."

"It's my fault." Obviously distressed, Allegra twisted her hands together. "I was going on and on about everything that's happening, and I upset her."

"It's not that. Really, I just got up too fast. Blood pressure drop. All good now." She pressed her lips to Max's. "Cold!" And laughed. "I'm making soup—and you can help me out by seeing if there's any tequila."

He stroked her face. "Tortilla soup? Funny you should ask. Hey, Poe, how about that tequila? Found some in the cabin we checked out."

"Like magic," Allegra said, and laughed.

Once Lana had her soup simmering, she added what the scouting party had brought in to her inventory list. She shared the list with Max while he built up the fire in the great room.

"What we have, if we're careful, should cover a couple of weeks."

Max nodded. "According to Kim, Shaun said there are a couple of small towns—very small—within a few miles. We might find more supplies there. The biggest issue is propane. Without the generator, we don't have heat, light, or a means to cook. Poe checked the gauge when they got here, and they started out with it full. It's down fifteen percent now. They've been wasting fuel."

He straightened, looked at her. "We should close off any rooms we don't need, cut the heat back and use the fireplaces. Kim said there's a good supply of candles and oil for lamps."

"Yeah. I've got them on the list."

"So we limit light use. And hot water. We need to work out shower schedules, keep them to five minutes."

"I didn't think about the water. I asked Eddie to do laundry."

"We're going to need to ration that, too."

"I know you're right, just like I know some of them aren't going to like it. They may not like being assigned certain roles and tasks. I'll take food—it's what I do—but there's cleaning, firewood, more scouting for supplies. And news, Max. We're so isolated here, Allegra was right about that. It adds safety, but how can we find out what's going on? No Internet, no TV, no radio."

He prowled as they talked, prowled, she thought, and considered options, directions.

"We'll try one of the nearby towns, see if we can find some sort of communication. Or people. We hit three cabins, Lana, and found no sign of anyone. We need to figure out how to self-sustain first, and yeah, you're right, try to find out what's going on."

"Eddie found something." Lana lowered her voice, glancing back to make sure they were alone. "When he walked Joe this morning, he found some sort of circle of stones back in the woods, and the ground in the center was burned. Not like a campfire. Something off with it, he told me. And Joe wouldn't go near it, and that he felt, well, he said it wasn't right, wasn't natural."

"It's easy to get spooked," Max speculated, "but we should take a look."

"I didn't say anything to the others. There's no point in raising alarm."

Absently, he brushed a hand down her arm. "Are you sure you're feeling all right?"

"Promise. In fact, I feel less dragged out than I did this morning. Making soup's therapeutic."

"Then let's get Eddie, go check this out. Anybody asks, we're getting some air."

"More firewood," Lana suggested.

"Even better."

She'd never been much for winter or tromping through the snow, and Lana could admit without shame she preferred urban hiking through Chelsea or the old Meatpacking District to a hike through a mountain forest.

But there was something astonishing about walking through snapping crisp air, the scent of pine and snow, the somehow majestic silence while an energetic young dog leaped and bounded.

An enormous buck stepped out of the trees to stare at them fearlessly, making her gasp.

"That's a lot of venison," Max commented, killing the wonder of the moment for her. "Sorry, but we have to think in practicalities. We found a rifle and a shotgun—both with ammo—in the cabins we went through. Kim suggested stowing them in the garden shed for now. It seemed like a good call."

"We have enough food for a couple of weeks" was all Lana said.

"You can see where me and Joe broke the trail through here." Eddie gestured. "Shaun's folks got some nice land. The going gets pretty steep that way, and I didn't feel all the way up for that much of a hike, so we headed off here. Hey, Joe! Dude! Come on back here."

The dog came back, but bellied through the snow to stick close to Eddie's side.

"He's figured out we're going back to the weird. Gives me the bumps of goose right with him."

"Way out of sight of the house," Max observed. "Did you see footprints?"

"Didn't, but it was snowing pretty good when we got here, so if whoever was back here was back here before that?" Eddie spread his hands, then lowered one to rub Joe's head. "Not gonna let any boogie shoes get you, doggie dude." Murmuring to Joe, Eddie continued to stroke and soothe. "He's shaking some."

"It's this way?"

"Yeah, up and around that bend—see where we went through before?"

"Yeah." Max nodded. "Why don't you wait here with Joe?"

"Don't mind using my pal here to wimp out. But if you need help, give a shout and we'll come."

"You stay with Eddie," Max said to Lana. "I'll go check it out."

"We'll check it out." She took his hand. "If it is magickal, two witches are better than one."

When she took the first step forward, he didn't argue.

As they approached the bend, she tightened her grip on his hand. "It's colder. Can you feel it?"

"Yeah. And the air feels thinner."

He saw it then. He'd expected to find some sort of botched amateur campfire—something like a survivor as inexperienced as himself might attempt. But he knew now what lay ahead hadn't been the result of an amateur attempt to provide heat and light.

What lay ahead was cold and dark and deliberate.

"Dark." Lana's murmur echoed his thoughts. "Max, what dark ritual would have done this?"

"We don't know enough. We don't even know enough about what's changed in us, what's growing in us. But someone knows about the black, and twisting the Craft to the dark."

"Out of sight of the house, but still, too close." She felt her skin shudder as they approached the circle.

Rough stones laid in a perfect circle, as if set on a line drawn by a compass. Within it the ground was spread black and slick as tar. And that, too, was spread in a perfect circle, without a trace of the snow that had fallen on its surface or the stones around it.

"I . . . Do you smell blood?"

"Yes." He kept her hand firmly in his.

"Do you think this was a blood sacrifice?"

"Yes. But for what purpose? For what power? Lana!" He tried to jerk her back, but she had crouched, reached out, touched a stone.

It jolted through her, that dark, grasping power. It stung her fingers, even through gloves. And in its flash, she saw blood pour into the circle, heard a voice raised in triumph call out.

"A deer. A young deer. Its throat slit." She turned into Max's arms when he yanked her away. "I could see it, and the way the blood pooled into the circle. Then the fire—ice-cold, consuming all. I heard . . ."

"What?" He held her more tightly as she burrowed against him. "What did you hear?"

"I couldn't really understand it—it was like a roar more than a voice. But it called for Eris."

"Goddess of strife. We need to try to purify it. The ritual's done, and we can't turn that back. But this *thing* still has power."

"And it's pulling power, I think. Or will, in the dark."

He opened the pack they'd filled with items from their supplies. Three white candles, his athame, a small container of salt, a handful of crystals.

"I don't know if it's enough, if we're enough."

"We've done pretty well so far," he reminded her.

He set the candles in the snow outside the circle while Lana scattered the crystals between their points.

"We don't know what to say." Still, she poured salt into his palm, then into her own.

"I think we need to call on powers of the light, ask for their help in basic purification."

"This isn't basic."

As she spoke, she heard the cries, looked up.

Crows circled in the hard winter sky. Something pulsed inside her that was both fear and knowledge.

"I dreamt of crows, do you see them? A murder of crows come to gloat, come to feed."

"Lana—"

"Light the candles white and bright, and their flames will turn this right. Spark the crystals, clean and pure, and their power will endure. Call to the north, the south, the east, the west, unite and from evil power we wrest."

The wind whipped as she spoke, sending her hair flying. Her eyes went opaque as she turned to him, lifting her arms.

"Call!"

He felt her power—the sudden flash of it—burn into him. Lifted his athame. North, south, east, west.

Above them, the crows screamed. Around them, the air pulsed.

Eddie came on the run, breathless, a hand pressed to his healing wound. "Holy fuck."

"Candles light." Lana held out a hand, and the three candles flamed. "Crystals spark." She threw it out again, and the crystals glowed as if lit from within.

"Here is light against the dark." Bending, she picked up a burning candle. "Take one."

"But I'm not—"

"Take one," she ordered Eddie again. "You're a child of humanity. You're of the light. Light burns through the dark." She tossed her candle into the circle. The ground rose up, writhed.

With a shaking hand, Eddie threw in his. Blood bubbled to the surface, fouling the air. Max tossed in his.

"And here is faith against fear." Lana scooped up the crystals burning against the snow, poured them in.

Smoke billowed.

With an audible swallow, Eddie plucked crystals from the ground, dropped them in. Then Max.

"It fights, it seethes, it snarls, and its creatures scream for blood. It will have blood, both good and ill. But it will never win. Now salt to smother what evil sought to free."

She stepped over, poured some into Eddie's hand.

"As I will." She threw salt into the pit. "As you will," she said to Eddie. "As we will." She looked at Max. "So mote it be."

Three scant handfuls of salt expanded and spread over the black in a white layer. Thunder shuddered from the sky, from under the earth. Then the circle filled with a white flash.

When it faded, the ground inside the stone lay bare, its scarred earth quiet. Overhead a single cardinal winged, and vanished scarlet, into the forest.

"It wasn't me, exactly," Lana managed.

"It was you." Max strode to her, pulling her close. "I felt you. I felt you in me, over me. Everywhere. Power awakened."

She shook her head, but didn't know how to explain. Now that what had risen in her had ebbed, she couldn't see any answers.

"Ah, hey, guys?" Eddie sat on the snowy ground, gathering Joe to him. "Am I, like, you know, a witch?"

Lana found she had an answer after all. Easing away from Max, she crouched down, stroked Joe with one hand, cupped Eddie's face with another.

"No. What you are is a good man."

"But, like, a regular dude?"

"I'd go with special, but yeah. You're a regular dude, Eddie."

"Cool." He heaved out a relieved breath. "That was way out of the awesome, but I'd like to get the flock away from here if it's okay now."

"What was done was done." Max looked back at the dead earth. "But it won't be done here again. We'll head back. We've already been gone longer than we intended. We should grab some downed branches on the way."

"For cover." Eddie accepted Max's outstretched hand, pulled himself up. "Because maybe one of them . . ."

"No point taking that chance."

CHAPTER THIRTEEN

Arlys Reid's childhood home sat sturdily on just shy of an acre in a neighborhood southeast of Columbus. People owned their homes here—the brick ranches, the tidy and old-fashioned split-levels, the bungalows, and the Cape Cods.

It was a neighborhood of screened porches and chain-link fences.

While most of the homes had been built in the post–World War II boom, generations of owners made changes. A deck, a bonus room, a second story with dormers, man caves, and great rooms.

She'd grown up riding her bike on the frost-heaved sidewalks and playing in the grassy park with its fringe of trees.

Until she'd left for college, it had been the only home she'd known in the quiet middle-class neighborhood that edged toward dull.

As their convoy of two turned onto her old street, nostalgia and hope squeezed her heart in brutal, twisting hands.

"Never would've pegged you for Midwestern suburbia."

She stared out the window, thinking of neighbors she'd known. The Minnows, the Clarkstons, the Andersons, the Malleys.

She remembered, clear as day, coming home from school to find her mother sitting with a tearful Mrs. Malley in the kitchen—and having herself shooed out.

Mr. Malley, father of three, manager of the local bank, and back-yard barbecue king, had fallen in love with his dental hygienist, had moved out that very morning, and wanted a divorce.

Small matters now, she thought as they passed houses with dark-ened windows, with curtains drawn tight on a street where no snowplow had passed for weeks.

She turned to Chuck. "It was a good place to grow up." Some-thing she hadn't appreciated until she'd left it behind. "There, on the right. Brick house with the dormers and the covered front porch."

"It's really pretty," Fred said from the back. "A really big yard. I always wanted a really big yard."

Inside Arlys, the low-grade stress that had lived in her through this last leg, with its detours, its inching progress, spiked. The really big yard Fred admired formed a white blanket, straight across the driveway, and piled at least a foot in front of the closed garage doors.

No one had shoveled the drive, the front steps, the walk.

The eyes of the front windows showed dark with tightly closed curtains. The azaleas her mother prized formed misshapen white lumps.

Chuck pushed up the drive in the Humvee so Jonah could fol-low in his tracks. Arlys shoved out, went nearly knee-deep in snow. Heart hammering, face burning hot, she waded through it.

"Hold on, Arlys." Chuck pumped his long legs behind her. "Just slow down."

"I have to see. My mother . . . I have to see."

"Okay, okay, but not alone." He had to wrap an arm around her shoulders to slow her down. "Remember, we all agreed? Nobody goes anywhere without a buddy. We're your buds."

"They haven't shoveled the porch, the steps, the walk. Somebody always shovels the snow. Why haven't they cleaned off the bushes? She'd never let snow pile on her azaleas. I have to see."

She pushed past one of the pink dogwoods her father had planted when a storm damaged the old red maple.

"Hold it right there!"

Arlys heard a hard slide and *click*. Chuck's arm released her as he tossed his hands in the air. "Take it easy, mister."

"Just keep your hands up. All of you! Hands up."

In a half daze, Arlys turned, stared at the man in boots and a flannel jacket who was holding a shotgun while his glasses slid down his nose.

"Mr. Anderson?"

Behind his silver-framed glasses, his eyes flicked from Chuck toward Arlys. Recognition sparked in them. "Arlys? Is that Arlys Reid?"

"Yes, sir."

He lowered the gun, broke the stock open, then plowed through the snow to reach her. "Didn't recognize you." His voice cracked as he wrapped one arm around her in a hug. "Didn't expect to see you."

"I've been trying to get here, trying to . . . My parents."

Because she knew, already knew, her throat narrowed on grief, then just closed.

Now his hand rubbed up and down her back, already comforting. "I'm sorry to have to tell you, honey. I'm sorry."

She'd already known, and still it came as a blow to the heart. For a moment she just pressed her face to his shoulder. Caught the faint scent of tobacco.

Remembered how he'd liked to sit out on his front porch after dinner, smoking a cigar, sipping a whiskey. How she'd seen him out there from her bedroom window, cold or heat, rain or shine.

"When?"

"I guess it's been two weeks, or near to three for your dad. Your mom a few days after. Your mom had your brother bring your dad home from the hospital. He didn't want to go there. And she, well, she never went. So, and I hope it's some solace for you, they died at home like they wanted. I helped Theo bury them in the backyard, between those weeping cherries your mom loved so much."

"Theo."

"Honey, I . . . I buried him myself not a week later. I wish I could give you better news."

She drew back, stared into eyes full of sorrow and sympathy. "I need to . . ."

"Sure you do. Listen, honey, the power's been out for a while now, so there's no heat or light, but I've got the keys right here if you want to go inside."

"Yes, yes, but I need to go out back. I need to see."

"You go ahead."

"We're on the buddy system," Chuck began as Arlys trudged away. "Should I—"

"She's all right," Fred told him. "I'll go after her in a minute, but she needs to be alone first. I'm Fred. I worked with Arlys in New York. This is Chuck."

"Bill Anderson. We lived across the street from Arlys and her family more than thirty years."

"These are our friends," Fred continued. "Rachel and Katie and Jonah, and the babies."

"Babies?" Some light moved into his face as he adjusted his glasses. "I'll be damned, three of them? We ought to get them inside. We shouldn't stand out here in the open too long."

He fished in his pocket, took out a huge ring with dozens of keys.

"Have you had any problems—violence?" Jonah amended.

"Had some trouble early on, and some spots here and there off and on. Nobody much left now," he continued as he kicked his way up to the porch. "Van Thompson down the block, he's gone a little crazy. He shoots at shadows, inside the house and out. Set his own car on fire a couple nights ago, yelling how there were demons inside it."

He picked through the keys, all labeled, pulled out the ones marked *Reid*, and unlocked the door.

"Feels colder in than out, but it's better to be inside."

The house opened to a traditional living room, pin-neat.

Bill let out a little sigh. "I cleaned out most of the supplies. Didn't see the point in leaving them. If you're hungry, I've got food and my camp stove and whatnot over at the house. I can bring it over."

"We're fine." Rachel pulled off her cap.

"I'm going to go out now, to Arlys. Thanks for letting us come inside, Mr. Anderson."

"Bill." He smiled at Fred. "As hard as it is, it's good to have people around."

Outside, under the skeletal branches of the weeping cherries, Arlys stood looking at three graves. Marked with crosses made from wood scraps. Had Mr. Anderson dug out Theo's old woodburning kit to write the names?

Robert Reid

Carolyn Reid

Theodore Reid

But . . . but . . . Her father had always been so strong, her mother so vibrant, her brother so young. How could they all be gone? How could their lives just be over?

How much had they suffered? How much had they feared while she'd been in New York telling lies and half-truths to a camera?

"I'm sorry. Oh God, I'm sorry I wasn't here."

Arlys squeezed her eyes shut as Fred put an arm around her waist. "I know you're sad. I'm so sorry."

"I should've come home. I should've been here."

"Could you have saved them?"

"No, but I'd have been here. Helped take care of them, given them comfort. Said good-bye."

"Arlys, you're saying good-bye now. And what you did in New York gave comfort to we don't know how many people. Being able to hear you and see you every day. And at the end? What you did? We don't know how many people you might have saved. You saved me," Fred insisted when Arlys shook her head. "I wouldn't have left, and maybe they'd have taken me to some testing place, locked me up. Chuck, too. Katie and the babies, all of them. You saved some who could be saved. It matters."

"My family—"

"Must have been proud of you. I bet they're proud of the way you figured out how to get out of New York, how you came all the way back here to stand over them now. It shows you loved them, and love matters."

"I knew they were gone." She had to take careful breaths to get the words out. "I knew in my head even before we left New York."

"But you came because you loved them. Is it all right if I pray their souls find peace? I feel like they have, but I'd still like to."

Undone, Arlys turned her face into Fred's hair. "They would've liked you."

She wept a little, knew she'd weep more, but now she had to decide—they all did—what to do next. She hadn't thought beyond coming home.

They went inside. Pangs twisted and pulled as she walked through the kitchen, saw her mother's wooden spoons in the white pitcher, the fancy coffeemaker she'd given her father for Christmas, the holiday photo of the four of them Theo had taken with a selfie stick centered on the kitchen corkboard.

She pressed the heels of her hands to her eyes, then dropped them.

"There are things we can use. We'll need to make room."

"You don't have to think about that right now."

"Yes, we do, Fred." She took the photo, slipped it into her coat pocket. "We all have to think."

She walked to the living room. Katie sat on the couch with a baby at each breast. The third slept in Bill Anderson's arms. Chuck peeked through a chink in the curtains.

"Rachel and Jonah?"

He glanced back at Arlys. "Outside. We don't want anyone happening by and getting our supplies. Sorry, Arlys. I want to say we're all sorry."

"I know. Mr. Anderson—"

"Make it Bill now."

"Bill, I didn't ask about Mrs. Anderson, or Masie and Will."

"Theo helped me bury Ava before he took sick. Masie, she . . . she's with her mom now, her husband and our two grandchildren with them."

"Oh, Mr. . . . Oh, Bill."

"It's been a hard winter. It's been . . . a horrible time. But Will was in Florida on business, and I have to believe, I have to hold on to hope he's all right. The last I heard from him he was okay, and trying to get home."

Arlys sat on the edge of the chair next to his. "I'm so sorry."

"A lot to be sorry about these days. Then you've got this." He brushed a finger over the baby's cheek. "You've got to hold on to it."

"How many people are still in the neighborhood?"

"Four last count, but Karyn Bickles took sick a couple days ago. I was going to check on her when you rolled up. Some died, some left."

On a fresh sweep of cold air, Rachel came in. "We're going to take shifts watching our supplies. I'm sorry about your family, Arlys."

"Thanks." There would be time, plenty of time, for sorrow later. "Bill says there are four left in the neighborhood, one of them sick. Bill, Rachel is a doctor."

"So she told me. The hard fact is a doctor won't help Karyn. She's got the virus. I've seen enough of it to know."

"I might be able to make her more comfortable."

"Well, I've got a key to her place. I can take you over."

Practical matters, Arlys thought. Next steps. "The rest of us should go through the house, see what we can use. What we have room for. We can't stay here without heat or water."

"Jonah and I were talking about that. We thought maybe south, maybe into Kentucky or toward Virginia," Rachel said.

Arlys nodded. Direction didn't matter to her, but south made sense. Get out of the hardest grip of winter in the weeks it had left.

"We could plot out a route—and alternates. Bill, you should come with us."

"My boy may be trying to get home. I have to be here when Will gets home."

"You can't stay here alone."

"You shouldn't." Katie looked at Rachel, lifted a baby for Rachel to take, burp while she shouldered the other. "You should come with us."

"We could leave the route for your son," Fred said. "Leave a big note or sign telling him where we're going. And, if we have to go off route, we can leave signs there that he could follow. I bet he's really smart, isn't he?"

A smile ghosted around Bill's mouth. "He is. He's smart and strong."

"He'll follow the signs," Fred told him. "He'd want you to come with us, and he'll follow the signs."

Bill shifted to look out the window, to his own house, his own porch and yard. "We bought the house when Ava was pregnant with Masie. It strapped us, but we knew what we wanted for our family. We had a good life here. A good life."

"I know how hard it is," Arlys consoled. "But we need to make a new place, and here we're too far from a water source, too exposed once the snow melts. I've seen things, Bill. It's not just the virus killing people."

She stood. "I'll start upstairs—there'll be blankets and linens and . . ."

Understanding her sudden distress, Bill rose as well, passing the baby to Fred. "Theo and I, we cleaned up, and he helped me do the same. Your mom and my Ava would've wanted that."

Tears rose up, spilled out before she could stop them. Bill simply hugged her. "It's all right, honey. Tears wash some of the worst away."

When she'd cried all she could, Arlys went back to her parents' room. Blankets, sheets, towels. Maybe they could get another car for supplies. She could drive it.

Bandages, antiseptics, more baby aspirin, more ibuprofen, over-the-counter sleep aids from the bathroom. Soaps, shampoos, razors, skin-care stock.

She slipped one of her mother's lipsticks into her pocket with the photo as a keepsake.

Scissors, sewing supplies.

Despite the circumstances, she found herself more than mildly mortified to find lubricant and Viagra in her parents' nightstand drawers. Rachel stepped in as Arlys stared at the bottle in her hand.

"Any meds—OTC or RX—for my stock?"

"It's, ah, Viagra."

"Also used in treating pulmonary hypertension."

"Oh. Well. I bet he wasn't using it for that." She laughed a little. "They had a good life here. Like Mr. and Mrs. Anderson. He has to come with us, Rachel."

"I think he's leaning that way now. The woman, Karyn? She was already gone. Another woman—I can't remember her name—gone, too. She hanged herself. There's a man several houses down, but we couldn't get close to the house, much less inside. Even when Bill identified himself, he threatened to shoot us dead—his term—if we didn't get the hell off his lawn."

"But you think Bill will come with us?"

"He's having a hard time with it, but, yes, I think he will. He's got a truck—four-wheel drive—and he and Jonah are working on fixing a tarp across the bed. Jonah's pushing the idea of it helping us out to have him and another vehicle. And the babies are a big draw."

"A good strategy, and truth, and, yeah, I can see the babies added some weight. One less thing to worry about then. We should go through the other houses, see what we can use. We're going to find more guns, and we should take them."

"Any here?"

"No, not that I know of, but upstairs there might be a compound bow. My brother—"

It slammed into her again, all the loss, nearly stole her breath.

"Theo," she managed. "Theo got on a hunting kick when he was a teenager. It didn't stick, but he had a bow. And if we can get another four-wheel drive, we should take it. We can take turns driving it."

When Rachel said nothing, Arlys tossed the medicine bottle onto the bed with the other supplies. "It helps me to just do what comes next."

"I know. I haven't lost anyone in this. Only child. My mother died two years ago. I haven't seen or spoken to my father since I was eighteen. That doesn't mean I don't understand how hard it is to come here, find your family gone, then do what comes next."

Tears clouded up again, but Arlys sighed them away. "It doesn't seem real, any of it. But it is."

By sundown, they had dry goods, canned goods, frozen foods in two ice chests packed with snow. Blankets, sleeping bags, numerous kitchen tools, four hunting knives, eight handguns, three rifles, an AR-15, two shotguns in addition to Bill's, and three compound bows.

Rachel packed two boxes full of medications and medical supplies. Another box held a variety of batteries. They gathered clothes, boots, winter gear, scored walkie-talkies—including a child's set. Fred put together a box of baby and toddler gear. Between Jonah and Chuck they siphoned enough gas out of tanks to fill their vehicles—and the brand-new Pathfinder they added to their convoy.

They hauled in a couple of kerosene heaters, cooked over Bill's camp stove, and plotted out the route south.

At dawn, they loaded up. Chuck led the way with Fred, Jonah's group followed. Arlys, the holiday photo tucked in the Pathfinder's visor, pulled out behind Jonah.

Bill, after one last glance at his home, at the sign he'd left for his son, drove after her.

After a full week, Lana took another inventory of supplies, and found them diminished beyond her calculations. As she—with the occasional assist from Poe or Kim—did the cooking, she knew damn well how much of every single item should have been on the shelves, in the cabinets, in the freezer.

They were light several cans of soup, ravioli, two boxes of mac and cheese—however deplorable she considered that—and some of the frozen foods. Bags of chips and snack foods, too.

She went through the inventory again, then stood seething in the kitchen as Max and Eddie came in, with Joe rushing to her with a snow-covered nose.

"We're light in food inventory," she said flatly. "Someone broke the agreement and has been sneaking food. Maybe more than one person."

Rather than ask if she was sure, Max hissed out a breath. "That goes along with the fact that the propane's down more than it should be. We're going to have to try to get that truck up here. We're below half. The way Kim calculated it, we should be well above that."

"How do you want to handle it?" Eddie asked.

"I'd say by kicking some ass."

Lana smiled thinly at Max. "I'm in the mood for kicking ass."

"Whose?" Poe wondered as he came in, still sweaty from his morning workout.

"Whoever's been pilfering the food supplies and using up propane."

"Propane? What are we down to?"

"Under half."

"But Kim said we wouldn't be down to half for another five days. She's never wrong. What food supplies?"

"Some of just about everything. Frozen, canned, dry goods, snack food, box mixes."

Poe scrubbed a hand over his face, eased down on a stool. "I'm going to tell you it wasn't me, but everybody's likely to say that."

"It wasn't you." Lana dismissed that with an annoyed flick of the wrist. "I've cooked with you. I've seen how carefully you measure things out, then check off the inventory list."

"It's not going to be Kim—and not just because I like her. Because she's no bullshit. And she's no sneak."

"Not the Kimster," Eddie agreed. "She always saves a little something on her plate to give to Joe. You don't do that, then steal. 'Cause, man, it's stealing."

Hands fisted on her hips, Lana scowled at the cabinets. "I'm going to have to recalculate meals and portions."

"We'll see about getting more supplies when we get the truck," Max told her.

"I'll go with you," Poe said. "You need at least two for driving, and three's better."

They turned as a group, looked at Shaun when he came in. He shoved up his glasses.

"What?"

"Food supplies and propane are down," Poe said.

"Yeah? Well, we've been eating and living, so supplies go down." He walked to the pantry, came out with a can of Coke. "This is my ration, and I don't drink coffee or tea."

"How much else have you taken out of there?"

"Why me?" he shot back at Poe.

"Because, brother, you've got guilt all over you."

"Bull. If anybody's taking stuff, it's probably you so you don't lose any frigging muscle tone. And you know what? I don't have to take this crap from you, from anybody. It's my damn house."

"One you wouldn't have gotten to without the rest of us," Poe reminded him, and stood, using his impressive height and build. "It's everybody's damn house now. It's everybody's supplies. And nobody takes more than his share."

"Screw you." But Shaun's eyes sparkled with more than defiance. Seeing it, sensing the anger building in Poe, Max stepped forward.

"Easy," he murmured to Poe, then turned to Shaun. "If I go up to your room, am I going to find food stashed?"

"You've got no right to go into my room. Who made you captain of the damn ship, anyway? You're only here because I did Eric a favor."

"Dude." Eddie let out a sigh. "Weak. And you just copped to it."

"So the frick what? So I took a fricking bag of fricking Doritos. I got hungry."

"That's bad enough, but it's more than that," Lana said. "There's more food gone than that."

"Fine, I made some damn mac and cheese one night. I couldn't sleep. Sue me."

"And the canned pasta and stew, the soup?" Lana asked.

"Not on me!" Now tears glittered on his lashes behind his glasses. "Canned stew's revolting. I took Doritos and the mac and cheese, and okay, a couple of the snack cakes. That's it. I get nervous at night. I eat when I'm nervous."

"What's going on?" The raised voices had Kim rushing in, with Eric and Allegra strolling in behind her.

"They're bent out of shape because I ate some Doritos."

"Because you took more than your share," Lana corrected.

"What else do you do when you're nervous at night?" Poe demanded. "Do you sleep with the lights on, turn up the heat in your room?"

"I *read*. Okay, I read, but I've got a book light. I use my book light. And I like the room cool to sleep. You could ask my fricking roommate if he wasn't dead."

Tears spilled then as he dropped down on a stool.

"Hey, chill, everybody." Smiling a little, Eddie held out his hands. "No big. So Shaun got the munchies."

"He took more than his share." Max's voice hardened. "More than we all agreed. We have to think of the group as a whole, not just ourselves. We're down food and propane because someone got selfish."

"It's not all on me! I didn't take any disgusting stew."

"Jesus, get off his back." Eric patted Shaun's knee. "It's not the end of the world because, hey, that pretty much already happened."

Hands clenched at his sides, Max stepped forward. He knew his brother. He recognized the attitude. "Did you help yourself, Eric?"

"What if I did? Are you going to vote me off the island? Who crowned you king around here? You bring this guy—who wasn't even invited—and his stupid dog. Without them, we'd have more food anyway."

"Harsh, dude," Eddie commented.

Because her temper jumped, Lana fought for calm. Shouting, she thought, accusations, ugly words wouldn't solve the problem. "We had enough for two weeks, now we don't. It's just that simple."

"So, get more." All defiance, Eric flipped a hand at Lana. "You're the one doing all the cooking. Maybe you got sloppy with it. For all we know you're helping yourself when you stir the pot, and guard this kitchen like you're fucking in charge."

Max clamped a hand on Eric's shoulder. "Careful."

After knocking the hand away, Eric rounded on Max.

In Eric, Lana saw more than temper. It shocked her to see something approaching rage.

"What're you going to do about it?" Eric lifted a hand. Little blue sparks snapped from his fingertips. "You want to try to push me around like you always did? Try it. Try it now and see what happens."

"What the hell's wrong with you?"

"Everybody's just stressed out." Allegra gripped Eric's arm, tugged. "Come on, Eric, come on now. We're all just penned in here and stressed out. Let's go for a walk, okay? I really want to get out for a while."

"Sure, babe." Eric's eyes held Max's, gleaming with rage, even as he let Allegra pull him away. "Let's get the hell out of here. Bunch of losers."

Allegra threw an apologetic look over her shoulder, and walked Eric into the mudroom.

"Dude's on something." Eddie blew out a breath. "Wish I had some."

"My parents wouldn't have drugs in the house. We didn't bring any."

"Shaun's right. I'm going to make some tea, okay?" Kim waited for Lana's nod. "Poe's body's a temple, and we'd have known if Eric had anything. We were on the road for days."

"It's not drugs, not like you mean. It's the power," Max said. "He's drunk on it. None of that was like him."

"Maybe, maybe not. Sorry," Kim added. "He's your brother. But the fact is, Shaun screwed up, and he's sorry."

"I get scared at night. I hear things at night. And I stress eat. I didn't mean to screw it up."

"Well, you did," Kim said flatly, "and you'll have to make up for it. Eric screwed up—and if he did, Allegra knew and was probably part of it. But he doesn't give a shit. That's going to be a problem."

"I'll talk to Allegra." Lana rubbed at her forehead. "I think I can talk to her. She seems to be able to calm him down, and he needs calming down."

"He's not handling the power," Max said quietly. "He doesn't know how, and that's another problem. I'll deal with it. But for now, we'll deal with the immediate and go try to get the propane truck. And we'll try to scavenge more supplies."

"Just let me grab a shower—I've got it down to ninety seconds," Poe added.

"We could use you," Max admitted. "But . . . I think I'd feel easier if you were here while we're gone."

On a nod, Poe glanced toward the window. "I've got it."

"I've got a wish list started upstairs." Lana signaled Eddie before she slipped out of the room. She waited until she'd reached her bedroom, then eased the door shut.

"Something up?" Eddie asked her.

"Yes, actually. Would you do me a favor? If you see a drugstore, a pharmacy, we can always use more first-aid or medical supplies."

"No sweat."

"And I need . . . I need a pregnancy test."

He did a comical hands-up, step-back. "Whoa."

"Please don't say anything to Max. I don't want to say anything until I'm sure one way or the other."

"Wow. Major. You feeling okay? You, like, ah, booting in the mornings?"

"No, it's other things. I didn't think about being late with everything going on. It just slipped by me until a couple days ago." She picked up the list, handed it to him. "Once it did, other things occurred to me. But a test would really help, if you find one."

"You got it. Ah, stick close to Poe and Kim, okay? They're solid. You can tell. Shaun, he's kind of a jerk, kind of a screwup. I've been one enough to know. But . . . I know Eric's like your brother-in-law, but something's just not right there."

"Don't worry. Just come back safe, both of you."

As she walked back down to see them off, Eddie's words echoed back to her. *Just not right.*

He'd said the same about the black circle in the forest.

CHAPTER FOURTEEN

The trip down the winding mountain road proved hairy in spots, and had Eddie wishing for the days of snowplows and road salt. Better, for the days of sitting out a couple feet of snow in his crap apartment listening to some Kid Cudi, maybe some Pink Floyd while he toked his brains out and munched on Cheetos.

But all in all, he preferred the slipping, sliding trip down to creeping past a few dead-looking houses before what he guessed served as the supply center for hikers, vacationers, and maybe a couple scoops of locals.

He spotted a pretty good-size grocery store with a sign showing a bear on one side, a big-ass buck on the other, with STANLEY'S PRODUCE AND PHARMACY in between.

The pharmacy part meant maybe he could do Lana that favor, help her find out if she had a bun in the oven.

Big wow if she did. He cast a sidelong look at Max before scoping out the rest of the half-assed town.

A log-cabin type of place stood directly across the two-lane road. Stanley's Outfitters, and beside that a skinny, glass-fronted place. Stanley's Liquors.

Beer, baby! Please let there be beer!

"I guess this Stanley dude's the big man around here. Gonna run over to the liquor store before we head back, see if there's any beer left."

"Wouldn't hurt my feelings."

"Pop the top of a cold one thanks to good old Stanley. But hey, there's something different. Ma Bea's Burgers and More. Maybe she's Stanley's ma."

Max eased to a stop in front of the market. Sat a moment, studied the lay of the land.

"We're the first tire tracks through since the last storm, but I see some footprints, so somebody's here, or somebody's been here in the last couple days."

"The quiet creeps me, man. I sure as hell don't want to get my ass shot again." Eddie lifted his chin toward the market. "I guess that's first stop. Food before beer."

"Food, beer, propane." Max got out, slung the rifle he'd brought with him over his shoulder. "Let's see what's left in the market."

The door, unlocked, opened smoothly. Two neat lines of carts stood across from four checkout stations. Metal handbaskets were stacked in a pyramid, as if waiting patiently for shoppers who just needed a few things. Max kept a hand on the gun at his hip as he scanned the store.

Floors gleamed clean. He could spot plenty of empty shelves down aisles, but what remained appeared to be in neat and orderly groups.

"Weird." Beside him, Eddie fidgeted. "It's like they're open for business, right, and expecting the truck to roll up so they can restock the shelves. Like, you know, normal."

"Stanley runs a tight ship."

At that Eddie snickered. "I guess we oughta do some shopping." So saying, he pulled out a cart with a rattle. "I'm gonna get some stuff for Joe. Bet they got Milk-Bones."

"Take the left, I'll take the right. We'll work toward the center."

Weird covered it, Max thought as he passed the produce section. Not a single leaf of lettuce remained, but the tubs sparkled clean. No milk or cream in the dairy section, but it surprised him to find butter, some cheeses.

He loaded the cart with what he judged most necessary and practical. Shelf talkers showed him what wasn't there. Anything perishable. No fresh fruits, no fresh vegetables, but he found flour, sugar, salt, baking soda and powder, dried spices and herbs.

Canned goods had taken a hard hit, but he still found soups, beans, cans of tomato paste and sauce. He picked up a can of Spam, grinning as he added it to his load because he knew it would make Lana laugh.

She could use a laugh.

He moved on to pasta and rice when he heard Eddie's voice.

"Hey! How's it going?"

Max drew the gun from his hip, felt the weight of the rifle on his shoulder. He moved, fast and quiet, toward the sound of Eddie's voice.

"Cool, 'cause I'm not looking for trouble. That's some awesome dog you got there. Maybe he wants a Milk-Bone. I just got some here for my dog."

Max heard the low growl, and Eddie's nervous laugh.

"Okay, maybe not."

Max eased around the back of the aisle, saw the back of a man—a boy, he corrected—and the big gray dog at his side. And though he didn't make a sound, both the dog and the boy turned.

"I'm not afraid of you, either."

Fifteen, maybe sixteen, Max judged, on the thin side with a shaggy, choppy mop of bark-colored hair and fearless eyes of sharp green.

When his canine companion growled again, the boy laid a hand on its head.

Going with instinct, Max holstered his gun.

"There's no need to be, as we're not looking to harm. We need supplies. We're not looking to hurt anyone or take what someone else needs."

"You're the one with the guns," the boy pointed out.

"Just being careful," Eddie put in before Max could speak. "I got shot awhile back just for walking my dog."

The boy looked back at Eddie. "Where?"

"Oh, it was back in . . . You mean on me," he realized, and tapped a finger under his collarbone. "One minute me and Joe are taking a leak, you know, and walking back to the car, and *bam!* I'd've been in shit city if Lana—that's Max's girl—and Max hadn't fixed me. Sewed me up with a needle and thread and took care of me even though they'd hardly just met me."

He rolled his shoulder gingerly as it throbbed with memory pain. "Let's see."

"Yeah?" Obliging, Eddie unzipped his jacket, unbuttoned his shirt, tugged down the waffle shirt under it to show off his wound. "Doesn't look so bad now, since Lana took the stitches out yesterday. Still hurts some. Back here, too." He jerked his thumb behind him. " 'Cause the bullet went clean through."

Dispassionately, the boy studied the wound. "It's healing well enough. Did you shoot anybody?"

"Nope. Hope I don't never have to. We, like, you know, come in peace."

"Where's your dog?"

"Joe? He's back at the . . ." He trailed off, looked back at Max. "It's okay, right, if I tell him?"

"I'm not talking to him yet," the boy said. "I'll talk to him later."

"Okay, well, see Max's brother had a friend who had a place up in the forest, so Max and Lana and me—and Joe—we made it there."

"Who's the friend?"

"Shaun— Shit, Max, I don't remember his last name."

"Iseler," Max supplied.

"I know the Iselers. They shop here. We stocked the cabin like we do every year." Obviously deciding he'd speak to Max now, the boy turned. "Are they up there?"

"They didn't make it," Max said. "Shaun did. We did. We're eight."

"And Joe," Eddie added. "What's your dog's name?"

"He's Lupa," the boy said, and smiled. "He wouldn't mind a biscuit."

"Sure." Eddie dug down in the basket, opened the box of Milk-Bones. "Ah, he's not going to take my hand off, is he?"

"Not unless I tell him to."

"Ha-ha. Don't, okay? Here you go, Lupa. Nothing like a Milk-Bone, right?"

Lupa studied Eddie with steady eyes of burnished gold, then nipped the biscuit out of his fingers. "He's some good-looking dog. Can I . . ." Eddie made a stroking motion.

"He'll let you know."

Cautious, Eddie held out a hand, eased it toward Lupa's head. When Lupa didn't growl or snarl, Eddie took the chance, ran his hand over the fur. "Oh, yeah, that's right. You're one beautiful bastard, yeah, you are."

"Have you got a name?" Max asked.

The boy said, "Yeah," and nothing more.

"Is this your place?"

"I guess it is now. It was my uncle's. He's dead."

"I'm sorry."

Now the boy shrugged. "He was an asshole. Knocked me around every chance he got."

"I'll be sorry for that instead. We can pay for at least some of the supplies."

"I'll put it on the Iseler account," he said and smirked. "Money doesn't mean dick anymore."

"No, but we can barter."

"You haven't got anything I need. You might as well take what you want."

"Are you alone here?"

"No. We're fine."

"Store sure is clean," Eddie commented.

"My aunt and I cleaned it up after . . . after. She's dead now, too. She did the best she could. You didn't come in to bust things up. Otherwise, Lupa and I wouldn't be so friendly, so you can take what you need."

"We're grateful," Max told him. "One thing we need is propane. Is there any chance we can take a truck up to the Iseler place, fill the generator?"

The boy's eyebrows lifted into the hair that flopped over his forehead. "The chance would be getting a truck up there on these roads."

"We'll manage, if we can take one."

The boy studied Max a moment, nodded. "All right. Load up what you're taking, and I'll show you."

"Is it okay if I check across the street, take some beer if there's any?"

"I don't like the taste of it. If you find it, you can take it."

Thinking of the boy, and whoever he might have with him, Max took less of everything than he would have otherwise.

"You should come with us," he told the boy as they loaded the supplies. "It's a big house, and we'll have supplies, heat, light."

"No. I like the quiet." He paused a moment. "But it's good of you to offer. I'll remember that."

"If you change your mind, you know where we are."

"I know where you are. You're going to drive to the other side of town, take the first bend to the left. Can't miss Stanley's Fucking Gas and Electric. You'll see three propane trucks in the back lot. The first one on the left's more than half full, so you should take that. Don't blow yourself up," he added with a half smile.

"Thanks." Eddie bent down, gave Lupa another enthusiastic pet. "See you around, boy, see you later. You ought to come on up and play with Joe. Thanks, man," he said again.

"If you need anything, or if there's trouble, find your way to us," Max told him. "Even if you just want a hot meal. My woman's a hell of a cook."

"We get by." The boy laid his hand on Lupa's head, stepped back.

Max got behind the wheel.

"Don't like leaving him," Eddie said.

"We can't make him come. But we'll drive down next week, check on him, bring him a hot meal, some of Lana's bread—I found plenty of yeast."

He glanced in the rearview, saw the boy standing in the middle of the road, watching them.

Saw the light shimmer around him, heard the voice clear and cool in his head.

I'm Flynn.

"His name is Flynn."

"Huh? How do you know?"

"He just told me. He has elfin blood."

"He has . . . He's an elf?" Mouth gaping open, Eddie swiveled around to look back. "Like, you know, Will Ferrell in the movie?"

With a delight he'd all but forgotten, Max laughed. "Christ, Eddie, you never fail me. No, not like that. He's magickal, and I have a strong feeling if we'd had any thoughts about causing trouble back there, we wouldn't be driving away with supplies and propane."

"Ain't that some shit? I met a fucking elf. Well, I guess he'll be all right then. And he's got that big dog, too."

"That's not a dog. His name says what he is. *Lupa*. Wolf."

"Now you're shitting me. You're not shitting me," Eddie realized. "I gave a Milk-Bone to a *wolf*? I petted a wolf? That is freaking awesome!"

"It's a brave new world, Eddie." Max made the turn at the bend. "It's a brave new fucking world."

At the house, Lana kept herself busy adapting her recipe for Tuscan Chicken to the ingredients on hand. Both Kim and Poe stayed in the great room while she worked and, as she'd waved off their offers of help, passed the time playing Scrabble.

"Treenail? Give me a break." Not for the first time in the match, Poe jabbed a finger at Kim's play. "What's that, a nail in a damn tree?"

Her lashes, long over exotic Asian eyes, fluttered. "Is that a challenge? Again?"

"You're bluffing this time. Playing off that *e*, using all seven fricking letters. And you hit a double word score? I call bullshit."

"Big, bad dictionary's right there. Challenge me. Lose a turn."

He actually pushed up, paced around a little, and distracted Lana out of her worried, angry mood enough to make her laugh. "How many challenges have you lost?" Lana asked him.

"Three, but . . . Hell. You're bullshitting, I just know it. I'm toss-ing down the glove."

"And you lose again." Kim picked up the dictionary, flipped through. "Treenail—one of its four spellings. A wooden peg, pin, or dowel used to—"

She broke off, unoffended, even smug, when Poe yanked the dic-tionary out of her hand. "Son of a bitch!"

When he flopped down again, Kim took seven letters out of the bag, lined them up, rubbed her hands together. "Now, let's see."

The game stopped as the door to the mudroom opened, closed again. Poe straightened in his seat, and his sulky face went blank and hard.

Eric came in, his hand holding Allegra's.

"Chill," he said when he saw Poe's face. "Seriously," he added when Poe got slowly to his feet. "I was a dick. A total dick. I'm sorry. Lana, especially to you, but all-around sorry. No excuses. I was a dick and, if it helps any, I feel like a dick."

"He really is sorry, and so am I. It's partly my fault."

"It's not." Eric let go of Allegra's hand to put his arm around her.

"It is. I've been complaining about being bored, feeling closed-in. Just being all-around bitchy. I pushed Eric into a mood, and he took it out on you. And he . . . he only took some of the food for me, to cheer me up. We both knew it was stupid and wrong. We won't do it again."

"You can cut my portions back until it evens out."

"Mine, too."

"No." Eric leaned over to kiss Allegra's hair. "I took the food, I turned up the heat."

"I said I was cold. I . . ." She heaved out a breath. "I whined about it."

"I turned it up."

"Let's put it away." Lana heard the cool briskness in her voice, but couldn't warm it. They'd behaved like selfish children sneaking cookies from a jar.

As the tone hit home, Eric hunched his shoulders. "I get it'll take more than words, but it's what I've got to start. Where's Shaun? I want to apologize to him, too."

"He's upstairs." Rather than look up, Kim kept shifting her tiles on the holder. "He was feeling pretty low. He took the dog and went upstairs."

"Okay, I'll wait till he's ready. Ah, Max and Eddie?"

"They went for supplies, and to try to bring up propane." There it was again, Lana thought. That tone. Annoyed parent to idiot child.

In a show of self-disgust, Eric rubbed his hands over his face. "Damn it. I should've gone with them, I should've helped out. Add that to the list of screwups. You're worried. I can see it. I can hike down, make sure they're okay."

"Eric, it's miles," Allegra began.

"Only a little more than five," Poe said easily. "According to Shaun."

"I'll hike down. Maybe they need a hand."

"No. They haven't been gone that long." Lana added a glug of wine to the stockpot. "We'll think about that if they're not back in another hour."

"Give me something," Eric insisted. "Actions speak louder."

"You're on bringing in firewood today," Lana reminded him, "and feeding the fires."

"Right. I'm on it. And I'll take kitchen cleanup tonight, whoever's turn it is."

He went back into the mudroom. Allegra bit her lip, then moved over to Lana as the outside door opened and closed.

"Honestly, Eric feels terrible. We both do."

"You should. If Max and Eddie don't find supplies, I have to cut portions, and even then we only have enough for a week at most."

"I wish we could take it back. We can't. Can I help you?"

"No. Thanks," she added.

"Is there anything . . ."

Lana turned from the stove, looked Allegra in the eyes. "You can go up, bring down whatever you and Eric stashed in your bedroom."

"Of course." Visibly drooping, she went out.

"I know I was harsh, but—"

"I'd have been harsher," Kim interrupted. "I know we're all finding ways to get through. You cook, Poe pumps iron. I kick Poe's sorry ass at Scrabble."

"Hey."

"I should've said hot and toned ass. Eddie's got Joe, Max plans and figures."

"Plans and figures?" Lana repeated.

"What to do, when and how to do it. What's next, what's needed. It's why he's in charge. It's why we're glad he is. Shaun—I know he screwed up—but he's messed up about his parents and doesn't want to show it. He's scared, and doesn't want to show it. He reads, he does puzzles, and he joneses because he can't play vid games. If he could . . ."

"What?"

"I know it's not essential or practical, but it's therapeutic." Kim smiled a little. "Like Scrabble. If Shaun could have an hour a day to fire up his Xbox, we could cut corners on fuel somewhere else. If you could ask Max—"

To cut Kim off, Lana held up a hand. It couldn't, shouldn't be all sacrifice, she thought. There had to be living, too.

"We don't have to ask Max on everything. But I will tell him I think it's a really good use."

"Great. Good. I'm going to finish by saying we all find our ways, but Eric and Allegra are acting—most of the time—like this is some party and they're a little bored with it, and us. So they get a little drunk, have a lot of sex, shrug off their assignments, have more sex."

"Have they been?"

"Having sex?" Poe put in. Snorted. "Rabbits are awed."

"No, shrugging off assignments."

"Look, we're not tattlers," Kim began.

"Speak for yourself." Poe jabbed a finger at Kim. "Yeah, most of the time. One of us gets it done because it's not worth the trouble."

"Party's over," Lana announced. "Everybody pulls weight, everybody follows the rules. And don't make me feel like the damn den mother."

Allegra walked back in, eyes damp, cheeks flushed with embarrassment. She set opened bags of chips, cookies, some sodas, a bottle of wine on the counter.

"You can check our room. I swear this is all, but you can check."

Lana said nothing, simply started to add the items to the inventory.

"I know it was stupid and selfish. It was childish. I'm sorry. I'm scared. I know I complain about being bored. I don't know how I can be bored and scared at the same time, but I am."

"We're all scared." The shrug in Kim's voice didn't offer much sympathy. "You get rid of boredom by doing something."

"It's easier for you— It is! You're all stronger or smarter or just more capable. I'm trying. I swear, I'm trying. But it's more, okay?"

She pressed her fingers to her eyes, swiped away the dampness. "I think I'm probably in love with Eric, but he scares me, too. He scares himself. What's happening to him, it's so much. It's so much, and it's so scary. Can't you understand?"

Lana thought of the moment on the bridge in New York, that slap of power, and softened a little. "I can. Max and I can help Eric."

"I know." Allegra turned to Lana, looked at her as if Lana held all the answers. "Eric knows. He's . . . Okay, he gets a little jealous and resentful of Max, but he's trying. And honestly, I promise, I'm helping him, too. I can make him laugh, or think of something else, or just let him vent, right? It's just, sometimes it's so much to handle, you know? And I swear I'm doing everything I can to keep Eric, well, level. I know taking the food was wrong, but it distracted him. And it was fun. I'm ashamed to admit it, but it was fun and it distracted me, too. It's so much to deal with, it's all so big, and I've never had to deal with . . . Everything that's happened, being here, cut off this way, what's happening with Eric, and how I feel about it. All of it. I'm just scared, and I'm trying."

She choked out a sob, covered her face with her hands. "Don't hate me. Maybe I'm just not a nice person, maybe I don't know how to do things like the rest of you, but I'm trying."

"Okay." Lana moved to her. "All right. But we all try together. And nobody hates you."

Sniffling, Allegra wrapped her arms around Lana, held tight.

"You piss me off." This time Kim offered a physical shrug, but kept her voice light. "But I don't hate you. Much."

On a watery laugh, Allegra drew away, breathed out. "Thanks, I really mean it. I'm just going to go up, pull myself together. Then I'll come down and do something, like Kim said. I'll do something."

When Allegra left, Lana walked back behind the counter. "It's hard," she said. "All of this is hard. I guess we need to give one another a break now and then."

"Sorry counts," Poe added. "And I guess I didn't really think about what it must be like to have all that power and stuff going on. You'd know more about it."

"It's a lot to handle. For those of us who do, and for those who don't."

Eric raced in with an armload of wood. "I can hear them. I heard them coming. It sounds like the truck. It sounds bigger than the car."

"Thank God." Grabbing a coat on the way, Lana ran outside.

Eddie drove the SUV, trying to pack the snow down further, to give Max and the truck better traction. They'd grabbed a couple of bags of sand from the gas place, laid them over the tailgate of the SUV so they spilled out sand—with Max's witchy-woo help—along the road.

But it was rough going.

He knew Max pushed it—with his Craft—and still the truck labored. As the incline steepened, he gritted his teeth as if pushing the truck himself, until sweat rolled down his temples, the back of his neck.

"Come on, Max, come on."

As he topped the incline, he saw the house. Felt a new flare of hope as Lana ran out. He saw some of the others sprint out after her.

"We're going to do it." Then in the rearview, he saw the truck slide a full yard back. "Fuck me!"

Lana threw out power, imagined it like a hook and chain, latching onto the truck, pulling it up the hill. Her heart hammered through a vicious tug-of-war, then she felt the chain snap tight and begin to pull.

"Help," she snapped at Eric. "You can help."

"Trying." His face went white, his eyes dark. "It's so damn heavy."

"Try harder. Pull!"

Another foot, then another, then she felt, finally felt, Max's power mate with hers. She focused all she had on the baby-blue truck with the big white barrel, with the man she loved inside.

"He's going to make it! He's nearly at the pull off." Poe ran, slipping and sliding along the path they'd dug in the snow.

"Don't let go yet," Lana told Eric. "Don't let him go."

"We've got him." Eric clamped a hand on her shoulder. "Look, look, he's at the pull off, he's at the generator."

When she saw Max was safe, she let go and ran.

Eric glanced back toward the house, saw Allegra, blew her a kiss. He spotted Shaun in his bedroom window, waved enthusiastically.

When she got to the pull off, Lana leaped into Max's arms. "You did it!"

"Touch and go." Breath labored from the effort, he rested his brow on hers. "Your touch turned the key."

"Man, getting that big bitch up here took some doing." Poe punched Max's shoulder, faked one at Eddie's. Then his jaw dropped when he saw the supplies loaded in the back of the SUV.

"What? You hit Sam's Club?"

"Grocery store."

"They had all that?"

"It's a story," Eddie told him. He wiped at his sweaty face. "Now we have to figure out how to get the gas out of the truck into the generator."

"Max will figure it out." Eric gave his brother an apologetic smile. "He got it here. Sorry, bro. Way, way sorry."

"We'll talk about it." But he laid a hand on Eric's shoulder, shook it. "And, yeah, we'll figure out how to fuel up the generator."

"I know how." Shaun lost his balance on the shoveled path, went down on his ass. His glasses bumped down his nose.

Poe stepped to him, took his arm, helped him up.

"A nerd's nerd."

His ass wet, Shaun still managed a smile. "Yeah. I used to hang out when the gas guy came up to top it off. I like seeing how things work."

"Show us how it's done, my man." Eddie stepped back as Joe sniffed manically at his boots and pants. "I'm going to get the supplies up to the house. Lana, why don't you ride with me? You can take a look."

She caught his exaggerated eye roll, gave Max a last squeeze, then climbed in.

"You hit the mother lode of supply stops."

"Yeah, we did. They had a drugstore, too. I slipped what you wanted in my backpack. Otherwise, Max would've wondered what the what."

"Thanks, Eddie."

"I'm just gonna say good luck, 'cause I don't know which way you want it to go. Front outside pocket."

"I'm going to take your pack upstairs with me. We have to unload first. I have to do inventory. We have to keep an account, then I'll go up."

"Go up now while most everybody's down below. It doesn't take long, right? There was this girl once, and she thought maybe. Wasn't, so whew, but I remember it doesn't take long. I'll say you went up to get some socks since you ran out in your shoes and they're all wet."

"Good. That's good." She slung his backpack over her shoulder, climbed out to go to the back and take a load in.

"I'd taken off my boots." Allegra grabbed a cardboard box. "I had to get them back on or I'd've been out sooner."

"That's too heavy. Take one of those bags instead. You, too, Lana," Eddie instructed. "And get out of those wet shoes, get something warm on your feet. We don't want anybody getting sick."

"You're right. Just start putting things in categories—canned food, dry goods, and so on. I'll be right back."

She ran upstairs, closed the door. Rushed into the bathroom, closed and locked the door. She already knew, but wanted—needed—verification.

She even knew when, she thought as she opened the kit, followed the instructions. That night she'd come home from work, they'd had wine. That night before everything had gone insane, when they'd made love, intense and wonderful. And then, as the glow spread, that flash, that wild, wonderful explosion inside her.

Life, she thought now. Light.

Promise and potential.

She set the stick on the dresser, pulled off her wet shoes, socks, her jeans wet to the knees.

Then gasped when the stick shimmered, sparkled.

She reached for it, lifted it, saw the bright flash of the plus sign.

What did she feel? Fear, yes, fear—so much death, so much violence, so much unknown. Doubt, too. Was she strong enough, capable enough? Shock, even though she'd known.

And over it all, under it all, woven through it all, what did she feel?

Joy. This, after all the misery, this was joy.

With a sign sparkling in one hand, she pressed the other against her belly, against what she and the man she loved had begun inside her.

And felt such joy.

CHAPTER FIFTEEN

S he also saw joy when she told Max.

She waited. Organizing and inventorying supplies topped the priority list. And to keep on top of supplies, she needed to finish dinner prep. Since she had what she needed, she took the opportunity to walk Poe—the most interested—through the basic steps of bread making.

Throughout it all, Lana hugged the knowledge close.

She didn't tell Eddie outright, but when he caught her eye with a question in his, she smiled and tapped a hand to her belly. And got a big, goofy grin in return.

A good day, she thought as Poe slid the loaves into the oven. A special day.

While Lana celebrated the news inside her, Max sat with Eric in front of the living room fire. They split one of the beers Eddie had scavenged from the liquor store.

"I'm going to find a way to make it up to everyone. I feel like shit. I know that's not enough, so I'll make it up to everybody."

While the anger of the morning faded, disappointment remained. Still, when Max studied his brother, he saw embarrassment as much as guilt.

And reminded himself that Eric was young, and had been pampered by their parents as a surprise, somewhat-late-in-their-lives baby.

"I hope you do, but the more important issue is the power that's growing, how you handle it, what you do with it. It's new, and it's exhilarating."

"Yeah. It's just . . . Man, it's wild. Maybe I used to be a little jealous that you had something, and I didn't. Now that I do, I got carried away. I know that."

"It's not surprising, really. Plus, you've never studied the Craft, its tenets, been a part of a group or coven."

"I didn't have anything before."

"Didn't know you did," Max corrected. "It must have always been inside you. I need you to understand, Eric." He leaned in now, determined to impress the vitality, the importance. "Excitement, that exhilaration's natural, especially since your power manifested so quickly. But having this gift requires bedrock respect and responsibility. And practice. The witches' mantra, 'An it harm none' is more than a philosophy. It's the foundation for all."

"I get that." Eagerness layered over the shame. "I get it, Max, absolutely."

With the worst of his doubts eased, Max nodded. "It's new for you. I get that. You need guidance, and Lana and I are here for you. None of us can know how far our powers will go, and we have to make certain, absolutely, that we control them. They don't control us."

"It's a rush. I mean, you've got to admit." Eric gestured toward the fireplace, making the flames leap. "I mean, wow."

"It's a rush," Max agreed, "but if you don't study, practice, and control, fire might get beyond you. Burn down a building, burn people."

"Jesus, now I'm an arsonist." Eric rolled his eyes, gulped down some beer. "Give me some credit."

"You don't have to intend to do harm to cause it. What I had before this was small, and wondrous. What's grown since, there's your rush. But I've had years to build that foundation, to study and practice. And, still, there's so much more to know, to learn. Why with so much dark has so much light bloomed? Or is that the reason itself?"

"We're filling the vacuum." Now Eric leaned forward, eagerness flushed in his face. "I've given this a lot of thought. Hell, not a whole lot to do around here, so I've spent a lot of time thinking about it. People like us are coming into our own because the virus took out the noise, the mind-sets against, the numbers."

"Those numbers were people. I can't believe, and won't, that what's a celebration of light, of love, of life, blossomed out of death and suffering."

"It's a theory." Eric shrugged. "We didn't cause the virus. The harm, the death. Think of it like power punched through."

"I've given it some thought myself," Max said dryly. "I think of it as a kind of balancing. We've been given more, or what we had already has surfaced so we can balance out the dark and the death. Help rebuild, help restructure a world with more light. More kindness, more tolerance."

"Pretty much the same thing."

"With practice and study, I think you'll see the difference."

As he slumped back, Eric's eyes went sulky. "So, what, I'm going to school, with you as the teacher?"

"Consider it a way to start making it up to everyone."

Eric had to smile, even toasted Max with his beer. "Boxed me right in on that one. Okay, okay. When do we start?"

"We already have."

With a nod, Eric studied his beer. "I haven't brought it up because I . . . But do you think Mom and Dad are alive?"

"I hope they are. I hope they're safe and well."

"They might be like us. They could be."

"They could." He'd never seen the smallest sign in either of them. Then again, he hadn't in Eric, either. "One thing I know is you're my brother. You're my family, and we're together."

"I was an asshole to you this morning."

"That's done now. We start here." Reaching over, Max laid a hand over Eric's.

"Okay."

Lana waited until Max sat back. Hearing Eric ask about their parents helped tamp down some of her lingering resentment. Besides, he was her child's uncle. Blood kin.

"Anybody hungry?"

Eric rose quickly. "I can set the table."

"Kim's already done it, but I'll take you up on the cleanup offer."

"You got it. I'm really sorry, Lana."

"I know. Why don't you tell Allegra dinner's ready? Eating together as a group, as a family, might soothe some bruised feelings."

"You're right. We've got to be a team, pull together. I'll go get her."

Max rose as Eric hurried out.

"You're still a little pissed at him, and I can't blame you."

"Not as much as I was. I'll get over it, especially if he doesn't pull anything like this again."

"We'll make sure he doesn't. He needs guidance, and he's willing to accept it."

"Good. I have reason to know he couldn't have a better mentor than you."

"He'll get annoyed and resentful, I'll get impatient. But . . ." Max crossed to her. "That's how we roll. You look happy."

"I am happy." Thrilled, she thought as she leaned into him, and a little terrified. "And I'll be happier if we can have a little time to ourselves after dinner."

"I've missed time to ourselves. We could take a walk."

"I was thinking more an evening alone, in our room."

"Were you?" He kissed her forehead, her cheeks, her lips.

"Yes. Let's go upstairs after dinner, Max, shut the door. Shut out everything but us."

"Then let's eat." He drew her closer, let the next kiss linger. "Fast."

The mood during dinner proved markedly different from the morning. If bygones weren't altogether bygones, they seemed well on their way. Maybe a good meal, Poe's pride in his fresh bread, and the bounty of supplies erased a lot of resentment. And Eric certainly made an effort.

He joked with Shaun until Shaun's gloomy face brightened, talked with Poe about splitting wood, challenged the group at large to a board game tournament.

"Dinner was great," he told Lana. "Thanks. And kudos on the bread, Poe. I'm on cleanup. Kim ought to figure out the rules and terms for the tournament. She's the big brain."

"That'll give Joe and me time to take our walk. Come on, dude." Eddie patted his thigh as he rose. Joe rolled over, crawled out from under the table.

"Lana and I will take a pass on game night." Max took her hand as he pushed back from the table. "I have a lesson plan to work out."

"Oh, man!" But Eric said it with a laugh.

"It's good." Lana glanced back as she and Max walked upstairs. "It feels like we've all turned a corner. Maybe we needed the blowup to clear the air, bring on some unity."

"They're young."

"And we're so old."

He laughed. "Younger. They can use a night of dissing each other over games, trash talking and bragging."

He drew her into the bedroom, and into his arms. "And we can use this," he said, took her mouth.

"There are things I want to tell you."

"We've got all night to talk. I've missed you, Lana." He drew out the pins she'd used to bundle her hair up while cooking. "I've missed shutting the world out so it's just you and me."

This first then, she thought. Yes, this first. The world shut away so all that remained was love.

He lit the fire; she lit the candles. And the glow of magick joined love.

From two feet away, she turned down the duvet with a sweep of her hand, making him laugh.

"A little something I've been working on."

"So I see. Well, not to be outdone . . ." He lifted his hands, drew them down in the air. Her clothes slid off to pool at her feet.

Delighted, she looked down at herself. "This doesn't seem like the act of a serious and sober witch."

"It's the act of a man who wants you. My lovely Lana. I haven't taken enough time to just look at you."

"We'll take it now." She opened her arms.

Yes, this, she thought. This time, with their hands on each other, their mouths meeting. She drew his sweater off to feel the shape of him—leaner than he had been, tauter. So much stress, she thought, so much work and worry.

She'd give him more than that tonight. So much more.

She thrilled at the way he swept her up, wrapped around her as they lay together on the cool sheets. He pressed her hand to his heart, then to his lips. She drew him down so their mouths met. Blessed, she thought, she was blessed to be so loved, to have such love inside her.

His hands, palms rougher than they'd been, roamed over her. He knew, he knew where she yearned to be touched, what glide and press would quicken her pulse. He knew where to taste to send the blood swimming under her skin.

Weak with love, she gave herself to him. Dizzy with lust, she shifted to rush kisses over his chest. His heart beat so strong, so vital. Hers galloped to match it.

She opened, took him in, held tight and close.

"This," she whispered. "Just this for a moment."

No movement, no urgency. Just held together, fitted into one. Just that moment of being with his eyes, that rich smoke, locked with hers.

Then she arched, lifted to him. Rose and fell with him, and let the moment, and the next, the next, the next, sweep them both away.

She thought of the night weeks ago, a world away, when they'd curled together like this, replete. When the light inside her had been struck.

With the fire simmering, the candles flickering, she combed her fingers through his hair. A little choppy, she thought with a smile, from her amateur attempt to trim it for him. She brushed her fingers over his cheek—rough with several days' worth of stubble.

So many changes, she thought, small and enormous for both of them.

And the most enormous she'd yet to tell him.

"Max." She rolled to sit up, realized then that he wasn't just replete, but half asleep. The day, full of stress, effort, strain—personal, physical, magickal—wore hard.

She considered waiting until morning, then decided no, now, before she put the candles out. Now, while the act of their love still hummed in the air.

"Max," she repeated. "I have something I need to tell you. It's important."

"Mmm."

"Very important."

His eyes flashed open. He pushed up. "What's wrong? Something happened when I was gone today?"

"Nothing's wrong." She took his hand, and with her eyes on his, pressed his hand to her belly. "Max. We're having a baby."

"A—"

She saw it, all the layers. Confusion, shock, caution.

"Are you sure?"

Rather than speak, she got up, walked to the dresser, drew the pregnancy test out from where she'd hidden it. It sparkled in her hand. Then in his when she gave it to him.

"It's what we made together. You. Me."

He looked up at her, and she saw what she'd most needed. She saw the joy.

"Lana." He drew her to him, pressing his face between her breasts. Breathed her in, breathed in the miracle of the moment.

"A child. Our child. Are you all right? Have you been sick? Do you—"

"I feel stronger than I ever have. I'm carrying what we made together. Our love, our light, our magick. You're happy."

"I don't have words," he told her. "Words are my business, but I don't have the words for what I feel." He laid a hand protectively over her belly. "Ours."

"Ours," she repeated, pressing her hand over his. "I want to keep it just ours for now. I don't want to tell the others. Well, Eddie knows. I didn't want to say anything to you until I was sure, so I asked him to get the test. But I don't want to tell anyone else."

"Why? It's momentous. It's beautiful."

"Ours," she said again. "Like tonight. Just ours. And maybe part of it is simple superstition. I think they say not to tell people until the end of the first trimester. And that's about all I know about being pregnant. God."

She sat beside him, immediately stood again. "And no alcohol. That's off the table. It might be why that glass of wine Allegra gave me smelled off. Anyway. God! It's not like I can just Google what to do and not to do, what to expect. I'm nervous about that part, about not knowing. And maybe I'm selfish and superstitious about not telling."

"Then we won't tell anyone else until you're ready. And we'll find out . . . whatever we need to."

"How?"

"We'll find a book. There has to be a library or a bookstore somewhere. In the meantime, we'll use common sense. Rest when you need to rest, good nutrition."

"I think there are special vitamins I'm supposed to take."

"Maybe we can come up with those, too. But women have had babies for thousands of years without them."

On a half laugh, she sent him a steely stare. "Easy for a man to say."

"It is, isn't it?" He reached for her hand. "I'll take care of you, both of you, I swear it. This is meant, Lana. How it happened, when we took every precaution. When it happened. This sign," he added, looking at the sparkle. "This child is meant. We'll learn what needs to be done to bring him or her into the world, and to make the world safe for our child."

She sat beside him again. "You always know how to keep me

calm. Give me confidence. I believe you. This is meant. We'll find a way."

He turned her face to his, kissed her. "I love you. I love both of you already."

"Max. I feel the same."

He took her hands in his. "I pledge to you, all I am, all I have or will have. I will protect you, defend you, love you with every breath. Be my partner, my wife, my mate, from this moment."

Her heart simply swelled. "I will. I am. I pledge to you, all I am, all I have or will have. I will protect you, defend you, love you with every breath. Be my partner, my husband, my mate, from this moment."

"I will. I am." He kissed their joined hands, then sealed the promise with his lips on hers.

"This is all we need between us, but I want to give you a ring. I want that symbol for us."

"Both of us," she said. "The circle, the symbol."

"For both of us." He lay down with her again, stroked her as they lay face-to-face. "I didn't ask if you know how far along you are."

"Nearly seven weeks."

She saw the understanding in his eyes. "Of course. It's meant," he murmured, holding his wife and child.

The mood stayed bright, a study in group cooperation, for two full weeks.

Max knew himself, and his brother. As predicted, they clashed more than once over practice and study. But Max reported to Lana they made progress.

Arguments broke out, but normal ones that ebbed and flowed as they might with any insular group.

An early March thaw melted some of the snow, and though it turned everything sloppy, the sign that spring would return some-day lured everyone outside for longer stretches.

Poe scavenged a hunting bow and spent an hour practicing every day. Lana often watched him from the kitchen window as he shot arrows into a target he'd drawn on a square of plywood.

He was getting better. To her relief, he had yet to aim one of his arrows at any of the deer that wandered freely out of the forest.

Shaun and Eddie bonded over fishing and Xbox.

Poe went down with Max, and reported the Wolf Boy, as he called the boy Flynn, didn't seem interested in joining the group.

Max slipped Lana some prenatal vitamins he'd found at the pharmacy.

As she entered her ninth week, Lana felt healthy and strong. She cooked, joined practices with Max and Eric, took long walks with Max or with Eddie and Joe, and participated—generally losing—in what became the three-times-weekly game night.

She knew Max pored over maps and routes, looking for the best direction for them to go in the spring. Though she'd begun to feel settled, even content, in their strange new home, she understood his reasoning.

They needed to find more people, a location they could defend rather than one with only one road in or out. And even with what they'd found in the little village, supplies wouldn't last forever.

"Why wait?" Allegra asked at a group discussion. "Why not leave now?"

"Because we have shelter and supplies. We have heat and light," Max reminded her. "We don't want to end up traveling without any of that and get hit with a snowstorm. Another month, we'll be past that."

"Another month." Allegra pressed her hands to her head, shook it. "I know I'm whining, but oh shit. We've already been here *for-*

ever. We haven't seen another soul—except for that weird kid you ran into. If the goal's to find people, we're failing big-time."

"And if we run into the wrong kind of people?" Kim asked. "When we're not prepared?"

"Okay, I know things were crazy back at college, and even on the way here. But that was weeks ago. For all we know things are getting back to normal. They've got to have come up with a vaccine by now. We don't know anything because we're in the middle of nowhere."

"She's got a point," Eric put in.

"Yeah, and I get we're in this box and don't know what's outside it." Shaun shifted in his seat. "But Max is right about snow through March into early April. We had a thaw, so we're getting antsy again, but it won't last."

"What, you're the new local meteorologist?"

He flushed a little at Allegra's swipe, but stuck. His friendship with Eddie had built his confidence, Lana thought.

"No, but I've spent a lot more time here than you. Than any of you. We were damn lucky to get here. We wait until we're into April, we'll have a better chance of getting out of the box without getting stuck or getting frostbite, and finding out what's out there."

"Tell them what you told me," Poe said to Kim. "Come on," he insisted when she stared at him. "We need to add it in."

"Fine. Big downer." She sat back in her chair, drummed her fingers on the table. "Back in February, we heard the report—Eddie heard the same one—out of New York. No progress on the vaccine, government in shambles, over two billion dead."

"We don't know if all of that's true," Allegra objected. "Or any of it."

"Empirical evidence supports. What we saw with our own eyes. You can try optimism and hope progress on the vaccine flew from that point, and within another week or so they had it. Then you've got to get it produced in mass quantities, and distributed when transportation is also in shambles. But sticking with optimism, the vaccine is created, produced, and distributed. That takes time," Kim pointed out. "People were dropping like flies. Would this vaccine immunize or would it cure? Would it cure someone already dying? At the rate those infected and not immune succumbed, we could realistically estimate another billion deaths. We could realistically estimate nearly half the world's population wiped out. And that's going with optimism."

"Give them the pessimist's version," Poe urged.

"The vaccine never happens. Using our own campus as the gauge, we could have a death rate of seventy percent—that's about five billion people."

"I'm not going to believe that." Allegra's voice shook as she groped for Eric's hand. "I don't believe that."

"Take the middle ground between optimist and pessimist." Kim paused a moment, but got a go-ahead signal from Poe. "Even with that middle ground, it's going to be a hell of a mess out there. Bodies not properly disposed of will spread other diseases. Panic and violent assholes will cause more deaths. Despair will lead to suicides. Add in failed infrastructure, spoiled food, lack of power, unreliable communication. Being stuck here for a couple months is going to feel like a picnic."

"What's your solution?" Eric demanded. "Just stay here for-fucking-ever?"

"No, we can't. We won't have enough fuel to get through another winter. We don't have enough defenses if somebody wants to take what we have. And we have to know," Kim added. "We need people, and we'd better hope some of the survivors are doctors, scientists, engineers, carpenters, welders, farmers. We'd better hope people still want to make babies. We need to form communities, safe havens.

"You know how many guns are probably in this state alone?" she continued. "We're not going to be the only ones armed. Jesus, think of the nuclear weapons, the bioweapons some nutcase could get hands on. So, yeah, we have to get out there, try to start putting things back together before somebody else blows it all the way up."

"I . . ." Allegra pressed a hand to her temple. "I've got a headache. Can I . . ."

Lana rose, went to their store of medication. "Scale of one to ten."

"An eight. Maybe a nine."

"Take two." She brought Allegra two Advil.

"Thanks." She downed them with her water. "I'm really not feeling very well. I'm going to go lie down."

"I'm sorry," Kim began, but Allegra shook her head.

"No." She shook her head again. "No."

"Do you really think it's that bad?" Eric asked.

"I think we have to be prepared for it, yeah."

"Jesus Christ." He shut his eyes, blew out a breath. "I'm going to go up, make sure she's all right." He started out, paused, looked at Max. "What about people like us?"

"Good and bad, just like anyone else."

"Yeah."

Eddie sat, kept stroking his hand over Joe's head. "I guess when we go, we ought to think about heading south, down toward Kentucky to start. I know that part of things. Like Poe said back when, we need to find someplace we can hunt, fish, grow shit."

"We're good at fishing."

Eddie grinned at Shaun. "Yeah, we are."

Bracing herself, Lana turned to Kim. "Optimist or pessimist? Don't hedge," she added when she saw Kim prepare to do just that.

"Pessimist. Look, the reporter wasn't some crackpot. I'd been watching her for a week solid before that last report. She held it together, even when she had a gun to her head, even when that guy shot his face off beside her. She said what she knew, what she believed, and what she felt people needed to know. The numbers at that point, the crumbling of the government? Martial law, all of it with no vaccine on the near horizon? Seventy percent, maybe more. Hell, if you get up that high in casualties, you're already fucked anyway."

"All right." She'd be clear-sighted, Lana told herself. For her child. "We all have our strengths. Poe's getting pretty good with the bow."

"We all need weapons training," Max said. "We all have to learn how to defend ourselves, and how to hunt, how to fish. How to cook."

Lana smiled a little. "I'm available for lessons there. I'll trade them for driving lessons."

"I'm a good driver. No Asian driver cracks, black boy."

Poe snickered at Kim. "It's the black part of you that can drive. We've got a month to work it all out."

"Then south." Max nodded at Eddie. "Warmer climate, longer growing season."

"We get power. Wind or water energy," Kim said. "We build a greenhouse—extend the growing season. There's got to be a lot of livestock out there. We herd up cows, chickens, pigs."

"Build ourselves a world?" Eddie asked.

Kim shrugged. "It's what we've got."

Lana slept poorly, chased by dreams.

Crows circling as they had over the black circle. And the flash of something more, something darker all but blanking out the sky. Bloody lightning flamed with it, and roaring thunder followed.

She ran, an arm cradled under her heavy belly, her breath whistling, sweat and blood running. When she could no longer run, she hid, crouching in the shadows while whatever pursued her thrashed, streaked, sneaked, slithered.

When the terrible dream night ended, she walked with her broken heart weeping inside her. She walked, armed with a knife and a gun, a woman the one she'd been in New York wouldn't recognize.

She walked, a mile, two, then three, with only one purpose. She would protect the child inside her at all costs.

CHAPTER SIXTEEN

For two weeks, time was divided between plots, plans, routes, alternates, and the kind of instruction Lana never imagined herself involved in.

She'd never held a gun in her life, and now knew how to fire a revolver, a semiauto, a rifle, and a double-barreled shotgun. Her accuracy improved—still needed work—but she doubted she'd ever overcome her visceral distaste for the shock that ran through her when she pulled a trigger.

Pulling that trigger fired a missile designed to tear through flesh. She hoped, with all she was, she'd never have to aim a weapon at a living thing and pull that trigger.

But she had stopped jerking away every time she fired a gun.

She preferred being the instructor: demonstrating, explaining, walking someone else through how to make a basic soup, how to combine a set number of ingredients into a palatable meal on the fly.

She worked on her archery, though she—and everyone else—

considered herself a miserable failure there. She learned how to change a tire and siphon gas, and took daily driving lessons. Those lessons comprised her favorite part of the day—an hour behind the wheel with only Max beside her.

It meant an hour learning a skill she actually liked owning, and time for them to talk about the baby.

Lessons had to be postponed when snow blew in, thick and fast. It melted under sunny skies, froze as night temperatures dipped, and left them with slicks of ice under and over the remaining snow. They spread ash they'd shoveled from the fireplaces to keep paths clear.

Lana sensed everyone, like her, longed for spring. And feared the unknown that would come with the greening.

With Max and Poe on a scavenging trip, Lana decided on a full-house inventory, making notes on what she thought they should take with them. Numerous kitchen items—the big stewpot, frying pan, manual can opener, a colander, bowls, the mortar and pestle Max found for her in another cabin. Her knives, of course.

They could make do with one wooden spoon, one slotted, a single spatula—but if they, as planned, took another car, she'd wedge in more supplies and equipment.

They'd designated finding and bringing back a truck or SUV as the top priority for today's scavenging trip. Putting her faith in Max to do just that, she earmarked more.

She looked up from detailing their medical and first-aid supplies when Kim came in. "These are holding up pretty well," she said, "but it wouldn't hurt to add to them once we're on the road. I can supplement these holistically once we're into spring. That, at least, is something I've learned about before."

"I know a little about it. My mother was big into holistic and Chinese medicine." As she spoke, Kim wandered to the window. "Listen, I really want to get out, get some sun. It's warmer today.

Are you up for it? I don't want to get a demerit for ignoring the buddy system."

"Sure. I could use a walk."

"We've had some more thawing, so it's sloppy out there, but—"

"Just let me get my boots." Setting down her pad, Lana went to the mudroom. "Are you feeling all right?"

Kim shrugged, grabbed her own boots. "Itchy. I guess it's knowing we're winding up our time here. Part of it's tedious, sure. Rinse and repeat. But routine gets comfortable. I want to go. We have to go, but—"

"I know." After choosing one of the lighter jackets, Lana added a scarf. "I think we all know."

"I've had this weird dread hanging over me all morning. My personal black cloud." Kim zipped up her jacket, pulled a ski cap over her lengthening wedge of ebony hair. "Probably caught it from Allegra. I'm not ragging on her," Kim claimed after Lana gave her an elbow poke. "She's been lifting her weight, and cut back on the whining. But, Jesus." She yanked open the door, took a deep inhale of air as they stepped out. "You can practically *see* her black cloud."

"My sense, from what I've seen and what she's said, is she came from privilege. Only child of well-off parents—divorced parents, and maybe a little spoiled by both as compensation."

"Yeah, WASP princess. Sorry, that *is* ragging on her, and I really barely knew her before all this, and only casually at best once she and Eric hooked up."

"Were you and Eric . . ."

"What? Oh, no." On her laugh, some of the stress in Kim's face lifted. "We had some classes together, and he dated a friend of mine for a while last year. I knew Shaun better—a couple of nerds. It was just chance, really, that the five of us ended up taking off together. We all ended up hiding out in the theater—the prop room. Poe had a car, Shaun had this place, so we decided to get the hell out. We had one more, my friend Anna. She didn't make it."

"I'm sorry. I didn't know you'd lost someone. You were close?"

"Dorm mates. We didn't have a lot in common, but we hit it off, and we got pretty tight. She was a theater major, and that's how I ended up in the prop room. She dragged me in there. She wanted to stay, ride it out, but I convinced her we had to go, we had to take off with the others."

"You were right to go, Kim. You couldn't have risked staying."

"I know, and I hang on to that. It was the first night out . . . We hadn't gotten very far, things were crazy. We actually found this empty house—a shack really. Anna was kind of a wreck, I guess we all were. In the morning . . . we found her in the morning."

Lana said nothing as Kim gathered herself, breathed in deep.

"She'd hanged herself from a tree branch. She used a bedsheet. And she'd pinned a note to her coat. It just read: 'I'd rather die.'"

Lana put an arm around Kim's shoulders. "I'm so sorry."

"I don't know why I've been thinking about her so much today. Part of that black cloud. Where's everyone else? I know Max and Poe are out car shopping."

Change the subject, Lana thought, and gave Kim a quick squeeze before dropping her arm. "I think Eddie and Shaun took Joe out for some exercise, maybe some archery practice."

"It's good for Shaun—Eddie and Joe, I mean. Even inside the circle of nerds, he's the one who usually got picked on or ignored. Eddie treats him like he's cool, and that's probably the first time in his life Shaun's approached the outer edges of the boundaries of coolness. And he's done more than pull his weight. We have the house because of him. Yeah, he screwed up, but since then he's not only toed the line, he's worked really hard."

"He has," Lana agreed. "He treats the cooking lessons like a science class, and that's not a bad thing."

Kim bent to pick up a thin, whiplike branch, swinging it idly as they walked. Restlessness pumped out of her.

"It's kind of awful to say, but all this shit that's happened? Freaking global plague, forced to adapt to survivalist mode? It could be the making of Shaun."

"It's going to make or break all of us." They stopped and watched a herd of deer stream through the trees. "I'd worried some that the situation, the dynamics, would damage Max and Eric's relationship. I still have moments when I can see Eric's resentment, but he swallows it, does what needs to be done."

"Max is the leader. Everybody knows it. Eric has more trouble with it, but he knows it, too."

"For me, then Eddie, Max taking charge was just natural. The rest of you . . ."

Kim whipped her switch, shook her head. "Look, I could and would have told everybody we had to ration the supplies, go out, find more, make a plan. And I'd have gotten Poe on my side of that because he's no idiot. But we wouldn't have been able to get everyone in line. Still, Eric sort of took point on the way here, and he's had to abdicate that role, you could say, since you and Max joined us."

She glanced over at Lana. "And we have supplies, organization, a plan because you did. Allegra? She's the princess, and Eric gets to be the knight. I guess it works for them. Where are they, anyway?"

"I don't know. They weren't in the house?"

"I didn't see them, and the stuff they usually wear outside wasn't in the mudroom."

"They probably needed a walk, too. It is warming out, and the sun feels good. I guess we could get more snow, but I'm going to believe winter's back is broken."

"I want to see things growing again, make stuff grow again." Kim tipped her face up, breathed in.

"An herb garden. It's the first thing I want to do. I grew herbs in Chelsea, in pots on the windowsill. I wish I'd brought them with me."

They circled back—following the rule not to wander too far from the house without everyone knowing.

"I'm glad you wanted to walk," Lana said. "I didn't realize how much I needed to get out, too."

They both turned at the sound of running, sliding footsteps. Lana gripped Kim's arm as she looked left. Nearly in sight of the house, she thought, close enough to see and smell the smoke from the fires left banked and simmering. If they had to run . . .

Then Joe burst out of the trees. Lana's instant relief, even the laugh at her own paranoia, faded as Joe pressed to her, shivering.

"What is it, Joe?"

Shaun slipped his way out of the trees, nearly face-planting in the melting snow before Eddie grabbed him, pulled him up again.

"What happened?" Lana demanded.

"Something way weird back there." Shaun pushed up his glasses, the lenses fogged from his own panting breaths. "Way weird. We should go back to the house. We should get Max."

"Just wait. Take a breath. What did you see?"

"Either of you bring walkies?" Eddie asked.

"No, we only went for a walk."

Shaun, face pink from running, breath still coming in pants, looked back toward the trees. "I'll get one. I'll contact Max—he took one—tell him to come back. We need him to come back."

"Like pronto," Eddie added.

Shaun took off in an awkward, slipping run.

"Eddie." Patience fraying, anxiety building, Lana spoke sharply. "What's going on?"

"Did you ever see *Blair Witch*? You know, like, the movie?"

"No," Lana said as Kim said, "Sure."

"I love spooky movies." Eddie comforted Joe with one hand, looking back over his shoulder. "Don't like living in one. You know how they had all those symbol-things hanging from trees?" he said to Kim.

"Yeah. Creepy."

"Well, you want to talk creepy? We've got a shit-ton of them back there. Hanging all over the hell. Off the track we use, but Joe started back that way, and we saw footprints, so we went to check it out. All these symbols, like—what it is?" He drew in the air with his finger.

"Pentagrams." Lana's chest tightened.

"Yeah, those, and these weird-ass little dolls, too. Made out of twigs and brush string and shit, and torn-up rags. I know some of it's from my Grateful Dead T-shirt. *Blair Witch*, baby, and it ain't good."

"I need to see."

Eddie shook his head. "It's bad, Lana. Bad like that black circle. You can feel it. And there's blood on the snow. It looked fresh. A lot of blood, and, you know, ah, entrails. Joe? He peed himself. Nearly did myself."

"What black circle?" Kim demanded.

"We'll explain later. I need you to show me. If someone's coming this close to the house, using dark magicks, I have to see it, counteract it."

"I knew you were going to say that." After scrubbing his hands over his face, Eddie dropped them. "Let's just wait for Max, okay?"

"Eddie, I need to see it. Then I can explain the symbolism to Max, and we can put together what's needed to counteract it."

"Okay, okay, but we're not going past where Joe peed himself and I almost did. Here comes Shaun."

Shaun rushed back, face red now with the effort, breath heaving. "I told them." Leaning over, he braced his hands on his knees. "They're coming. Ten or fifteen minutes, but they're coming."

"Good. Now take me back, and in ten or fifteen minutes Max and I will figure out what we have to do."

"Back?" Still bent over, Shaun lifted his head. His face went pale beneath the red. "In there? I'm not going back in there. No way any of us should go back in there. Max—"

"Isn't here," Lana pointed out.

"Would you rather wait here by yourself?" Kim asked, taking a step forward.

"Hell no." He fell in behind Kim, head swiveling side to side. "I just don't think this is a good idea."

"Neither is leaving up black magick symbols," Lana shot back. "Last month we found a ritual site—dark, dangerous. And again too close to the house. We purified it. And that's what we'll do with whatever this is."

"You didn't tell us," Kim accused.

"No, and maybe that was a mistake." When Eddie stopped, she looked at the trampled snow to the left. "Angling closer to the house."

"Yeah. It's rough going—a lot of brush, downed branches, rocks. It's why we stick to the trail."

"If we wait for Max—"

Kim rounded on Shaun. "Lana's as much a witch as he is."

To settle it, Lana moved forward on the broken snow. She'd gone no more than two yards before she stopped. She felt it pulsing, pumping, oozing. Darker and more potent than the circle, she realized as her skin went clammy.

That had been an offering. This, she feared, a realization.

She pressed a hand to her belly, to her child, and swore she felt a pulse in there as well. The light beating.

Trusting it, she continued on.

Blood, death. Sex. She smelled it all, mixed and smeared together.

Then she saw. Inverted pentagrams dangling from branches. Thirteen by thirteen by thirteen. Blood splashed red over the white snow, and the gore was piled on a makeshift altar of stones where something had been gutted.

The dolls: six human dolls and one four-legged.

With the black beating against her, the white pulsing inside her, the absolute silence of air gone bitter-thick and still, she knew.

And grieved.

To test, power to power, she lifted a hand, pressed her light to the dark, felt the shock as it all but licked greedily at her palm.

"We need to go back," she said with absolute calm. "There are things I need." Max was one of them.

"Good idea!" Shaun took a step back, but froze at the sound of thrashing.

"Jesus Christ, Jesus Christ, that's a *bear*." Kim took a stumbling step back.

"Something's wrong with it," Eddie stated. He unstrapped the rifle from his back as Joe stopped quivering and growled low.

The bear twitched and convulsed as it plodded forward. Its eyes gleaming a sick yellow as it snapped at the air.

"You're not supposed to run." With a shaking hand, Shaun gripped Kim's arm. "Don't run, or he might chase you. And he's faster. Maybe just back up slow, give him room, but stick together so we look bigger. It's a black bear, and they're not aggressive, but this one . . ."

"It's not right." Eddie breathed slow. "Is anyone else packing?"

"I am." Kim fumbled to get the gun from her hip.

"Shaun's right about not running. Let's try the backing up. Nice and easy," Eddie added. The bear reared onto its hind legs, roaring.

"Shit. Shit. That didn't work."

"It's infected. You have to kill it. Shoot it," Lana ordered, throwing out sharp power.

The first shot struck its chest. It screamed, dropped to all fours, and charged.

Shots—the rifle, the handgun—blasted. Lana pressed a hand to her belly, drew on what she'd been given, and hurled a jagged sphere of light.

The bear howled, letting out a cry of pain that tore through the air as its front legs crumpled. With pity, Lana saw its eyes go blank—not with death, not yet, but with fear.

Then Eddie ended it.

"Back to the house," Lana ordered. "Everyone back to the house. There may be more." Going with instinct, she threw out a hand, setting the hanging symbols ablaze. "Hurry."

"Eric and Allegra," Kim managed as they ran through the wet snow. "They might still be out here. We need to find them, get them inside."

"Eric and Allegra did that. Hurry," Lana repeated.

As they broke into the clearing around the house, Eric and Allegra stood on the path, their hands linked.

"You've spoiled our surprise." Allegra tossed back her hair, smiled.

"You held back on us." Panic skidded down Lana's spine. She didn't have to test power to power here, not when she felt it churning.

She needed Max. They all needed Max.

"I didn't want to brag." On a laugh, Allegra tipped her head to Eric's shoulder. The flirty, female gesture in contrast with the cold pleasure on her face. "It was so much fun to watch you play with your inferior talents while ours grew bigger, darker, sweeter. Now."

She circled a finger in the air and ringed them all in a circle of black fire. "We'll just wait here for the last of our happy group to get home."

Lana held up a hand as Kim raised her gun. "It won't get through the circle, and may hit one of us."

"You're so clever. We'll sacrifice you last." His face flushed with power and glee, both deathly dark, Eric smiled. "Max is first."

Everything inside Lana feared, everything inside her sickened as she met Eric's gaze and saw his glee.

"He's your brother."

"Fuck a brother." With a flick of his fingers, he shot darts of black light toward the sky. "All my life he's come first, and I was supposed to just follow along behind him, never quite measuring up. The good son, the dean's list, the important writer. The power. I'm so much more than he is now. And he thinks he can lecture *me*? Teach *me*? Train *me*?"

He shot out a hand, tossed an oily black bolt at a pine at the edge of the forest. It cleaved in two, and the jagged halves smoldering in the blackened snow.

"He thinks his soft, white, weak power can measure to mine?"

"He—he's gone to the dark side." Shaun stuttered it out. "Like, like Anakin Skywalker."

Mouth curling into a sneer, Eric flicked a black dart at the fire ring. "God, you're such a fucking geek."

"This isn't you, Eric."

He turned that sneer on Lana, then looked at his hand. Now something black and sinuous curled around his arm. When he lifted it, crows streamed over the sky, began to circle.

"It is. Finally, it is, and I have what should've always been mine. Humanity's dead. I'm standing on its rotting corpse, and *am*. We are," he said, turning to Allegra. "We are what lives now."

"Thrives and takes. Whatever we want. Whoever we want." Leaning into Eric, Allegra rubbed her cheek to his. "Maybe we should keep one for a pet."

"You're sick, man." Eddie gripped Joe's collar to keep him close. "You're way sick."

"Maybe him," Allegra considered. "After we roast his dog on a spit."

"Let's do one now. Our rule-making hero's taking too long. Let's just do one now, have some fun. You pick, baby."

"Hmm." Allegra stepped forward, pale hair streaming behind her as she strolled around the circle. "It's hard to choose. They're all so *boring*. Except her." She stopped in front of Lana. "But she needs to be last—her and that bitch she's growing inside her. She needs to see the rest die."

"I thought you were just a little stupid."

Off balance for a moment, Allegra blinked at Lana. "What?"

"You heard me." Whatever it takes, Lana thought, she'd protect her child. So she smiled dismissively. "A little stupid, a lot whiny, and mostly useless. I can see I underestimated you. You're really stupid, whiny, and useless. I'm not sure what that makes Eric, as you've been able to use sex and some clumsy power to pull him in with you."

"A man," Kim said from behind Lana. "A man who loses his shit over a pair of tits. Sorry, guys, but we've got a case in point here."

As she stood, legs spread, Allegra's hair began to fly in a rising wind. "You have no idea what I am, how long what's in me has waited for this day. But you'll know, before I rip that wriggling mass of cells out of you, you'll know. You'll see."

Allegra spread her arms, and they became wings, pale as her hair, with edges toothed and keen. She rose up on them, spun. In the whirl of wind, smoke rose from the flames.

"There she is!" On a laugh, Eric lifted his arms. His wings were black, oily like the bolt, gleaming in the haze.

"What are they?" Shaun choked out. "What are they?"

"Death. The dark. Desolation," Lana murmured. And arrogant, she thought.

While they, like their crows, circled, Lana drew on what she was, what she had, prayed it would be enough.

"When I say run, run. To the house."

"We're trapped here," Shaun began.

"We won't be."

She cast out her light, beat it against the circling dark. Cracked it. "Run," she snapped, shattering it.

She dug for more, hurled it upward. She heard a sound, like the sizzle of bacon in a hot skillet, a roar of pain and insult, as she ran with the others.

Those bolts rained down from the sky, turning the house into an inferno. The heat, the blast, knocked her back. Before she could push herself up, one of Allegra's singed wings swooped down. Desperate, Lana gripped it, twisted it, even as the teeth pierced and bit into her hands. Beyond pain, she heaved up power. Eric leaped to gather Allegra to him, pulling her clear.

Eddie yanked Lana to her feet. "Max, Max and Poe. They're coming. We've got to run for it."

She heard gunshots, ran in a blind haze with blood dripping from her hands. She saw Kim stop, try to pull a stumbling Shaun upright, and fire, fire, fire with one hand. With horror, Lana saw that singed, mangled wing slice down toward Kim. As Lana fought to find enough to defend, Shaun shoved Kim away. The jagged teeth tore through him, face, throat, chest, gut.

Whirling, Allegra let out a cry of triumph as life spilled out of him.

"No, no, no." Kim crawled through the blood, already a pool of it. "Shaun!"

"He's gone." Choking it out, Eddie dragged Kim away, down the muddy, slushy mire of the road as Max drove up.

"In the car. Everybody." As he shouted, Max pressed his hands up, fighting to create a shield. Teeth clenched, Poe stood beside the car, firing a long gun. "In the car."

"Not without you." Sheet white, shivering, Lana yanked her arm from Eddie's grip. "Never without you. They're strong, Max. More than either of us can stop alone. Eric . . ."

"I know. I need you to get in the car." Sweat rolled down his face as he strained to protect his family. "It won't be without me, but we need to move fast."

"We'll move faster together."

"Eric." His arms trembled, his muscles screamed, but Max held the shield.

"Look what she did." Allegra turned her face into Eric's shoulder. "She hurt me, Eric. She has to pay."

"She'll pay. They'll all pay."

"Eric, you have to stop. Why are you doing this?"

"Because I can! Because your rules don't apply anymore." He hurled bolts against the shield. "Because your time is over, and mine's finally here. Because it fucking feels good!"

"You're twisting what's in you. You—"

"Oh, shut the fuck up and die!"

The blast knocked Max back against the hood of the car, bloodied his nose. With his ears ringing, he looked at his brother's face, saw only hate and greed.

He made his choice.

"Poe, behind the wheel. Lana, in the back. I can't hold it much longer." He inched toward the passenger side and got in, keeping his gaze locked with Eric's.

In the back, Lana held up her bloodied hands while Kim wept.

"Lana, you need to help Poe. Poe, reverse, and fast. Just go. Lana, keep us on the road."

They would never outrun what was coming, she thought. Eric and Allegra whirled together, forces joined. The wind shook the car and, around it, the ground began to crack. On the hill the house blazed. They had only to fire the car the same way, to push through Max's shield and send a black lightning bolt streaking toward the car.

Lana pressed one torn hand to her belly, praying for her child, and turned her other raised hand to guide the car as Poe shot backward at a crazed speed.

"I'm sorry, Max," she murmured.

"So am I. God, so am I."

As they whipped past the propane truck, Max dropped the shield, throwing that power and all he had toward the tank. It met the bolts Eric hurled.

In an instant, Lana saw the shock and alarm on Eric's face, then the explosion spewed fire, metal into the air. She heard screams, terrible, terrible screams, through the rocking blast.

"Turn around as soon as you can." Max stared straight ahead. "Head into the village. We can't leave Flynn there, or anyone who's with him. If they survive that, they'll go after whoever's handy."

"She killed Shaun. They killed Shaun. He pushed me out of the way, and they killed him. He never hurt anyone, and they killed him."

Eddie hugged Kim close as Poe managed a three-point turn at a pull off. "Dude was a hero. A fricking hero."

Joe laid his head in Eddie's lap, let out a mournful howl.

"Lana's hands are bleeding pretty bad." Poe kept the wheel in a vise grip. "We should have something back there to bind them up."

"She tried to kill the baby. I couldn't let her. I can stop the bleeding." Lana pressed her palms together, closed her eyes. Opened them again when she felt Max's hand cover hers.

He stared into her eyes, his own filled with grief, with guilt, with unspeakable sorrow.

"You saved us," she told him.

"I lost him. How could I have looked at him and not have seen I'd already lost him?"

"You loved him."

"What I loved died with the rise of the dark. What I loved . . . the Doom killed. The baby? Is the baby all right?"

"She's fine. I'd know."

"She?"

"Allegra thought so. Seemed to know, and I feel it."

"I guess congratulations." Kim knuckled tears away. "She wanted to kill you and the baby most. Eric wanted to kill Max most. The rest of us were just entertainment. And we'd all be dead, all of us, if it wasn't for Lana, and for Max."

"Sorry, man, about your brother. But . . ." Eddie wiped at his own tears. "I hate that we had to leave Shaun back there that way."

"He was a hero." Exhausted, Lana let her head drop back. "The light will take him. I . . . know it will. He won't be alone. He gave his life for a friend. He won't be alone."

"We weren't fast enough. We have to learn to be faster, to be more." Max opened his window, leaning out to look back. "Nothing's following that I can see or sense. But there'll be more like them. We need another vehicle, and supplies. Weapons."

"We got another SUV going," Poe told them, "but we left it after Shaun— When he called us on the walkie, we left it and came back as fast as we could. Goddamn it." Tears, rage, and grief glimmered in his eyes. He punched a fist to the wheel. "Goddamn it."

As they drove into the village, Flynn and his wolf walked out to stand in the middle of the street.

Max got out.

"We need supplies, another vehicle, and you and whoever else is here need to come with us. There are dark forces that may come here."

"We have protection here."

"Not enough. My wife was injured," Max began.

Flynn's gaze flicked away, settling on Lana as she climbed out of the backseat. His gaze stayed locked on her as he walked forward and gently took Lana's hands.

"Protecting her. Defending The One. They'll heal, but you should wash the blood away."

"I will. Please listen to Max. It's not safe here, not now."

"We're ready. We were only waiting." He turned, looking one way, then the other.

People came out of buildings, mostly children. Some very young, some teens. A woman about her age, a man, white-haired and wearing a butcher's apron. A woman who looked ancient and leaned on a cane.

Twenty-five, maybe thirty people, Lana thought, all standing in waiting silence.

Joe leaped out of the car, racing to Lupa to wag and sniff. Lupa stood a moment, stiffly dignified, then lowered his front-quarters, pranced in a playing dance.

One of the little girls broke into a giggle and clapped her hands as the dog and wolf wrestled.

"Here is the woman who holds The One inside her. The time of waiting's done, and the next time starts. We'll go with them."

"We're gonna need more than one other car," Eddie said. Flynn smiled.

"We've got more than one. And a trailer for the cow."

"You've got a cow?"

"Cow means milk. I can take you to clean your hands," he said to Lana.

"Thanks." After a glance at Max, she fell into step beside him. "How did you know about the baby, about her?"

Flynn shot her a long, quiet look. "How did you not?"

CHAPTER SEVENTEEN

Arlys sat in what had been the den in a two-bedroom house, painstakingly—emphasis on *pain*—transcribing her notes on an ancient Underwood typewriter. Bill Anderson had hauled it over to her from a junk store titled Bygones. It was big, heavy, clunky, but with it she could produce a page or two of community news every day.

She was still a damn reporter.

She called her effort *The New Hope Bulletin*, and hoped to Christ that Chuck made good on his determination to bring back the Internet.

She shared the little white brick house, with its wide front porch and narrow backyard, with Fred. Chuck lived next door, having claimed—big surprise—the basement of the redbrick house as his own, while Bill and Jonah took two of the three bedrooms.

Rachel, Katie, and the babies lived in the bigger, two-story corner house on the other side. They'd grouped together by habit and instinct, and the location convenience of having the elementary school just across the street.

There Rachel and Jonah had set up a kind of medical center— administration offices were the exam rooms—a community center in the cafeteria, and a combination of day care and education in the classrooms.

They'd traveled south, and Arlys documented every stage of the journey. The winter storm just shy of the West Virginia border, where they'd taken shelter for two days in an abandoned garden center that smelled of soil and rot.

The garden center that had provided them with seeds, seedlings, fertilizer, and tools.

The first group they'd come across, hiking east, joined with them. Tara, a first-year kindergarten teacher, now seer; Mike, age twelve with a badly set broken arm; and Jess, age sixteen.

They'd made room, and eventually found an urgent-care facility where Rachel had reset Mike's arm.

From that facility, they'd gathered medical supplies, some equipment, and a truck.

They'd detoured twice, avoiding the sound of gunfire, found others hiking, driving, sheltering. Not all joined them, but most did.

Their group—seventy-eight people—entered the town of Besterville, Virginia, population eight hundred and thirty-two according to the sign (on which someone had rechristened the town as Worsterville with spray paint) on the Ides of March. They found a ghost town, one where it seemed the majority of the people had simply vanished. While the doors had been locked, and the handful of shops and businesses along the main street had been shuttered, they found no signs of vandalism or looting.

And there they stopped. Even after seven weeks, Arlys wasn't sure why it had been this place at that time. They'd passed through other towns and housing developments, rural areas and urban sprawls.

But they'd stopped, and now numbered at two hundred and six. The number changed week to week, sometimes day to day, as others came in, as some moved on.

They'd renamed the town and replaced the signs at the town borders. And New Hope became home.

Though there were days she woke physically aching for the life she'd known, she remembered the fear, the horror of the tunnel, the bitter cold. And the bodies found along the way, the bodies found in houses in the place they'd claimed as theirs.

So she wrote her bulletins on the old Underwood on an antique desk with the photo of her with her family at Christmas framed and facing her.

In today's news she'd announce that Drake Manning, electrician, and Wanda Swartz, engineer, continued their work to provide electric power for the community. As her own reporter, editor-in-chief, and publisher, she debated whether or not to include the statements from their newest community members that Washington, D.C., was essentially a war zone between military authority, organized Raiders, and factions of the Uncanny.

She weighed the public's (such as it was) right to know against human panic. Then added reality. Gossip spread like butter over hot toast through the community. Better to write up the statements.

She added some local color: mentioned the progress on the community garden—Fred's baby—in the town's pretty, sprawling park; announced Story Time for kids of all ages; reminded readers to bring found books that they didn't want to the town library (formerly First Virginia Bank).

She posted announcements for volunteer sign-up lists—gardening, the food bank, the supply center, the clothing exchange, sentry duty, supply runs, animal husbandry.

Taking her two-page bulletin, Arlys walked out into the living room. While the furnishings struck her—and likely always would—as Early American Tedium, all that faded with Fred's touch.

A half dozen little vases held spring flowers, stones rubbed smooth by the nearby creek filled shallow bowls, bits of colorful fabric, ribbons, buttons arranged in a frame created fanciful art. In the scrubbed-out hearth, an arrangement of candles added a welcoming touch, and light in the dark.

Gone were the ugly old drapes from the two front windows. In their place, Fred hung strings of colorful beads that caught the sunlight in rainbows.

She sought to inform, Arlys thought, Fred instinctively brightened. She wondered which one of them truly provided the best service.

She stepped onto the porch. Fred had pressured her into helping paint two old metal chairs a sweet and silly pink. On the table between them sat a white pot holding a single white geranium.

Around the doorframe Fred had painted her magick symbols.

A pair of pink flamingos guarded one side of the porch steps, a family of garden gnomes the other. Wind chimes tinkled in the spring breeze.

Arlys thought of it as Fred's Faerie House, and found herself surprisingly content there.

People walked along the street or rode bikes. She knew the faces, most of the names, could point out their community skills or flaws. She spotted Bill Anderson up and across the street, washing the display window of Bygones. He'd taken over the shop, organized it. People took what they needed, and most bartered their time, their skills in exchange.

There would come a time—she and what she thought of as the core group had talked about it often—when they would need a more defined structure, rules, even laws—and laws meant punishments.

Some would have to be in charge—and there were one or two already pushing to take control.

She walked across the street to the single-story schoolhouse. Katie sat at a table out front nursing one of the babies while another slept in a PortaBed, and the third cooed in a baby swing.

What Arlys knew about babies, she'd learned almost entirely in the previous weeks, but she knew when she looked at a trio of happy, healthy, and seriously pretty ones.

"I swear they're bigger every time I see them."

"Good appetites, all three of them." Katie lifted her face to the sky. "It's too pretty a day to be inside, so I set up out here." She adjusted a paperweight on one of her sign-up sheets as the breeze fluttered. "The fresh air's good for all of us. I just saw Fred."

It was a pretty day, Arlys thought, and took advantage of it by sitting down next to Katie. "I thought she was down at the gardens."

"She came by for her baby fix. New *Bulletin*?"

"Yeah, hot off the idiot typewriter. If Chuck ever performs his IT miracle I'll kiss him on the mouth. Hell, I'll offer the sexual favor of his choice."

"I'm starting to miss sex." Katie sighed. "Is that disloyal? I loved Tony so much, I—"

"It's not. It's human."

"Maybe it's because I'm starting to feel settled, the last couple of weeks especially. I don't wake up every night in the dark scared. It feels . . . settled to wake up in the same place every day, to have purpose every day. I know I don't do as much as the rest, but—"

"That's not true. You're feeding and raising three babies."

"I have help. Everyone helps."

"*Three* babies," Arlys repeated. "You're running our census and the sign-ups. I realized today, I don't know everyone's name anymore. Faces, yes, but not names. You would. I've seen you charm people into signing up or heading a task, an activity. You're good with people. A natural community organizer."

"It's hard to say no or to bitch at a nursing mother. Speaking of charming people, we could use another sign-up for morning yoga. It's good for stress, and you have too much stress. Don't say you don't have time. We all do."

"That woman's weird, Katie."

"What's weird about a fifty-year-old faerie calling herself Rainbow?" Katie smiled. "Besides, she's a good instructor. I took a couple of classes myself, and can vouch she's patient and knowledgeable. Try one, okay? Just try one. If you hate it, I'll never bug you again."

"Fine, fine. Did I say charming? *Nagging*'s more accurate." But Arlys scrawled her name on the sheet. "How many faeries does that make now?"

Katie reached down into her diaper bag, pulled out a notebook. She flipped through the tabs to her list. "Eight, but that doesn't count the little ones who come and go. I saw some last night—middle of the night—when Duncan was restless. Just lights dancing around the backyard. And, Arlys, this morning, there are flowers blooming along the fence line that weren't there yesterday. I have to ask Fred what they are, but it's . . . Maybe another reason I'm not scared all the time."

With a smooth, maternal grace, she shifted the baby—Duncan, Arlys realized—from breast to shoulder. "Anyway, eight faeries. At least eight comfortable enough to claim it. Four elves. I'm not sure what the difference is there. Twelve that fall into the witch/wizard/sorcerer group. And we've got twenty-eight who list some sort of ability. Like Jonah. I've got five with prophetic dreams, two shapeshifters—verified, and you can bet that's a jolt to watch. We've got four with telekinesis, an alchemist, two seers, and so on."

So many, Arlys realized. She hadn't been keeping up.

"Looking at the math, that's more than twenty percent of the community with magickal abilities."

"I think there are even more. I think there are some who aren't saying, who're afraid to." On Katie's shoulder, Duncan let out a small, distinct burp. "We've also got a percentage—small, but it's there—who are, well, magick bigots."

"Kurt Rove."

"He'd be president of the anti-magick coalition. I'm glad he's taken over working at the feedstore so he's not in town all that much."

"Even there, he's a pain in the ass from what I hear."

"I don't understand people like him, or the handful who hang around with him. Rachel told me that Jonah had to go out and deal with Don and Lou Mercer when they got after Bryar Gregory."

"Got after her?" Bryar, Arlys thought, quiet, composed, and on Katie's list as a seer.

"She went out for a walk, couldn't sleep. Apparently the Mercers were sitting out on their porch, having a few beers—maybe more than—and spotted her. They followed her, taunting her, blocked her way, were generally obnoxious and disgusting. Jonah happened to see it, went over to stop it. It might've gotten ugly—two against one— but Aaron Quince, the elf, and I think he's sweet on Bryar—came along. The Mercers backed off. Aaron walked Bryar back home.

"I don't understand it," Katie went on. "A few months ago, people were literally dying in the street. Every one of us lost family, friends, neighbors. We're all we have left, but people like the Mercers, like Kurt Rove, belittle and bad-talk those of us who, well, have something that might help get all of us through. Because they're different."

"I have a theory," Arlys began. "Major, monumental crises bring out the best or the worst in us—sometimes both. And sometimes those major, monumental crises have no effect on certain types. Which means, no matter what the circumstances, assholes remain assholes."

"Huh. That's a good theory." She cuddled Duncan. "Arlys, I think Duncan and Antonia . . . I think they're different."

"Why do you say that?"

"They dream. All babies do—Hannah dreams—but they . . . It's different. I said Duncan was restless last night, but it was more like excitement. Whatever he dreamed excited him. And one night last week, I heard Hannah crying. She'd stopped by the time I got to the nursery. And Duncan was in the crib with her—awake. I usually put Antonia and Hannah in one crib together, Duncan in the other, and I had. But he was in with the girls, and he and Antonia just looked at me and smiled. Him on one side of Hannah, Antonia on the other. Like they'd soothed her back to sleep."

"That's sweet."

"It is. They are. They look out for her. Sometimes I'll have them in the playpen together, and I'll go out for a minute. I'll come back and there'll be a toy in there I didn't put in. And just last night, when I was nursing Duncan, I started thinking about Tony. How much he'd have loved the babies, how much I missed him. And Duncan put his hand on my cheek. He stroked my cheek. When I looked down, he was looking at me . . ."

Tears filled her eyes, and Arlys saw the baby stroke his mother's cheek. "He was looking at me just like he is now."

Bending her head, she kissed him. "I'm all right, baby. Everything's all right. I'm blessed, Arlys, with these three beautiful babies. They're blessed. And when I think of people like Rove and the Mercers, I'm afraid. There's hate in them. You don't have to be magickal to see it, to know it. There's hate in them for anyone who's different."

"It's fear, too. They hate what they fear and don't understand. But there are more of us, Katie, than there are of them. We'll keep looking out for each other, just like Jonah looked out for Bryar. We're building something here. I don't know what the hell it is yet, but it's ours. And we're keeping it.

"I'm going to go post this, check in with Rachel. And I think we're going to have a bonus *Bulletin* later. An editorial. On assholes."

Now Katie laughed. "You would, too."

"Damn right."

Arlys headed into the school, stepping into light as odd as the fifty-year-old faerie. Magickal light cast a faintly golden glow. She posted the *Bulletin* on the corkboard, scanned other notices. Offers to barter one skill for another or for a mechanical part. Others looking for interest in a book club, a crocheting circle, a softball game.

People, she thought, reaching for people.

That's what they were building, she thought, despite the handful of morons who couldn't see past their own bigotry.

She walked on, made the slight turn to the offices. Through the glass window she saw Rachel and Jonah huddled together at the desk.

Didn't Rachel see the way he looked at her? Arlys wondered. Couldn't she feel it? The man was so obviously in love even Arlys, who considered herself inexpert and mostly disinterested in such matters, could spot it at a mile.

She rapped her knuckles on the jamb of the open door.

"Arlys." Rachel dropped her pencil, rolled her shoulders. "New *Bulletin?*"

"Just posted. We're going to have a bonus edition this afternoon. On bigotry versus acceptance. On decency versus assholery. My editor cleared me to use harsh language. I heard about Bryar and the Mercers. She's lucky you were around, Jonah."

He shrugged. "I'm pretty sure I'd've gotten my ass kicked if Aaron hadn't come along. They were drunk and belligerent enough to start swinging."

"My money's on you," Rachel said. "Writing it out, harsh language included, might stir up more resentment. But bringing that boil to the surface, lancing it might be better than letting it fester."

"It might take more than words." Jonah got up, rolled his chair around the desk for Arlys. "Have a seat," he said, then leaned on the desk. "I think we need to have a meeting, a serious one. You, Rachel, Katie, Chuck, Fred, Bill. I'd add Lloyd Stenson, Carla Barker."

"Lloyd was a lawyer, Carla a sheriff's deputy," Rachel put in. "Lloyd's, for lack of a better term, one of the animal whisperers, so that brings in three, with Jonah, from the magickal side of things—and all with good heads."

"We need to talk about official laws, rules, consequences," Jonah began. "We need to write up some sort of community constitution, I guess. Once we do, we need to take it to a full community meeting. People are settling in, and that's a good thing. By and large, we're working together, but that business with Bryar isn't the first trouble, and it won't be the last."

"Every one of us is armed, one way or the other," Rachel put in. "What happens if, human nature being what it is, somebody takes a shot at someone instead of a swing? What would have happened if the Mercers had hurt Bryar? We need to figure it out before it happens."

"I agree." Hadn't she just mulled over moving toward a more formal structure? Arlys thought. "Some won't like it—the rules or the consequences—so we'd need to make it simple and clear. And if we have laws, that means we need someone who will enforce them."

"I'm hoping Carla will take it on," Jonah said. "She has experience, she's steady. And maybe we could ask Bill Anderson to work with her."

"Bill?"

"Steady again, and people like him, respect him. I'm not sure he'll want to take that on, but we will need more than just Carla. Anyway, it would be a start. Right now, heading up committees, I'd guess you'd call them, is volunteer, and it can cycle."

"We need to make that more formal." Rachel tapped her pencil on the desk. "Since we haven't had any patients this morning, Jonah and I have been trying to work on an agenda. Up to now we've had to focus on food, shelter, security, medicine, supplies. Now we need structure."

Arlys nodded. "And with structure comes laws, mores, a line of authority, consequences. And information."

"On the list," Rachel told her. "We're going to need to send out scouting parties. Right now it feels like we're all there is in the world. But people are still trickling in so we know we're not. We have to know what's out there. Maybe Chuck can get communications up again, but we don't know who we'd communicate with, or what we'd risk if we contact the wrong people."

"Human nature being what it is," Arlys murmured. "And extra-human, too. Being extra isn't an immunization against being violent. It just adds a layer. What the hell do we do if we set up laws and one of our Uncannys breaks them?"

"We better figure it out."

Arlys looked at Jonah, blew out a breath. "All right."

"My place? We've got the room, and Katie can put the babies to bed." Rachel glanced at Jonah. "Tonight?"

"Sooner the better."

"I'll tell Fred." Arlys pushed to her feet. "And I'll go up to talk to Bill, talk to Chuck. Katie's right outside. I'll tell her on the way. Say nine?"

"It works. Carla's working the community garden." Jonah slid his hands into his pockets as he looked at Rachel. "Since we're clear, do you want to walk down, talk to her? We can round up the others while we're out."

"Sure. Let me grab a walkie." Rachel pulled them from the desk drawer, set one on the desk with the sign saying the doctor is out but available, hooked the other to her belt.

They walked out together to where Katie changed Hannah and the twins lay on a blanket squealing, waving hands, kicking feet.

"They act like I just gave them each a pound of chocolate." Laughing, she scooped up Hannah for a nuzzle.

Jonah laid a hand on Rachel's shoulder. "Do you hear that?"

"Hear what— I do now," she added when the sound of approaching engines reached her. "Someone's coming."

"More than one someone." Jonah walked down to the sidewalk. He saw others looking as well, coming out of their houses, the other buildings. Shielding his eyes with the flat of his hand against the glare of the sun, he stared.

"Holy shit."

Rachel pulled out her squawking walkie, scooped up a baby as she answered.

"The sentry cleared them," she called out to Jonah, and walked down to join him.

"I don't know if he'd have had much choice. That's got to be fifteen cars, trucks. And a damn school bus."

Katie, two babies in tow, and Arlys stepped down to the sidewalk. So together they all watched Max lead his group into New Hope.

CHAPTER EIGHTEEN

Both wary and curious, Arlys studied the man who got out of the lead car. Tall and lean in jeans and a black T-shirt, dark hair curling choppily over the collar, boots worn and scarred. He struck her as hard and handsome, with the scruffy look of a man who'd been on the road for days, maybe weeks.

He had an air about him, she thought, one of confidence and power. He pulled off his sunglasses with one hand, held the other up in a wait signal. More cars and trucks rolled in—more than the fifteen Jonah had estimated. Some with what she thought were horse trailers.

The man scanned the street, the people, appearing to judge whether they held welcome or aggression. He seemed prepared for either.

Beside her, Jonah shifted, then stepped down to walk to him.

"Jonah Vorhies." After the briefest hesitation, Jonah offered a hand.

"Max Fallon." Max accepted the hand. "Are you in charge?"

"Ah—"

Arlys went with instinct, speaking as she walked down to join them. "We were the first here. Arlys Reid."

A woman got out of the passenger side—earning a quick, warning glance from Max.

She wore her long, dark blond hair in a ponytail. A T-shirt bagged over her small baby bump.

"I know you," she said as she skirted the hood of the car. "I watched your broadcasts. Clung to them right up to the day we left New York. I'm Lana. Max and I lived in Chelsea."

Lana laid a hand on Max's arm. "We followed your signs," she added. "From . . ."

"South of Harrisburg," Max said when Lana glanced at him. "We picked up people along the way."

"Yeah, I can see that." Jonah held his ground as a skinny guy and a tail-wagging dog climbed out of the backseat. "How many are you?"

"Ninety-seven people, eighteen of them under fourteen. Eight dogs—two of them pups—three dairy cows, two Holsteins and a Guernsey, and a bull calf. Two Black Angus calves. Five horses, including a pregnant mare, eight cats, about a dozen chickens, and a rooster."

Jonah blew out a breath. "That's a lot. You're the biggest group we've ever had come in even without all the livestock. Are you looking to settle here?"

"New Hope. Following your signs gave people that." Max looked back as a muscular black man and a tough-looking white man started down the line of cars.

Arlys flicked them a glance, then focused. Her heart literally bumped in her chest. "Oh my God. Oh God. Will? Will Anderson." Flying on joy, she rushed him, flung her arms around him.

She felt him stiffen, start to draw back. "It's Arlys, Will. Arlys Reid."

"Arlys?" He yanked her back, stared at her with stormy blue eyes. "Jesus. Jesus. Arlys. My dad? Where's my dad?"

She gripped his arm tight, felt it quiver, and pointed up the street where Bill walked down the line of cars.

"Dad!"

Bill stopped and, as his legs buckled, braced on the side of a truck, a hand extended toward his son. Will took off running.

"New Hope," Lana murmured as she watched father and son embrace. "It's what we all need. What we're all looking for."

"Bill never gave up." Jonah let out a sigh. "It looks like we've got our first New Hope traffic jam. I guess we'd better figure out how to handle it. We've got a system. It's still got kinks, but it's a system. Maybe we can start with pulling some of these vehicles into the school parking lot."

"Is there somewhere we can unload the animals?" Max asked. "They're going to need food and water."

"Ah." Jonah scratched the back of his neck. "Rachel, we should contact whoever's out at the farm. It wasn't actually a farm until recently," he told Max. "There are a couple, but they're too far from town for safety so we're improvising. We've got a couple of cows, a couple of horses, a nanny goat, and some chickens. We've got a feed-store, but we're going to need more feed with what you've brought in. We've got some hay going. I can't tell you much about that. I'm no farmer."

"We've got two with us."

"Better and better. Aaron!" Jonah signaled a man across the street. "Can you get a couple of people to help lead the trailers to the farm, get them set up?" He bent to pet the dog who came over to sniff at him. "Good-looking dog."

"Best dog ever. He's Joe. I'm Eddie. I can lend a hand with the animals," he told Max. "I saw you on TV, too," he said to Arlys. "Got yourself some good-looking rug rats," he added with an easy grin as he looked at the babies. "We got a handful of our own on the wagon train."

"Let's get some of these vehicles into the lot. Pass the word down the line, will you, Poe?"

"Sure thing."

"Once you do, we've got a sign-up system. We're trying to keep track of people. Names, ages, skills." Jonah gestured. "Katie's in charge of that. I think she could use some help with this many."

"I've got it," Katie said. "How far along are you?" she asked Lana.

"About four and a half months. Are they . . . triplets?"

"They're all mine."

Lana let out a shaky breath, rubbed her bump. "Wow." Looked at Max. "Wow."

He put an arm around her shoulders, kissed her temple. "Let's get the cars out of the road."

"You do that. I'm fine here. I can . . . sign us in. Max." She patted a hand on his heart when he hesitated. "Trust goes both ways. We've had trouble along the way," she said.

"We all have. Any medicals with you?" Rachel asked.

"A retired nurse—he's great. Go ahead." Lana gave Max a nudge. "A nursing student, and she's coming along. A vet. A firefighter and two cops with emergency training. No doctors, but—"

"Rachel's a doctor," Katie put in. "And Jonah's a paramedic."

"A doctor." Now Lana pressed a hand to her belly, looked at Rachel with eyes full of relief. "Max."

He stroked a hand down her back. "I'll be right back. She'd feel better if a doctor examined her and the baby."

"That's what we'll do. Lana, you said?"

"Lana Bingham." Lana held out a hand to Rachel as she walked up. "I'm twenty-eight. I'm a chef—was a chef. I—"

Surprised, she jerked when Duncan reached for her. Babbling, he wiggled in his mother's arms, straining toward Lana.

"I know next to nothing about having a baby or what to do after I have one." With obvious nerves, she took Duncan.

He laid a hand on her heart, and those nerves dropped away. She felt his light as cleanly as she felt the light inside her.

She found herself staring back into deep infant blue eyes, but with green edging in the sunlight.

"He's special—I mean, he's beautiful." She continued to look at him as she spoke. "If you don't want Uncannys in New Hope, it's best if you tell us now."

Duncan curled his hand around her finger, and light shimmered.

"He's special," Katie said calmly. "So's his sister, Antonia. So is Jonah, and many others in the community."

Tears swam into Lana's eyes as she lowered her cheek to Duncan's head. "Sorry. Hormones—that's what Ray, our nurse, tells me."

"Katie, why don't you write down Lana's information. A professional chef?" Rachel asked.

"Yeah, and believe me, I know a lot more about fileting a Chilean sea bass than pregnancy, childbirth, or being a mother."

"A lot of parents start off that way. I'm a terrible cook. We can barter the OB-GYN services for cooking lessons. And besides being a chef?"

"Witch."

"And you're with Max?" Katie, behind her table, wrote out her information in such an easy, practical way, Lana smiled.

"Yes. He's the father, and my husband. Max Fallon. He's thirty-one. I can tell you without exaggeration, he can do whatever has to be done. He's kept all this together, all these people. He's a writer, but—"

"Max Fallon." Katie looked up. "It didn't click. My husband loved his books. I know we have some in our library."

"You have a library?" Lana asked, and her eyes swam again.

"We have a library, a community garden, a day care, and medical facilities. Does Max also have other abilities?"

"Witch."

"Would you like Max to be with you for the exam?" Rachel asked her.

"Yes, please."

"Send him in, Katie. I'm going to take Lana inside, get her comfortable."

Jonah took Duncan, watched Lana go in with Rachel. "They're healthy." He set Duncan on the blanket. "I couldn't *not* see. Healthy and strong. The baby . . . there's something bright. I don't know how to describe it. Something . . . more." He cut himself off as Max strode up.

"They just went in. I'll show you."

Lana changed into an exam gown while Rachel explained that they'd scavenged supplies and equipment from hospitals and clinics en route.

"We still need more, but at the time we didn't have room to take more. And some of what we have we can't use until we get power up again. Fingers crossed there. Come on in, Max. First, you estimate four and a half months, so eighteen weeks?"

"She was conceived on January second. That's certain."

"Date of your last period?"

"I honestly don't know, but I know the conception date."

"All right." Rachel walked to a calendar on the wall, flipped back, counted. "Eighteen weeks, three days. That puts your due date at . . . best estimate going forty weeks from conception, at September twenty-fifth."

"But, nine months would be early September."

Rachel let the calendar flip back down, smiled. "It's actually ten months' gestation. Forty weeks."

"Then why do they say nine? See," she said to Max. "I know nothing."

"You know now."

Rachel gestured toward the scale. "Do you know your weight pre-pregnancy?"

"A hundred and sixteen. Oh God, I have to get on there, don't I?" Resigned, Lana stepped on the scale, but closed her eyes.

"Height, five feet, six and a quarter inches. Weight one-twenty-six."

"Ten pounds?" Lana's eyes popped open. "Ten?"

"Is excellent for your stage of pregnancy. With your height and build, a twenty-five- to thirty-five-pound weight gain would be very good. But everyone's different, so don't stress about it."

"Did you say thirty-five pounds? I thought Ray was exaggerating."

"Why don't you sit up on the table—don't cross your legs. We'll get your blood pressure. How are you sleeping?"

"It depends. I have dreams."

"We haven't always been able to stop or find the best shelter at night," Max added.

"Mmm. Blood pressure's good." Rachel noted it down. "Morning sickness?"

"I never had any. A little light-headed now and again, and I'm hungry all the damn time."

"Allergies, medical conditions, medications?"

"No, nothing."

"Is this your first pregnancy?"

"Yes."

Rachel asked questions, Lana answered. Max wandered the room.

"Have you felt any movement?"

"I think—I felt . . . When we saw the sign? The one that says New Hope? She moved. It felt amazing really."

Max turned back. "You didn't say."

"You were on the walkie with Poe. You were worried. We didn't know if we'd be welcome here, or what to expect. And it wasn't like the butterflies I felt before. Ray called that quickening. It wasn't like that. It was excited. Is that normal?"

"At eighteen to twenty weeks it's good to feel movement. You'll feel more, but don't worry if you don't feel movement every day right now. 'Don't worry' is the mantra."

Rachel glanced at the ultrasound, sighed. "I need you to scoot down, feet in the stirrups." She walked over, took gloves from a box. "I need to do an internal. Once we get things running, we'll do an ultrasound."

Max pointed. "That?"

"Yes. Once we can use it, you'll be able to see the baby on the monitor, hear the heartbeat. I can measure weight and length, check a lot of things. I might be able to—if you want—determine sex."

"It's a girl. I know that the same way I know the conception date. I know she's healthy and strong, but—"

"You still worry."

"An ultrasound would show you things that would help with that worry?" Max asked.

Understanding expectant parents worried about everything even under normal circumstances, Rachel sent Max a reassuring smile.

"Babies have come into the world healthy and strong long before ultrasounds."

"But?"

"I'm a doctor. I'd love to have all the tools available."

"I can help with that."

Max stepped to the machine, laid his hand on it. Rachel felt the air vibrate around her before the machine hummed to life.

Lana reached out a hand to brush Max's arm. "Max has a talent for machines, motors, engines."

For a moment, professional equanimity lost against a celebratory fist pump. "Oh, hell yes! We have an engineer and an electrician—and an IT guy—who are all going to want to meet you as soon as possible."

"Can you use it now, for Lana and the baby?"

"Let's find out. If I'd known this was an option, you could've kept on your underwear."

"If you think modesty's a factor, it's not."

"All right then."

Rachel pulled out a tube of gel, snapped on the gloves. "I'm going to put this on your abdomen." She lifted the hem of the gown.

"Will this be painful?" Max asked, and took Lana's hand.

"Pain*less*." Mentally crossing her fingers, Rachel rubbed the transducer over the gel. "There." She nodded toward the monitor. "There's your baby."

"I can't really . . . Oh God, I can!" Lana's hand clamped on Max's. "I can see her. She's moving. I can feel her moving."

"Hear that sound? That's a good, strong heartbeat. And from the size, I agree with your conception date."

"She's so small." Max reached out, traced the image with his finger.

"I've seen bigger bell peppers," Lana agreed. "Is she growing all right?"

"We've got her at right about five and a half inches, and seven ounces. She's growing exactly right. And you're right again. It's a girl."

"I see her fingers." Lana's voice broke. "She has fingers."

"Eight fingers, two thumbs," Rachel confirmed. "We're going to take a closer look—at her heart, her brain, her other organs—but I'm going to say I'm seeing a perfectly formed eighteen-week fetus, female. How long will this stay on?" she asked Max.

Still tracing the baby, he brought Lana's hand to his lips. "How long do you need it?"

Rachel felt a bit like weeping herself. "If I didn't say it before, let me say it now. Welcome to New Hope."

Lana came out clutching a list of do's and don'ts. A line of people snaked out from Katie's table. Lana zeroed in on Ray, walked over to hug him.

"Told you, Mama."

"The doctor said she's perfect. We're perfect. She's hoping to talk to you and Carly after you're settled a little. I liked her, Ray. I really liked her."

He gave her a pat on the cheek with his big, broad-palmed hand. "You were right to follow the signs."

"Hey, I'm Fred." She bounced up, beaming. "You're Lana, right, and Max? You brought Bill's son. He's so happy. They're up at Bygones. I think they need a little time together. But Jonah said I should show you around, and let you see the house he thinks will work for you. If you want."

"I really need to check on some things," Max told Lana. "Some people."

"Go ahead. I can go with—Fred? Is that short for Fredrica?"

"Short for Freddie. My mom was like a huge Freddie Mercury fan. You know, Queen?"

Lana let out a laugh. "Yes. And I'd really like to look around, see the house."

"It's right across the street. See?" She pointed over and up a few houses to a two-story white brick with a porch. "It used to be bigger. See?" she said again. "They made the other part of it into apartments. They're kind of dated and need work, but the house part's pretty good."

"I'd love to see it."

Lana tipped her face up to kiss Max. "Do what you have to do." And she went with Fred.

"I live right there. Arlys and I share that house."

"Did you meet her on the way here?"

"No, we worked together in New York. I was an intern at the station. Chuck lives over there—he has the basement, and Bill and Jonah live there, too. Arlys and I got to Hoboken to Chuck—he's a hacker, he was her main source."

"How did you get to Hoboken?"

"Through the PATH tunnels."

Lana stopped in the middle of the street. "You went through the tunnel? Just you and Arlys?"

"We had to. It was bad. Some of it was really bad, but it's over now, and we got to Chuck, and he has a Humvee, and we got out. He's trying to get communications up again. If anybody can . . . We met Jonah and Rachel and Katie and the babies on the way. I love babies. And we went all the way to Ohio because Arlys's family—but . . ."

"I'm sorry."

Dangling earrings with multicolored beads swayed on Fred's ears. "But we found Bill, and he came with us. We left signs for Will. And we met Lloyd and Rainbow and . . . I know I'm talking a lot. I'm excited."

"So am I."

Steps led straight off the sidewalk to the porch. Fred opened the door. "Somebody remodeled it, that open floor plan thing."

"Yes."

It was airy, Lana thought, and had decent light even with the small front windows.

"You can switch out the furniture if you want. Nobody minds if you switch things with another of the empty places. There won't be so many empty now. I'm glad."

"I can work with this. I'm so grateful for this."

Whoever lived there had had clean, simple tastes. A sofa covered in a gray that made her think of Max's eyes, chairs in a pattern of gray and navy blue. Tables of dark wood on a floor of golden oak. A fireplace with a wide mantel over it.

But the kitchen pulled at her. They'd carried the flooring through so it read as one flowing space, areas defined by a counter of cream-colored wood covered in deep gray granite.

She wandered in, clutched her hands together at the six-burner stove, the stainless appliances, the generous counter space. Double ovens, she thought, and wide atrium doors to bring in more light.

"It's a good kitchen."

"Everything's dusty, but—"

"We'll clean it. It's a good house. There's a nice yard. They said there's a community garden. Are there herbs?"

"Sure. We had to start a lot of them from seed, but we've got lots of herbs."

"I wonder if I can get some seed, or transplant some. Who would I ask?"

"I'm sort of in charge of that, so sure. Do you want to see upstairs?"

"Yes."

"Katie said you were a chef in New York."

"I was. A sous chef—an under chef," she explained. "I worked at Delray's. Three and a half years."

"I know Delray's!" Fred led the way to the stairs at a bounce. "I mean, I read some reviews. I couldn't afford to actually eat there, but I read reviews. It was a hot spot."

"Those were the days," Lana murmured. "I'll cook for you."

"Really? If I get you cheese, can you make lasagna?"

"If you get me cheese, I'll make you the best lasagna you've ever tasted."

"We've got milk cows and a goat. If you have milk you can get cheese and butter. Cheese is harder, but I'm working on it. I found a book, and I'm using nettles and thistles for the— What is it?"

"Rennet. That's damn clever, Fred."

"I made some cottage cheese, and it wasn't too bad. I'm a faerie, by the way."

"I should've known. You have a brightness about you."

"Your baby's bright. Jonah said. He sees things like that. I can feel it, but he can see it, too. This would be a really nice nursery."

Thinking about the baby, about the light, Lana looked in what had been a guest room doubling as a home office. But Fred was right. It would make a nice nursery. Not too big, not too small, with good light from a window that faced the backyard.

"We can move this out and get baby stuff."

"I don't even know what a baby needs."

"I'll help you, and Katie. Katie knows all about babies now. And she has clothes from when her babies were just born. We have a crochet circle just starting. They'd love to make you baby things."

"A crochet circle." A cheese-making faerie, a doctor, a house with a good kitchen, and a pretty backyard. "It's like a dream."

"There's some bad. We have to have guards, in case. And most everybody accepts us, and most are happy to have us because we can help."

Lana didn't have to hear a *but* to know one was there. "Not everybody accepts Uncannys."

"Not everybody, even though they don't say so to your face. But there's more good than bad. The other bedroom's bigger, and it's fixed up pretty nice. The bathroom up here—it's just a half-bath deal downstairs—must've been redone not long before because it's updated and all. Not like the apartments."

Lana walked in, sat on the side of the bed.

"Are you tired? You can lie down awhile."

"I'm not tired. I'm overwhelmed. You can start to doubt there's real kindness left. Then you find there is. We're so grateful."

"We're all we have. We should be kind." Fred sat down beside Lana. "You're adding to the community, and it makes us all stronger. Can I touch the baby?"

"Sure." Lana took Fred's hand, pressed it to her belly.

"She's kicking!"

"She just started doing that today."

"She's happy, too. Are you hungry? We have ready-to-eat supplies at home."

Kindness, Lana thought. The utter simplicity of kindness. "I'm always hungry—or she is. But what I'd really like is to see the gardens."

"Yeah? It's a nice walk. We can stop off, get you a snack on the way."

"Queen Fred," Lana said, making Fred giggle. "I'd like that. It's been awhile since I took a walk just because it was nice."

At the elementary school, Rachel reviewed new patient information— she'd seen twenty-two out of Max's group—and made some additional notes.

Jonah, walking back from the nurse's office, where they kept additional supplies, stopped. Just looked at her through the glass.

She'd let a woman—Clarice, who'd once owned a hair salon— cut her hair. He loved the way it sort of exploded in corkscrews around her face.

They'd set up the clinic together, often worked there side by side for hours. While his respect for her as a person and a doctor had grown, he'd learned more about her. Little things, he thought.

She liked science fiction novels, had lettered in track and field in high school, had never ridden a horse, and harbored a mild fear of them.

She'd collected PEZ dispensers—something he found ridiculously endearing.

He knew she'd lived in a group house with other interns for a year, and the daily soap opera had caused her to cut her budget to the bone so she could afford an efficiency apartment on her own.

He knew when she needed a break, five minutes to herself. And he knew his feelings for her, about her, had changed. What he felt now wasn't a crush. What he didn't know was what to do about it.

She looked up then. He saw the fatigue in her eyes, and the mild puzzlement.

To cover the fact he'd been staring at her, he stepped to the doorway.

"Sorry. I didn't want to break your focus."

"Just finished up. Or will be once I file all these."

"I've got that. Take a break, Doc. Ray's going to take some of the load off, don't you think?"

"He's willing, and he's able. Carly, the nursing student? She got some practical experience on the trip here, but needs more training."

He continued to file the patient information as she sat, rubbing at the back of her neck.

"Headache?"

"Just overload," she said. "We've got a type two diabetic. They've done well managing that, and finding oral meds, but the supply's low. Some of the group is on medication—hypertension, chemical balancing, beta blockers, blood thinners, asthma inhalers, and so on."

He nodded, finished up the filing. "I was coming in to let you know we're going to need more supplies. Even the bare basics are running low after today. We're in decent shape," he said as he turned to her. "But we just added nearly a hundred people. It's time for a scavenger hunt."

"I'll go with you."

"We need you here. We can figure out who'd be best to go along, nudge them into volunteering. I think we need to postpone the meeting—at least a day. Too much going on. And when we do hold it, if we're comfortable with them by then, we should probably include Max and—it's Lana, right?"

"Yes, and I agree about including them. Bill's going to want his son there."

"I'll get a better sense of Will. He's moving in with us. My initial take on him? He traveled hundreds of miles to find his father. That says something about heart and character."

"Again, I agree. Here's where I don't. I don't think we can or should postpone the meeting. Katie worked the sign-up, and Lloyd helped her with it for a while. Both of them came in to tell me Kurt Rove, the Mercers, and Denny Wertz stood across the street, watching. And Katie saw the Mercers stroll over and start on some kid—a teenager with a dog. Apparently one of them made noises and threats about putting the dog down when it growled at them."

"Crap. Why didn't Katie have someone come get me?"

"She was about to when Rove strutted across, and people in Max's group had words to say back. Max walked up. Whatever he said or did had Rove and the Mercers backing off.

"We need those rules, Jonah. We need the order. And we need them yesterday."

"All right." He scrubbed at his face. "Okay. We've got about three hours. Add Max, Lana, and Will Anderson?"

"I think it's the way to go. I can stop by and tell Max and Lana. You can talk to Will."

"You need a break, Rachel. When did you eat last?"

"It's been a long day, Dr. Vorhies."

He opened the desk drawer, took out a protein bar.

"Why can't they make these in hot fudge sundae, or rare roast beef au jus?" She unwrapped it, took a bite. "They're just terrible. Good news is, they won't last forever."

"Could be like Twinkies."

She laughed a little. "*Zombieland*. Love that movie. The other good news is: However much the world is screwed, we're not having a zombie apocalypse."

"Yet."

On a sigh, she ate more of the protein bar. "You sure can cheer me up, Jonah."

"How about we take a walk? You could use some air, some just out-of-here time. We'll go tell Max about the meeting, tell Bill and his son. Maybe walk down to the gardens."

"I could use a walk."

She got up; he forgot to step back. And he reminded himself he'd delivered twins under desperate circumstances. He'd gotten those twins, Hannah, their mother, and Rachel out of New York City. He'd done things during the past four months he never believed he could or would.

So why couldn't he just make a move here?

He didn't step back, and realized neither did she.

"I want to ask you something."

She kept her eyes on his. "All right."

"If none of this had happened, if things were just the way they used to be, and I'd asked you out for a drink, or maybe out to a movie, would you have agreed?"

She waited a beat. "What kind of movie? It matters. If you'd have asked me to go to some foreign art film with subtitles, I'd have said no. That's no way to relax after a day in the ER."

"I've never seen a foreign art film with subtitles."

"Then maybe." Those dark chocolate eyes stayed steady on his. "Sometimes it's hard to go back there, to try to remember the way things were. But maybe. Why didn't you?"

"I was working up to it."

"Well, the way things stand now, you missed your chance for movie night. Got anything else?"

"I don't want to mess anything up, make things weird between us. We've got to work here, and we've got to build that structure. So, if you're not—"

"Oh, for God's sake."

She rolled her eyes as she clamped a hand on the back of his head, pulled him down until his mouth met hers.

He felt his mind melt. Just melt. All that longing, all that wishful thinking beat into reality. He held there, beat, beat, beat, until he felt her hand press against his pounding heart.

"I don't feel weird." With her big, beautiful eyes on his, she breathed out, slowly. "Do you?"

"I'm not sure. I should make sure."

He lifted her to her toes, took her mouth again. He didn't ask himself why he'd waited so long. Why question what seemed perfect?

"No. I don't feel weird."

"Good. We should take that walk. Talk to Max, talk to Bill."

"Right." He let her go, reminded himself they had priorities.

"Then we should keep walking. To my place."

His gaze sharpened on hers. "Your place."

"My bed. We've got a couple hours. Like you said, I need a break. I think you need one, too."

"I've wanted you a long time."

"Maybe not as long for me because I'd have been surprised if you'd asked me to a movie. But somewhere in Pennsylvania, not long after we met Arlys and Fred and Chuck, I started wanting you."

"We should close up."

"Yeah."

She set up the walkie as she always did in case of a medical emergency.

"Rachel?" They went out, closing the door behind them. "I ought to tell you, I'm pretty, well, pent up."

"Hmm." She tipped him a smile as they walked together through the odd light to the front entrance. "Lucky for you, I have a cure for that."

Within the hour, Jonah considered himself cured.

CHAPTER NINETEEN

In the big living room with its comfortable sofas and beautiful old chestnut floor, Max accepted the offered beer. He wasn't sure what to make of this invitation, but calculated Jonah and the others gathering tonight wanted to get a better sense of him and Lana.

Since he wanted to get a better sense of them, it worked out well.

He hadn't brought up any of the reservations circling through his thoughts. Not when he could all but see the stress sloughing off Lana, not when he saw the pleasure she'd gotten from putting flowers in a vase in what was—for now—their bedroom.

Not when he'd seen the child—their child—moving inside her.

He could keep his concerns and doubts to himself for now, at least until he'd gotten a better lay of the land here. But the incident with Flynn, the ugliness that had rolled off the men who'd made a point of trying to bait the boy, that stuck with him.

"Katie and Fred will be down in a minute." Rachel lit a few more candles before sitting beside Jonah on the facing sofa. "They're getting the babies settled down. Arlys just went over to pry Chuck away from his continuing quest for Wi-Fi. We appreciate you coming over. I know you're still settling in yourselves."

"How about the rest of your group?" Jonah asked.

"Sorting it out."

"Good. I can give you a hand with that tomorrow. Furniture, supplies, that sort of thing."

"We appreciate it."

"You and Katie and the babies live here," Lana said.

"There weren't as many of us when we first got here," Rachel told her. "But we ended up sticking pretty close. We're here. Jonah and Chuck and Bill—now Will, too—next door, Fred and Arlys on the other side of them. We've been together the longest."

"Lloyd Stenson took an apartment across the street, and Carla Barker's in one of the apartments over Bygones. They'll be here tonight." Feeling his way, Jonah studied his beer. "We'd already planned to meet tonight. We decided, after you came in, your group should be represented."

"In what?"

Jonah's gaze flicked up to Max's. "We're just over three hundred now. For the most part people get along. Everyone contributes."

"And everyone's still dealing with trauma," Rachel continued. "What they lost, what they've gained, you could say. What they've been through. Some get together for a kind of group therapy, rotating houses. Others find different ways to cope. Working the gardens, crafting circles, hobbies. Lloyd builds things. We're working on a greenhouse—that's a community project. And he cleaned up the playground equipment so the kids can play while people are planting or weeding. We've got some putting bands together, a book club, prayer groups."

"We've got people who rotate looking after the animals," Jonah added. "We'll need to add to that with what you've brought in."

"You're saying that, for the most part, people have found a way. Found their place." Lana sipped water, considered. "But not everyone."

"People are what people are," Jonah commented.

"Such as the bunch who went after Flynn today."

Jonah nodded at Max. "Don and Lou Mercer? They're just basic assholes."

"Flynn's not. If he were, they'd have been seeking medical attention."

"It's not the first time they've looked for trouble," Rachel told them. "Or found it. Which is the reason for this meeting."

She glanced over as she heard the door open, heard voices. "Arlys and Chuck."

"I need power. I get power, I can dig in deeper. They get me power, I can maybe get over to the AOL headquarters again, see about pulling out the Net."

Max watched the gangly man in his early twenties with a scruffy goatee and a tangled mess of hair—white-blond with purple streaks—stop dead, gape.

"Holy shit! Max Fallon! It's fricking Max Fallon."

"I told you," Arlys began.

"Huh? I wasn't listening." He bolted over, grabbed Max's hand, pumped like he expected water to gush from a well. "Major fan. I went to your signing at Spirit Books last year, even though I mostly read e. *Under Siege.* Awesome! Personal favorite."

It threw Max off stride. It had been awhile—too long, he realized—since he'd thought of himself as a writer. "Thanks."

"Max Fallon," Chuck said again. "This is wild."

"And this is Chuck," Arlys said. "Our basement dweller."

"That's me. You got beer? Cold?"

"Fred chilled them down," Jonah told him.

"Excellent." He got one, twisted the top. "So, you're the Max and . . . sorry, I wasn't listening. Lucy?"

"Lana."

"Max and Lana. You brought in close to a hundred people? More awesome." He chugged some beer. "What's it like out there?"

"We followed your signs, your route, so the way was clearer than we expected. Trouble spots here and there. We avoided when we could, dealt with it when we couldn't."

"Raiders? Bunch of assholes. Kill you dead for a can of beans."

"Here and there," Max said again.

"We ran into some outside of Baltimore. We lost three people. It would've been more, but . . ." Chuck trailed off, glanced at Jonah.

"It's all right. We had Uncannys with us who set up a fire wall. It drove them back."

"The torched motorcycle and Jeep," Lana murmured. "The charred remains in the Jeep. We went by there."

"Avoid when you can," Jonah said. "Deal when you can't. We have sentry posts, manned around the clock. Harley was on the north road when you came in, and you got through because . . ."

"We read each other." Max heard the door again, more voices, relaxed a little when one of them was Will's. "He knew we weren't Raiders or looking to harm."

Max rose when Will came in with a man obviously his father. Same jawline, same eyes. Max gripped Will's hand. "You found him, just like you said you would."

"Yeah. Dad, this is Max and Lana. They helped me get here."

Bill Anderson didn't shake hands but took Max, then Lana, into bear hugs. "Anything you need, anytime. You gave me my boy back."

"With or without us, he wouldn't have stopped."

"Means the world to me." Bill held up a bottle of wine. "From my private cellar." Grinned and winked.

Fred danced down the stairs. "You're Will. Bill's Will." She dashed to Bill, hugged hard. "I'm so happy for you. I'm Fred." She tipped her head to Bill's arm, smiled at Will. "I helped make the signs. With a little faerie power."

Will took her hand, kissed it, making her giggle. "Oh, I bet that's Lloyd and Carla. I'll get it. Katie's coming, and we'll all be here."

Max let it flow around him, taking stock. Clearly Lana enjoyed the moment—people, conversation, no worry about where they might be the next day, the day after.

He judged Lloyd about the same age as Bill, hovering around sixty, with a wiry, almost springy look about him. Carla, sturdy of build, hair hacked short, took stock of him, Max thought, as he did her.

Katie jogged down the steps, already apologizing. "Sorry. Restless babies. Are you moved in next door?" she asked Will.

"Lock and stock. Wasn't that much stock anyway."

When she dropped down beside Jonah on the sofa, Will eased down on the arm of Arlys's chair. "Maybe we can find time to catch up."

"Sure we can." She lowered her voice. "I'm sorry about your mom, your sister."

"I know." He laid a hand over hers. "And your parents, Theo. A hell of a lot to be sorry for."

On the sofa, Rachel tapped Jonah's knee. He shifted, looked a little reluctant, then shrugged.

"Okay, I'll start. Rachel, Arlys, and I had a conversation this morning, even before we added ninety-odd people and livestock. We survived, and we've gone a long way toward making New Hope home. I know getting power up's a priority, and so's security. We need to add supplies to that—medical especially—and that means scavenger and scouting crews."

As he spoke, Arlys pulled out a notebook, a pencil.

"It might be time to have a town hall," Lloyd suggested. "Introduce our newest neighbors, call for more volunteers."

"Yeah. Before we have, I guess what we'd call a public meeting, we want to talk some things over. I guess everybody heard about the Mercers giving Bryar a hard time last night, then Aaron."

"I heard if you hadn't gone out, moved them along, it might've been more than trash talk from the Mercers. Troublemakers," Carla added. "Some are just born that way."

"Maybe. They tried to cause some trouble with a boy in Max's group today."

"I heard about that, too." Carla studied Max. "And how they backed off when you got toe-to-toe."

"Troublemakers and bullies. Some are just born that way."

"We need to ask ourselves what we'll do if it's more than giving a hard time. So far this sort of thing's mostly been words, a couple punches." Jonah paused. "But Bryar shouldn't be afraid to take a walk at night. Nobody should."

"Almost everybody's armed," Carla put in, "even people who—and I'll hit the Mercers again—shouldn't be."

"Kurt Rove," Bill added. "Sharon Beamer. A few more I could name."

"We need a plan. We need structure." Rachel laid a hand on Jonah's knee. "Rules, laws."

"Once you have laws, you need those who enforce them, and those who litigate and legislate." Lloyd frowned over steepled hands. "Some will object to being told what they can and can't do. Who writes the laws, who enacts and enforces them, who decides on the consequences for breaking them?"

"We're starting with a blank slate, right?" Jonah asked. "Maybe we start with broad strokes. With common sense."

"An it harm none," Lana said, then held up a hand. "Sorry, I don't mean to interrupt. It's our first rule."

"Sounds like a good one." Bill smiled at her. "We'd have to break it down some. Harm to another person, harm to property, harm to animals. Hoarding supplies, because that causes harm."

"We can lay it out as for the common good." Arlys continued to write. "But that takes us back to enforcing, and consequences."

"Policing," Jonah said and looked at Carla.

"I was a small-town deputy, so yeah, I know about small-town squabbles and dynamics. It's a little dicier when you've got more weapons than people—and when some of the people have what we'd call unconventional weapons."

"How much trouble have you had from Uncannys?" Max asked.

"Not much. A couple of kids raising a little hell," Jonah explained.

"They're mostly testing their abilities," Fred put in.

"Yale Trezori blew up a tree, Fred," Chuck reminded her.

"I know, but he didn't mean to, and scared himself. He's only fourteen. I think . . ."

"Go ahead," Rachel prompted.

"I think if we could set up a kind of school or training center for the kids, or even people really new to abilities."

"Hogwarts," Chuck said, poking her in the ribs.

"Sort of. Bryar would really be good at it. She's so patient."

"Do you have anyone in your group who'd qualify?" Rachel asked Max. "Who'd be willing to teach and corral kids?"

"Yeah, we've already started that." He looked at Arlys, gave her two names.

"We could set it up at the American Legion hall," Fred said. "It's only a block off Main so the kids could walk. I could talk to Bryar and if she's willing, Aaron would be. He'd have an excuse to be with her."

"It's a good idea." Jonah looked back at Max. "Would the people you named help structure it?"

"I'll talk to them."

"Great. Carla, are you willing to do the policing?"

"I'm willing, Jonah, but will people be willing to accept the authority? Also, I've never been in charge, and I couldn't do it alone."

Though he'd initially thought of asking Bill, Jonah had reassessed. "I was hoping Max would be willing."

Max lifted his eyebrows. "Why?"

"Because you know how to be in charge," Jonah pointed out. "And for it to work we need everybody represented. You have a couple of police in your group. That would round it out."

Max shook his head. "Mike Rozer, yes. He was a big-city cop, about a decade of experience. He's steady. The other's Brad Fitz, and he's got experience, but he's a hothead. And he's bitter. It's not a good combination."

"Okay. Would you do it?"

Before Max could speak, Lana touched his arm. "You got us here safe. You kept people from losing their heads. Everyone, almost a hundred people, who came here with us knows that, and looks to you for that. With you as part of this, they'll feel part of this."

"You'd want me to do this?"

"I . . . I think you're meant to do this."

"All right." He took her hand. "All right, we'll try it. But you should choose another from your people, and an Uncanny. It gives balance."

"Diane Simmons," Arlys said without looking up from her notebook. "She's quick-thinking, stable, and doesn't tolerate bullshit."

"Shapeshifter," Katie added.

"I agree, Diane and Carla are sensible women," Lloyd began. "And first impressions here say the same about Max. But spelling out the laws, and having the community at large accept them, accept the authority of the people we've named, is another matter."

"I was hoping you'd spell things out," Jonah said. "You're smart and you're fair, and nobody here would say otherwise. People respect you, Lloyd, so if you lay it out—and it might not be the fair way, but it's the best way right now—like it's just a done deal, most people are going to accept it."

"And the ones who don't?"

"Are going to get overruled."

Lloyd rubbed the back of his neck, pinched the bridge of his nose. "Let me fiddle with that some. What do we do, if we manage this, with violators? Lock them in a closet?"

"A locked door wouldn't stop some magickal violators," Max pointed out. "Lana and I had a different method."

"We called it Quiet Time." Lana laughed. "Part of that was to make them feel like idiots, and this was, for the most part, frayed tempers, a fistfight or . . . some magickal bitch-slapping. We kept the same rule for either. A designated span in Quiet Time."

"Inside the circle for a designated amount of time," Max explained. "No communication. Time to cool off, time to think about being an ass. It worked fairly well."

"I had ten minutes inside," Will admitted. "Early on in our relationship. It's mortifying, and isolating. The first minute in, all I wanted to do was get out and kick Max's ass. Nine minutes later, I had a different perspective."

The grin Max sent him mirrored the easy affection between them. "You were a quick study."

"Well, let me think about this," Lloyd said. "Try to work up some language, and an approach."

"Good enough." Jonah looked back at Max. "Meanwhile, we're hoping you'd work with the power crew tomorrow. And give us some people for scouting and scavenging."

"I can go. I'm not sure what I can do on power when we're talking an entire town, but we'll see. For scouting, you can't do better than Flynn and Lupa."

"That's the boy from today," Rachel said. "Lupa?"

"His wolf."

"Do you mean an actual wolf?"

"I do. An elf and his wolf who kept a village of nearly thirty people safe and fed for more than two months. I'd send Eddie and Joe—Eddie's dog—along there."

"A regular dog?"

"A regular dog and a good man. For scavenging, Poe and Kim. Eddie, Poe, and Kim moved into the apartments attached to our house," Lana told them. "They've been with us the longest. They're not magickal, but they're smart, and they're steady."

"Send a magickal with them," Bill suggested. "It's been an advantage there."

"Aaron for now?" Rachel turned to Jonah. "And you should go. Medic—in case there's trouble, and you'll know what's needed in medical supplies."

As he'd thought the same, Jonah nodded. "Can you have your people ready, Max? First light?"

"I can."

"I think . . ." Fred looked around the room. "I think they shouldn't be Max's people. If we're together, everyone's together. Everyone's our people."

"Fred's right, as she usually is." Arlys closed her book. "And that's a pretty big agenda for what seems to be the first meeting of the New Hope Town Council."

When Lana kissed Max good-bye at first light, it felt almost normal. Her man heading off to work, her own list of chores and errands lined up in her head.

"Good luck. You might have better if I went with you." She took his hand, linked fingers.

"Let's see how it goes. And let's be optimistic. You should make sure everything's turned off. No point bringing the power up if we end up blowing it out."

"Good point. I'll do that. Then I'm going to go down and work in the community garden in exchange for bringing some herbs home."

"Nothing too physical." He laid a hand on her belly. "Very precious cargo."

"Rachel said sensible exercise is good for me and the baby, so I'll be sensible. Then I'm going to check out the food supplies. Arlys said the American Legion, where they're going to set up the training center for the kids, has a big kitchen. I might be able to organize a community kitchen there. Make breads and basics."

He leaned in, kissed the top of her head. "You're happy."

"Yes. Aren't you? Sheriff?"

With a laughing shake of his head, Max pulled back. "I think we'll pin that one on Mike." From where they stood on the front porch, he scanned the street, the buildings. "Strange times, Lana."

"You'll write again. You'll write about strange times. People need stories, Max, and the ones who tell them. So I'm going to set you up an office."

"So far, it sounds like your day's going to be busier than mine."

The door at the far end of the porch opened. Joe dashed out to greet Max and Lana. Eddie sauntered after. "Howdy, neighbors."

"You're set?" Max asked him.

Eddie tapped his backpack, shifted the rifle over his shoulder. "Yep. Poe and Kim are right behind me. Speaking of."

Lana gave Joe another rub as Poe and Kim came out. A good thing, she thought, out of all the tragic. They'd found each other, and seemed to fit so well.

"Anything you need for the apartments?" she asked them. "Bill Anderson said he'd help with that."

"Joe and me are all good."

"We figured to live with it awhile." Kim glanced up at Poe. "If this ends up being home base, I wouldn't mind slapping some paint on the walls. And there's some really ugly wallpaper that just needs to go."

"No argument on that. We want to get a better feel," Poe added. "No complaints so far. Who's this Aaron we're going out with? We met Jonah. Do they know their shit, Max?"

"It's clear Jonah does, and since he suggested Aaron, I'd say yes to both."

He spotted Jonah walking up the street with another man. A bit younger, slighter, moved like a dancer, Max thought. "You can get acquainted. Be safe."

"Could use some more Milk-Bones," Eddie said.

"We'll see what we can do. Anything on your wish list?" Kim asked.

"Actually, if you come across a decent set of kitchen knives."

"Like the ones you had in the mountains?"

"Anything remotely close to those would be great. In fact, any decent kitchen tools."

"We're on it." Poe nudged Kim's arm. "Let's go shopping."

"I'll go scoop up Flynn and . . . Shit, there he is. You never know when that dude's going to show up."

Flynn stood, silent as smoke, in the middle of the street, Lupa beside him. Joe let out a happy bark, flew down to have a morning tumble with the wolf.

"Ready to rock and roll?" Eddie called out.

Flynn nodded, then smiled. "I'm driving."

"Hell." Eddie pulled off his ball cap, scratched at his mass of hair, replaced it. "We'll be back if he don't run us into a tree. Elves can't drive for shit," he added before he strolled down.

"That must be my group."

"Good luck." Lana lifted her face for another kiss. "Be safe."

"Don't overdo it," he warned.

She watched the three groups merge, then walk to the lot beside the school.

She told herself not to worry. Worry didn't help. And Max had gotten them all here. Through storms, through raiding parties, through roads washed out by spring floods. He'd led, she thought, because someone had to. Because one by one, those who'd joined them had looked to him, trusted him.

And he'd done it while grieving for a brother who'd gone mad with power.

Yes, she'd set up an office for him, she decided as she added a haze of light, began to unplug cords. They both had to take back at least a part of who they'd been. He'd become a leader, a man of authority through circumstances. A witch whose power had grown with every mile of the journey.

And he was a writer. He was someone who could write about what had happened in the world and to it, who was left and how they fought to rebuild even while others still fought to tear down.

He needed to write, to take that time for himself. And wouldn't it help him with the grief he still carried?

Just as she needed to make her place in this strange new reality. To make a home for their child, to find work—not just that had to be done, but that satisfied her needs.

So she'd organize a kitchen. She'd cook. It's what she did best.

He'd asked if she was happy, and she was. Happy to have a chance to make a place for herself, for him, for the baby. If part of her wondered whether she would forever miss New York, the life she'd known, she understood she had to put it aside.

That life was the fairy tale now.

CHAPTER TWENTY

Jonah navigated the road, weaving through abandoned cars.

"We've already passed some houses," Kim pointed out. "Abandoned houses almost always have something useful."

"We can hit some on the way back. Medical supplies are priority. There's a hospital about ten exits up. We got what we could about six weeks ago. We need more."

Poe scanned the road, the scatter of houses. "We'll have room for more in this UPS truck, but if we run into trouble, it's sure not going to burn up the road."

Jonah had weighed that in before deciding on the big box truck. "We need to avoid trouble. A couple of gas stations at the interchange up ahead. We might be able to fill the tank and the ten-gallon cans we brought. On the way back."

Kim leaned up in her seat, gestured. "Is that a mall?"

"Yeah. Indoor/outdoor place. Kind of an outlet."

"Could be handy. Have you hit it yet?"

Now Aaron turned slightly in his seat. "We tried a few weeks ago. Another group had claimed it. They weren't friendly."

"You'll find Aaron has a tendency to . . . underplay," Jonah decided. "They started shooting at us before we'd even turned into the parking lot. About, what, twenty of them?"

Aaron moved his shoulders. "About. What they lacked in strategy, they made up for in firepower. If they'd waited until we'd gone into the lot, they might have picked us off."

"It's worth another look, right? Twenty people probably didn't strip it," Poe pointed out. "And maybe they've moved on. I mean, why live in a mall when there are houses?"

Jonah sent Aaron—who said nothing—a sidelong look. Sighed. "Aaron's mentioned that, a few damn times. We'll circle back after the hospital."

As Jonah's group turned off toward the hospital, Eddie stared out the side window of the scouting pickup. "There should be more people. And yeah, I know I've said that before, but, man, there should be more people. How far have we gone?"

"Twelve miles. Not far."

"Maybe another ten, then we should check out some of the side roads. Maybe we'll find another settlement like ours, get some word of what the fuck from anybody who's come up from the south."

Before Eddie had finished the sentence, Flynn whipped the wheel right, rattled the truck onto a skinny road that immediately curved hard right.

"Jesus, Flynn! I said—"

"Engines." He pulled the truck off the road, stopped it where the curve and the trees blocked it from the main road. "Wait."

Flynn jogged over a hillock, then—and though he'd seen it plenty now, Eddie still gaped when Flynn simply merged into one of the trees.

Sort of . . . became the tree. A weird-ass, and, hell, pretty damn cool elf thing.

But it still gave him the way-out willies to watch it happen.

"Just hold on, boys. Stay," Eddie ordered Lupa and Joe as he eased out of the truck, crouching beside it with his rifle ready.

He heard the engines now, bikes mostly to his ear. That deep, throaty roar. Coming hard, coming fast. By the tree—in the frigging tree—Flynn would have an unobstructed view of the road.

Eddie hoped he wouldn't have to use the rifle; was resigned to using it. He'd shot a man—a big, burly Raider—during an attack on their group south of Charles Town, West Virginia.

It wasn't a moment he'd ever forget. It wasn't an act he wanted to repeat.

But . . .

The roaring built, blasted, then began to fade. On a shaky breath, Eddie pushed to his feet.

Flynn slid out of the tree. "Raiders."

"You sure?"

"Five motorcycles—three of them doubled with women riding pillion. A truck, four inside, two in the bed. A camper. I could only see two in it. Skull and crossbones painted on the side. They had a naked man strapped to the roof of the camper. Dead."

"Christ. Just when you think the world can't get more fucked-up. Good ears, dude."

Elf ears, Eddie thought, which meant he might not have to kill anybody today.

"They're heading away from New Hope, so that's something." Relieved, Eddie looked back toward the truck. "Might as well keep on this road, right? No point taking a chance of them turning around. No point taking on that many."

"We should walk first."

"Because?"

"They can hear engines, too. And some of these plants?" Flynn gestured to the small grove of trees. "The wildflowers and weeds? They can be useful. We should dig some up."

"Supposed to be scouting, not gardening." But Eddie signaled to the dogs so they leaped out of the bed of the truck as Flynn moved into the trees. "Gotta be some houses back through here," he continued as Flynn crouched down to dig with his knife. "Not on scavenging either, but it doesn't hurt to look. Somebody might be holed up. It ain't right nobody's nowhere."

Lupa let out a soft, warning growl that had Flynn rearing up, stumbling back as the girl flashed out of a tree, knife slicing.

Eddie lifted his rifle, lowered it as Flynn danced back a second time. "Uh-uh, just no. I'm not shooting at some kid!"

"She's old enough to slice me open," Flynn snapped back.

Lupa solved the problem by leaping up, knocking the girl back, standing on her shoulders while she sucked in the air the fall had stolen.

Flynn moved fast enough to blur, wrenched the knife out of her hand before she could jab it at Lupa.

"He won't hurt you. We won't hurt you."

She aimed a fierce look at Flynn out of golden brown eyes. "Don't touch me. If you do, I'll hurt *you*."

"Nobody's touching nobody." Eddie swung the rifle back over his shoulder, held both hands up. "Everybody chill, okay?"

Joe bellied over to her, licked her face. Her lips trembled as she closed her eyes.

Flynn sheathed his knife, stuck hers in his belt. He crouched, put a hand on Lupa's head.

And spoke to the girl's mind.

I'm like you.

Her eyes flew open. *Lies, lies.*

No. I'm like you. I'm Flynn. Eddie isn't like us, but he's with us. We're not like the ones who went by on the road.

"Come on, Flynn, call Lupa off. Let the kid up."

"We're talking."

"You're . . . Oh. Okay, cool."

You don't have to run. But if you need to, we won't chase you. We have some food in our packs. You can have it.

"Is she hungry? She's pretty skinny." Skinny, dirty, and pretty damn pissed to Eddie's eye. "You want some food, kid?"

Flynn smiled. "You see? He's with us. She's thirsty," he said, pulling off his pack and drawing the bottle of water from the side pouch. "It's all right, Lupa."

The wolf backed off, sat.

"Don't touch me."

Saying nothing, Flynn set the water beside her, rose, and stepped back.

"Look, she's, like, twelve. We can't just leave her out here by herself."

"Fourteen," Flynn said, reading her thoughts.

"Whatever. It ain't safe, man."

"She can take care of herself. But there's no need to be alone," Flynn continued as she snatched up the water, drank. "Unless you want alone. We have people, good people."

"Girls," Eddie said. "It's not just guys and stuff. You ought to come with us."

"I don't know you."

"Yeah, stranger danger, but still. Out here alone ain't safe."

"We won't hurt you. You'd know that if you look."

She watched Flynn as she drank again. "I don't know how. I don't know why I can hear you in my head."

"Or become the tree, the rock?" He smiled at her again. "It's what we are. I can help you learn. We won't make you come, but you should."

"Maybe you got lost?" Eddie suggested. "If you've got people, we can help you find them."

"They're dead. All dead!"

Flynn took her knife out, laid it on the ground. "The rest of us have to live. We're going to walk to the houses nearby, see if anyone is alive and needs help. If no one is, we'll take supplies if we can find them. Come with us. There are more like us where we live now. More like Eddie, too."

She grabbed the knife, got to her feet. Her hair, nearly the same color as Flynn's, nearly the same color as the bark of the tree, hung in matted tangles. Her eyes, big and dark, projected belligerence more than fear.

"I can leave when I want."

"Okay." Flynn turned and started to walk. Though it made him nervous to have some wild girl with a knife behind him, Eddie fell into step with Flynn.

"Does the dog have a name?" she asked.

"He's Joe. He's a great dog," Eddie said. "And Lupa's a good dog, too, for a wolf."

Flynn didn't bother to glance back. "Do you have a name?"

When she laid an unsteady hand on Joe's head, the dog sent her a happy, tongue-lolling grin. Her lips nearly curved, nearly smiled for the first time in weeks.

"Starr. I'm Starr."

Using the back entrance of the hospital—out of sight from the road—they loaded up the truck. Kim kept watch in the front of the building.

Since the last trip someone else had gone through. Someone more interested in opiates and morphine than sutures and bandages and antibiotics. Jonah loaded in an EKG machine, a fetal monitor, and—remembering the twins' delivery—scavenged all he could from the NICU. Poe rolled out more on a gurney, and Aaron followed with more, including an autoclave.

As before, Jonah ignored the dried blood spatters on walls, on doors. At least this time there were no bodies to be carried out and burned in a mass pyre.

But the stench of death took a long time to fade.

"It's a good haul," Jonah decided once they'd loaded the box truck. "Poe, can you drive this?"

"Sure."

"Aaron, let's see about taking an ambulance. It wouldn't hurt to have one, and whatever we can load inside from the rest of the fleet."

Poe pulled around the front. "They're trying for an ambulance."

"Smart." Kim hopped in.

"Yeah. I'm feeling better about them."

"Max trusts them, and that goes a long way. I want to hit that mall, Poe. It's too good an opportunity to miss. How much room have we got back there?"

"Enough, especially if they can get . . . And here they come. Nice." He shot Kim a smile, pulled out behind the ambulance.

Max stood in a room full of computers, switches, and monitors while the man and woman with him—armed with flashlights—talked about grids, junction boxes, amps, transformers, overhead and underground cables.

He understood them less, he thought, than they understood him.

And for the most part that was not at all. They had tools, and obviously knew how to use them, and ignored him while they did.

Chuck, in his new version of a basement, sat muttering to himself while he performed surgery on the guts of a computer. The gist of the muttering, as far as Max could tell, involved getting the computer running on a jury-rigged battery long enough for him to hack into the system.

Things were fried, compromised, undermined. A shutdown, as far as Max could discern, that had rolled like a wave, killing the power not only in the station but across that grid, burning out every transformer.

Max didn't know about watts or amps or outdated cables, but he knew about power. About how power could be used to ignite.

He ignored the talk about going down to the bowels again, fusing something, clamping off something else, and studied the board in front of him.

He held out a hand, imagined transferring power. Flipping a switch, lighting a light. Too much, too big, he realized, and narrowed the point. A step, he thought, one candle in the dark.

He hesitated a moment, another moment. What if this push of power destroyed what progress skill and technology had managed so far? Knowing how to light a light was far from knowing how the light actually worked.

He narrowed a bit more. Starting an engine, he thought—he didn't know how to build one, but he knew how to use what he had to bring one to life.

Faith, he thought. Believe. Accept. Open.

The monitor he faced blinked on.

The discussion—not an argument, but a tech-heavy discussion— rolled on. Max tapped Chuck's shoulder, gestured to the monitor.

"Can you work with that?"

"What? Huh? Whoa, baby."

Chuck shot his rolling chair down the counter. His fingers dived toward a keyboard, stopped an inch away. "Man, it's the first time I've ever been nervous with tech. Hold on to your hats, boys. And girl."

Drake Manning gave Chuck a punch in the arm. "How'd you get it on?"

"I didn't." Chuck took a hand off the board long enough to wag a thumb at Max.

"You wooed it on?"

"You could say that."

"Son of a bitch." Manning—his belt showing worn notches from steady weight loss, his graying hair in tufts under a Phillies ball cap—let out a cackle. "How long will it hold, Mr. Wizard?"

"I don't know. It's my first day on the job."

"I'm in. I'm in." Chuck did some jazz hands over the keyboard. "Yeah, baby, haven't lost my touch."

"Can you get the power on in here?" Manning demanded.

"Do bears shit in the woods? Give me a mo or so. Jesus, I've missed this. Missed the hell out of this."

"That." Manning leaned over Chuck's shoulder, tapped a section of the monitor. "Just that. If we bring everything back on line, we'll end up blowing the system. Just this station. We've got everything shut down. Bring it on line, and we'll test it. One step at a time."

"And done. Probably."

Manning let out a breath. "Try the lights, Wanda. Just the lights."

When at the flip of the switches they flashed on, Chuck pumped a fist in the air. Manning just pressed his fingers to his eyes. Then he dropped his hands, looked at Max. "At the end of your first day on the job, I'll be buying the beer."

He turned and met Wanda's grin with one of his own. "Okay, team, let's get the lights on."

In the parking lot of the mall, cars lay on their sides, or on their roofs like turtles on smashed shells.

Crows, vultures, rats pecked and gnawed on carcasses of dogs, cats, deer. And what had once been human. The air reeked with the stench of decay and garbage.

Jonah drove past the remains hanging from a noose. A cardboard sign still draped around the neck.

UNCANNY BITCH BACK TO HELL

As he circled the lot, he saw no signs of life other than the gorged birds and well-fed rats. At some point, he thought, they'd send a crew of volunteers to burn or bury the dead, clean up the garbage, dispose of the piles of feces.

He pulled up at the front entrance, in front of shattered glass doors, and wondered what made some portions of the human race so foul.

He got out as Poe pulled in beside him.

"They're long gone." Kim got out, standing with her face like stone. "The bodies have to be at least two or three weeks old."

"Could come back," Poe said.

"Why? It's a big, empty world. Plenty of other places to desecrate and destroy. I wish we hadn't come."

When her voice cracked, Poe put an arm around her. She stiffened her shoulders. "But we did. We should get whatever we can."

"The dead deserve better."

Jonah nodded at Aaron. "We'll give them better. We'll come back as soon as we can, and give them better."

He thought of the body hanging. They'd cut it down before they left. They could do that much now, then come back for burial or burning.

"First we have to look after the living."

Lana took Fred's advice and transplanted some herbs in pots. Setting them in the sun near the kitchen door gave her a happy moment. She knew seeing them, smelling them, harvesting them would give her many more.

She'd gardened for the first time in her life. Helping hoe and weed rows of carrots and beans, being taught how to stake tomatoes. She'd seen hillocks of potatoes, the trailing vines of squash and pumpkin, eggplants. The growing stalks of corn.

And she'd heard children playing while she worked.

Best of all, after a thorough inspection of what she determined would be a community kitchen, she had plans.

She opted to work on them while sitting on the front porch with a glass of sun tea. Absently, she laid a hand where the baby kicked, then looked up when she saw Arlys.

"I heard you've been busy."

"I had a wonderful day. Do you have a minute? I've got sun tea."

"Sounds good."

"I'll get you a glass."

Even more wonderful, Lana thought as she went inside, to have a visitor, to just be able to sit and talk without worrying about what danger might lurk on the next mile of road.

"No ice, but I chilled it." Lana wiggled her fingers as she offered Arlys the glass.

"Thanks. Wish list?" She tapped a finger on Lana's legal pad.

"A couple of them. The community kitchen project. Do you know Dave Daily?"

"Sure. Big guy, big laugh."

"He was a short-order cook and he's all in on the project. And we've got a couple of people who have experience in dressing game. I'd love a smokehouse—ham, bacon, and so on. I actually found a book in the library on how that works."

Impressed, interested, Arlys studied Lana over the rim of her glass. "You have been busy. I spent some time with Lloyd, working on the agenda for the public meeting."

"You're worried about it."

"There are bound to be objections, people who don't like being told what they can do, what they can't. But we need it, and we need it before something happens, and we don't have a solid structure to deal with it. I did an editorial bulletin on tolerance versus bigotry, on acceptance versus outdated fears. It didn't hit the mark with everyone."

"I worked at the gardens this morning. Almost everyone's friendly and helpful. But a couple of people kept their distance. From Fred, too. How anyone can look at Fred and see anything but light and joy is beyond me."

"She was my first personal experience with the magickal. Maybe that's why it's been easier for me than for some. For some, their first experience was with the frightening, the deadly. The Dark Uncanny. It's harder to convince them to accept that those who have abilities beyond ours aren't built to harm."

No, Lana thought, not all magicks were of the light.

"Max's brother. His own brother. He turned. He and the woman he was with. I think she was always dark, and she turned him. They killed one of our group. A harmless man—a boy really. Would have tried to kill all of us, especially . . ." She pressed a hand to her belly.

"Max had to make a choice, and he chose light. He chose what was right even though it meant destroying his own brother. He loved Eric, but he chose light."

"It must have been horrible for him."

"It was, and still is. I've never seen power like that. Huge and black." It still haunted Lana's dreams. "They were giddy with it, drunk on it."

"Fred and I saw it in the tunnels, getting out of New York." Thinking of the . . . *thing* flying through the tunnels, she nodded at the words. "Huge and black."

"Then you know. It's not hard to see why anyone who faced that has fear."

Lana turned her head, then rose as she saw the pickup. "That's Eddie and Flynn."

Arlys stood beside her. "Someone's with them."

When he spotted them, Flynn pulled up in front of the house.

These are good people, he told Starr.

I don't know them.

You never will if you sit in the truck.

She got out reluctantly as the women came down. Lupa and Joe leaped out.

"This is Starr. She doesn't want to be touched."

A ragged shirt, torn jeans over a bone-thin frame, Lana noted. Hair tangled and matted. Suspicious eyes.

"I'm Lana. This is Arlys."

Starr hunched her shoulders as others wandered closer or stopped to stare.

"I only got here yesterday," Lana continued. "I know it's a little scary at first, but—"

"I'm not scared, and I don't have to stay."

Fred jogged up, rhinestone-studded pink sunglasses perched on top of her bouncy red curls. "I saw the truck come back. Hey, hi!"

"This is Fred." Arlys laid a hand on Fred's arm, warning her back. "Starr doesn't want to be touched."

"Oh." Fred's face went to instant sympathy. "It feels weird, right, everybody looking at you and wondering? But this is a good place. Maybe you want to come with me—Arlys and I live right down there. You could come inside, clean up a little."

"I don't have to stay."

"Well, even if you leave, you could have some clean clothes and maybe something to eat first. Then you can decide." Fred stepped back, gestured. "Come on."

Starr took a step forward, then another. Then followed Fred down the sidewalk.

"Full of light," Lana acknowledged.

"Glad she's off our hands." Eddie rolled his eyes. "I don't think she'd stick that knife of hers in my ribs, right, but it made for a nervous ride back, man. Jittery ride."

"She won't hurt Fred. She's afraid, and she's wounded." Flynn tapped his heart.

"She took a swipe at you, but yeah, you're right. We found her about fifteen miles north. Flynn says she's like him."

"She's afraid of that, too. We saw a party of Raiders, headed south. They didn't see us. We found no one but Starr. Some dead, but no living. We brought some supplies, but we felt we should bring her back. We can go out again tomorrow."

"I don't know if that's . . ." Lana trailed off, then gestured. Beside the door of a house across the street, a light flickered on.

"Hot damn! And I'm talking hot food, hot showers, and hot *damn!*" Eddie slung an arm around Flynn's shoulders. "Dude! Let there be some frigging light."

———

In the kitchen of the house she shared with Arlys, Fred set out a snack bag of potato chips and a can of Coke she chilled.

"You should probably have something healthy, but this is quick, and what I'd want. I'm a faerie," she said easily as she got a bag of chips for herself. "But you're like Flynn, right? I've gotten pretty good at guessing."

Starr eyed the chips suspiciously. And longingly. "I don't know what I am."

"Oh, that's okay. I was totally freaked when I first got these." She brought her wings out, fluttered them while she munched on chips. "People wanted to hurt me, too, and Arlys. But we found more people, good people. Now we're here."

Helpfully, Fred opened Starr's chips, popped the tab on her Coke.

Warily, Starr reached in, took a single chip. After a tiny, testing bite, she stuffed it into her mouth, grabbed more.

And began to weep fat, silent tears as she ate.

"I'm not going to touch you." In sympathy, Fred's eyes filled, spilled over. "But you could imagine I'm giving you a hug. I'm sorry for whatever happened to you. I wish bad things didn't happen."

"It's all bad."

"No, it's really not. But it can feel like it."

"It killed my father, my little brother, the bad. The Doom."

"I'm hugging you again. Your mom?"

"*They* killed her. The ones that hunt us."

The shiver jumped up Fred's spine. "Raiders."

Starr shook her head. "Not them. Others. We tried to run, but they caught us. They raped us, again and again. And laughed. We're Uncanny, and they can do what they want to us."

Fred's wings drooped, receded. "I'm going to sit down with you. I won't touch you, but I need to sit down."

"And they hurt us." The words tumbled out of Starr, bitter and barbed. "Kept hurting us. My mother said—inside my head, she told me to run, and go into the tree. To stay until it was safe. Not to come out, no matter what."

Starr swiped at her face, smearing dirt with tears. "My mother screamed and fought and tried to run—away from me so they left me to hurt her. And in my head she screamed, *RUN!* So I ran and ran. When I heard them coming after me, I went into the tree. I heard her screaming, but I didn't come out. I didn't come out until they went away.

"They killed her. They hung her from a tree."

"Oh, Starr, I'm so sorry. It's not enough, but I'm so sorry. Your mom loved you. She wanted you to be safe."

"They killed her because I ran away."

"No." Fred got up, dug up a paper napkin, tore it in two to share. "They'd have killed both of you, and she knew it. She loved you and made sure they didn't kill you."

"I didn't have a knife then, so I couldn't climb the tree and cut her down. But I found one, and I went back. I tried to find them so I could kill them. But I couldn't find them."

"I think your mom was as brave and loving as any mom ever. I think she'd be glad you're here with us now. You could live here with me and Arlys if you want. We have room."

When Starr just shook her head, Fred tried to think of the best solution. "Maybe, at least for now, you'd rather have your own place. We have apartments. You could have one. You'd be with us, but on your own, too. I can show you one, and get you some clothes and supplies. You could, you know, clean up, get some real food, maybe rest for a while."

"I can leave whenever I want."

"Sure, but I hope you won't want to. New Hope's a good place to . . ." She trailed off, glanced up at the ceiling light. "Are you doing that?"

"I'm not doing anything."

"The light's on. If you didn't . . . Holy cow, I think they got the power back." Fred swiped her tears away, smiled. "I think that makes you our lucky Starr. The day you come, we get the power back on."

When Max and his crew rolled into town, cheers greeted them. People rushed out to flock around the truck.

Max saw Lana laughing, running toward him.

Caught her when she jumped into his arms.

"You did it."

"I gave them the spark. They did the rest."

She pressed her lips to his ear. "We're going to take a hot shower. Together."

"Best prize in the box."

Someone thumped him on the back; someone else pushed a beer into his hand.

Eddie whipped out his harmonica. A woman sat on the curb with a banjo. When Jonah drove in, people danced in the street.

"Power's on." Jonah said it like a prayer. "They got the power on. Go on, Aaron, find Bryar, and give her a whirl. We'll get this unloaded later."

"I will." Aaron opened the door, glanced back. "Don't carry it with you."

Jonah turned the ambulance into the school lot. Got out, turned to Poe and Kim. "Go on and celebrate. We'll have plenty of volunteers to help unload in a bit."

He shot them a smile that faded the minute they joined the crowd. He couldn't take the crowd, not even to go through them to get to his house and close himself in. So he went in the side entrance of the school. He sat down behind the desk, dropped his head in his hands.

He didn't hear the door open again, or the voices. He was too far away in his mind. He heard nothing but his own tortured thoughts until Rachel touched his arm.

"I couldn't find you. Poe said he saw you come in here. So we . . ."

"We'll step out." Max took Lana's hand.

"No. No, don't." Pale, eyes deep with misery, Jonah sat up.

"What happened?" Rachel demanded. "Poe didn't say."

"We got plenty of supplies and equipment from the hospital. No trouble there. And then we went to try the mall, the one where we had trouble before."

"Raiders?" The hand on his arm dug in. "You ran into Raiders?"

He shook his head. "No, they'd gone. Trashed a lot, inside and out. Christ, pissed on stacks and racks of clothes. Kim bagged them anyway. Piss washes out, she said. Found the usual vandalism. Broken glass, obscenities painted on walls, garbage in heaps and piles.

"And bodies. People mutilated, rotting. Animals, too. Inside and out. Rats and carrion tearing at them. We . . ."

He stopped, cleared his throat. "We need to take a crew back, dig graves or . . . maybe another mass pyre. The bodies have been there awhile. I . . ."

He looked at Max and Lana.

"The place can be cleansed and purified," Max said. "We can do that. The souls of the lives lost can be blessed."

"It needs to be. Aaron felt it, too. We didn't talk about it much, but he felt it. And I, and I— Don't we have some whiskey?"

Rachel walked to a cabinet, took out a bottle, a glass. She poured two fingers.

Jonah downed it, breathed out.

"I don't think it was all Raiders. There . . . something else. And whoever, whatever, it felt worse. They hanged a woman—an Uncanny. We all felt we couldn't leave her like that. We had to at least cut her down. We got a ladder. I climbed up to cut the rope.

"I see death," he told Max and Lana. "That's my *gift*. Death, physical trauma, sickness. I climbed up to cut the rope, and what was there of her turned, brushed my arm. I saw her life. I saw flashes of who she'd been. I saw what they did to her. I heard her screams. I saw her death."

He pressed his face to Rachel's breasts when she put her arms around him. "Her name was Anja. She was twenty-two. She was like Fred. They hacked off her wings before they—"

"Don't." Rachel stroked his hair, his back. "Don't."

Max pulled up a chair, sat beside the desk. "This is new for you, seeing the life of the dead?"

"Yeah. Just one more gift."

"It's hard for you, but I think it is a gift. A gift to those who lived. Someone remembers them. It's something all of us want. For someone to remember us. We can help you. Lana more than me."

Max looked at her when Lana said nothing. "You have an empathy. A healing touch."

She stepped up. "I think you have what you have, Jonah, because you do, too."

"What does it mean that if I could find the ones who raped her, mutilated her, murdered her, I'd kill them without a single qualm?"

Max rose. "It means you're human. I'll go back with you and bury her."

"When you mark her grave with her name," Lana said, with a hand on the child who stirred inside her, "when you say the words over her, you'll free her soul. You'll ease your own. Mark her grave with her name, say her name." Lana looked at Max. "I feel that."

"Then it's right. Then it's what we'll do. I'll go with you now. We can send a crew for the rest tomorrow."

Jonah nodded, rose, and shook Max's hand. "Thank you."

Late in the dark of night, Max lay awake with images ripe and clear in his head. He hadn't seen, hadn't felt what Jonah had as they'd buried the desecrated remains of a young woman who'd done no harm.

He hadn't seen her life, the brightness of it. He'd seen only death, cruelty, only waste. And had imagined too well the fear, the agony of the end of that life as Jonah laid the stone at the head of the mound, as he himself had used fire to carve the name.

Mark her name, say her name. So it was done, and Max hoped the young woman who'd done no harm found peace.

He believed Jonah had, at least for now, in the ritual of respect.

But in the dark of the night, in the silence, in the void between the what-must-be-done, Max found none.

He thought of Eric, how fascinated he'd been with his brother as a newborn, amused by him as a toddler. He remembered how frustrated Eric had been at five and six, desperate to keep up with a brother eight years his senior.

Yet it had been Eric with whom he'd first shared the secret of what he was, what he had. Because there had been trust between them. Brotherhood.

How could he have not seen the changes? How could he have been so blind to them? If he had let himself see, there would have been enough time for him to pull Eric back from the edges of the dark before he'd leaped into it.

He should have looked after him. He should have been more aware. Instead, he'd killed his brother.

What he'd become at the end couldn't erase all he'd been before. Just as the horror of her end didn't erase all the girl they'd buried had been.

But he'd never have the chance to bury his brother, to mark his name, say his name. To send his soul to peace.

To live with the choice he'd made, he pushed along the path of what had to be done next. Food, shelter, movement. Following the signs. He'd killed again, to defend the lives of those who'd become his responsibility. An it harm none, a vow he believed with every cell of his being. He'd broken it, made that choice because he saw no other choice, and accepted he might have to make that choice again.

He had a chance now to build a life here, with Lana, with their child, with the children that might come after. So he would do what had to be done next.

Beside him, Lana stirred in sleep, as she often did now. Dreams dogged her sleep, dreams she couldn't remember. Or claimed she couldn't remember. But this time instead of curling toward him, she turned away, and got out of bed.

"Are you all right?"

She walked to the window, stood naked in the blue moonlight.

"To make the Savior is your fate. Life out of death, light out of dark. To save the Savior is your fate. Life out of death, light out of dark."

He rose, went to her. He didn't touch her, didn't speak as she stared through the window with eyes as deep as the night.

"Power demands sacrifice to reach its terrible balance. It calls for blood and tears, and still it feeds on love and joy. You, son of the Tuatha de Danann, have lived before, will live again. You, sire of the Savior, sire of The One, embrace the moments and hold them dear, as moments are fleeting and finite. But life and light, the power of what will come, the legacy within, are infinite."

Lana took his hand, pressed it to the sweet mound of her belly. "She is. A heart beating, wings fluttering, light stirring. She is the sword shining, the bolt that strikes true. She is the answer to questions not yet asked.

"She will be."

Lana kept his hand, walked back to the bed. "She is your blood. She is your gift. Sleep now, and be at peace." Lana drew him down, lay beside him. Rested a hand on his cheek. "You are loved." She closed her eyes, sighed. Slept.

And so did he.

DARK TO LIGHT

And the light shineth in the darkness;
and the darkness comprehended it not.

—John 1:5

CHAPTER TWENTY-ONE

The self-appointed town council decided there'd never be a better time to hold a public meeting. Having the power back up boosted morale and mood, but it wouldn't take long before that minor miracle faded into the expected.

They agreed to strike while the spirit of gratitude and appreciation rode high.

Spreading the word posed no problem, nor did finding volunteers to set up row after row of chairs at the Legion's hall, as the school cafeteria wouldn't hold the expanded population if, as expected, most showed.

They set up long tables on the platform while Chuck got the sound system up and running.

Arlys stood in the empty hall, imagined it full. Imagined countless scenarios—raging from pretty good to ugly chaos.

"Do you think we're ready, Lloyd?"

"As we'll ever be, I guess." He looked down at the binder in his hands. "It's a good agenda, a sensible one. Doesn't mean it's going to fly. Starting with asking everybody to stow their guns in the vestibule out there. Some won't."

"And I'm worried the some who won't are the ones most likely to cause trouble. But we have to start somewhere." She turned as Lana came in carrying a huge basket. Then sniffed the air. "My God, what is that amazing smell?"

"Bread. Fresh baked." She set the basket on the platform, one full of small rounds and loaves. "We've got a variety. I've got a lot of different starters going. We had packaged yeast, but that won't last forever, so I'm making more right now. And I'm going to try my hand at making dry yeast."

"You can make yeast?" Arlys all but buried her head in the basket.

"Yeah. It grows on fruits, potatoes, even tomatoes. I'm going to experiment. Somebody else has to figure out how to mill flour."

"If I don't have a chunk of that"—Lloyd breathed in hard through his nose—"I might just die right here and now."

"Help yourself. The idea was having some for every household. They're small, I know, but—"

"Praise Jesus," Lloyd said with his mouth full.

"Community action at work." Arlys broke a chunk of her own from Lloyd's round. "We're going to have rules, we're going to have structure, but . . ." She bit in. "We're also going to have bread that brings a tear to your eye. It's still warm!"

"Bread symbolizes hospitality. We break bread together." Lana smiled at the basket. "I liked using the community kitchen for the first time with this symbol."

"Will you marry me?" Lloyd broke off another little chunk.

"Hey!" Arlys jabbed him with her elbow. "Get in line."

Laughing, Lana wiggled her hand with the ring Max had slipped onto it one quiet spring night.

"Already taken, but I'll bake bread for you. Next up? Fred and I are going to get serious about making cheese."

"If you can do that, we're going to crown you the queens of New Hope."

Laughing at Arlys, Lana fluffed at her hair. "I'd look good in a crown. I'll be back with more."

Arlys sat beside the basket. "We're going to do this, Lloyd."

He sat on the other side, broke what remained of the round, offered half. "Damn right."

By eight, the hall buzzed with voices. Some had muttered about leaving their weapons, and some had just ignored the edict. But most left them outside the hall.

The holiday feeling still rang out, confirming the sense of timing the meeting. Arlys watched Kurt Rove—gun still on his hip—stride in. He gave the crowd a hard look before making his way to where the Mercer brothers had saved a seat for him.

If trouble came, she knew, it would center there.

Arlys took her seat at the long table, flipped open her notebook. She expected to have a lot to record.

Fred leaned over to her. "Some are already angry."

"Yeah, I got that."

Jonah stepped to the podium. His opening, "Um," reverberated in the room, surprising everyone into silence, then laughter. "We have a sound system thanks to Chuck." He waited out the applause. "And we've got that because we have power back thanks to Manning, Wanda, Chuck again, and Max."

Applause thundered; cheers and whistles rang.

Arlys noted Rove just folded his arms over his chest.

"We're going to ask everybody to conserve that power. Those of you who don't have a washing machine in your place, Manning's bypassed the coin-op at the Laundromat. We put a sign-up sheet in there for rotation. We've got detergent in inventory, for now, and Marci Wiggs is heading up the committee making soaps. Marci, why don't you stand up, let us know how that's coming."

Smart, Arlys thought as the woman stood, began to speak. Touch on other basics, on cooperation.

He called out other volunteers. Candle making, clothes, firewood, animal husbandry, the gardens, the greenhouse project, community maintenance.

"Some of you might not know Lana—can you stand up, Lana? She's been organizing the kitchen here at the Legion into a community kitchen to provide basics for those of us who can't boil water."

That brought out some laughter, more applause.

"She's starting that providing tonight. Lana?"

"I've had a lot of help getting this started." She rattled off the names of the cleanup and organizing crew. "We've got some new equipment thanks to Poe and Kim, Jonah and Aaron, and we're going to put it to use. Dave and Mirium and I decided to christen the kitchen with the most basic, and the most satisfying. Bread."

She picked up her basket. "A symbol of life, of hospitality, of communion. We have enough for each household to take a loaf." She tipped the basket so the crowd could see the contents, smiled at the cheerful response. "We'll have baskets in the vestibule. Take your share when you leave. Meanwhile, we have—"

"I'm not taking anything of hers." Arms still crossed, Rove stared at Lana, actually curled his lip. "How do we know what she put in it? Who says she can take over the kitchen here? Next thing we know she'll have a caldron going."

"I'm fresh out of eye of newt," Lana said coolly. "But I do have some starters, and some recipes printed out for anyone who wants them."

"I'll take Kurt's share!" somebody called out.

Lana waited for the roll of laughter to subside. "We'll also start on constructing a smokehouse behind the kitchen. If anyone has experience smoking meats, I'd really like to talk to you. Dave and I will be making venison sausage and bologna over the next few days. Arlys will announce in the *Bulletin* when it's ready. We hope to have the kitchen open six days a week, and we're always available for lessons for those, like Jonah, who want to learn how to boil water."

When she sat, Max rubbed her leg under the table.

"Thanks, Lana. The woman can cook," Jonah added. "I had some of her newt-less pasta last night. Rachel, can you give us an update on the clinic?"

She rose. "Appreciation again, to Jonah, Aaron, Kim, and Poe. We now have a fully stocked ambulance, and some solid equipment. And due to the work of the power team, the clinic will be able to run that equipment. Our over-the-counter and prescription medication stores are well stocked again. We also have a good start on the holistics, thanks to Fred, Tara, Kim, and Lana."

Briefly, she glanced at her notes. "Jonah and I will continue to give instructions in CPR the first Wednesday evening of each month at seven, and first aid courses every Monday evening at seven for anyone who signs up. As always, the clinic is open daily at eight, and either Jonah or I will be available for medical emergencies twenty-four-seven. We now have Ray, a nurse, and Carly, a nursing student, and Justine, a healer, added to the clinic staff. We'll work together to keep New Hope healthy."

"Healer, my ass," Lou Mercer shouted. "What's she do, lay hands on you and fix your broken arm?" He snorted out a laugh, had some join him.

"You're free to request the medical of your choice," Rachel told him, her tone as cold as February. "Just like you're free to sit there and be a dick. We'll still treat your hemorrhoids."

"Look, bitch—"

"Dr. Bitch," she snapped back. "And, as the only doctor in the community, I'm going to tell everyone here, the traditional medication we have will eventually deplete. It will expire. Without a chemist, a pharmacist, a lab, without the means, we'll have to depend on other types of medicine and healing, and those who have the ability and the skill to provide it. We need to live in the world we have."

"I've got diabetes." One of Rachel's new patients rose. "And I'm not the only one with a medical issue that needs daily medication. I'm damn grateful a group of my neighbors went out and found more of what we need. And I'm damn grateful to know when there isn't more, there's somebody who'll try to keep me alive and well. That's all I have to say."

"I think that says it all." Rachel stepped back, sat down.

Jonah stepped back, gave the room a moment to mutter. "Anybody who doesn't want to hear what needs to be said tonight doesn't have to stay. Just as anybody who doesn't like what needs to be done to build this community and keep it safe doesn't have to stay in New Hope. We survived to get here. Surviving isn't enough anymore, so I'm going to turn this meeting over to Lloyd."

Lloyd crossed to the podium, opened his binder before taking cheaters out of his shirt pocket, adjusted them on his nose. He peered out over them at the audience.

"I came into New Hope on April first. April Fool's Day was a bitch of a day. Cold rain, some sleet, a lot of wind. I came in alone, after the group I'd been traveling with for a few weeks got hit by Raiders. We got separated, and I guess I got lucky because when we were running in all directions with no plan, I fell into a gully. Knocked my head some, banged up my leg. So I lived. I don't know about the others, because when I came to and managed to crawl out, I was alone. A lot of us have been alone since the early days of January.

"We're not alone anymore."

Some applauded.

"I got lucky," he continued. "I limped away, and on that first day of April, I limped into New Hope. It was Bill Anderson on sentry duty that day, and he took me straight to the clinic, where Rachel treated my leg, gave me a bottle of water. Young Fred over there brought me an orange and a Milky Way bar. And I'm not shamed to say I cried like a baby. It was Arlys who brought me a change of clothes, and she and Katie saw to it there were blankets and some food and water in the house Chuck took me to. The house where I live today.

"I was hurt, and they tended to me. I was hungry, and they gave me food. I wasn't naked, but by God, I was ripe and ragged, and they clothed me. They gave me shelter. They gave me what every one of us has here today. Community."

He paused, adjusted his glasses. "Every one here has a story not so different from that. I want you to think back to it. I want you not to forget you're lucky, because Jonah's right. Surviving isn't enough. When I limped into New Hope, there were thirty-one people living here. Now we're more than three hundred.

"The group I'd been with ran, without a thought—and I was one of them—when we were attacked. We had no leader, no sense beyond our own survival. We had no plan, and no structure. New Hope already has more than that, and we're going to build on it. We've already talked about some of the ways we have built on it, and plans for how we'll go forward. Now we're going to talk about how we keep our community safe from Raiders and those who threaten the peace from outside, as well as from those who break that peace from the inside."

He took off the cheaters, absently polishing them on his shirt-sleeve. "We've had some incidents, and we could call them minor in the big scheme. Fistfights, threats of violence, and physical in-timidation. Our own Bryar was threatened, intimidated, and ha-rassed by two men when she took a walk along Main Street. Little Dennis Reader had the bike Bill fixed up for him stolen off the porch of the house where he's living. Ugly words were painted on the door of the house where Jess and Flynn and Dennis and some other children live. Our oldest resident, who we affectionately call Ma Zee and lives in the apartment across from mine, came home after work-ing in the gardens—eighty-six, and she puts her time in—to find her place ransacked."

He paused again, laid both his hands on the sides of the podium. "So I'm going to ask you right now: Are we a community who's going to sit and do nothing while a young woman can't take a walk in peace, while an old one's home is wrecked, or a little boy has his bike taken off his front porch?"

The shouts of "NO!" and the hard or surreptitious glances at the Mercers gave Lloyd just what he wanted.

"I'm glad to hear that." He held up a hand to quell the noise. "I'm glad to hear that. I agree. The founders of this community agree. The people who took you in, tended your wounds, gave you food and shelter agree. We survived, and we work every day to secure our homes against any who'd come here to do us harm. Now it's time to implement laws to keep us all safe from any in our com-munity who seek to cause harm."

Rove surged to his feet. "Laws? Getting here first doesn't give any-body the right to tell the rest of us what to do, how to live. We've got bigger things to worry about than some kid's bike, for Christ's sake. Look who's sitting up there, lording it over the rest of us. Half of them aren't like us."

"You've got a pot to piss in because of the people up here. You want to piss somewhere else, no one's stopping you." Lloyd's voice didn't rise, his tone didn't sharpen.

And his words carried weight.

"Like anybody else who's chosen to move on, you'll be given supplies and wishes for a safe journey."

"That's the way it's going to be?"

"That's the way it's going to be."

"But who decides?" A woman in the front raised her hand. "Who writes the laws, and what happens when they're broken?"

"That's a good question, Tara. We're starting off with what I believe every reasonable person in this room will support. Laws against violence, against theft and vandalism. I've written up the laws we agree are most essential. We're going to pass out copies of all that rather than have me stand here and go over every one. I'm just going to example killing."

He took a sharp breath in through his nose. "Now, we'd agree the taking of a life can't be tolerated. But what if the taking of that life was in self-defense, in defense of another? That has to be determined. The first line of that determination is law enforcement. We have Carla, who served six years as a sheriff's deputy, Mike Rozer, who served ten years in law enforcement, and Max Fallon, who led nearly a hundred people safely to New Hope, willing and able to serve the community in this capacity."

This time Don Mercer leaped to his feet. "I'm not taking orders from some bullshit girl deputy who probably sat on her fat ass eating doughnuts, or some asshole cop nobody around here even knows. And I'm sure as hell not taking nothing from his kind."

He pointed at Max. "His kind's what caused all this anyway, and most of us know it. What's to stop that fucking weirdo from striking down any one of us if he gets the itch? It was one of his kind killed your man, wasn't it, Lucy?"

A thin woman with short, graying hair nodded. "It was his kind killed Johnny. Swooped in on us like a demon from hell. I barely escaped with my life."

"Probably his kind that wrecked the old lady's place. Probably disappeared that kid's bike, too. Laws, my ass. Just another way for them to screw with actual human beings."

Max got slowly to his feet, barely spared Rove a glance when Rove rose with a hand on his gun. "It was human beings who killed three of our group, who ambushed us and killed three human beings before we could stop them. If you want to separate us into sides, both sides have dark in them. I know. It was one like me, and not, who caused the death of a young man who'd given us shelter. Who turned against everything we who embrace magick believe. He and the woman who turned him took a life, would have taken the life of my wife and child, my friends. He was my brother, my flesh, my blood, my family, and to stop him from killing, from using what was a gift to destroy, I took his life."

His gaze shifted, latched cold and gray on to Rove. "Believe me, if you draw that gun and threaten anyone here with it, I will stop you. If one who has the gift seeks to harm, I'll stop them.

"You insulted my wife, who used her talents to give the simple gift of bread. But that's not a crime, it's just ignorance. Draw the gun, if you're determined to learn the difference."

"This is bullshit!" Lou Mercer jumped to his feet. "Where does he get off threatening to use his mumbo-jumbo to go after one of us?"

"Where does Kurt get off threatening anybody with a gun?"

Kurt swung around toward Manning. "My gun's holstered."

"Be smart to keep it there and sit the hell down."

"It's all bullshit." Lou waved his arms. "Bullshit laws they get to make up? A half-assed police force coming down on us, and all started because some of those up there got here before the rest of us. It's bullshit. I say we vote on it. We're still in fucking America, and we get to vote. We don't just get told."

"You might want to peruse the laws before—"

"Just shut the hell up!" Lou shouted at Lloyd. "You've got no more right than me. I say we vote on this bullshit. We vote if we're going to let a bunch of assholes tell us how we've gotta live."

"All right, Lou, we can call for a vote. We'll do a show of hands," Lloyd suggested. "All those who want no structure of law in New Hope, no designated authority to enforce said laws, and no system of justice to enact consequences for the breaking of said laws, raise your hand."

He scanned the room. He'd already had a pretty good idea where he'd see hands raised, and was pleased to note he remained a good judge of character.

"I count fourteen against. Arlys?"

"Fourteen against," she confirmed.

"That's bullshit," Lou began.

"You called for a vote. We're voting. All those in favor of a structure of law in New Hope, a designated authority to enforce said laws, and a system of justice to enact consequences for the breaking of said laws, raise your hand."

He nodded. "As it's clearly more than two hundred for, which is the majority, the vote carries for the structure of laws. Eddie, Fred, would you mind passing out the lists so people can read what's being proposed?"

As they went to hand a stack for each row to pass down, Rove shoved his way forward, snatched a paper from Eddie's hands, crumpled it, tossed it down.

"Dude, don't be such a dick."

Eyes fired up, Rove jerked his arm back, fist balled. He punched it at Eddie's face, where it rammed two inches away. The fire died to shock, frustration. Then disgust.

"I knew you were one of them."

"He's not." Lana got to her feet. "Not in the way you mean. I blocked your punch, Mr. Rove," she continued as she walked down. "Because I'm not going to let you bully and physically assault a friend."

"Aw, Lana, I can handle myself."

She patted Eddie's shoulder. "I know it. Go ahead and pass out the stacks." As Eddie moved on, Lana stepped into his place.

She tapped a finger in the air in front of Rove's fist. He rolled his shoulder, dropped his arm.

"Would you like to take a swing at me, Mr. Rove?" Without looking around, she held up a hand as Max pushed to his feet. "Or are you going to leave it with insults and bigotry?"

She knew hate when he stood in front of her, and could read through that hate, the humiliation that stained it, just how much he wished to hurt her. And just how much he feared her.

Several more people rose as he stood, his fist still balled at his side and trembling there. Some moved to stand beside her, behind her.

"Go home, Kurt," Manning advised, and gently drew Lana back. "Go home and cool off."

Rove turned on his heel, strode toward the back. Of the fourteen who'd raised a hand with him for the nay vote, only nine walked out with him.

"You got balls," Manning told Lana. "If you don't mind me saying so."

"I don't mind, since I haven't had them very long."

CHAPTER TWENTY-TWO

For a week, then two, as May blended into June, New Hope built.

A greenhouse, a smokehouse, a picnic area behind the gardens. Twice people wandered in—a group of three, another of five.

With power restored, Chuck combined his brand of magic with Max's to bring the Internet on line. It was slow and spotty dial-up, supported only a handful of what they'd designated as priority locations, but it added another layer of hope.

Many with missing loved ones lined up daily at the new town library to send e-mails and check religiously for any response.

Even though none came, hope lived.

Though Chuck continued his quest, communication with the outside world remained a void. Arlys might not have been able to surf the Web, but she had the software to publish the *Bulletin* without hammering at the old Underwood.

And Max wrote.

Jonah quietly moved into Rachel's bedroom.

The gardens flourished, and if they benefited from a little magickal help, no one complained.

"It feels like we found balance." Lana sat on her front porch—in a chair painted a cheerful red—and enjoyed sun tea and a sugar cookie from the batch she'd made with her share of supplies.

Arlys sat with her, as she often did at the end of the day.

"It's like an idyll," she continued. "And this is from the lifelong city dweller. We've got fresh cherries, grapes—"

"Which makes you think yeast."

"I also think tarts and jams and jellies. We're already getting some tomatoes, some vegetables, lovely fresh lettuce and greens. Bill hauled two cases of Mason jars and lids to the kitchen. I'm watching corn grow, which is amazing to this lifelong urbanite. Rachel said the baby is perfect—and over a pound now. I swear she feels a lot heavier, then I imagine swallowing a pound of sugar, and see the correlation."

On a contented sigh, she stroked her belly. "Speaking of yeast, we made and dried some. And thanks to Chuck I don't have to write recipes out until my hand cramps. Plus, Rove and the Mercers and that pissy Sharon Beamer haven't caused any trouble since the public meeting."

"Give them time."

"Oh, no spoiling my happy mood. There's Will." Lana waved a hand, signaling him over. "How are things going there?"

"Going where?"

"With you and Will?" Deliberately Lana wiggled her eyebrows. "I've felt some definite vibes."

"Your vibes are off. We're just friends, with a shared childhood history." Arlys took a sip of her wine, watched Will cross the street. "But he is nice to look at."

"Ladies."

"We're out of beer," Lana told him. "But we've got wine."

"I wouldn't mind some. We're just back—hunting party."

"Don't tell me I'm going to be making more venison sausage."

"It's good stuff."

"Oh well. I'll get you a glass."

"Sit," Arlys ordered. "I'll get it. Pound of sugar," she added as she got up, went inside.

"Pound of sugar?"

Lana tapped her baby mound. "Have a cookie."

"Wouldn't mind that, either." He took one, bit in. Shut his eyes. "Oh man, that's really good. You could make a living."

"Those were the days."

Arlys came out with the glass, poured him one. Will leaned back against the fence post. He glanced back as three deer trotted down Main Street.

"It's a good thing Fred thought of putting that invisible fence around the gardens," he commented. "We don't have to go more than half a mile to bag a deer."

"Also good we approved the town ordinance against deploying a firearm within town limits," Arlys added. "Or we'd end up with more windows being shot out by accident."

"You got that. We're thinking of invading Rachel's place tonight for some DVD roulette. Are you in?"

Arlys raised her brows. "Who are 'we'?"

"Dad and me—and Chuck if we can pull him out of the basement—a few others. They've got that big screen and the player. Entry fee's a snack or beverage."

"I could be in," Arlys said, smiling at him. He really was nice to look at, she thought as Lana got up and walked to the other side of the steps. "What about you, Lana? An evening of DVD roulette sound appealing?"

"Something's coming. It all changes. Something's coming. It always was. Something's coming. It ends. It begins."

Will stepped toward her, then rushed to her as she swayed.

"Hey, hey, hey." He shoved his glass at Arlys and steadied Lana.

"I'm all right. Just got dizzy."

"I'll get Rachel. I'll find Max."

"No, no, I just got dizzy. I'm fine."

"I'm getting Rachel," Arlys insisted, and bolted across the street.

"Here." Will carried her to the chair, set her down. "What's this?"

"Ah, sun tea."

"Okay, that's probably good. Drink a little. You really went pale. What's coming?"

"I don't know." She laid a hand on the baby. "It was just this feeling of inevitability. And sorrow. I practice, but not as much as I should. I don't know how to control or interpret as much as I should."

Rachel, in a T-shirt and cargo shorts, crossed the street at a fast clip. "What's all this?"

"I just had a moment," Lana said as Rachel took her pulse. "It came and went. I feel fine."

"Your pulse is rapid."

"It scared me. It was one of the feelings I get. They just cover me. I don't know how to explain. They pour out of me and saturate me. It's not physical. Not in the usual way."

"I'll find Max."

"Oh, don't." As he stepped back, Lana pleaded with Will. "Don't worry him. I'm fine."

"He'd kick my ass—and I'd have to help him do it—if I didn't go get him."

"All right, all right. I can't be responsible for you and Max both kicking your ass. Rachel, really, you just examined me and the baby this morning. I know what it was—it's not medical, and it passed."

She took Rachel's hand, then Arlys's. "Something's coming, and soon. That's all I know for certain."

"'It all changes,'" Arlys repeated. "'It ends. It begins.'"

"Did I say that? It's a little like being outside myself. Or inside. I'm not a seer." She looked down at her belly. "But she might be. I can't see what she sees. I just feel it."

She heard the sound of running feet, but saw Chuck not Max rushing along the sidewalk.

"I got something!" He waved the paper he held, jogging onto the porch. "Contact. Sort of."

"Internet contact?" Arlys snatched the paper out of his hand before he'd caught his breath.

ATTENTION ALL GOD-FEARING HUMANS

If you are reading this, you are one of the chosen. No doubt you have lost those dear to you and have felt, may still know, despair. No doubt you have witnessed firsthand the abominations that have desecrated the world Our Lord created. You may believe the End Times are upon us.

But take heart!

You are not alone!

Have Faith!

Have Courage!

We who survived this demonic plague wrought by Satan's Children face A Great Test! Only we can defend our world, our lives, our very souls. Arm yourselves and join The Holy Crusade. Will you stand by while our women are raped, our children mutilated, while the very survival of humanity is threatened by the ungodly, by The Uncanny? The future of the Human Race is in our hands. To save it we must soak them in the blood of the demon.

Gather together, Chosen Warriors! Hunt, Kill, Destroy the
EVIL that threatens us. "Thou shalt not suffer a witch to
live," so sayeth The Lord. This is the time of retribution! This
is the time of The Slaughter! This is the time of
                    The Purity Warriors!
I am with you. I am of you. I am filled with the light of
righteous vengeance.
          Reverend and Commander Jeremiah White

"Bad copy," Arlys managed. "Overwrought and fucking terrifying."

"Purity Warriors." Lana gripped the porch rail. "Flynn said he
finally got Starr to talk a little more. The gang who killed her mother
called themselves Purity Warriors, and had tattoos. Crossed swords
with a *P* and a *W* under the *X*."

"I know. Just like I know this Jeremiah." Arlys handed the paper
back to Chuck. "He was already stirring up calls for bloodshed back
in January, in the early weeks of the Doom."

"He's got a rudimentary site up," Chuck told them. "I stumbled
on it while I hunted for communications. There's more. He's up-
loaded some photos—they're pretty graphic. And he's got one up
of the tattoo you're talking about. He calls it the Mark of the Chosen. Bat shit, man. Sick and bat shit. He claims he's working on
putting up a message board. I hacked in, and he's got more than
two hundred hits. Less than fifty individuals, so people go back,
check the site again."

"Fifty's not many," Arlys murmured. "But . . ."

"It says we're not the only ones with power and Internet," Chuck
finished.

"We wouldn't be the only ones appalled by the sick and the bat
shit," Arlys commented. "But . . ."

"Some will revel in it." Eyes grim, Rachel nodded. "Including a handful in New Hope. Could you tell when he is, or was, posting? Where the site's based?"

"I think he's mobile—adds more scary because I don't know how he could be. Still, now that I found it, I can monitor it. Everything else I've found, so far, is pre-Doom. It's stuff that's been up since before it all fell down. But if there's one—the bat shit—there's going to be more."

He broke off as Max pulled up to the curb in a truck. Max got out one side, Will the other.

"I'm fine," Lana said quickly.

"Will said you fainted."

She aimed a frustrated look at Will. "I got a little dizzy."

He cupped her face, studied it. "You had a vision?"

"No, not . . . It's hard to explain. I think the baby did, and it somehow filtered through me."

"You're connected physically," Rachel pointed out. "Your health, the baby's. I don't know anything about this other side of things, really, but it seems to me that connection could go there."

"It's not the first time," Max concurred. "Could it harm her?"

"I'd say driving's out."

Appalled, Lana stared. She'd learned to love driving. "Come on!"

"I'm going to side with the doctor," Arlys said. "You went off, Lana. You were somewhere else. I'd give a pass on driving, operating heavy equipment," she added, trying to lighten the blow.

"You're a terrible driver anyway." Max kissed her forehead.

"You'll pay for that later, but we've got more to worry about. Chuck?"

As Chuck handed the paper to Max, began to explain, Lana sat again, thought again. No risks, she decided. Whatever affected her, affected the baby.

And apparently vice versa.

Rachel poured out more sun tea. "Hydrate. And I want to know if you have more dizzy spells. If you have any unusual feelings, physical or otherwise. There's no point stressing over what Chuck found. One fanatic, and a very big country."

"That helps, but as we said, we have a handful right here who might, probably would, take up that call."

"Most aren't here." Max reread the paper. "Mike and I went out to check on Rove. Just take a look. He's pulled out, and so have the Mercers, along with Sharon Beamer, Brad Fitz, Denny Wertz."

"That explains why we haven't seen them around in the past few days." Arlys nodded. "And they haven't picked up any supplies or reported for any details. Well, it doesn't hurt my feelings."

"I'm glad they're gone," Lana said. "I'll sleep easier knowing they are."

"It also explains why we're two trucks shy," Max went on. "Twenty gallons of gas, food supplies. Weapons. That's why we went out to check." He ran an absent hand down Lana's arm while he scanned the street. "Still, I imagine most would consider that loss a win against having them moving on."

"Meanwhile, I'm going back down, see if I can find somebody else who's back online." Chuck pulled his fingers through his scraggly beard. "Hitting the downer button here, but figuring all the techs and hackers in the world before the Doom, and how I'm getting all but zilch on the surf?" His shoulders lifted and fell. "You gotta do the math, right? You gotta figure more than fifty percent—a lot more than fifty—wiped out in the Doom.

"Anyway." He let that trail off, then wandered away.

"He's right." Max stroked his hand—comfort, reassurance—up and down Lana's arm. "We can judge that by what we all saw getting here, and by the fact that the number of people coming in to stay or even to pass through has trickled down to nothing in the last two weeks or so."

"It makes building and maintaining our own even more important," Arlys put in. "Law, order, education, water, and food supplies."

"Security," Max added. "A big world, one fanatic," he repeated. "But one with followers. Add Raiders, Dark Uncannys. Whatever outside laws and government might still exist doesn't reach here. And whatever outside laws and government might exist? We don't know who or what might be in charge of it. So we have to protect our own."

"I agree. I agree with all that," Rachel said, hands in her pockets, looking out at the street. At the peace. "We've made a lot of progress in a short amount of time. Even having the framework of a system of rules, of community responsibilities has given people a foundation. Maybe, having those who don't want that foundation—like Rove— leaving adds to it. It is a big world, and we've got the chance to make this part of it safe and solid."

"It has to be more than rules and responsibilities. We're alive." Lana laid a hand on her child as she stirred. "So many of us have been grieving, even while doing what has to be done." She looked at Will. "So many of us lost pieces of ourselves. But we found pieces, too. Found things inside ourselves we didn't know were there. We're alive," she repeated. "Maybe it's time to celebrate that. It's nearly the solstice."

Max smiled at her. "The longest day. A time for celebrating."

"Yes, and some of us will. I think it may be too soon—only a few days away—for a full community celebration. We need more time to plan that, and I think that's just what we need."

"Fourth of July was always my favorite holiday growing up."

Arlys turned, smiled at Will. "I remember. Barbecue, marching bands, hot dogs, and fireworks."

"My mom's cherry pie."

"I fondly remember your mom's cherry pie."

"A New Hope–style Independence Day. We've got like three

weeks to set it up," Will pointed out. "And the setting up will get people juiced up, right?"

"The all-American holiday." Arlys cocked her head. "Food, games, crafts, music, dancing. I like it. I really like it."

"We could start the day with a memorial for those we've lost." Lana reached for Max's hand. "To honor friends and family who aren't with us. And end the day in celebration."

"Now I like it even more. I'm going to work on a *Bulletin*," Arlys decided. "I'll get it out today."

"I've got a couple of ideas on that," Will told Arlys. "I'll walk down with you. This is a good thing, Lana. It's a good thing."

"I'll go give Jonah the heads-up. Will's right." Rachel tapped Lana's arm. "This is a good thing."

Alone on the porch with Lana, Max sat looking out on the town. "You're happy here? It's just us," he said before she could answer.

"It's not the life I ever imagined for us. And there are still times I wake up expecting to be in the loft. There's a lot I miss. Just walking home in the noise and the crowds. I remember how we'd just started to talk about taking a couple of weeks and going to Italy or France. I remember, and I miss. But yes, I'm happy here. I'm with you, and in a few months, we'll have a daughter. We're alive, Max. You got us out of a nightmare and brought us here.

"Are you? Happy here?"

"It's not the life I imagined, either, and there's a lot I miss. But I'm with you. We're having a child. We're both able to do work that satisfies us, and have powers we're both still learning to understand. There's a purpose. We're alive, and there's a purpose. We'll celebrate that."

The day of the festival dawned soft and pink.

Lana spent the beginning of it, as she had the day before, in food prep with her kitchen team. She focused in on her area, leaving the decorations—with Fred leading that charge—to others.

She'd made countless patties of venison and wild turkey while listening to musicians practicing and hammers striking nails. In the hall outside the kitchen, Bryar and others worked with groups of children to make Chinese lanterns—red, white, and blue—and paper stars that bore the names of loved ones lost.

As the blue washed away the pink, Lana stepped outside, moved to see so many gathered while a newly formed choir sang "Amazing Grace."

She watched Bill and Will Anderson hang their stars on the old oak at the edge of the green. How they stood with Arlys when she hung hers.

And so many others who stepped forward with those symbols until they crowded the lower branches.

It touched her to see Starr step forward to hang her own.

The lanterns the faeries would light as dusk circled the park. Garlands of flowers decked lampposts and newly constructed arbors. Grills formed a line in a designated cooking area.

By noon, musicians played in a gazebo volunteers had finished painting only the night before. Those grills smoked.

Crafts lined tables—all up for barter. Kids got their faces painted or took pony rides. Others played boccie or horseshoes.

The gardens offered a banquet—tomatoes, peppers, summer squash, summer corn (Rachel said the baby was as long as a healthy ear of corn now).

The weather, bright and hot, had many sprawled in the shade, drinking cups of the gallons and gallons of sun tea the community kitchen provided.

She heard talk of putting together a softball team, one for adults, one for kids, and using the Little League field half a mile outside the town proper.

More talk of expanding the farm, moving it to one of the farms a mile out.

Good talk, she thought, hopeful talk.

She danced with Max over the green grass in a summer dress that billowed over her belly. Basking in the sunlight, she gossiped with Arlys while Eddie jammed on his harmonica. On the swings, Fred and Katie swayed back and forth with babies on their laps.

Was she happy? Max had asked her a few weeks before. On this day, at this moment, she could give him an unqualified yes.

She lifted a hand to wave at Kim and Poe, and sighed. "We'll do this every year, won't we?"

"I think that's a definite yes. And," Arlys added, "we'll put something together for the holidays—Christmas, Hanukkah."

"Yes! Winter solstice." Lana rubbed circles over her belly. "It'll be her first."

Arlys lifted her face, shook back her hair—a sassy swing with highlights again thanks to Clarice. "You still haven't come up with a name for the baby?"

"We're playing around but nothing's sticking yet. Last summer, I was just moving in with Max. It seemed so huge, so amazing. Now, here we are, expecting a child. Max is playing horseshoes. I'd bet my entire supply of baking powder he's never played that before in his life."

She let out a laugh when he threw one, had it pause and revolve in midair, backtrack, then drop neatly onto the post.

"And he cheats!"

The maneuver had Carla—his partner—cheering, and Manning—one of his opponents—erupting in mock outrage. Max lifted his hands in an innocent gesture, then glanced at Lana. Grinned, winked.

"He was also so serious about the Craft. He'd lighten up with me, but he would never have played like that before. It's good to see him relax. I'm going to go pick more corn—and give the other team a little boost on the way."

"I'll give you a hand."

Lana pushed herself up, wandered toward the horseshoe pitch. More corn, definitely, she thought as she scanned tables. And tomatoes. She'd check on the supply of wild turkey and venison burgers.

But first she guided Manning's flung horseshoe to the post, had it execute a trio of flips before hitting with a clanging ring. Gave Max a grin and a wink.

Manning let out a laughing hoot, did a little dance, then blew her a kiss.

Yes, she thought, it was good, so good, to just play.

"Hey." Will ran up, tugged Arlys's arm. "We need another for boccie."

"I was just going to—"

"Oh, go ahead. I'm an expert corn picker now."

"I don't know anything about boccie."

"Good, neither do I." Will grabbed her hand, glanced at the stars swaying on the branches. "It's a good day." On impulse he leaned over, kissed Lana's cheek. Then turned Arlys to him, kissed her, slow and easy, on the mouth. "A really good day."

Lana smiled all the way into the corn.

It smelled green and earthy, and the music, the voices, the ring of metal on metal followed her as she twisted ears of corn from the stalks. She heard children laughing, a magical sound to her ear, carried on the gentle sigh of the summer breeze.

Everything felt so peaceful, the blue sweep of sky, the tall green stalks, the brush of them against her skin.

She stood a moment, her arms filled with corn, giving thanks for what she had.

The baby kicked—a fast flurry of kicks—that nearly had her bobbling the ears. She heard one of Katie's babies cry out, long and shrill over the music and voices. As she turned to start back, something fluttered to the ground in front of her.

She glanced down. Froze.

It was scorched, its edges curled and blackened, but she recognized the photo of her and Max together, the photo she'd packed before they'd left New York. The photo that had been in the house in the mountains when . . .

Overhead, in a sky going thick, going gray, black crows circled.

"Max!" Corn thudded to the ground as she ran, as she shoved through the verdant stalks. As she heard the first cracks of gunfire.

Screams echoed as she fought her way clear.

People ran, scattered, dived for cover, returned fire.

She saw Carla sprawled on the ground, eyes wide and staring. And Manning, oh God, Manning bleeding on the soft dirt of the horseshoe pitch.

Her own scream clogged in her throat as Kurt Rove smashed the butt of his rifle into Chuck's face.

All around her men fired guns and arrows indiscriminately as men and women she knew grabbed children to shield them or to rush them to safety.

Rainbow, who taught yoga every morning, threw a shimmering shield over a woman with a toddler. Then her body pitched forward from a bullet in the back.

Lana saw a man—tall, lean, his golden mane of hair rippling—lift a rifle, aiming it up as Fred rose, wings furiously batting, one of the babies wrapped in her arms.

In seconds, only seconds, the world changed.

Lana had no weapon but her power, and threw it out, all instinct. The rifle aimed at Fred and the child flew out of the man's hands. And he turned his crazed blue gaze on her.

"There." He pointed. The man beside him, dark and muscular, the purity tattoo bold on his biceps, lifted his hands. He held a gun in each. "Kill the witch!" he shouted.

Even as Lana lifted her hands to fight, to protect her child, thunder blasted. The ground shook with it.

"Ours!"

Rising behind the building, wings scorched, faces scarred, Eric and Allegra loomed.

Everything seemed to stop. An illusion as she heard the screams, the gunfire, even the slicing *swish* of the stalks as some ran to hide there.

They'd survived. They lived. And she saw death in their eyes.

She gathered all she had to fight.

Max sprinted to her, shoved her back. "Run!"

"Where?" Spewing black bolts toward the sky, Eric let out a laugh. "Nowhere to run, nowhere to hide. Step aside, brother. We don't want you this time."

"We want what's inside her." With a flash of wings, Allegra swooped lower. Max thrust out, pushed Lana back.

"Run. Save our daughter."

"Together. We're stronger. We have more." Lana gripped Max's hand.

"There's no need for this, Eric, for any of it," Max shouted. "You're aligning yourself with a madman who hunts our kind. He'll turn on you. They'll all turn on you."

"Wow, I never thought of that." He shot Allegra a surprised look. "Maybe we should think about this. Except . . . Yeah, I forgot one thing. You tried to *kill* me. I was wrong, Max. We do want you. Dead."

"Both of them. The three of them!" Pale hair flying, Allegra shouted. "We call the dark. We rule the dark! And with it cut off the light."

As Lana did with Max, Allegra gripped Eric's hand. Snarling thunder, black lightning. With Max, Lana blocked the blows, shoved them back.

And felt the power quake the ground under her feet.

Blood bloomed on Max's arm where a bolt slipped through. Across the field, others ran toward them. Flynn and Lupa, Jonah, Aaron.

For a moment, her hope leaped. Together, all of them, they'd push back the dark.

"They're coming to help. We just have to—"

Lana saw the wave of black, felt the first biting edge of it before Max spun her around. His eyes met hers, held hers as he cloaked her, cloaked their child with his body.

He took the full force of the hate, of the dark. The shock jolted through him into her as they flew together, fell together into the stalks. Blood ran from the gash where that keen edge caught her arm.

Breath gone, head spinning, she crawled free, rolled, tried to drag Max to safety.

He lay covered with blood from countless wounds, his skin scored from burns.

"No. No. Max." She knew, even as she dragged his body into her arms, even as she pressed her face to his, she knew he was gone.

Gone. Taken. Murdered.

The rage, the grief, the roaring fury spewed up in her. Covered in his blood, spilling her own, she released it on a scream that cleaved the air like a blade.

It gushed out wild and red against the oily black.

She heard her scream answered with howls of pain.

Run. He'd told her to run, but she hadn't listened. He'd told her to save their child, but he'd given his life to save them both.

Nowhere to run, nowhere to hide. Choking on sobs, she dragged Max's gun belt free. Tenderly, she drew the ring from his finger, pushed it onto her thumb. She kissed his face, his lips, his hands.

Save the child, whatever the cost.

She heard his voice in her head, in her heart and, sobbing, pushed through the stalks toward the forest. She began to run.

A movement to her right had her whirling, hand thrown up to fight, to defend. Starr flowed out of the tree.

"You're hurt."

Lana could only shake her head.

"You hurt them more."

As Starr gestured back, Lana looked toward the park. Whatever had exploded out of her, that mad, red, raging grief, had leveled some of the attackers. She saw no sign of Eric or Allegra other than a thin haze of smoke smearing the sky.

It twisted the raw edges of her already shattered heart to see Arlys limping toward Carla's body, Rachel kneeling beside an unconscious and bloodied Chuck. Others she knew, cared for, rushing to help, or racing toward the street, guns in hand.

"Katie, the babies?"

"Jonah got them inside. They killed Rainbow. She was good. They came for you. For her," Starr said, reaching out and for the first time in weeks touching anyone, touched a hand to Lana's child.

"I can't stay. They'll come back. I can't . . . They killed Max."

"I'm sorry. He was good." Starr bowed her head. "They want us dead, all of us, but the Savior most."

"She's not the Savior," Lana said fiercely. "She's my daughter."

"She's both. I could hear them." Now Starr pressed a hand to her head. "Hear all the hate. It hurts my head, so I ran and hid, like I did with my mother. I didn't fight, but I will next time. I will. They'll help, they'll protect you. Her."

"I have to protect her. I can't stay. They'll try again. They'll come back and try again."

Starr nodded. "Then you have to run. You have to hide. I can still hear them in my head. I'll put Max's name on the tree for you."

Blinded by tears, Lana ran. She ran into all the dreams that had haunted her nights.

CHAPTER TWENTY-THREE

Lana kept off the main roads for days. She took shelter where she could, scavenging remote houses for clothes and supplies. Along with clothes she found a chain and threaded it through Max's ring to wear around her neck.

She ate what she could find, and worried about the baby.

Whenever she saw crows circling overhead or heard their call, she changed direction.

Once, exhausted, she dropped down at the base of a dead tree, too steeped in fatigue and grief to go on. Staring at the sky through its skeletal branches, she drifted away, she dreamed. Dreamed of a slim young woman with gray eyes and black hair telling her to get up, to move, to keep going.

So Lana got up, moved, kept going.

One terrible day blurred into every terrible night.

With no sense of time or distance, she slept in an abandoned car on the side of the road, and woke in the shimmer of dawn to the sound of engines.

Her first instinct was to call for help, but the stronger one ordered her to stay still and quiet. The stronger one had her skin shivering as those engines stopped.

Car doors opened, slammed. Men's voices floated through the windows she'd left open in hopes of a breeze.

"We ought to go back to that shit-hole town, level it. Somebody there knows where the bitch is."

"The Rev says she ain't there, she ain't there."

She heard footsteps coming closer, tightened her grip on the gun she slept with. Then the distinctive sound of a zipper, the sound of water striking asphalt.

"Waste of gas, you ask me, and if those two freaks want her so bad, they should've taken her out when they had the chance. Instead we lost six good men. We're supposed to be killing freaks not working with them."

"Don't see nobody asking you. The Rev knows what he's doing. He's got a plan, and I expect we'll be taking those freaks out after we do the woman. Fucking witch. I got a score to settle with her now."

"Aw, did she mess up your pretty face when she cut loose?"

"Fuck you, Steed."

A quick laugh, the jerk of a zipper. "What I know is the freaks are hurting more than you, which is why we're driving all over hell and back looking for some knocked-up demon whore."

"I find her first, I'm putting a knife straight through her and the brat inside her."

"Witches have to hang or burn."

"That'll come. We oughta go through these couple of cars here, see if there's anything worth taking."

"Forget that. We got a gas mart about twenty miles east. Better pickings."

Lana kept her grip tight on the gun as she felt the car rock.

"Piece of shit anyway."

She held her breath as the footsteps moved on, as doors opened and slammed again. She lay still as an engine roared to life, tires squealed.

She counted the knocks of her heart one by one even after the car sped off, as silence fell again.

"I wouldn't have let them touch you," she murmured as she crawled out of the backseat on trembling legs. "East. They're going east, so we'll go west."

But not on foot. However long she'd walked and wandered, she hadn't put enough distance between her child and those who wanted to harm her.

She'd risk the road, for now she'd risk it.

She got behind the wheel, laid the gun on the seat beside her. It took a moment to gather herself, to pull up the power she'd set aside since the day it had ripped through her in a red, killing rage.

When she held her hand out, the engine didn't roar to life. It sputtered, knocked, caught. With the sun rising behind her, she drove.

The sun hung high when the car died. Leaving it where it stopped, she walked again with mountains rising around her.

Time blurred, walking, driving when she found another car, scavenging for food, for water. Though she asked herself how far would be far enough, she avoided any towns where people might have gathered.

How would she know if they held friend or enemy?

She closed away her old life, killed rabbit and squirrel, dressed them, roasted the meat over a fire made by power to feed herself and her baby.

She who'd once believed food could be, should be, art, ate to live, ate to feed what lived inside her.

Her world became trees, rocks, sky, endless roads, the pitiful thrill of finding a house that had fresh clothes, boots that nearly fit.

Comfort became feeling the baby move inside her. Joy became finding a peach tree and tasting the sweet, fresh fruit, having the juice run down a throat parched from the summer heat.

Safety became hearing no human voice but her own, seeing human shape only in her own shadow.

In those weeks since New Hope, she became a nomad, a wanderer, a hermit with no plan except movement, food, shelter.

Until.

She topped a rise thick with trees, then immediately crouched for cover.

A house sat on land that gently rolled, then flattened again. On the flat an expansive garden spread at summer peak. She dragged at the pack she'd scavenged, pulled out binoculars.

Tomatoes, red and ripe, peas, beans, peppers, carrots. Rows of lettuce, cabbage, hillocks of squashes, eggplant. The rising field of corn brought back the scent of blood, of death.

Of Max.

She curled up a moment, fighting off waves of sorrow and grief, then made herself lift the glasses again.

A couple of horses stood together, fenced off from a black-and-white cow, another fence line and black cows—beef cows along with a calf.

She scanned over a pen where five pigs lolled.

Chickens! The idea of eggs nearly brought tears to her eyes.

The house itself stood square and sturdy, simple white with a wide porch. A small, traditional barn stood cheerfully red.

She skimmed over a shed, a small, squat silo, a pair of windmills, a greenhouse, some ornamental trees and shrubs, what she thought might be a beehive. Beyond it more fields. Wheat, she thought, wheat, and maybe hay.

Obviously not abandoned, she thought, and, as a truck sat outside, someone was probably inside.

Eggs, fresh vegetables, fruit trees.

She could wait.

Waiting, she dozed.

The barking woke her, sent her heart leaping into her throat.

A pair of dogs raced around the front of the house, bumping together, tumbling over a patch of grass.

She lifted the glasses again as a man came out. Tanned, strong-looking in faded jeans and a T-shirt. He wore a ball cap over a shaggy mop of brown hair and sunglasses that obscured his eyes.

He loaded a couple of bushel baskets full of produce into the truck, walked back into the house. He came out again with two more before whistling to the dogs.

They both jumped into the back of the truck. After loading the other baskets, he got into the cab, drove away.

She counted to sixty, then counted again before rising.

She could hear nothing but birds, chittering squirrels. Using a hand to support her pregnant belly, she picked her way down the rocky slope, eyes trained on the house.

If he didn't live alone, someone might be inside. Though she wanted to make a run for the garden, she approached the house cautiously, circling it to peer in windows.

Another porch ran along the back, and in the bold sun grew herbs. Pulling her knife she cut basil, rosemary, thyme, oregano, chives, dill, reveled in the scents as she pushed them into a plastic bag from her pack.

Someone could be inside, on the second floor. But she'd risk it.

She ran as quickly as her skewed center of gravity allowed and plucked a tomato from the vine. Bit into it like an apple, swiped the juice from her chin.

She picked pea pods, a handful of string beans, a glossy eggplant, tugged up a carrot, a bulb of garlic. She picked lettuce, ate a leaf while she gathered what she could carry in her pack, her pockets.

Apples, a little on the green side, went into her pack along with a cluster of purple grapes from a vine. She ate some where she stood looking down at two stone markers under the shade of the apple tree.

Ethan Swift
Madeline Swift

They'd died in the plague, Lana noted, in February, two days apart.

And someone—the farmer?—had marked their graves and planted a sunbeam-yellow rosebush between them.

"Ethan and Madeline, I hope your souls found peace. Thank you for the food."

Eyes closed, she stood in the dappled shade, wished she could curl up under the tree and sleep. Wake in a world without fear and constant movement. Where Max could put his arms around her, and their baby would be born in peace and safety.

That world, she thought, was done. Living in this one meant doing what needed to be done next.

She glanced toward the clucking, humming chickens, imagined sautéing chicken in one of the pats of butter she'd hoarded, flavored with fresh garlic and herbs.

And figured while the farmer probably wouldn't miss the vegetables, he'd surely miss a chicken. And since she might want to stay in the area for a day or two, she'd come back, relieve him of one of the hens before she moved on.

For now, she'd settle for a couple of eggs.

She walked through the pecking chickens into the open coop,

where she found a single brown egg under a single roosting bird who seemed as wary of her as Lana was of it.

"He gathered the eggs earlier," she murmured. "I'm lucky you held back."

"She usually does."

Lana whirled, the egg clutched like a grenade in one hand, her other thrust out ready to throw power and defense.

He held his hands up, away from the gun on his hip.

"I'm not going to give you grief over an egg, or whatever else you helped yourself to. Especially since you're eating for two. I've got water if you need it. Milk, too. A little bacon to go with that egg."

She had to swallow before speaking the first word to another human since she'd left New Hope. "Why?"

"Why what?"

"Why would you give me anything? I was stealing."

"So was Jean Valjean." He shrugged. "He was hungry, too. Look, you can take the damn egg and go, or you can come inside, have a hot meal. It's up to you."

She lowered her hand, laid it on her belly. Thought of the baby.

He'd planted a rosebush for his dead. She would take it as a sign.

"I'd appreciate a hot meal. I can barter for it, and for the fruits and vegetables I took."

He smiled then. "Whatcha got?"

"I can work for it."

"Well." He scratched the back of his neck. "We can talk about that."

He stepped back, gave her plenty of room.

She could still run, Lana thought.

"Lady, if I wanted to hurt you, I'd have already done it."

Now he turned, walked to where she saw the dogs—prancing and wagging—just outside the chicken wire.

"How did you know I was here?"

"I caught the flash of the sun on your field glasses. Or what I figured was field glasses. The dogs and I decided we'd head out, stop up the road, and walk back to see what you were up to. They won't hurt you."

As if to prove it, both dogs—big with thick, creamy fur and madly happy eyes—moved in to rub their bodies against her legs. "That's Harper, that's Lee. *Mockingbird* was my mother's favorite book."

She saw him glance toward the apple tree, the graves. Feeling foolish holding on to it, she handed him the egg. "Your parents?"

"Yeah. Yeah," he said again, starting toward the house. "Those boots have some miles on them."

"They did when I found them."

Accepting that, he continued out, walked onto the porch, opened the unlocked front door. When she hesitated, he let out an impatient breath.

"I was raised in this house by the two people I buried out there. They lived here for thirty-five years, made a good life for themselves and for me. I'm damn well not going to disrespect them by pulling any crap on a pregnant woman under the roof they gave me. In or out?"

"Sorry. I've forgotten people can be decent."

She stepped inside, into a wide, comfortable living room with a big stone fireplace, easy furniture that mixed styles in a cheerful, welcoming way.

It boasted considerable dust and dog hair.

Stairs made a jog up. A laundry basket full of jumbled sheets and towels sat on the bottom step.

He continued down a hallway, paused when she did at a room lined with shelves jammed with books and trinkets.

"My mother was a fierce reader. I've been catching up on reading lately myself."

Like a dream—was she dreaming—the room drew her in, the memories of a life she'd once had. And more, as she reached out, took a book from the shelf, the love.

"Max Fallon. She liked his stuff. I haven't tried him yet. Are you a fan?"

She looked up, eyes drenched, clutching the book, her love's picture, to her heart. "My . . . my husband."

"He was a fan?"

"Max." She began to rock, to weep. "Max. Max."

"Shit." He pulled off his cap, raked hands through his hair. "Maybe you should sit down. You can keep the book. Just . . . I'm going to, ah, bring the truck back. So . . ." He gestured, eased out of the room.

She did sit, on the edge of a big chair of navy blue leather, and wept herself empty.

He hiked up the road for the truck, came back, put a kettle of water on.

She'd looked wound tight in the henhouse, he thought. Ready—and he suspected able—to hold her own. Eyes—big and summer blue—exhausted but fierce. And the pregnant—really pregnant—had struck him then as adding a fertile warrior angle to her.

But there, in his mother's library, all that had fallen away, leaving her frail, vulnerable, broken.

He did better with the fierce and able.

When he heard her coming, he put a frying pan on the stove.

"I'm sorry," she said.

"Losing somebody sucks. Pretty much everybody left knows how much." He went to the refrigerator, took out bacon wrapped in cloth. "Max Fallon was your husband."

"Yes."

"Did you lose him in the Doom?"

"No. He got us out of New York. He got us away and kept us safe. They killed him. His brother killed him."

"His brother?"

"His brother turned to the dark, his brother and the twisted witch who turned him. His brother, and the men who hate us because we're not like them. They wanted to kill me. Her."

She wrapped her arms around the mound of her belly. "Max saved us. He died for us. They killed him. Eric, his brother, and the Purity Warriors. They killed Max, killed people we were building a life with. Tried to kill more. I had to leave because they wanted me and would kill whoever stood in their way. They hunted me. They may still be hunting me.

"They'll try to kill you if you help me."

He nodded, said, "Huh." Then turned back to the stove. "You want the eggs scrambled or fried?"

She'd worked herself up again, was nearly breathless with it. Her hands clutched at her sides. "Who are you?"

"Swift. Simon Swift. In another life I was Captain Swift, U.S. Army. In this one, I'm a farmer. Who are you?"

Slowly, she took off her pack, set it aside. "Lana Bingham. I was a chef. I am a witch."

"I got the second back in the coop when you gave me a little punch."

"I didn't mean—"

"Just a little. Bet you've got more. A chef? Why am I cooking?"

She let out a breath, took in another, then crouched by her pack. She took out herbs, a tomato, a pepper, a couple of spring onions. "Would you like an omelette?"

"Sure."

"It's a nice stove. It's a nice kitchen."

Her voice shook again. He could see as well as hear her fight to steady it. "How do you get the gas?"

"Gas well."

"A what?"

"Natural gas well." He gestured vaguely toward the window. "It's piped into the house. We've got gaslight, gas stove, gas every damn thing. Some wind power, too."

She washed her hands in the farm sink, then the herbs and vegetables. "I need a few things. More eggs, a small bowl, a whisk."

"I've got it."

After heating the skillet, she put on bacon. She took a chef's knife—serviceable—from a block, pulled over a cutting board, and began chopping while it sizzled.

Cooking. Normal. How could anything be normal?

And yet, chopping herbs, she felt more herself than she had in weeks.

"You were in the army."

"Yeah, for about ten years. I'd had enough, but I got out primarily because my mother got sick. Cancer. They needed help around here while she was fighting it. She fought it, beat it. And then . . . Well, fucking Doom."

"I'm sorry."

They worked together in silence for a few minutes. He got her the can he used to store bacon grease, the plastic tub he used for kitchen compost. And watched, mildly in awe, as she cooked.

"How long have you been on the road?" he asked her.

"I don't know. I lost track. It was the Fourth of July when . . . I left."

"About six weeks. Where'd you start?"

"We were in a place we called New Hope, in Virginia. I think south of Fredericksburg. Where am I now?"

"You came a ways. This is Maryland, western."

"What are the mountains?"

"The Blue Ridge."

"Are there other people?"

"Some. There's a town—more a settlement now. We do some

trading. I was taking produce in. There's a mill. They're making flour. Got some sheep, a loom. A blacksmith, a butcher. You work with what you've got."

She nodded, folded the egg over the vegetables. "Is there a doctor?"

"Not yet. A vet assistant's as close as we've got."

She lifted the omelette onto one of the plates he'd set out, cut it in half, slid half onto the second plate.

"Are there any Uncannys?"

"A few sprinkled in. Nobody has a problem with it. Do you want that milk?"

"I hate milk, but yes, it's probably good for the baby."

He got out the jug, poured her a short glass.

They sat at the kitchen counter, a classy and mottled gray granite. The first bite had her closing her eyes as her system absorbed.

He took a heftier bite. "Okay, you were serious about the chef deal. I haven't had anything close to this good in a hell of a while."

Calculating, she ate slowly. "If I could stay for a couple of days, I could pay you back with cooking. And we had a garden in New Hope, so I learned how to garden. I could help there. A couple of days should be safe."

For both of us.

"Then what?"

"I don't know. I haven't thought about anything but moving, getting away, keeping the baby safe."

"When's she due? You said she, right?"

"Yes. The last week of September."

"You figure to deliver her on your own, on the road?"

She knew how it sounded, had worried about it constantly, but hadn't seen a choice.

"I hope to find a place and . . . do what I need to. I won't let anything happen to her. Whatever it takes, nothing's going to hurt her."

"There are women in the settlement—houses scattered around."

"I can't . . . I can't risk so many people. The Purity Warriors, you don't know."

A pretty park, a happy celebration. Bodies scattered, smoke rising. Max's blood soaking the brown earth.

"Yeah, I do. Some of them came through the settlement a few weeks ago. They didn't get a warm reception."

Fear jumped back into her voice. "They were here."

"From what I hear there are some of them traveling around, looking for others who think like they do. Like I said, they didn't find that here."

He ate, considered. Between the Purity Warriors, Raiders, and general assholes, the road wasn't close to safe for a woman alone. Add in that that woman was due to give birth in about eight weeks.

And fierce or not, she apparently had a target on her back.

He scooped up the last of his eggs, turned to her. "You should think about staying here. You can take over the kitchen, that's for damn sure. You should think about staying at least until after you have the kid. Four bedrooms upstairs. I'm only using one."

"They could find me. Eric—"

"That's the brother?"

"He's mad with power. There's something about my baby, something special. Important. I don't know. But Eric and Allegra want to kill her."

"Well, if she's special and important it's just more reason to get her here safe. I don't like people who start trouble, start wars, look to generally fuck things up. However they're built, I don't like it."

"You don't even know me."

After nudging his empty plate aside, he shrugged. "What the hell difference does that make?" Nothing, nothing he could have said would have reassured her more.

"I'm so grateful. And I'm so tired. I'm just so tired. Can we take it a day at a time?"

"Sure. You can pick a bedroom. It'll be clear which one's mine." He rose, started to clear.

"I'll do the dishes. Part of the deal."

"Next time they're all yours. No offense, but you look pretty done. So go up, pick a bed, tune out. I need to get the produce into town. You ought to take my parents' room. It's one of those master deals. Got its own bathroom."

"Simon. Thank you."

He carted dishes to the sink. "Can you make meatloaf?"

"If you have the meat along with what I've already seen, I can make amazing meatloaf."

"You put that together for dinner, we're square."

CHAPTER TWENTY-FOUR

Lana found the master suite with its four-poster bed at the top of the stairs. A duvet of deep forest green covered it along with four thick shams in the same color edged in a quiet and dull gold that matched the walls.

His parents had died here, she remembered. He'd put their room to rights again, cleaned what must have been heartbreaking, cleared the room of all signs of illness.

Even through a gnawing fatigue, she recognized that his caring to restore the room to how his mother certainly would have wanted it said something about the son.

A man who'd given her food and shelter. It made her think of Lloyd, what he'd said at that first full community meeting.

Still, she locked the door behind her, adding a charm to block entrance. She didn't consider it overkill to carry a chair over and prop it under the doorknob.

She wanted to sleep, just wanted to go away for a while. On clean sheets, with pillows, under a duvet of forest green. Thinking of his mother, she considered the dirt and grime she carried from the trail, and stepped into the adjoining bath.

She wouldn't disrespect the woman whose home offered sanctuary by besmirching her bed.

Here, too, he'd put things to rights. A stack of fluffy towels on clean, if dusty, counters. Setting aside her pack, she opened the glass door of the shower.

Shower gel, shampoo, conditioner, even a woman's shower razor. As her own supplies had dwindled, Lana ignored the niceties as she stripped down. She'd use whatever she needed now, apologize later.

If she wept a little as hot water beat down on her, as she watched the dirt—that quick washes in streams and creeks hadn't touched—spiral down the floor drain, she told herself she was entitled to a few tears.

She indulged—who knew how long this bounty would last?—wrapped her hair in a towel, her body in another.

Soft, so blissfully soft.

Turning, she studied herself in the mirror. Her breasts, her belly, so ripe. She must be at thirty-three or thirty-four weeks now. With all her heart she believed her daughter remained healthy and strong. She felt that light, that life—both depending on her.

If that meant *she* had to depend on the largess of a stranger, she would. Cautiously, but she would.

She eyed the baskets on the open shelves beside the mirror.

Body lotion, skin cream, all so wonderfully female.

"Madeline Swift," she murmured. "I'm grateful, and hope you don't mind."

She slathered herself, all but felt her thirsty skin gulp in the moisture. As nothing in her pack resembled clean, she borrowed the robe hanging on the back of the bathroom door.

Trembling with gratitude, she turned down the duvet, slid into the sheets. She slept, and slept dreamlessly.

Awoke with a jerk, her heart pounding as she tried to remember where she was.

The farmhouse, the man with the tough face and careless generosity. She got up as quickly as her heavy belly allowed, tidied the bed, rehung the robe. Dressed.

The sun told her it was after noon—she'd gotten good at gauging the time. So she'd slept at least two hours. If she wanted to stay the night—God, she wanted to stay the night—she had to earn her keep.

Curious, she moved quietly along the second floor, found another bathroom, smaller than what he'd allowed her, and obviously what he used.

A towel hung over the shower door, a toothbrush stood in a cup on a small vanity.

She found a guest room—as she didn't imagine Simon Swift slept under a cover dotted with pretty violets—another room, a spare bedroom and sitting room combination, she supposed, with a sewing station under the window.

Lastly, his room—unmade bed, a shirt tossed over a chair back, and air that carried the faint hints of earth and grass.

She noted the shotgun propped in the corner, respected his choice to keep a weapon close while he slept.

She didn't find him downstairs, so she looked out windows until she spotted him working in the garden. Sweat dampened his shirt as he hoed between rows. The dogs slept under the apple tree, by the grave markers, and the horses watched him with their heads over the fence.

Her first thought was to go out and offer to help, but she noted the dishes they'd used that morning sat, clean, dry now, beside the sink. She saw no other signs he'd made a meal while she'd showered, slept, explored.

So she'd earn her keep by scouting through the kitchen and making him lunch.

When he came in, hot and hungry, the dogs bursting in ahead of him, he saw her at the stove. Something smelled damn good, and some of that, he realized, was woman.

She'd wrapped her hair up somehow or other, and it shined like butterscotch candy. When she turned, her face struck him. Quiet and wary beauty.

The wariness for him, he thought, as the charge of the dogs, their manic tail flapping didn't appear to bother her.

He kept it light. "What's cooking?"

"Stir-fry—vegetables and rice. I thought you could use lunch more than a hand in the garden."

"Good thinking." He moved to the sink, washed the dirt off his hands and arms. "Where'd you cook? For a living?"

"New York."

"Big city."

"It was." She plated the food, added one of the cloth napkins she'd found in a drawer, handed him both. "I saw some sourdough starter in your refrigerator."

"Yeah, my father liked to bake bread. He couldn't cook anything else worth a damn, but he liked baking bread. I've been feeding it, but . . ."

"I'll bake some bread if you want."

"That'd be good." He sat. "Aren't you eating?"

She nodded, but didn't get a plate, or sit. "I want to thank you—"

"You already did."

"I haven't had a real shower in . . . I'll apologize if I get emotional. Some of it's hormones. But being able to wash my hair . . . I used your mother's shampoo, and her shower gel. And she has—had—skin cream. It was open, and I used some. I just used it without . . ."

"You could do me a favor and not cry over that."

He looked at her as he ate with annoyed hazel eyes. Eyes that blurred green and gold together. "It'll put me off this stir-fry, and it's damn good. She wouldn't care, and I sure don't. Look, I dealt with my dad's stuff like that. I couldn't seem to go through hers. So use what you want."

"She has backups. Unopened. You could barter them."

"Use it." This time his tone snapped a bit. "If I'd wanted to barter her damn face cream, I would have."

Understanding pain, and loss, she said nothing more until she'd plated some lunch for herself and sat.

"If you'd tell me if there are any off-limits rooms in the house while I'm here."

"Other than the locked room in the basement full of the mutilated bodies of my victims, no."

She scooped up some stir-fry. He was right. It was damn good. "All right, I'll stay out of there. Do you have any food allergies?"

"I'm temperamentally allergic to spinach."

"Then I won't put any in the meatloaf."

Simon gave Lana plenty of space. He expected she'd stay for a couple days, pull herself together. He didn't have a problem giving her that time and space, especially since, Jesus, the woman could cook.

Plus, she carried her weight, no question, during those couple of days. Maybe he hadn't noticed the dust and dog hair—but he noticed when it was gone. Maybe he hadn't had a problem snagging clothes or towels out of a laundry basket, but it didn't hurt his feelings to find them all folded and where they belonged.

The dogs liked her. He'd walked by the library late one night and had seen her sitting in the dark—grieving for her husband—with Harper's head on her knee, Lee sprawled over her feet.

He figured to take her into the settlement once she'd gathered herself, turn her over to one of the women he knew. Any one of them would know more about dealing with a pregnant woman and delivering a baby than he did.

As for her insistence that the baby she carried was both special and a target of dark forces, he'd reserve judgment. While he couldn't deny he'd gotten used to looking out for himself alone, and the farm, he couldn't just turn her out.

He'd been raised better than that. He *was* better than that.

She wasn't much for conversation, and that was fine, too, as he'd grown accustomed to the quiet.

He thought of her as a kind of temporary, live-in farmhand who put together three solid meals a day, and dealt with the house so he didn't have to.

One who didn't look to be entertained, one who wasn't hard on the eyes, especially since after a couple of days she'd lost most of the living-on-raw-nerves edge that had haunted her eyes.

In truth, he had to admit he'd miss knowing he'd come in after the early chores to a hot breakfast—and having someone who knew their way around tending crops.

She wouldn't go near the cornfield, and he didn't ask why.

By day four, they'd fallen into a routine, one comfortable enough it worried him. Routines led to depending on each other.

Best thing all around? Nudge her into moving to the settlement, nesting there until she had her kid.

He started to ease her in that direction over a dinner of fried chicken and potato salad—his request.

"I'm going to take a load of produce into the settlement tomorrow."

"If you're bartering, you could use more flour."

"You've got a better sense by now what we're low on in the pantry. You ought to come in with me. It'd give you a sense of things."

Her gaze shifted up—deep, sad blue—met his. "I can make you a list."

"You could. There're probably things you need. Personal things."

"I don't need anything. If you're ready for me to move on—"

"I didn't say that." Thought it maybe, but that was different. "Look, there are women in there who've been through what you're going through. Who've, you know, had babies. Plus, people pass through. Some stay. Maybe somebody's come in who has medical experience."

Her fingers moved restlessly over the ring she wore around her neck. "I've still got time. I can do more until—"

"Christ, Lana." He rarely used her name, and did so now in pure frustration. "Give me a small break. I'm saying you'd be better off with people who know what they're doing when the kid decides she wants to come out. If you're not nervous about that, you're made of fucking steel."

"I'm scared to death. Terrified. Even knowing, absolutely knowing, she's meant to be born, meant to live and shine and do amazing things, I'm terrified."

Studying her face, he sat back. "You don't look scared."

She kept her gaze steady, laid a hand on the baby mound. "Before I looked down, saw the farm, whenever I was tired and hungry, I couldn't let myself be scared. If it snuck through, I had to shove it away again or I'd have stopped. Just stopped and given up. I told myself I'd find a place, a safe place to bring her into the world. Then I looked down, and saw the farm. The house, the fields, the animals—like a painting of before the world stopped."

Now her hand made slow circles over the baby.

"Still, I didn't let myself hope. It was just the immediate. Tomatoes on the vine, bees humming, chickens clucking. I thought, Food, because I needed it. I didn't let myself think shelter or rest. Until you spoke to me. You told me to come inside and eat, and then I began to hope.

"It's not fair to put my hopes on you, but I am. Because she needs me to."

No, she didn't look afraid, he thought. Neither her voice nor her face held a plea. He'd never have resisted a plea. Instead they held a quiet, steady strength.

That, to him, was even more irresistible.

"How about we compromise on it? I'll bring one of the women back with me—her name's Anne. Grandmotherly type, and she'd probably kick my ass for saying that. You could meet her, see how you feel then. I know she's had kids. When the time comes I could go get her, have her help you out."

"She comes into your hands first."

"Huh?"

Her eyes changed, seemed to stare straight into him, now dark as midnight.

"Into yours on the windswept night. And lightning heralds the birth of The One. Will you teach her to ride, and think she was born knowing? I teach her the old ways, what I can, but she has so much more. Safe, time out of time, while the dark rages. Until in the Book of Spells, in the Well of Light she takes her sword and shield. And with the rise of magicks she takes her place. She will risk all to fulfill her destiny, this precious child of the Tuatha de Danann. For this she grows in me, for this she comes into your hands."

She'd gone very pale, and now reached an unsteady hand for her water glass.

"What was that?"

"It's her." Lana sipped slowly until the dizziness passed. "I don't know how to explain it. Sometimes I see her, as clearly as I see you. She's so beautiful." As she sipped again, Lana's eyes filled, but the tears didn't spill. "So strong and fierce and lovely. Sometimes I hear her, a voice in my head. I think I might have given up a dozen times without that voice telling me to keep going. And sometimes, like now, she speaks through me. Or lets me know enough to speak for her."

In that moment, Simon believed her. Absolutely. "What is she?"

"The answer. When I'm afraid, I'm afraid for her, for what's going to be asked of her. I know what I'm asking of you," she began, and the dogs scrambled up from their evening naps.

"Yeah, I hear it." With his eyes still on hers, Simon rose. "Somebody's coming. You should go down into the root cellar until I see who it is. Take the shotgun with you," he added as he retrieved the 9mm he'd set on top of the fridge for the meal.

Walking to the front of the house, he grabbed the rifle propped by the door. Stepped out on the porch to watch the unfamiliar truck spit gravel on its way down the farm lane.

He ordered the dogs to sit, to hold, waiting until two men, both armed, got out of either side of the truck.

"Evening," he said easily, watching their gaits, their hands, their expressions.

He recognized trouble, prepared to deal with it.

One had a viciously scarred face, as if claws had raked across it, right to left, just under the right eye to the jawline under his left ear.

It twisted his mouth into a curled sneer.

"Nice place you got here." The one with a scraggly, graying beard spoke first.

"Yeah. I like it."

"A lot of stock, a lot of crops for one man to handle."

"Keeps me busy. Something I can do for you?"

"We're looking for a woman."

Simon flashed a grin. "Who isn't?"

The bearded one laughed, took a paper out of his front pocket, unfolded it. "This one in particular."

Simon looked at the paper, at the excellent sketch of Lana. "She's a looker. I wouldn't mind finding her myself."

"She's pregnant, 'bout seven or eight months. We got word she might be wandering around this way."

"I think I'd remember seeing that face, and a pregnant woman, wandering around here. How'd you lose her?"

"Ain't none of your business," the scarred man snapped.

"Just making conversation. I don't get many visitors."

The bearded one pulled his nose. "It must get lonely, out here on your own."

"Like I said, I keep busy."

"Still. You're pretty out of the way, kind of . . . cut off. Looks like you've got enough food going here to feed an army. It happens we've got one. We'll take that trailer of yours, along with two of those cows."

"I'm not looking to trade, thanks all the same."

"Nobody said nothing about trading." The scarred man pulled his gun. "We're taking. Now you go on and hitch that trailer up to the truck."

"You know, that's not very friendly of you."

Simon moved fast. The scarred one held his gun like some B-movie cowboy, all show, no sense. Simon slapped his forearm out, jabbed his other elbow into the bearded face, and had the scarred man's gun in his own hand in three smooth moves.

"I'd shoot you both where you stand," he said, his tone pleasant and skimmed with ice. "But I'm not in the mood to dig the graves.

You're going to want to think before you reach for that gun," he warned the bearded man. "Now take it out slow—two fingers— and set it down on the porch. Otherwise I'll just gut shoot your friend and let you haul him away to bleed out in your truck."

"Didn't say he was my friend."

Simon could have handled it, intended to. Then he heard Lana's voice.

"I don't mind digging graves."

Lana's voice, Simon thought, trying not to react, as the woman standing with the shotgun pointed at the uninvited guests looked nothing like her.

A sturdy build—not a pregnant one—short, dark hair instead of the long butterscotch-candy blond. Wearing a sneer that suited the tough, lean face.

"It's not like we haven't done it before."

"Now, don't shoot them unless you have to, honey." Putting amusement into his voice, Simon yanked the gun out of the second man's holster. "We just painted the damn porch last spring. She's meaner than I am," Simon commented. "And the men upstairs, out in the barn? The ones with guns trained on you? They're meaner than she is—that takes doing. An army you said. Yeah, we eat pretty well here. Now, we'd've been happy enough to give you some food to take on your way, but bad manners can't be rewarded. Right, honey?"

"You know how I feel about it, and that one's already bleeding on the damn porch. Maybe I'll just shoot the other one in the leg."

"Told you she's mean. Now, if I were you, I'd get back in the truck and head back the way you came. Otherwise, she's going to get irritated and shoot you. That'll whip up the rest of them, and they'll Bonnie and Clyde the shit out of you."

"I'd like my gun back."

"Consider the loss a consequence of poor manners. Get the fuck off my land or I'll let her put a hole in you. Then I'll sic the dogs on you."

At the word *sic*, both dogs bared teeth, growled.

The men backed off the porch, got into the truck. Simon saw the move, and still waited until the scarred man jerked another gun up to the side window.

He shot him, center of the forehead, tracked his aim toward the driver. The truck reversed fast, tossing up gravel and smoke, spun around to speed up the lane. When he stopped, Simon switched handgun for rifle, then held off when the passenger door opened, and the driver shoved his dead companion out.

"Hell, looks like I'll be digging after all."

He waited until the truck vanished over the rise.

"You didn't say you were a shapeshifter."

"I'm not." Lana lowered the shotgun, then staggered the few steps toward the porch. Dropped heavily on the step. "It's an illusion," she said as it faded. "Just like a . . . costume. I've never tried it before. It took a lot.

"You killed him."

"His choice, not mine."

She nodded. "They were in New Hope, part of the attack. His face—the dead one—I did that to his face. I don't know how. They nearly found me awhile back."

"I told you to go down to the root cellar."

"And do what?" The fierceness snapped back as her head jerked up. "Tremble and wait, expect somebody to protect me and mine? I've been finished with that for a long time now. Feels like a lifetime ago. I thought if I let them see me—the illusion—they'd have more reason to believe you hadn't seen me. They'd leave you alone. Then I heard what they said about taking, and knew they weren't going to leave."

She sat in silence when he released the dogs and sat beside her as the dogs bumped against them for attention.

"I'll leave in the morning. I'd like to be sure he's a good distance away first."

He'd been careful not to touch her, not once since she'd walked into his world, but now he took her chin in his hand, turned her face to his. "You're not going anywhere. I offered you a place to stay because you needed it. God knows you've earned it. I believed *you* believed people were after you and the kid. But I'm going to admit, I thought you were mostly being paranoid. I was wrong."

"He could come back, bring others back."

Shifting to scrub hands over the dogs, Simon shook his head. "That type looks for easy pickings. Now he knows we're not. You can put your hopes on me. I can handle it."

He rose. "Like I could've handled those two," he added.

"I know. I saw that. What did you do in the army?"

He smiled. "Followed orders."

"And gave them. Captain, you said."

"It's been awhile. Now I'm a farmer." Sitting back down on the step, he looked out at the fields, the crops. "But I know how to protect my land, my home. What's in it."

He'd been a warrior, she thought. He had that controlled danger under the easy. She'd seen that control in Max, seen him develop it as he'd led people, had them depend on him.

Now she sat with another warrior, another leader.

"People are stronger together. I know how to defend, too."

"I got that impression. I've had it since I found you in the henhouse."

"I didn't always. In New York—was it really only months ago?—I liked to shop, to plan dinner parties. I liked to dream about opening my own restaurant one day. I'd never held a gun, much less fired one. And my power . . . it was barely a whisper."

"It seems you've found your voice then."

"It's more being found. If you hadn't come back to help your parents, would you have stayed in the army?"

"No, it was time to get out."

"What did you want to do?"

He realized they were having the longest and certainly the easiest conversation they'd had to date. With a dead man a few yards away. Christ, he wondered why it didn't strike him as strange.

"I thought about starting a business maybe, in the town up the road that's not a town anymore."

"What kind of business?"

"Making furniture. That was kind of a hobby of my father's, and I picked it up. A little business working with my hands, on my own time, in my own way, close to home because I'd spent so much time away."

The light began to settle toward twilight, and he found it too easy to just sit, talk with her about old dreams as night approached.

"Anyway, I've got to dig a hole."

He walked off to get a shovel.

Lana stayed where she was, crossed her hands over her belly. Despite the death, the violence, the threat, she felt safe.

CHAPTER TWENTY-FIVE

In the end, Lana had her way. She couldn't go into the settlement, nor have anyone come to her. Either might put lives at risk if the Purity Warriors came back.

Her child had spoken to her, and through her. For now, she believed things were as they were meant to be.

She cooked, gardened, gathered eggs, and took comfort in the simplicity of the quiet.

As summer waned toward fall, she harvested vegetables, canned them for winter use. Made jams and jellies while Simon mowed and baled hay, cut wheat for the meal, hauled corn to the silo or the kitchen.

One day he brought back seeds he'd bartered for—three each from the fruit of dwarf orange and lemon trees. She found them as priceless as diamonds.

"Could work," he said as they potted them for the greenhouse. "Lemonade on the porch next summer."

"Duck à l'Orange next fall."

"Maybe we'll find lime. Tequila shots."

She laughed, carefully covered a seed with soil.

"You must like tequila," he commented. "That's the first time I've heard you really laugh."

"I'm planting orange seeds in dirt sweetened with chicken poop and imagining knocking back some tequila. It's pretty funny."

"My dad always said a little chicken shit'll help grow most anything."

"I guess we'll find out."

Curious, she went with instinct, held her hands over the pot. She let it flow through her, in her, of her, out of her.

She felt the rise, the pulse, and the power.

A tender green sprig broke through the dirt, reached toward the light.

She laughed again, a sound that began on amazement, ended on joy. Beaming with it, she looked over at Simon, found him staring at her.

"That's a hell of a thing," he managed.

"If you'd rather I didn't—"

"Do I look stupid to you?" he demanded, eyes firing green under gold. "The world is what it damn well is. As it is, I'm a farmer who's got a witch who can give the crops a boost. Have you got a problem with what you are?"

"No, but—"

"Why should I? The way I see it, the biggest problem we've had, right from the get, is people pointing fingers and worse at ones who aren't just like them. We ought to try to do better this time around. It might be our last chance to get it right."

He tapped another pot. "Do this one."

She let it come, all joy now. Then stepped back from the tender sprout.

"I don't know if it's me or her or us. But I know she changed me. If I woke tomorrow, and all these months had been a dream, I'd still be changed. Oh!" Once again she laughed as she pressed a hand to the side of her belly.

Those kinds of moves and gestures made him twitchy. "You okay?"

"Yeah. She's kicking." Surprising them both, Lana took his hand, pressing it to her stomach.

He felt a jolt, one that went straight into him. Life kicking against his hands, and for reasons he couldn't comprehend, into his heart.

Someone grew inside there, he thought. Someone innocent, help-less. Yet from the strength of the kick, fierce.

"She's . . . got some sass."

Now he stepped back as Lana's face was nearly as luminous as it had been when she'd brought life out of the dirt. The look of her, bold and glowing, stirred something in him just as the child stirred in her.

He'd been careful, damn careful, to avoid that.

"I've got work I need to get to. Can you handle the rest of this?"

"Yes."

When he left, she stood quietly with the scent of dirt and grow-ing things.

Simon kept busy, and treated Lana like he'd have treated a sister if he'd had one. Twice in September groups passed by. She stayed in the house and out of sight, wary.

He gave them supplies, directed them to the settlement. Some would stay, others he knew would continue on. Searching for some-thing else, something more. Just searching.

After he saw the second group off, Simon came into the kitchen to find her stirring stew on the stove with the shotgun propped beside her.

He moved it to the back door.

"Eight people. One of them had wings. I can't get used to seeing that. They skirted around D.C. a few days ago."

Since the table was set—she tended to fuss with that sort of thing—he washed up in the sink.

"They heard gunfire, saw smoke. One of them was getting the hell out when he hooked up with them. He said, word is— God, what's her name?" He paused, rubbed his temple. "MacBride's still alive, and what's left of the government's trying to hold the city. Every time they get communications up, somebody takes it out again."

"It seems like another world. Like a story about another world."

"Yeah, it does. But it isn't. There are rumors about people in camps and labs."

"Magickal people?"

"Yeah, but not just. The estimate is . . ." He'd considered saying nothing to her, had nearly convinced himself to take that tack.

But he couldn't.

"I'm telling you because it's not right you don't know, but it's not confirmed, okay?"

She turned to him. "Okay?"

"They're saying the plague's finished, run its course. That's the good news. The bad is they're estimating it took about eighty percent of the population. That's world population. That's more than five billion people. It could be more."

"I need a drink."

He went to the pantry, got a bottle of whiskey, poured two fingers.

"I heard the same a few days ago." He downed half the whiskey. "There's a guy with a ham radio in the settlement, and he's been

able to reach a few others—even a couple in Europe, and it's no better there. Adding the ones who offed themselves, the ones killed
for the fucking hell of it, you can up the percentage. New York . . .
Do you want to hear this?"

"Yes. But more, I need to hear it."

"New York's under the control of the Dark Uncannys. There's
talk of human sacrifice, of stake-burning people like you—who
aren't like them. The military's holding some areas, especially west
of the Mississippi, but from what I get, the chain of command's
pretty fractured. There are offshoots, and they're posting bounties
on all Uncannys: dark, light, doesn't matter."

"The Purity Warriors."

"They're leading the charge. Raiders are keeping mobile, doing
hit-and-runs. And they're bounty hunting."

Calmly, she ladled stew into one of his mother's fancy dishes—
she did like to fuss. "So it's bad for everyone, but for someone like
me? We're hunted by all sides. It's hard to believe what you said the
other day about getting it right this time could happen."

She carried the bowl to the table.

"I have to believe it."

Now she ladled stew from the dish to the bowls.

She sat, waited for him to join her.

"When I was in New Hope, I saw what people could and would
do together. I saw how others tried to destroy that. You were a soldier."

"Yeah."

"So was Max, at the end. He made the choice to fight, to lead
because it needed to be done. You did the same, killing to protect
someone you barely knew. You gave the people who were here food
you worked to grow, and that was a choice. The people who try to
destroy won't win because there will always be people like Max, like
you, like the people I left behind who make the choice."

She held a brighter view than he did at the moment. He didn't mind the balance.

"I read one of his books. Not the one you have," he said, when she stared at him. "One of the others. It was good. He was a good writer."

"He was." She smiled over the ache in her heart. "He was good."

Habitually after a long day, after the evening meal and the evening chores, Simon worked in the barn. He usually wound down before bed in his mother's library for an hour or two with a book.

He missed TV, and wasn't shamed to admit it, but books made up for it. He missed beer, and had high hopes the group trying to put together a little brewery would succeed. He settled most nights for tea, and had—almost—acquired a taste for it.

That didn't make up for the lack of beer.

The dogs generally settled down with him, making it a nice, easy way to end the day. He'd let them out for a last round before heading up.

The book took his mind off the work, the world, the woman sleeping upstairs. The work would always be there, he couldn't do a damn thing about the world. And he limited his thoughts regarding Lana to a very narrow window.

The last few nights he studied. Books were good for that as much as entertainment.

He'd done plenty of scavenging in the months since his parents died. Running a farm the way things turned out was a different prospect than growing up on one the way things had been.

He'd added considerably to the library.

Books gave him instructions on beekeeping, on butchering—though he'd happily turned that task over to the settlement—on making butter, cheese, holistic medicines and treatments.

Cooking—before Lana had come along.

So he did what he thought of as his homework with a mixture of fascination and horror—laced with a good dose of dread.

When he heard her coming, it surprised him enough to have him slap the book shut and rise. She never stirred out of her room once she'd gone in, shut the door.

But she stepped in now, her hair tumbled over her shoulders, the big, baggy T-shirt flowing over Baby Mountain and barely reaching the middle of her thighs.

She had damn nice legs, he thought, then immediately shut that part of his brain down.

"Sorry. Couldn't sleep."

"No problem. Do you need something?"

"I thought maybe a book . . ." She trailed off as she caught sight of the one he held. "*Home Birthing Guide?*"

She'd distracted him, he realized. Her legs had distracted him, and he'd left the cover facing out.

"They've got a lot of books at the settlement you can borrow. I stole this one because I couldn't figure out how to explain borrowing it. I figured I should know what the hell to do when the time comes."

"Good idea, because that'll make one of us." She pressed a hand to the aching small of her back. "I talked to Rachel some—the doctor in New Hope—and we were going to start birthing lessons in September. That was the plan. Anyway, I thought maybe a book, and I'd make some tea."

"I'll make it. No, you look a little ragged."

"I'd be insulted except I feel the same. Should I read that?"

"Not if you want to sleep tonight." He added a smile that made her laugh.

And press a hand to her side. "Whoa."

"Must be hard to sleep with her kicking you from the inside."

"I don't know—I don't think. Rachel said Braxton-Hicks contractions are like a preview of coming attractions." Her voice hitched through the words as she braced on the back of the sofa.

"You're hurting?"

"It's just . . . It's not that bad. Enough to keep me up." She let out a breath, straightened.

"Maybe it's . . . the thing."

" 'The thing'? Labor? Oh, no, it's just those fake contractions. I'd know. I mean, I'd have to know. I think some chamomile tea and a book. Maybe just the tea, actually."

"Okay." He tossed down the book, went to the kitchen with her. "I can bring it up."

"Thanks, but being up feels pretty good. I'm just restless. Looks like the dogs are, too. Should I let them out?"

"Yeah, go ahead." He put on the kettle as she opened the door. Wind moaned in.

"It's really blowing," she murmured, standing for a moment and letting the cool air blast over her. "Might be a storm coming in."

He turned away from the vision of her hair flying, the shirt dancing high on her thighs, appalled by the attraction.

Pregnant woman, he reminded himself. A woman who trusted and depended on him. A woman grieving for the man she'd loved.

"Dark nights full of wonder when magicks poise to rise. Max wrote that, or something close to that. It's what tonight feels like."

On a quick sound of shock she wrapped an arm around her belly. And her water broke.

They stood, her at the door, the wind blowing, him at the stove, the kettle steaming, and stared at each other in complete shock.

"Oh my God. My water broke. Did you hear it? Did you? It went *ping*. Oh, Jesus *Christ*! I don't think these are the fake ones."

"Okay, okay. Wait." He turned the kettle down. He'd need the boiling water to sterilize . . . Don't think about it yet.

"I don't think waiting's an option."

"I don't mean wait. I mean . . . Okay." Military training kicked in. He simply put himself in combat mode.

"Let's get you upstairs."

"My water broke all over the floor."

"I'll mop it up later. I've got what we need upstairs."

"What we need?"

He solved the let's-get-you-upstairs issue by picking her up. A hefty load, but he could handle it. "I read the book, right? Clean shower curtain, towels, blankets, stuff. I've got this."

"I need to have this."

"I've got a stopwatch. We need to time the contractions. So, you've had a couple—about what, five minutes apart?"

"I don't know how many. I thought they were the other kind. Why are there another kind? Whose idea was that?"

One of them, at least one of them, had to keep calm. "Give me a ballpark on how long."

"A couple of hours I guess. I'm an idiot."

"A novice is different than an idiot." He carried her into his parents' room, stood her beside the old four-poster. "I'm going to get the stuff. Can you hang on here?"

"Yes. I feel okay."

Since he didn't know how long that would last, he made it fast. He had the stackable containers, came back with them, spread out the shower curtain, piled up the towels.

" 'Cause it gets messy. Ah, I can get you another shirt. That one's wet."

She looked down at herself, up at him. Closed her eyes for just a moment. "I guess it's past time to worry about being embarrassed."

She pulled it off, stood in the dim glow of gaslight looking to his eyes like some sort of fertility goddess. Ripe, beautiful, unearthly.

What she was, he reminded himself, was a woman in labor.

And he was the designated medic.

"I'm going to help you into bed, then I've got to get the rest of the stuff."

He eased her onto the bed, spread a blanket over her, switched on the little gas fireplace his mother had loved.

"Be right back. Ah, breathe through it, right? In through the nose, out through the mouth. Wait, here." He pushed a stopwatch into her hand. "Time the next one. How long it lasts, then start timing how long between."

He moved fast, sterilized scissors, lengths of sturdy string, a cup of ice, a bowl of warm water, and cloths. He scrubbed his hands, under his nails, wished he'd thought to scavenge some doctor's gloves from somewhere.

He organized everything while she breathed through a contraction.

"They're harder. Really harder. That was like a minute after four minutes between."

"Got it. So, the book says when you're getting close I can see the kid's head pushing against . . . down there. I should, ah, look. The next contraction."

Propped up against pillows, she stared straight into his eyes. "When's your birthday?"

"My birthday?"

"I need to know something more personal about you."

"Weird, but June second."

"Your middle name."

He smiled a little. "James."

"The first time you had sex."

"Come on."

"I'm serious. You're about to study my vagina." She arched her eyebrows when he winced. "If you're going to study it, you should be able to handle the name for it. And compared to that, I asked a casual question."

"I was sixteen. Before you ask, her name was Jessica Hobbs, and we fumbled through it one night in my thirdhand pickup on the side of the lane. Second time was better for both of us."

"All right." She looked toward the window. "Did you let the dogs back in? It's really blowing out there."

"Yeah, they're in. Sleeping in my room. Do you want—"

She pushed up on a gasp. "Here it comes."

He lifted the blanket, gently shifted her legs so the flats of her feet sat on the bed.

Don't think, don't react, he ordered himself. He'd seen cows calve, mares foal. He'd . . . Holy God.

"I don't see her yet, so we've got some time."

He dampened a cloth, wiped at her sweaty face, and wondered why the female of any species agreed to the process of perpetuating it.

Three insane hours later, he knew damn well there had to be a better system. Technology, medical science should've found a way. As the contractions came harder, closer, he wiped at her sweat with his good hand. She'd pretty much crushed the bones in the other gripping it each time the pain peaked.

He fed her ice chips like the book suggested, ran down for more between bouts. Every few contractions he checked for the money shot, and wondered if he'd ever be able to have sex with a woman again.

He breathed with her as the wind screamed outside, as her pain-glazed eyes stared into his—as he sacrificed the future use of his right hand—Jesus, the woman had a *grip*.

Toward hour four she collapsed back against the mound of pillows, the ring she wore on a chain glinting between her breasts.

"Why won't she come *out*!"

"The book says the first one especially can take awhile." At a loss, he brushed the sweat-dampened hair back from her face. "I remember my mom saying I took about twelve hours."

He hadn't appreciated his mother enough, not nearly enough.

"Twelve? *Twelve?*"

He understood he'd taken the wrong tack when she reared up, teeth bared, gripped the front of his shirt, hauling him closer, and snarled, "Do something!"

"You need to stay calm. We're going to get through this."

"We? We? Get me some pliers, get me some damn pliers so I can yank a couple of your teeth out without Novocain, then you can say *we*. Don't tell me to stay calm, you fucking lunatic . . . Oh God. Oh God, here it comes!"

"Breathe, breathe. Come on, babe. I'm going to check. Keep breathing. Holy shit, I see her head! I see her head. She's got hair." For some reason that delighted him, and he grinned as he looked up while Lana blew out breaths.

"Then pull her out! Just pull her out!"

Then she collapsed again on a long moan. Her eyes shut.

"You really saw her head?"

"Yeah. Hair looks dark. It's wet, but it looks dark."

Shifting, he dumped some of the ice in a cloth to cool it, stroked it over her face. "Okay, listen up. You're doing great. I know it hurts. I don't know why the hell it has to hurt so much. It's a crap system, but we're getting closer to the payoff. You can do this."

"I can do this. Sorry about the 'fucking lunatic.'"

"It's okay. I feel like one."

"Well, you're not, and in case I call you one again, or worse, I'm telling you now, you're a hero. You are," she said when he shook his head. "I know heroes. Oh, fuck!"

He'd been in combat. He'd led men, lost men, killed men. Nothing had prepared him for the rigors of helping a laboring woman as she fought to push a child into the world.

He knelt on the bed, bracing her feet against his hand, pressing his weight against them as she bore down, time after time.

That fierceness pulsed from her now, sharpening her eyes, glowing on her face—and her cries were those of war, not of pain. When sweat soaked through his shirt, he stripped it off, tossed it aside.

Like Lana, he wore a chain, and he carried a medal bearing the image of Michael the Archangel.

"Breathe it out, breathe it out." He swiped his forearm over his brow as she lay back and gathered herself. "We're really close."

Lana curled up, gulped in air. Pushed while the first rumbles of thunder joined the howling wind.

"There's her head. Jesus, Lana, look. There's her head. No, pant, don't push. Wait, pant, don't push. Okay, yeah." Carefully, he lifted the cord from around the baby's neck. "Let's get the rest of her out here. Ready?"

Tears mixed with sweat as she rode the birth pangs, watched Simon guide one shoulder, then the other.

The room, the night sky burst with light. On the mantel over the little gas fire, the candles flashed to flame.

On a mother's fierce call, the baby slid into Simon's hands. And with her first breath, loosed a cry like triumph.

"I've got her." Stunned, awed, overwhelmed, Simon stared down at the wriggling infant. "I've got her. Wow."

"She's beautiful. Oh, isn't she beautiful!"

As Lana reached out, Simon gave her the child. "Damn right she is. You gotta hold her head lower, the book said. Drains the fluids. I'm gonna clean her up some, okay? And we need to keep her warm."

Laughing, weeping, Lana pressed her lips to the infant's cheek. "It's my baby. She's here. She's beautiful." Lightning flashed again as she looked at Simon. "Out of me, into your hands, and into mine. She's yours, too."

Because he couldn't speak, he nodded.

Dealing with the practicalities steadied him. Birth was a messy business, and by the time he'd cleaned up, the sun shimmered pink through the windows. And the baby nursed at her mother's breast.

That was a picture he would carry in his head for the rest of his life.

"How about I scramble up some eggs, get you that tea we never got around to?"

"I could eat." She stroked a finger over the baby's hair. Max's dark hair. "I don't have the words, Simon. I just don't have them."

"What are you going to call her?"

"Fallon. She's Fallon. Born in the Year One. Conceived and saved by one man, delivered into the hands of another. I know she'll honor them both. I know it."

He brought her food, made sure she was comfortable before going out to deal with the stock. The fields would wait.

He checked on them, found them sleeping, and took the time to grab a shower where he braced his hands against the tile while the water beat on him and tried to sort out his feelings.

Too many to sort.

He went out to the barn, brought back the project he'd worked on in the evenings for weeks.

The cradle stood waist high, built with pine he'd stained a deep, rich brown. It rocked gently at the push of his hand.

The baby opened her eyes. The dark, somehow magickal infant blue seemed to see straight into him.

"Man," he murmured, using a fingertip to stroke her cheek. "You look like you know everything there is and more. I'm going to catch a couple hours of sack time myself. So . . ."

What if they needed him?

With a shrug, he stretched out on the bed beside Lana.

If they needed him, he thought as he drifted off, he'd be right there. The baby whimpered, had him blinking his eyes open again.

"Don't wake her up, okay?" he whispered, gave the tiny rump a couple of awkward pats. "In her place, I'd sleep a month."

When she whimpered again, stirring restlessly, he shifted.

"Okay, let's try this." He gathered her up, and when she curled against his chest, rubbed her back. "Yeah, that's better. That's better. That's my girl."

As he slept, Fallon watched him. Knew him.

EPILOGUE

On the last day of the first year Lana stood at the window watching a light, pretty fall of snow. She cuddled Fallon as she wondered what the New Year would bring.

A year before she'd been with Max at a party in SoHo, drinking wine, laughing, dancing while thousands gathered in Times Square to watch the ball drop.

She thought of Max often. She had only to look at Fallon, the already thick raven-dark hair, the eyes slowly turning from infant blue to smoky gray.

The pang had lessened, and the baby was part of the healing.

So, she knew, was Simon.

Just as she knew his feelings for her, as she knew his unquestionable love for the baby.

She'd end this year, this first year, with memories of the man she'd loved, memories she'd always hold precious. And she'd begin the next giving her heart to the man she'd come to love.

"You're the link between us, my baby." She brushed her lips over Fallon's hair. She lifted the baby high, making her gurgle and kick her legs. "You're the everything."

She heard the dogs bark and, lowering the baby, saw a man on horseback riding down the lane toward the house.

Fear came first. Would it always?

She ran to get the sling she'd made, secured Fallon in it to free her hands before she retrieved the shotgun. Ready to protect, defend, she watched as Simon walked toward the horseman.

The man dismounted. He wore a long, dark coat, held the bay's reins in one gloved hand. He wore no hat, and snow fell over his wavy mane of hair. His beard, trim and dark like his hair, carried a white streak.

They spoke. Simon glanced toward the house, then left the man standing in the snow with his horse.

"Who is he?" Lana demanded when Simon opened the front door. "What does he want?"

"He says his name is Mallick. He says he's come to pay tribute to The One and her mother, and won't come in without your invitation. He claims he has things to tell you. He's not armed."

"He knows about the baby?"

"He knew the night she was born, Lana. He knew the hour. He knows her name. He says he's sworn to her. I believe him." Simon took the shotgun from her. "But I'll tell him to go if you don't want to talk to him."

"He has power," she said. "I feel it. He's letting me feel it so I understand he won't use it to harm. I wish I didn't have to talk to him. I wish she was only a baby, my baby. But . . ."

Lana stepped to the door, looked out. "Please, come in."

"Thank you. Is there a place my horse can rest out of the weather? We've traveled a long way."

"I'll take care of it." Simon brushed a hand over Fallon's hair, ran it down to give Lana's arm a reassuring squeeze. "Nobody's going to hurt her."

"Bring him into the kitchen. I'll make him something to eat."

She heated soup, made tea, warmed bread. And steeled herself when Simon brought Mallick in.

"Blessings on you," Mallick said. "And on the light you've brought to the world."

"There's food."

"And kindness. May I sit?"

She nodded, but kept one arm protectively around the baby in the sling. "How do you know about my daughter?"

"Her coming has been written, sung, foretold. One year ago today, the fabric ripped, the scales tipped when the blood of the damned defiled holy ground. So the purge followed, and magick strikes back. You have nothing to fear from me."

"Then why am I so afraid?"

"You're a mother. What mother doesn't fear for her child, especially one who has hints of the child's destiny. May I eat? I've fasted three days in honor of The One."

"Yes. I'm sorry."

"Here." Simon lifted Fallon out of the sling. She immediately babbled at him, tugging at his hair. Then she looked solemnly at Mallick.

"She still remembers some of the waiting time, and sees some of what's to come. Knows these times as much as the here and now. You see that, too," he said to Lana.

Heavy with the weight of destiny, Lana sat. "Is there no choice for her?"

"Oh, she'll have many choices, as do we all. If Max had chosen to go north instead of south, if you had chosen to stay rather than to think first of the child and your friends, if Simon had chosen to turn you away, we would all be somewhere else now. Instead we're here, and I break my fast with this excellent soup."

He studied Fallon as he ate. "She'll be a great beauty—that is not a choice, of course. She takes much from you, from her birth father. You'll teach her what you know, as her life father will teach her. As will I, when the time comes."

"You?"

"It's my task. And my choice. Let me comfort you first. For thirteen years she will be safe. They will hunt, they will scourge the land, but they won't find her. When you see me again, you must entrust her to me for two years."

"I won't—"

"It will be your choice, and hers. Two years to teach her what I know, to train her to become what she was born to be. In those years, the world will burn and bleed. Some will build, some will destroy. How much easier it is to tear apart than to mend. How many years beyond those before she's ready, before she takes up sword and shield, I can't see. But without her and those she leads, the suffering is endless."

"And if we say no," Simon demanded. "That's the end of it?"

"You have thirteen years to weigh the choice. To prepare to make it. As does she. I have gifts for her."

He turned his hand over, and held a pure, white candle. "Only she can light it, and it will guide her through the dark." He set it down, once again opened his hand. Held a ball of crystal. "Only she can see what it holds, and it will show her the way."

He set it beside the candle. "And . . ." He held a candy-pink teddy bear. "Because not all should be duty. I hope it brings her comfort and joy. Know she'll have my sword, my fist, my power, always. I'm honored to be the tutor, the trainer, the protector of Fallon Swift. Thank you for the food."

He vanished.

Simon took a full step back with the baby. "He just . . . Who does that? Can you do that?"

"I've never tried."

"Maybe don't. And despite the vanishing act, nobody's going to take her if we say screw you. Nobody's going to make us turn her over to some wizard for a couple years in some magickal boot camp."

"I knew when I was carrying her," Lana murmured. "She knew. Thirteen years. She'll be safe."

"I'll keep her safe every day of my life."

"I know it. I know." She rose, turned to him. "The day she was born, I woke up and you were sleeping beside me, exhausted, and you were holding her. And I knew. You'd made her a cradle with your own hands, thinking of her even before she was born. And I knew.

"He called her Fallon Swift. Will you give her your name?"

"I . . . sure. I'd give her anything, but—"

"I loved Max. And she will, too. I'll tell her everything I can about him."

"Of course you will."

"What led me here, Simon? Was it her?" She stepped closer, smiling when Fallon gripped her finger, tried gnawing on it. "Was it me? Was it Max, pushing me toward someone who'd love and protect? Who he could trust and respect. Maybe it was all of that. Maybe it was something in you pulling us here.

"You're her father, too. You're the father who walks her at night, who'll help teach her to walk and talk. Who'll worry about her, be proud of her. She's so lucky to have two good men as fathers. She has Max's name. I'd like her to have yours."

"She's got it." Emotion all but drowned him. "I'm proud to give it to her."

"Fallon Swift." Lana lifted the chain, Max's ring, from around her neck. "This I'll save for her now." She laid it beside the gifts on the table. "And this . . ." She drew her wedding ring off her left hand, slipped it onto her right. "I'll wear to honor the man I loved. Can you accept that?"

"I don't know what you're getting at."

He wouldn't reach for her, she thought, wouldn't cross that line. Because he understood honor. Because he lived honorably.

So she reached, she crossed, she touched a hand to his cheek as she rose up, leaned in, laid her lips on his. "I'm lucky to have loved and been loved by a good man. Lucky to love and be loved by another. Do you love me?"

Fallon snuggled her head on his shoulder, and Simon was lost. "I think since I caught you with an egg in your hand. I can wait," he began, but she kissed him again.

This time, he pulled her in, the baby between them, and let himself feast.

"The year's ending," she told him. "The terrible, miraculous, bitter, and joyful year. I want to start the next one with you. I want to look toward all the next ones with you. I want to be your family."

She felt the joy of it when he held her, the blessed heat of it when their lips met again. Life to be lived.

The child bounced between them, cooing. Joyful.

And waving her hand out, set the candle to flame.